FLING WITH THE DOC NEXT DOOR

ALISON ROBERTS

SOUTH AFRICAN ESCAPE TO HEAL HER

BECKY WICKS

MILLS & BOON

First published in Great Britain 2023
by Mills & Boon, an imprint of HarperCollins*Publishers* Ltd,
1 London Bridge Street, London, SE1 9GF

www.harpercollins.co.uk

HarperCollins*Publishers* Macken House, 39/40 Mayor Street Upper,
Dublin 1, D01 C9W8, Ireland

Fling with the Doc Next Door © 2023 Alison Roberts

South African Escape to Heal Her © 2023 Becky Wicks

ISBN: 978-0-263-30605-7

05/23

MIX
Paper | Supporting
responsible forestry
FSC™ C007454

This book is produced from independently certified FSC™ paper
to ensure responsible forest management.
For more information visit: www.harpercollins.co.uk/green.

Printed and Bound in the UK using 100% Renewable Electricity
at CPI Group (UK) Ltd, Croydon, CR0 4YY

FLING WITH THE DOC NEXT DOOR

ALISON ROBERTS

MILLS & BOON

CHAPTER ONE

BEING FACED WITH a potentially life-threatening emergency on her first day in a new job, let alone with her very first patient, was not something that Dr Ella Grisham had been anticipating.

She'd been a specialist obstetrician for long enough now, however, to know that the first signs of an emergency could appear at any time. They could also escalate rapidly and, when there were two lives involved, the stakes—and the tension—could reach overwhelming levels surprisingly rapidly.

Ella was quite aware that, in hindsight, she might excuse what was happening for that reason but, right now, the brusque demand from the man who'd burst through the door of this delivery room, after stopping suddenly to stare through the window on the corridor side, was alarming for everyone, including Ella.

Especially Ella?

'What's going on?' He was glaring at her. 'Who are you?'

'Ella Grisham.'

'Ah, right…our new locum. I'm Logan Walsh.'

Ella simply nodded. She had expected to meet the head of department here in the Queen Mother's Maternity Hospital—a separate wing of a large general hospital in Aberdeen—before she actually started her first shift but he'd been away presenting a course in obstetric emergencies the day of her interview last month and was apparently running late this morning due to an urgent administration issue that needed his attention. Nobody had time for introductions, anyway, because a midwife was asking for an urgent consult on a woman in labour.

A woman that Ella was currently still examining. She had the transducer of a portable ultrasound machine in her hand and she turned back to the screen.

'No obvious signs of a placental abruption,' she said.

Judy, the midwife, gave Ella a cautiously relieved glance but they both knew that even massive internal blood loss could stay hidden for some time. She turned back to the tympanic thermometer she was holding as it beeped. 'Thirty-seven point six,' she reported. 'Heart rate's up to one ten.'

'Blood pressure?'

'One forty over sixty-five.'

'Can someone tell me what's going on, please?' The words were clipped enough to be a command rather than a request. It only took a couple of steps of Logan Walsh's long legs for him to be beside the CTG machine being used for continuous monitoring of both the baby's heart rate and the mother's contractions. He ran the strip of paper, that was long enough to have puddled on the floor, between his fingers.

'Lauren's a thirty-two-year-old primigravida,' Ella told him. 'She's coming up to thirty-seven weeks gestation. No concerns with the pregnancy other than the baby being breech but he seemed to decide it was time to turn around by himself a couple of days ago.'

Lauren leaned back against her pillows, her face almost as pale as the hospital linen. 'It felt like I was being turned inside out,' she put in. 'It was my midwife that told me what had happened and she said it was a good thing because it meant I might not need to have a Caesarean.'

'Lauren came in about half an hour ago with sudden abdominal pain,' Ella continued.

'I checked her,' Judy put in. 'Waters were intact, she wasn't having any contractions and there was no bleeding or dilation on an internal exam.'

'Judy had just called for an urgent consult when I arrived on the ward,' Ella added.

'Why?' Logan's gaze flicked up from the graph paper to land on Judy.

Ella wanted to suggest that it had probably been more than seeing a staff member he didn't recognise that had brought him barging into this room after barely more than a glance through the window. It was more likely to have been an instinct—the same kind that was making the hairs prickle on the back of her own neck. Something wasn't right here.

Judy didn't get the chance to respond to the HoD because Lauren let out a cry. Her husband reached out to put his hand on her forehead.

'What's wrong, babe?'

'That pain's getting worse. It hurts in my shoulders now, too.' She pulled in a sharp breath, and then another, as if it was suddenly becoming difficult to breathe. 'And I think I'm going to be sick.'

Ella had started wiping the gel off Lauren's abdomen at the same time she'd cried out in pain and she had caught her own breath as she felt the rigid muscles beneath the tissues in her hand. She couldn't miss being the sudden focus of Logan's attention either, despite Judy reaching past him with a container in case Lauren was about to vomit. His stare had the intensity of a laser beam.

'Abdomen was soft five minutes ago,' she said quietly. 'And only slightly tender.'

'Blood pressure's dropping.' Judy was watching for the figures to finish appearing. 'Seventy-eight over forty. Heart rate's up to one-forty.'

The blood pressure was suddenly dangerously low and the heart rate too high. Ella didn't need to check the recording being spat out from the CTG to know that the unborn baby was having a deceleration because she could hear the blips of his heartbeat slowing ominously. She picked up the transducer of the ultrasound with one hand and squeezed a new blob of gel onto the stretched skin of Lauren's belly with the other. It took only seconds to find something that hadn't been obvious even a minute or two earlier.

'There's free fluid in the abdomen.' Most likely blood. A lot of it, although Ella didn't pass on either of those thoughts aloud. Logan was the only person who needed to know just how serious this situation had suddenly become.

Lauren was sobbing, between agonised groans.

'Do something,' her husband begged. 'Please…'

'We're going to take Lauren up to Theatre.' Logan's

tone was deceptively calm. 'We can get her pain under control there and start giving her some fluids at the same time as getting her ready for surgery.'

'Surgery?'

'It looks like there's some internal bleeding going on,' Ella told him. 'So the sooner we deliver baby, the better.'

'Can I stay with her?'

'We'll see how it goes.' Ella couldn't make promises. In the event of a major surgical emergency you didn't want family members in there watching. 'You can certainly come up as far as Theatre with us. We'll need you to sign the consent forms for a Caesarean section.'

'Are you going to do the operation?'

'No,' Logan said. 'I'll be doing that.'

'You're in the best hands,' Judy assured them as she began opening both doors to the room to allow for the bed to be wheeled through. 'Dr Walsh is our top consultant.'

Ella was blinking at having her first patient whisked from her care like this. Okay, this man was her new boss and maybe he hadn't read her CV and had no idea that she was more than capable of handling an emergency C-section herself but to dismiss her like this, in front of a patient and one of her new colleagues was…well…rather stunningly rude.

She'd probably decide it was mortifying when she gave herself time to think about it and maybe that would be in only a matter of seconds when everybody else had vanished through those doors, leaving her in an empty delivery room.

Lauren was still sobbing as the bed started moving,

beside herself now with the fear on top of her pain. 'But I want Ella to look after me…'

'She's coming too,' Logan said, his tone suggesting that it was a given. He turned as he reached the door, his brows lowering as he saw her still standing beside where the bed had been positioned. 'Any time you're ready, Doctor…?'

'Grisham,' Ella muttered as she followed the bed. Not that there had been much point in answering the query. He'd probably forgotten he'd even asked by now. Her HoD was holding onto the rails on one side of the bed, Judy on the other, as they sped towards a lift that another staff member was already holding open for them, the tension of an escalating emergency clearly contagious.

Ella squeezed herself into the small space remaining in the lift as the doors began to close. She found she was still holding her breath as they slid open again a very short time later, giving them access to the theatre suite. She got out to allow room for Lauren's bed to get past and, to her horror, Ella could see a bright red bloodstain beginning to spread on the hospital gown that had become tucked between her legs.

This was definitely the most dramatic start to any job she'd ever had and maybe the worst part was that she was clearly not going to be allowed to take an active role in making sure it didn't become a catastrophe. Ella could only hope that this tall, rugged-looking man who'd simply assumed command—and who, in fact, was the reason she'd chosen to come to this particular hospital in the first place—was every bit as good as his reputation suggested.

* * *

At least she knew better than to make idle small talk at an inappropriate time—like when you were scrubbing in for an emergent situation where every second counted.

It seemed that this new locum was every bit as focused as Logan was on the woman they'd just left in the hands of the anaesthetic team to put in a spinal block and the theatre technicians to drape and prep Lauren's skin. A sideways glance as Logan pulled on a hat and tied his mask showed him that Ella was already well into the detailed process of decontamination. She was rinsing off the first soaping by holding her hands up to let the water stream down towards her elbows. He noticed that her nails were short and practical and that she wasn't wearing any rings, although anything other than a plain wedding band had to be removed for surgery anyway. What was far more important was that Ella had just demonstrated skills far more useful than not interrupting his concentration.

'That was good work,' he said gruffly. 'Getting wide bore venous access for fluid resuscitation when someone's that shut down isn't easy.'

'Can the blood bank here do a full group and hold within forty minutes?'

'Of course. And we'll have O negative packed red cells, platelets and plasma here by the time we've run two litres of saline.' Logan used his elbow to dispense the liquid surgical scrub onto his hands and then interlaced his fingers to start a ritual he was so familiar with it was automatic. 'Did you get the chance to do a detailed history?'

'Enough to know she had no red flags for a placental

abruption.' Ella had taken the soap-impregnated brush from its sterile packaging and was starting to scrub her nails. 'Her blood pressure's been normal at every antenatal visit, she doesn't smoke and she hasn't experienced any recent traumatic event.'

'What makes you so sure it's a placental abruption?' Logan clasped his arm with his other hand and rotated it as he moved his hand towards his elbow. 'Why wouldn't you think it could be a uterine rupture?'

The glance he got then was wide-eyed. 'Because the chances of that in a primigravida with no history of trauma or surgery are virtually non-existent. What's that saying about thinking of horses when you hear hoofbeats and not zebras?'

'When you're the only maternity hospital for a very large catchment area, maybe it pays to remember there might be a zoo nearby.' It was Logan's turn to reach for the nailbrush.

Ella was unfolding the sterile towel to dry each hand and arm. 'Lauren's not an older mother, she's less than forty weeks gestation with a baby of normal weight.' She picked up the gown on the top of the opened sterile pack, giving it an expert shake before pushing her arms into the sleeves without letting her fingers come through the cuffs. 'As far as anyone knows, she doesn't have a malformed uterus and hasn't got a placenta praevia. She's never had a C-section or surgery for fibroids. She's not even in labour...'

Logan said nothing as he let her finish demonstrating her knowledge of known risk factors for the major complication of a ruptured uterus. While it wouldn't change the initial management of getting both this mother and baby out of danger, it was disappointing that this new colleague was dismissing what was always top of his own list of potential diagnoses with this kind of presentation. He stayed silent as he put on his own gown and gloves. Ella was turning to wrap the tie of her gown around her body while a nurse held the end. She tied it in a bow, clasped both gloved hands in front of her body and stood back, clearly waiting for him to lead the way into Theatre. Her gaze was steady.

'You're quite right,' she said quietly. 'About keeping even the rarest of things in mind.' She didn't let go of his gaze.

Logan was still silent for a heartbeat but then he gave her a single approving nod. 'Let's go and find out, shall we?'

He was right.

Against those unbelievable odds, Logan Walsh had picked the correct cause for the sudden life-threatening deterioration of Lauren's condition. The massive amount of blood that had been lost became dramatically obvious the moment the abdomen was opened and at least a litre of blood spilled out to soak the drapes and trickle onto the floor of the operating theatre.

'Suction, please.' Logan's voice was deceptively calm.

Ella held the tube of the suction unit and could see the collection chamber filling rapidly with another litre of blood. Lauren's husband, sitting on the other side of the screen and holding tight to her hand, couldn't see the operating field but he went several shades paler as he saw the blood on the floor.

It was only when Ella had suctioned even more blood out of the abdomen that the tear in the uterus became evident. For a split second she caught Logan's gaze and it was a silent acknowledgement that, from now on, she would always be more prepared for even the most unlikely diagnosis.

It was impressive just how calmly Logan was dealing with this. Within a remarkably short period of time he was lifting a completely motionless baby from the damaged womb and placing him onto towels that a paediatric registrar was holding. Ella took another glance as the baby was placed on the trolley in front of the senior neonatal paediatrician and a bag mask was fitted over the tiny face to begin an attempt to resuscitate the newborn.

'Is he all right?' The baby's father had twisted his neck to watch but could see nothing past the backs of so many people.

'Can I see him?' It was Lauren's voice this time. 'Just for a minute?'

'Not just yet.' Logan's voice held a note that Ella hadn't heard before. 'He needs a wee bit of help but he's in the best hands.'

He wasn't just being reassuring without making promises that might not be possible to keep. There was something deeper in that tone. A hint of an empathy that Ella could actually feel rather than hear.

'Suction, thanks.'

This time Logan's tone told Ella not to lose focus on the task ahead of them now—to stop the blood loss and hopefully be able to repair the uterus so that Lauren wouldn't lose the chance to have another child in the future. It didn't look promising with the distortion she could see in the uterine structure but, as the minutes ticked past and more blood products and then whole blood were hung for transfusion, Logan worked with the utmost concentration and a skill that Ella recognised as being possibly the best she'd ever seen to repair the jagged damage.

Even better, the ominous silence from the corner of the theatre where the paediatric team were working to resuscitate the baby was finally broken by the warbling cry of an infant who sounded as if he'd got over the shock of his tumultuous entrance to the world and he wanted everybody to know he wasn't happy about it.

His parents both burst into tears and Ella could feel herself welling up too, because the survival of a tiny baby against the odds was always going to be something that squeezed her heart hard enough to push a lump into her throat and tears into her eyes, but she had to blink them back. Fast.

How embarrassing would it be if her new boss caught her crying right now? He was already unimpressed that she'd picked the wrong potential cause for a dangerous internal bleed in a pregnant woman. She kept her head down, using the swab she had clasped in some forceps to clear a small pooling of blood, but that wasn't the reason Logan paused his meticulous stitching for a moment. Ella could feel, for that heartbeat, that he was staring at her.

She also had the distinct feeling that he knew just how easy it was for her to get a bit too emotionally involved with her cases. And that he was even less impressed with her because of it.

'I can't thank you enough, Ella.'

But Ella shook her head. 'It's not me that deserves the thanks, Lauren.' She smiled down at the young mother, propped against her pillows, who was holding her sound asleep baby boy in her arms. 'You were lucky enough to be in the hands of one of the best surgeons I've ever worked with—and I've worked with a lot, given that I never stay in one place for long.'

'What made you come to Aberdeen?' Lauren was still too pale and obviously exhausted but happy enough to be smiling back at Ella. 'Can't possibly be for the weather.'

Both women—and the nurse who was tidying Lauren's bedside table—looked towards the window of the room, where the rain was coming down in sheets that would have been thick enough to blur the view of the old grey stone buildings in this older western area of the Scottish city even if the daylight wasn't rapidly fading.

'My grandparents used to live here and I visited frequently as a child. Maybe I felt the need for a place that felt more like home for a change. I've been in California for the last six months, doing some advanced training, and I had a condo right on the beach.'

'Some people have all the luck,' the nurse muttered, but her smile was friendly.

Lauren shook her head sadly. 'You won't want to live on any beach around here.'

'No… And I'm only here for three months, filling in for someone on maternity leave, so it's not worth even looking for my own place.' Ella picked up the chart on the end of Lauren's bed to check the latest vital sign recordings, taking a glance at the catheter bag on the way. Bladder injuries from a uterine rupture were not uncommon and it was reassuring not to see any tinge of pink in the bag. 'I've been given a room in the doctors' residence,' she said when she'd taken in recordings that were all within normal limits. 'Which was another good reason to come here. Not the most important one, of course.'

'What *was* the most important one?' Lauren sounded curious.

'Working with the surgeon who did your operation,' Ella told her. 'He's had some papers published around his mission to reduce the risk of obstetric emergencies, especially in remote areas. He's developed a course to train paramedics and supply refresher courses to GPs and midwives. He also heads a response team that's available to be in the emergency department when a serious case is brought in or they ride out with the crew on ambulances or with helicopter rescue teams if there's enough time. They work with a NETS team as well, which is the neonatal emergency transfer service if an incubator is needed. I'm really hoping I can get involved with the programme while I'm here.'

'You might be out of luck this time...' It was the nurse who was shaking her head now. 'I know people who'd happily give up an eye tooth to get in on that front line obstetric stuff, including the doctor you're filling in for, who's never been included. He's very picky about who gets to work with him, is our Dr Walsh.'

'Hmm...'

Ella's tone was noncommittal but yes…she'd got the impression that her new boss might be rather picky about quite a few things. This morning's emergency hadn't been the time to even think about him on a personal level but those first impressions had been surfacing somewhere in the back of her mind over the course of the rest of the day which had, fortunately, been full of perfectly routine, easy to manage obstetrical tasks, including two straight-forward deliveries and an antenatal clinic that had taken up most of the afternoon.

The impression that stood out above all others was the sheer presence of the man. If she'd been a fly on the wall, watching the way he simply assumed command of a situ-ation he'd chosen to walk into, she might have labelled it arrogance but, even though she'd been the person who'd been pushed aside, it hadn't felt as if Logan Walsh was a self-centred or uncaring man. Quite the opposite, really. It was just that what he cared about so fiercely had nothing to do with what others might think of him or the feelings of colleagues he might be trampling on. The intensity of his focus—that, in hindsight, was a perfect match for his very Scottish kind of ruggedness and the dark, slightly unkempt waves of his hair—had been on what actually mattered in the moment, however, and that was saving the lives of this young mother and her first baby.

'It's so good to see you looking so much better,' Ella said to Lauren. 'You had us all worried there for a little while this morning.'

'I was kind of terrified myself.' Lauren's smile was full of joy now, though, as she gazed at the scrunched-up face of the tiny boy in her arms. 'But he's just perfect, isn't he?'

'He's gorgeous,' Ella agreed. 'But how are you? How's the pain level?'

'The pain's not too bad. I'm just so tired...'

'We had to replace almost your whole blood volume,' Ella said. 'It's only to be expected that you'll feel like you've had the stuffing knocked out of you for a few days but you're doing very well and I can see you're being extremely well looked after.' She smiled at the nurse. 'I'm about to brave that filthy weather out there and find where I'm going to be living because I came straight here from my hotel this morning and left my suitcase at Reception. I don't think I'm far away, though, so if there's any problems overnight I'll be available.'

'The doctors' residence is just across the road from the back of this part of the hospital buildings,' the nurse said. 'But it's Dr Walsh who'll be on call for Lauren. He makes a point of being available for all his own surgical cases.'

Ella blinked. How could any surgeon, let alone a head of department, find the time to do that, on top of running an emergency service for obstetric cases that could be activated at any time of the day or night? Did the man have no life of his own? No need to sleep?

Not that she was about to criticise his lifestyle. Or tread on his toes. She needed some sleep herself after a huge first day on top of the travel and general upheaval that came from shifting her life from one country to another. It would have been sensible to have another night at the hotel with the convenience of the restaurant for an evening meal but it was too late to go back now. Her suitcase—and the keys to her self-contained apartment in the doctors' residence—were waiting for her at the main reception desk.

The weariness, as well as hunger, were even more noticeable by the time Ella had changed out of her scrubs into jeans, sneakers and a warm jumper over her tee shirt. Any thoughts of finding a nearby supermarket were easy to dismiss when all she wanted was to unpack essentials, have a long, hot shower and crash into bed. Passing a vending machine in one of the corridors on the way to Reception, she stopped and selected a ham and salad sandwich in a plastic triangle. At least she'd found an easy way to prevent herself getting any hungrier.

There was no way to stop herself getting very, very wet as she followed the directions they gave her at Reception, dragged her overly large wheelie case across a main road at the first set of traffic lights and looked for an old stone building with a brass plaque above its front door that had the impression of a crown and the grand title of 'The Lodge'.

The mosaic tiling in the foyer was magnificent. So was the ornate ceiling, the chandelier and the sweeping staircase of what must have once been a grand private home. The common areas on the ground floor like the big sitting room to one side seemed to be deserted and Ella's heart sank a little as she realised there was no lift available. She checked the tag attached to the keys she'd been given to both the front door and her own space. Apartment Seven, she confirmed. Second floor.

The big suitcase thumped against every step. Ella stopped to catch her breath on the first-floor landing and then started again, aware that she was still leaving a trail of dripping water from her sodden anorak and the long braid hanging down her back. She was also starting to feel unpleasantly cold.

Apartments Five and Six were the closest to the stairs but the end of the hallway had a wonderful arched window that had the sparkle of lights behind a curtain of the relentless rain so maybe Ella's apartment would have a nice view of the city. It was a huge relief to park her suitcase beside the door with a shiny brass number seven screwed to the dark wood. She fished in her bag for the key and fitted it into the lock.

Or rather she tried to fit it into the lock. She tried both keys. She tried many times but it was quite obvious that there was no way she was going to open this door. She found her phone and tried to call the woman called Jean who'd been so charming when she'd made the arrangements for this accommodation during a phone call from California.

'It'll be perfect for you, Dr Grisham, I promise. You'll find breakfast supplies like tea, coffee and milk, along with all the linen you'll need. The bed will be made up and ready for you and you have my number if there are any problems.'

The response to the number was a message that suggested calling back during business hours on weekdays between nine a.m. and five p.m. As Ella hung up she noticed the warning message of low battery power on the screen of her phone. The option of searching online for a number that would get her through to the hospital's reception desk wasn't looking promising. She was going to have to go out into that horrible weather again, wasn't she?

Ella never normally used swear words but she used one now. Quite loudly. She was tempted to kick the door of Apartment Seven but settled with glaring at it instead. And then she made a growling sound, snatching up her shoulder bag as she turned to head for the staircase again. She hadn't quite finished the turn when the door opposite her own flew open and she froze instantly.

At least she didn't swear again. Out loud, anyway.

This day had started on an undeniably mortifying note when Ella's albeit unknown level of skill had been summarily dismissed in the face of a life-or-death emergency. She'd then offered her senior colleague an inaccurate diagnosis of what was causing that emergency. And now... oh, dear Lord...now, she could almost *feel* him thinking that she was not only demonstrating a lack of control in a frustrating situation but total incompetency in not even being able to unlock a door.

Had she done something terrible in a previous life to earn this kind of karma?

What else could explain this appalling development of discovering that the occupant of Apartment Eight, her closest neighbour, was none other than Logan Walsh?

CHAPTER TWO

IT SHOULDN'T HAVE been so startling to find his new locum standing in the hallway outside his apartment. This was, after all, a residence that was normally used for precisely a situation like this—a locum who was only going to be working at Queen's for a short period. Or the arrival of a new permanent staff member who needed time to find a property to rent or purchase.

Being faced with someone who'd only arrived at his workplace this morning—someone who was going to be working in his own department—made Logan Walsh suddenly realise what it might look like to Ella to find that her HoD was living in what was only intended to be a temporary residence. He could imagine her wondering what sort of consultant doctor, presumably a member of staff who wasn't about to resign, would both work and virtually live in the same building?

But she wasn't looking particularly curious. More like…thoroughly dismayed, with those wide eyes and her lips twisted somewhere halfway between a smile and a scowl. As if he was the last person she'd expected—or wanted—to see right now?

She was also looking like a drowned rat.

A rather angry drowned rat with a dripping tail hanging over her shoulder. Logan could feel an embryonic smile hovering at one corner of his own mouth. He liked that she would choose anger rather than crying if she was in trouble because he'd long ago discovered that it was a far more useful emotion as long as it could be well controlled.

'I...um...heard you,' he said mildly. 'Is there a problem?'

Apart from her being soaked and looking completely exhausted and at the end of her tether? There was more to the way she looked than being either angry or dismayed, he thought. Vulnerable, that was the word for it.

'I can't open my door,' she told him. She sounded as if she was speaking through gritted teeth.

'Shall I try?'

Logan held his hand out for the key without giving Ella a chance to respond and thought he caught a flash of something like a resigned eyeroll before she handed him the key and seemed to find something interesting on the ceiling to stare at. Perhaps it was the decorative plaster rose on the ceiling that provided the anchor for that wonderful antique chandelier he was so familiar with he barely gave it a second glance these days.

The key slid inside the lock easily enough but it wouldn't turn. 'These old doors can be a bit tricky,' Logan said. He rattled the handle and tried again. Then he checked the tag attached to the key ring. 'I think there's been some sort of mix-up,' he suggested.

'Oh...r-really?' Any note of sarcasm was undermined by the way Ella's teeth were starting to chatter so Logan chose to ignore it. He could at least be polite to his new locum.

'You'd better come into my apartment,' he said. 'You can't stand out here in this draughty hallway in the state you're in. I'll ring the concierge and he'll be able to sort it out for you.'

The central heating inside these apartments was efficient and he could see the way Ella closed her eyes in a moment of relief, after dropping her shoulder bag on the floor and starting to remove her soaked anorak. She was wearing a woollen jumper underneath in a golden-brown shade with...good grief...was that a row of llamas across the front of it? Fortunately, Ella didn't notice the direction of his gaze. She was letting her own drift around his apartment as if she was wondering where to put her coat.

'Give it to me,' Logan ordered, grateful for a reason to turn away. There was something about that vaguely childlike oversized jumper that, oddly, had made him curious about the shape of Ella's body beneath in a way that a baggy scrub suit would never do. 'I'll hang it on a chair beside the radiator. There's a stack of clean towels in the bathroom if you want one to dry your hair a wee bit. I'll find the number for Dougal, the concierge.'

He was ending his call as Ella came out of the bathroom, squeezing water from her braid with a towel.

'Dougal's on his way back but he's about fifteen to twenty minutes away, I'm afraid. He actually lives in a small ground-floor apartment, for future reference, but this happens to be the day he takes his elderly mother grocery shopping on the other side of the city. He's very apologetic.'

The band holding the end of Ella's braid had slipped off and the movement of the towel was loosening the tight control of her hair. It was wavy, he noticed as tresses began to break free. As dark as her eyes and it was long enough to be able to cover her breasts if that ridiculous jumper wasn't already doing that job so well.

Logan cleared his throat, a sound that did the trick of stamping on whatever direction his thoughts were trying to go because he had a feeling he was about to get a mental image of Ella riding a horse naked, like Lady Godiva—with her hair protecting at least part of her modesty.

'Apparently the housekeeper who got your apartment ready yesterday pointed out that some of the key tags were unreadable,' he continued hastily. 'So he put new ones on last night and must have put them back on the wrong keys.'

She gave him one of 'those' looks. The ones women were so good at, where they barely moved their eyebrows but could make you feel like a bit of an idiot. It might be a paler version of the glance he'd received when he'd suggested that she might have been given the wrong key in the first place but, added to the way she'd reacted when he'd offered to help, it was impossible not to get the impression that his new colleague didn't find him very likeable.

Not that it mattered. He didn't care what she thought of him personally but it might be awkward to work closely with someone who obviously disliked him.

'Can I get you a cup of tea or coffee? Or a whisky? That might warm you up a bit more quickly.'

'I hate whisky,' she said. 'My grandfather used to reek of it and it put me off for life.'

'Tea, then?'

'No, I'm good. But thank you.'

It was the first time Logan had seen her smile, which was hardly a surprise. The circumstances of their first meeting hadn't exactly been something to smile about, had they? Even that moment of relief in Theatre, when they'd heard the first cry of an infant who clearly intended to survive, hadn't made her smile like this, with that curve of her lips generous enough to crinkle the corners of her eyes. No...she'd quickly avoided looking at him at all in that moment and he'd been relieved that she hadn't been distracted from what they were doing in that complex job of controlling a dangerous amount of blood loss and repairing a ruptured uterus. Thinking back over the hours since then made Logan think he might understand a tension between them that was almost bordering on animosity.

'Your assistance was greatly appreciated this morning,' he told her. 'I enjoyed working with you.'

'Even when I was hearing horses' hooves instead of zebras'?'

Horses' hooves? For a horrible instant Logan wondered if Ella might be telepathic and had caught a fleeting glimpse of that Lady Godiva image. Then he retreated into the comfort zone of the profession that was his life.

'You were quite correct in assuming it was more likely to be a placental abruption from her presentation and lack of risk factors.'

'But it was obvious that she had blood in the peritoneum. And I know that can happen with blood that's backed up through a fallopian tube from a placental abruption, but that's just about as likely as a rupture in an unscarred uterus, isn't it?'

'You reacted quickly and appropriately,' Logan told her. 'And both our mother and baby survived.'

'Lauren tried to thank me when I went to see her this evening but I told her that you were the person she should be thanking. The way you handled a situation that could have easily become catastrophic was very impressive. I can see why you've earned the reputation you've got, Dr Walsh.'

'Logan,' he muttered. The formality felt like some kind of reprimand but he didn't say anything else. Ella had no idea at all of why or how he'd become so good at his job and so capable of managing exactly those kinds of emergencies and he wasn't about to start telling her. Because he didn't want to be reminded of what he'd left behind so many years ago.

He knew the silence had gone on a shade too long by the anxiety he could see surfacing in Ella's eyes at his lack of response on top of the frown of self-recrimination that was already there. He cleared his throat, which had long ago become his go-to method to change the direction of his thoughts and move on.

'You were a pleasure to work with in Theatre,' he said. 'And I don't think I've ever been able to say that to someone on the first occasion I've worked with them. I'm sorry I didn't get a chance to tell you that before now, but I was caught up in some high-level meetings. We're rather desperately hunting funding to extend our ability to keep operating our OERT—the obstetric emergency response team.'

'Oh…'

Logan could see Ella's expression changing like ripples on water from a stone being thrown into a pond. She had the most expressive face he'd ever seen. The anxiety and self-recrimination faded. Any hint of animosity evaporated. Ella was looking interested now. Very interested, with a hopeful undertone.

Interested in *him*…?

It hit him somewhere deep in his gut with the force of…a horse's hoof, maybe? Or was that a zebra, given that Logan didn't remember when he'd last felt a degree of sexual attraction quite like this?

Whatever.

It wasn't welcome. Logan could feel his brows lowering as he tried to think of the best way to make sure this wasn't going to go even a step further.

Oh, *help*…

What had been shaping up to be a disaster was suddenly an opportunity to talk about what was a part of the main attraction of coming here to the Queen Mother's Maternity Hospital in Aberdeen—the education programme and skilled response team that was becoming a gold standard for managing emergency obstetric interventions both in and out of hospital.

Except that Logan was scowling at her.

But hadn't he just been complimenting her on her management of Lauren's case and the assistance she'd provided in Theatre?

Ella should have been confused. Or intimidated but, to her horror, she could feel a curl of sensation that had absolutely nothing to do with either of those perfectly reasonable reactions.

No… She was looking at this tall, craggy man who was earning an international reputation for being at the top of his field—which also happened to be *her* field—and she was…oh, *God*…attracted to him? Yeah…she recognised that knot of something deep in her gut, that was not unlike excitement or the pleasure of anticipation, currently firing off tingles like microscopic skyrockets in all directions. It was easy enough to ignore, however, because there was something more important to focus on.

Ella swallowed hard as she felt her smile vanishing. 'I didn't say this in my interview because you weren't there, but the real reason I was so keen to take up this locum position is that I would love the chance to get involved with your OERT. It's…' Ella remembered what Lauren's nurse had said about how picky he was about squad members and decided to throw herself on Logan Walsh's mercy. She took a deep breath and smiled at him again—her best smile this time. 'It's a bit of a dream of mine to join one on a semi-permanent basis, to tell you the truth. To be able to use my skills in genuine frontline situations so I could be confident taking up locum positions in more remote areas.'

He didn't smile back.

'You're here for how long? Three months, while Kirsty's on maternity leave?'

'Yes.'

'We struggle for resources to meet our targets for the

training days and extra hours for staff members to be on call as it is.' Logan gave a single shake of his head. 'It would be a complete waste to use any of them to train someone who'll disappear as soon as they're remotely familiar with our protocols and setup.'

The disappointment was surprisingly crushing. 'I might stay longer if it's as good as I've heard,' she said quietly. 'I just spent six months in California doing some advanced training in obstetric emergencies and that involved some out of hospital work with an ambulance service.' Disappointment was morphing into something that she didn't need, added to the frustrations the day had already thrown at her. 'You never know,' she went on, a little more sharply than she had intended. 'I could be a resource myself that your team members might appreciate more than you.' Ella picked up her coat and walked towards where she'd left her bag. 'I'll wait for the concierge by my door,' she told Logan. 'He can't be far away now.'

She snatched up her bag but missed one of the handles. Things fell out, including that plastic triangle of sandwiches, a packet of tissues, her phone and a book that had been in there since her plane trip from the States yesterday. It was Logan who picked up the book.

'Are you kidding?'

'What?' Ella had crouched to pick up a slice of hardboiled egg and some rather wilted lettuce that had fallen out of the salad sandwich to stuff them back into a now dented plastic container. Her intended dinner was no longer even slightly tempting to eat. She'd laugh about this one day, wouldn't she? The final straw in a first day she'd never forget...

Logan was reading the title of her book aloud. *'Architectural Authenticity in the Conversion and Restoration of Historic Buildings.'*

She got to her feet and let her breath out in a sigh. 'I was reading it on my flight yesterday. That subject happens to be my hobby. If I hadn't become a doctor, I would have been an architect.' Her smile felt wry. 'Or maybe I would have just rescued dogs. And ducks.'

Logan was looking at her as if she'd just revealed herself to be an alien from an entirely different planet to his own.

'You wouldn't like to buy an old barn that's ripe for conversion by any chance, would you? One that just happens to have a large duck pond?'

Taken off-guard, Ella let out a huff of laughter. 'Why? Have you got one for sale?'

'As a matter of fact, I have.' Logan waved a hand to encompass the small sitting room of his apartment. 'The reason I'm living here is because I was stupid enough to buy an old barn a couple of years ago that I haven't found time to even think about converting. My last architect gave up on me months ago after I postponed one too many meetings.'

Ella was staring at him. Wondering if he knew that when he wasn't being completely professional and somewhat surly it took his sexiness to a whole new level?

'I'm only here for three months, remember? It would be a waste of time to get involved.'

'But…' There was a hint of a curve to one side of Logan's mouth that grew into a lopsided smile. 'It might be so good you'll want to stay longer.'

Damn it…

That *smile*…

Ella took the book out of his hands and shoved it back into her bag. 'If you're hitting on me, Dr Walsh, it's doomed to failure, I'm afraid. As tempting as an unconverted barn with its own duck pond might be, I'm not the settling down kind.'

Well, that certainly wiped the smile off his face and, like a punctuation mark, the knock on the door signalled an end to their conversation.

'Dr Walsh?' The voice on the other side of the door was a little muffled. 'It's Dougal here. Is Dr Grisham with you, by any chance?'

'Coming.' Logan went to open the door but the glance he threw over his shoulder had a hint of something that might have been respect in it.

'Good to know,' he said to Ella. 'And don't worry. You're perfectly safe as far as I'm concerned.'

It was the tomato slice that did it.

The one that Logan found beneath the chair he'd used to hang her anorak near the radiator, when he was moving it back to the table. A scrap of food that Ella clearly hadn't seen when she'd been gathering the spilled contents of her bag. Had that sad-looking sandwich been left over from her lunch or was it what she was planning to eat for her dinner?

Not that it was any of Logan's business but he found himself feeling sorry for her.

And guilty about how he'd treated her.

Not when he'd taken over the management of the patient she'd been called to see this morning, mind you. Apart from his personal mission in life to try and ensure that no mother or baby died if medical intervention could prevent the loss, he was the senior consultant on duty and, aside from the glowing reference that had crossed his desk, he had no real idea how competent this new locum was.

No. He was feeling bad about his reaction to her expressing such a fervent desire to be part of the department's emergency response team. He'd seen that hopeful light in her eyes die a rapid death when he'd dismissed any chance of her being allowed to be involved. And she was right. It was very likely, with her experience of different facilities and protocols, that she did have something to offer the team. On top of that, it wasn't easy to find people with the necessary skills willing to take on the disruption to their lives that an extra commitment like being on call for the team represented. So why on earth hadn't he been prepared to even consider it?

Because he was attracted to her and it had caught him so off-guard?

Well, that was his problem, not hers. Ella had made it quite clear that she wasn't interested in being 'hit on' as she'd so succinctly summed it up, so how unfair was it that he was punishing her for how *he* felt?

It was still a niggle in the back of his mind as he ate a microwaved meal for one without even tasting it while he skimmed a recent article on the incidence and management of gastroesophageal reflux disease during pregnancy.

He'd managed to consign what felt like something that

needed to be fixed to a mental list of things he would give further thought to in the near future by the time he fell asleep but, weirdly, it was the first thing he thought of when his phone rang at three o'clock in the morning because he knew there was only one reason for that to happen.

Someone in the hospital or the emergency services control room was fielding a call for a potential obstetric emergency and wanted his advice. It would be Logan's call whether the OERT got activated. The conversation was brief but the information received meant that the decision was an easy one. A pregnant woman was in serious trouble and that meant her baby was also in danger.

Logan was well practised in getting himself dressed in the shortest possible amount of time. He usually closed the door of his apartment and then slipped out of the building as quietly as he could to avoid disturbing anyone else who would be getting some probably well-deserved rest but this time, as he shut the door behind him, Logan stopped and stared at the door on the other side of the corridor. He could see Ella's face and the way it had been so alive with the hope that he'd snuffed out.

Two strides and he was tapping on that door.

Just quietly. If she didn't hear him, that was fine. He would still feel as if he'd done the right thing.

But Ella did hear him and she must have woken up instantly to have blinked any traces of sleep from her eyes by the time she opened the door.

'An OERT activation's just come in,' Logan told her. 'ETA of ten minutes to A&E. How fast can you get some clothes on?'

CHAPTER THREE

ELLA HAD BEEN wearing the leggings and a big tee shirt she wore as pyjamas. It took thirty seconds to pull her warm jumper on and jam her feet into her sneakers.

She had to run to keep up with Logan. She might have only had a few hours' sleep but, as she raced down the stairs and out into the night, it felt as if her sneakers had grown a pair of wings. Not that she could keep up a conversation, but she didn't need to. Just an affirmative sound was enough to let Logan know she was taking in the information as they ran along the street and around the corner to the main entrance of the emergency department. Fortunately, the torrential rain of earlier in the evening had stopped for now.

'The paramedic did a course with us not long ago and called this in early while he was still on scene,' Logan relayed. 'Thirty-eight-year-old primigravida, thirty-one weeks gestation with sudden onset preeclampsia symptoms including pulmonary oedema. Oxygen saturation down to eighty-eight percent and blood pressure through the roof.' Logan was starting to sound a little out of breath himself and his pace slowed as his phone started ringing.

His responses were terse and he ended the call swiftly.

'Patient's having a seizure en route,' he told Ella. 'Last

blood pressure recording was one ninety over one twenty. ETA four minutes now. Someone from Neonatal Paediatrics is on the way in case we need to deliver.'

They could see the big red sign with a white *H* and *A&E* beneath it beside an arrow pointing towards the entrance. Staff were waiting with packs containing scrub suits and booties to go over their footwear and it seemed like only seconds later that they were heading into the main resuscitation area. Ella tucked her hair under a cap and tied a mask around her face. There were people coming from all directions and the tension in the department shot up as a nurse gave them the latest update from the crew rushing the pregnant woman towards them.

'She's gone into cardiac arrest. CPR underway. ETA less than two minutes.'

Logan was suddenly centre stage, giving clear and calm directions.

'Start the clock,' he said, and someone pushed the button on a clock that began a time count from when their incoming patient had gone into cardiac arrest.

'We need three resus teams,' he continued. 'One to cover CPR, another one to set up a neonatal resus area and I'll cover the obstetric side of things along with my registrar, Dr Grisham.'

Ella could feel curious gazes on her but only in passing as people swiftly responded to further rapid instructions from Logan.

'CPR protocol to stay the same as normal for both chest compressions and ventilations except that the hand position for compressions is a few centimetres higher on the sternum. Patient to stay supine. You'll need an extra set of hands to provide left uterine deviation. We'll need to set up for a potential resuscitative hysterotomy.'

Ella could hear Logan checking off the equipment that needed to be set up in a sterile area. A scalpel, blunt scissors, clamps, a suction unit, sutures, antiseptic.

'Just a bottle of iodine'll do,' he was saying. 'We might not have time for any other skin prep.'

The neonatal team was on the other side of the resus area, setting up a space that would be used to resuscitate an infant that could well be shocked, with supplies like airways and a tiny bag mask unit, oxygen, umbilical IV access equipment and a baby warmer. A ventilator was being pulled into position at the head of the main bed, along with a defibrillation unit and an IV trolley. The pace was enough to make Ella's head spin but she was more likely to get in the way right now than help find and set things up in an unfamiliar setting. She found herself watching Logan and becoming increasingly impressed with how calm he was and how everybody was following his lead without hesitation. She thought she heard the sound of a siren in the distance and her thoughts went instantly to a pregnant woman heading towards them who was, unknowingly, facing what had probably been unthinkable even a few hours ago—a very real risk of losing both her own life and that of her unborn child.

Resuscitative hysterotomy was the new term for what used to be called a perimortem C-section. Getting ROSC, or return of spontaneous circulation, in a pregnant woman was far more difficult because the uterus compressed veins and arteries and reduced venous return and cardiac output during resuscitation. That was what the clock was ticking up to. If they didn't achieve ROSC within four to five minutes of the heart having stopped, the decision would need to be made to get the baby out as quickly as possible to improve the chances of survival for both mother and baby. Current research suggested that the time frame could be extended and still achieve good results but the sooner it could happen the better.

Ella saw that the decision had been made the moment the doors of the ambulance bay opened and a stretcher came towards them at speed, with a paramedic still doing his best to keep effective CPR going. She saw Logan glance at the clock, which was now reading three minutes, ten seconds. Twenty seconds by the time the stretcher was in Resus and hands were reaching to transfer the woman to the bed.

'On the count of three… One…two…*three*…'

Emergency department medics were ready to take over the CPR, with one person doing compressions, pausing for only a matter of seconds to allow the airway physician—an anaesthetist—to intubate her and position the bag mask unit, now attached to the hospital's overhead oxygen supply, over her nose and mouth. A third doctor placed his hands on the side of the woman's huge belly and pushed the baby towards the left to take pressure off major vessels and allow blood to return to the heart. Information was being relayed as rapidly as possible. There had been two cycles of CPR completed en route. Drugs had been administered. Defibrillation had not been successful.

Logan absorbed the handover information but another minute had ticked past and he'd already made the decision. He had a gown over his scrubs and shoved his hands into a fresh pair of gloves.

'Stand back, please, everyone. We're going to do an RH. Ella? Are you ready?'

'Yes.' Ella, also gowned and gloved, stepped up to the side of the table opposite Logan.

A nurse tipped iodine over the stretched bare skin of the woman's belly and Ella heard a gasp from behind her as Logan used the scalpel to make a long incision that opened the abdomen in the midline from the pubic symphysis to the umbilicus. She had the blunt scissors ready to hand him to get through the muscles beneath the skin and then to open the uterus. She held her breath as she watched him feeling for the closest part of the baby he could find through the incision and then getting a firm enough grasp to be able to apply traction.

'Fundal pressure, please, Ella.'

Ella pushed down on the top of the uterus to help Logan pull the baby out. She grabbed the clamps to close off a section of the umbilical cord for Logan to cut through and then held out a towel for him to put the baby on, turning in almost the same instant to hand a totally limp newborn over to the neonatal team, less than sixty seconds from when Logan had made that first incision. They rushed the tiny boy to the resuscitation area they'd set up on the other side of the room and he was lost to view within seconds.

CPR was in progress again on the mother.

'Stand clear,' someone warned. 'Shocking...'

The woman's body jerked but the static on the overhead monitor settled to reveal no change to the ominous wavy line of ventricular fibrillation.

'Still in VF,' Logan stated calmly. 'Ella, draw up a bolus dose of oxytocin, please. I've almost got the placenta now.'

She handed the new bag of saline to a nurse to hang, moments later, with the drug added that would help prevent excessive bleeding from the uterus by causing it to contract.

Logan wanted to control any immediate blood loss as well. 'Let's clamp any actively bleeding vessels here and then we'll pack the abdomen.'

Ella had never tried to operate while chest compressions were ongoing. She handed clamps to Logan and watched the way he carefully timed the moment of trying to clip them onto a bleeding vessel at the point of the pressure on the sternum being lifted. The two minutes before the next shock was due to happen seemed to pass in a blink.

'Stand clear… Shocking…'

And this time, perhaps helped by CPR after the dramatic intervention to remove the baby and relieve the pressure on blood vessels, the mother's heart started beating again. Just a few uneven spikes could be seen initially but then it settled into a more regular rhythm.

The airway doctor had his fingers against the woman's neck. 'I've got a pulse,' he said. 'Just. BP still not recordable and she's not trying to breathe for herself yet.'

'Let's get some sedation and analgesia on board,' Logan directed. 'I don't want her waking up in pain.' He and Ella were packing gauze into the gaping wound on the abdomen, ready to cover it and move their patient. 'Have we got a theatre on standby?'

'Yes. They're ready and waiting.'

'Good. Let's move.'

Ella took a look over her shoulder as they headed to Theatre. She could see the neonatal team still working on the baby that had an endotracheal tube in place with his lungs being inflated by someone holding the miniature bag mask. Someone else was using only two fingers to provide gentle, rapid chest compressions.

It wasn't looking good.

Logan gave Ella the lead role in the surgery they needed to do to repair the aftermath of the resuscitative hysterotomy but he was going to be right there and he wouldn't hesitate to step in if he thought it was necessary.

It was something of a miracle that they'd got this far with this patient still alive and now they needed to scrub in properly and manage a complicated case on someone whose name they still didn't know. They also had no idea whether this first-time mother had brain damage from lack of oxygen when her heart had stopped functioning, whether she might have suffered a devastating stroke from the uncontrolled blood pressure or could be facing a dangerous infection from a less than ideal operating environment in the emergency department, but Logan liked that Ella was approaching her work with the assumption that everything she did was as important as it would be on an otherwise healthy patient.

'So...' Her glance was direct as they scrubbed in, side by side, as they had for the first case they'd worked on together. Was that really less than twenty-four hours ago? Oddly, it felt like he'd known Ella a lot longer than that already. 'Where do you stand on the double-layer versus single-layer closure for the uterus?'

'Where do *you* stand?' he countered. This was his chance to find out a lot more about Ella professionally. He'd already put a lot of trust in her by bringing her on board for a QERT callout but, he had to admit, he was yet to feel that it might have been an unwise decision. She was calm and competent under a high level of stress and she provided an extra set of hands that almost felt like an extension of his own with her ability to anticipate what was needed.

'I know there's still debate but I think the evidence is leaning towards a double-layer closure improving uterine scar healing and reducing the risk of a scar defect in a future pregnancy. I also know it takes more time.'

'We're hardly under pressure to clear Theatre for the next patient at this time of night.' Logan rinsed the soap off his hands and arms. 'And our patient's stable from a cardiovascular point of view. I'd do a double layer.'

Ella's nod was brisk. She was already thinking in broader terms than the task ahead to close the surgical wounds.

'I'd like to get another of bloods off stat and get a full picture of current liver enzymes and kidney function. And a platelet count. We need to start antihypertensive and anticonvulsant treatment for the eclampsia and what protocol do you have for obstetric post-cardiac arrest here? Do you hand her over to Cardiology?'

'We'll have a full team onto it by the time we've got

her settled into the intensive care unit, including Neurology and Anaesthesia while she's being ventilated.' Logan reached for his sterile towel. 'But first things first. You focus on patching her up.'

Which Ella did. As competently as Logan was already coming to expect from her work. Her sutures were neat and her hands deft as she juggled forceps and a needle holder and demonstrated well-practised movements as she looped and locked the stitches. At some point, as the first blood test results got reported back to the team in Theatre, they heard that the baby was alive and had been transferred to the NICU and they finally learned the name of this young mother.

'Iona McTavish,' Ella repeated. 'That's such a pretty name.'

Something in her tone changed the atmosphere in Theatre. The patient whose body was being meticulously mended by Ella had, a little disconcertingly, just become a real person. A young mother with a tiny baby who was fighting for his life in another part of this hospital.

'And so Scottish,' Ella added. 'I've been to the island of Iona and it has to be one of the most beautiful places in the world, I think. Do you know there are forty-eight Scottish kings buried there?'

No. Logan didn't know that, and he didn't want to think about anything other than clinical information and that included the threat of a painful tug on his own heartstrings that was hovering ever since the news that Iona's baby was still alive. He knew that keeping a professional distance was key to providing the best care possible for his patients. What he did know and needed to focus on was that Iona McTavish's blood pressure was still too high but improving and there had been no further seizure activity during the surgery. Even better, her heart rhythm had remained stable and they were finally able to meet with her family and tell them that things had gone as well as they could have hoped for so far.

They didn't need to warn the shell-shocked partner, Gregor, or Iona's parents how critical the condition of their loved one still was, however. The bank of monitors around the bed where she was lying so motionless amongst a tangle of tubes and wires, with people adjusting infusions and ventilator settings and recording measurements, made it frighteningly clear that she was still in danger.

'We'll be keeping her in therapeutic hypothermia for another twelve hours or so,' the intensive care consultant was explaining to Gregor. 'And we'll keep her sedated and ventilated until we get everything under control. We won't be able to make any predictions about the extent of any potential brain damage until we know more. We'll arrange for an EEG to be done to assess brain activity in the next few days.'

It was Ella who broke the impersonal clinical atmosphere after a whispered conversation with a nurse. She touched Gregor's arm and Logan caught the glance that was offering a level of empathy that was as disconcerting as the way she'd talked about Iona in Theatre.

'You can come back to be with Iona soon,' she told Gregor softly. 'But would you like to come and meet your son? We've been told it would be okay, just for a quick visit.'

Gregor had his hand pressed to his mouth, struggling with his emotions, and Logan could see the way Ella drew in a deep breath. 'I could come with you,' she said.

Gregor nodded and it was only then that Ella's glance caught Logan's. The way she caught a corner of her bottom lip between her teeth suggested that she might be worried she'd overstepped a boundary but he echoed Gregor's nod. It would be a good thing to dial down the emotion in this space that Ella was contributing to more than he would have liked. He'd get someone to take Iona's parents to the relatives' room too, and then he would be able to focus on doing his job to the absolute best of his ability.

The way he always did.

He nodded again.

'Take your time,' he added quietly, stepping towards Ella as she followed Gregor from the room. 'And then grab some rest before our day shift starts, if you can. I'll stay here for a while.'

He could see that Iona's husband was waiting for Ella to join him in the quiet corridor that connected each space in this intensive care unit to the central desk. He needed to be shown how to get to the neonatal intensive care unit, of course, but there was more in his glance than waiting for a guide. He'd bonded with Ella as Iona's doctor, Logan realised. Had it been that moment of palpable empathy between them, when she'd touched his arm? Or was it just the way Ella was—like how she'd instantly made a connection when she'd learned the name of the patient she was operating on?

She was his complete opposite, Logan realised.

So how on earth had it felt as if they fitted together professionally so well? Was it a case of two sides of the same coin?

Whatever...

Logan turned back to the screens and it might have been deliberate that he was thinking of this patient as their post-cardiac arrest case, rather than by her name, as he focused on the information that multiple monitor screens were providing.

What actually mattered, as far as his new locum was concerned, was that she was competent. So much so that he would be happy to involve her to whatever degree she wanted in the OERT while she was here at Queen's. The intensity of working on this case with her tonight had done more than he could have hoped for. They'd not only been successful against huge odds, but the professional connection between them had strengthened enough to make any personal reaction to this woman irrelevant.

That blip of physical attraction had been dealt with. It would not be a problem again.

The baby's name was Finlay and Ella fell in love with him the moment she stood beside the incubator when his father was taken in to see him for the first time. The tiny baby looked so vulnerable with nothing on but a disposable nappy that looked far too big and a little woollen beanie that covered his head. He had heart-shaped electrode stickers to monitor his heart on a chest where you could see every rib and tubes and wires everywhere. Big tubes for the ventilator, a smaller nasogastric tube and narrow cannulas that disappeared into the bandage holding a splint onto an arm so tiny it looked like a twig.

Gregor was only allowed a brief visit that first night but Ella took a photograph of him with his face beside Finlay's head on the other side of the plastic barrier so that he could show Iona's parents. And Iona, when she woke up.

If she woke up...

That was another reason that Ella's heart went out to this particular baby who might never know his mother and she found herself heading towards the NICU every chance she got over the next few days. She was there when they took him off the ventilator and watched through the window as the neonatal team removed the invasive tube inside his airway that was attached to the ventilator, replacing it with a CPAP device that covered his nose and supported his own efforts to breathe instead of doing it for him. She stood there for long enough to see that his team were happy with how he settled afterwards and she crossed her fingers, hoping that his mother would be able to start breathing for herself soon as well.

Ella sat beside the incubator for a while, the day after the CPAP was in place, when Gregor was sitting with Iona and that was when she saw Finlay open his eyes for the first time. Just for a few seconds before he drifted back to sleep but it felt like he was looking straight back at her and Ella had to wipe tears from her cheeks, hoping that none of the NICU staff had noticed. It was one thing for a doctor to be interested in following up on a baby they had delivered under circumstances that were still the talk of the hospital but she knew nobody would approve of becoming this emotionally involved.

She didn't approve of it herself. But she knew she could avoid it affecting her ability to do her job.

And, sometimes, she just couldn't help it.

Logan could see her through the window.

Sitting beside that incubator.

She had a mask and gown on and even a cap over her hair, which should have been quite enough of a disguise, but he knew that it was Ella and not one of the NICU nurses watching over this baby. Weirdly, he could actually *feel* it was Ella but he didn't realise why until he saw her lift her hand to wipe tears from her face and he remembered what he'd seen in that moment they'd heard the first cry of that baby who had been lucky enough to survive being in a uterus that had ruptured. In the split second before Ella dipped her head he'd seen her eyes begin to fill with tears. He'd seen—and felt—the emotional connection she already had with that case.

And, while he couldn't fault her performance so far, it was early days and this intensity of her involvement with a patient was decidedly disturbing. Logan would never, ever allow himself to have that kind of connection with a patient—adult or infant.

With anybody, actually, patient or not…

With good reason, because you couldn't do your job as a doctor to your best ability if you couldn't keep a professional distance from your patients and, on a personal level, he was well aware that out-of-control emotions could influence how you thought or behaved, even if it was subconscious.

Logan had long ago built protective barriers to ensure that he was safe from the kind of danger that could come from losing a professional distance but, for a worrying moment, he wondered if they weren't as strong as he believed them to be. Could something make them crack?

Something like seeing Ella not only wiping tears from her face but smiling at the same time, as if something joyous was happening? A kind of joy that Logan never experienced in his work. A very pleasing sense of satisfaction, of course, or relief that could be quite intense was the closest he got to letting go.

And that was exactly how he liked it to be.

So he was horrified to feel a lump in his throat. Something jagged and unpleasant which, if allowed to get any bigger, might threaten to bring tears to his own eyes. He could feel himself scowling as he pushed back against such an unwelcome ambush but he wasn't quite fast enough and he could feel a shaft of that despair escaping before he could slam a familiar mental door.

That newly qualified doctor who wasn't experienced enough to recognise the danger. The pregnant woman in the emergency department who was in the process of losing her baby and bleeding to death herself because the diagnosis of *her* ruptured uterus was taking too long.

Logan had to physically turn away to shut down what could only be a destructive line of thought. He'd find the neonatal consultant and get her to fill him in on the McTavish baby's progress. He should have simply picked up the phone in the first place and stayed well away from this particular area of the hospital—like he usually did. He didn't turn away quite quickly enough, however. As if she felt him glaring at her, Ella had turned to look at the window and, in that split second before he kept moving, he saw her eyes widen enough to convey that she was startled. Shocked, even?

Not that he was about to let that bother him. Logan was her boss after all and Ella was simply a locum consultant who might be proving herself very good at her job but the jury was still out on whether that emotional involvement with her patients might affect her performance. For everybody's sake, he needed to keep an eye on her, Logan decided.

From a safe distance, of course.

CHAPTER FOUR

As ELLA'S FIRST week anniversary of starting her locum at the Queen Mother's Maternity Hospital rolled around, she was still waiting for another chance to work with Logan Walsh on the obstetric emergency team. Or even in the day-to-day routine of working in a busy obstetric hospital, for that matter.

It almost felt as if he was avoiding her, which would be weird but, on the other hand, the last time Ella had seen him in days was when he'd been glaring at her through the windows of the NICU when she'd been visiting Finlay. Mind you, she'd been incredibly busy with deliveries and surgeries, outpatient clinics and high-risk pregnancy patients who'd been admitted for monitoring. Even a CEO was allowed days off too, although she hadn't seen Logan in the hallways of the doctors' residence either.

And, she had to admit, she'd been keeping her eye out for an encounter and *not* seeing him in the residence or working with him in the hospital was adding a frisson of mystery that was having the effect of making him rather more interesting.

Okay...attractive. But she wasn't going there. Not after that cutting little comment about how safe she was from him hitting on her. Good grief...the man couldn't even take a joke and she'd only been trying to lighten the atmosphere after he'd rejected her request to join his specialist team so bluntly. To get such a curt rejection on personal grounds as well could have made working with Logan Walsh unbearable but he'd more than redeemed himself by inviting her to assist with the resuscitative hysterotomy case, so Ella was quite prepared to forgive his grumpy quirks—including the way he'd been glaring at her in NICU.

She really had nothing to complain about in this new chapter of her life.

Especially today. She'd been in this very delivery room on her first day last week, feeling like the new girl at school and not even that welcome when her management of her first patient here had been overridden so presumptively. But things had only improved from that point and Ella was now loving this new position.

That first patient, Lauren, had been discharged yesterday, after making a good recovery from her complicated delivery with the uterine rupture. Ella had been delighted to hear this morning that Iona McTavish—her even more dramatic case in that first twenty-four hours here, was now making good progress. The high blood pressure that had caused the complications in her pregnancy was finally under control, any seizure activity had stopped and her liver and kidney function was improving. While she still hadn't regained consciousness, and had had a setback with a chest infection, her sedation was being lightened so that she could be carefully weaned off the ventilator. An EEG that had been done had been reassuringly normal and her family were desperately hoping she would wake up without evidence of significant brain damage.

Baby Finlay was proving to be a little champion. When Ella had popped into NICU to see him this morning she found him having some skin-to-skin time with his dad, Gregor, with his adorable little button nose visible for the first time because the CPAP device had been removed. Ella was acutely aware that the family's relief—and cautious joy—in the survival of Iona's baby was providing, at least to some degree, a balance for the awful anxiety of their vigil for Finlay's mum. She was feeling it herself...

Best of all, however, Ella's current patient was the perfect way to celebrate the end of her first week at Queen's because it was a twin birth and multiples were her absolute favourite kind of deliveries. This was a woman she'd already met at an antenatal clinic this week, as well, so she was not only now familiar with where everything was in her new hospital and knew most of her colleagues, she had had the chance to discuss Melissa's desire to have as little intervention as possible when she gave birth to her twin girls. The mother of two young boys had already agreed to give up her dream of a home birth in order to have specialist help and facilities on hand but she was still hoping to deliver both twins without the need for a C-section, even though one twin was in a breech position.

The room was getting crowded because there were two midwives here and extra paediatric staff to cover the newborn checks for two babies. Ella was already in the room as the consultant on hand in case the breech position for the second twin led to any complications but, for the moment, she was keeping in the background.

Judy was one of the midwives involved and she was kneeling on the floor, peering up to see what was happening as Melissa squatted beside the bed, being supported by her partner, Hamish, who was rubbing her back and adding to Judy's verbal encouragement and reassurance, but Melissa was groaning so loudly with the pain of the strong contractions she was experiencing it was doubtful she even heard the support.

'The baby's crowning...' Judy told her. 'No...the head's gone back in again. She's playing turtle...'

Melissa's groan got louder and she bent her head as she kept pushing.

'Here she comes... One more big push...'

'Push, Mel,' Hamish chimed in. 'Push, push, *push*...'

Moments later, Judy caught the slippery infant as it emerged and then passed it through Melissa's legs so that she could pick up her baby and hold it to her chest with the umbilical cord still attached.

'Oh...oh...' Melissa was in tears now. 'Look, Hamish...isn't she beautiful? Get your buttons undone on your shirt. You're going to hold her while I push out her sister, remember?'

The second midwife put the bean bag down beside Melissa. 'Are you still okay in this position?' she asked as she helped shift the newborn girl into her father's arms and tuck a blanket over them both. 'Do you need a break? Would you prefer to get on the bed for number two?'

Melissa opened her mouth but couldn't say anything as a new pain hit her. Gasping, she sank down onto her knees and put her hands on the floor as the contraction grew stronger. Ella moved so that she could see what was going on. The waters from the second twin had clearly broken and the legs appeared as the contraction faded. The baby was half out, in a sideways position, and its legs were moving in a cyclic motion.

'Big push with your next contraction, Melissa. Baby's trying to help. You're almost there…'

Ella moved in as she realised the baby wasn't rotating as expected with the next contraction and she knew exactly what was going on.

'Your baby needs a bit of help,' she told Melissa calmly. 'I think one of her arms is trapped and that's stopping her being able to come out. I need to move her a little. Are you okay with that?'

'Yes…' Melissa sounded frightened. 'Please…just help her come out…'

'Do whatever you need to do, Doctor,' Hamish added.

Ella knelt behind Melissa. This was a procedure she had done before, but it needed to go smoothly or the situation could deteriorate rapidly.

'You'll feel my hands going in to hold baby,' she told Melissa as she slipped flat hands onto the baby's torso, her thumb tucked beside her fingers, one in front on the tiny chest and the other behind on the back, her fingertips in far enough to almost touch the unborn head. She gently pushed the baby back into the uterus a little to give her room to manoeuvre. 'And now I'm turning her.'

She rotated the baby forty-five degrees in the direction it was facing, using her bottom hand to sweep the baby's anterior arm across its face and body to release it under the pubic arch.

'There we go…' she said quietly. 'Almost there. You're doing *really* well, Melissa…'

She rotated the baby back, far enough for it to be in the correct position for a normal breech birth and then, with a simple shoulder push, the head was delivered and the baby was born.

Twin number two began crying immediately and Ella could feel a collective sigh of relief coming from everybody in the room. The midwives were helping Melissa to a position where she could hold her second born to her chest, against her skin, and she ended up leaning on the beanbag beside her partner, the baby tucked into her arms, its head almost touching that of its twin in the father's arms.

The medical team backed off for a moment. Ella and the midwives were watching for any undue postpartum bleeding and the imminent arrival of the placenta. The neonatal specialists were keeping a close eye on these babies and it would be time to cut the umbilical cords and give them a thorough check and another Apgar score very soon but, even if it was only for a matter of seconds, this time for a brand-new family to be connected like this and bonding in a wash of pure joy was too precious to take away.

Ella knew she had tears on her cheeks as she watched the parents' heads touching as they both gazed down at their infant girls but she didn't care. Even when she looked up to see that Logan had slipped into this delivery room at some point during the tense moments of delivering the second twin. She was by no means the only person present who didn't have dry eyes right now and that hint of a crooked smile on Logan's face before he turned and left the room again suggested that he was just as happy with the outcome as everyone else, even if he had no intention of showing it.

Ella was quite professional enough to keep things hidden herself. Okay, showing a bit of emotion witnessing the overwhelming joy these parents were experiencing with the arrival of two healthy, beautiful babies was fine. But that knot of sensation Ella was experiencing thanks to seeing not only that hint of a smile on Logan's face but the way he'd caught and held eye contact with her for a heartbeat before he'd left the room was most definitely not something she wanted anybody else to notice.

She was planning to ignore it herself, in fact. She'd been quite confident that she had a lid on that very unexpected—and unwelcome—attraction she'd felt to her new boss when she'd first arrived and…okay, maybe she'd been thinking about him and keeping an eye out for him, but she wasn't thinking about him in *that* way. This fizzing sensation deep in her gut was because of the atmosphere in this room. The miracle of two new lives beginning and the satisfaction of successfully navigating the kind of medical challenge that could make obstetrics a bit of a rollercoaster but also made it one of the more exciting specialties to be part of.

She was happy, that was all it was. The kind of happiness that would have made her do a little dance if she'd been somewhere nobody could see her. But she wasn't alone and she was completely professional so she simply smiled instead.

'The cords have both stopped pulsating now,' she said. 'Are you happy to have them cut now, Melissa?'

Good *grief*...

Logan had turned into the corridor that led to the staff-rooms with lockers and showers and changing facilities at the end of a particularly hectic day and the last thing he'd expected to see was someone ahead of him...*dancing*?

Not just someone.

Ella Grisham.

Still in her scrubs and clearly unaware that anyone was behind her. She had her arms in the air, her head bobbing and...yes...her feet were doing a kind of skippy thing. Just for a few steps and then she straightened her back and lifted her chin as if she was collecting herself before she bumped the door of the locker room open and went inside.

Logan paused long enough to take a steadying breath as he felt surprise morph into a shaft of sensation that went straight to his groin. That...sexual attraction. Unwelcome, because Ella didn't fit into any category of what he considered to be safe—or possibly even acceptable—liaisons with women. This was a woman who wore her heart on her sleeve, for goodness' sake. She got too emotionally involved with her patients and cried easily. She also wore childish jumpers and wanted to rescue ducks. Maybe the surprising thing was that Logan *hadn't* seen her dancing before this. Or was the biggest surprise that he couldn't deal with that inappropriate attraction as easily as he would have preferred?

When he emerged from the locker rooms having

changed out of his scrubs and saw Ella ahead of him going outside through the main hospital doors, despite knowing that he might be playing with fire, Logan found himself lengthening his stride to catch up with her. Or perhaps he needed the challenge to reassure himself that he was still in control?

'Looks like we're heading in the same direction,' he said.

'I know. Weird, huh?'

There might have been the tiniest note of sarcasm in her words but Ella was smiling. Radiating happiness, in fact. She was walking perfectly normally beside him but Logan could almost imagine her starting to skip at any moment and…it was rather nice to be close to someone who was this happy.

'You look like you've had a good day.'

'The best.' Ella nodded.

'You did well with that nuchal arm delivery on the twins.' Logan cleared his throat. 'I hope you didn't think I was interfering by poking my head in.'

'Not at all.' Ella's smile was understanding this time. 'I would have done the same thing. Multiple births are a lot more common these days but they're still magical, aren't they?'

The signal to cross the busy road began flashing red as they got to the traffic lights so they stopped, side by side. Logan was shaking his head.

'They're risky,' he said. 'The chance of complications for both the birth and the babies are also multiplied. Stuff of nightmares for both the doctors and the parents.' He pressed the button again, as if it might make the traffic lights change more quickly. 'And that's only the start. I can't imagine how hard it must be once they leave hospital.'

'It's magical,' Ella said firmly. 'I love everything about them.'

'Maybe you'll be lucky enough to have some yourself.'

'No, thanks.' Ella set off as soon as the lights changed. 'Been there, done that.'

'*What?*'

'Oh, not me, personally.' She threw a grin over her shoulder. 'It was my mother who had the babies. The fertility treatment she had worked a bit too well and she had non-identical triplet boys. Mick, Jimmy and Eddie. I was eight when they turned up.'

'Wow...'

'I adored them,' Ella said. 'Mum needed all the help she could get and I was kind of like another mother. When they started crawling, they'd follow me round like a row of little ducks.'

An eight-year-old who was being a second mother? Logan had to wonder how much Ella had missed out on a normal childhood after her siblings had arrived en masse. Her adolescence must have been rather different to her peers as well. Had she been babysitting while her friends were all out having a good time?

'Where are they now?'

'All over the place. Mick and Jimmy are both junior doctors, currently being overworked in London and Newcastle but they're planning to move on soon. Eddie's a paramedic and working in Australia.'

'Sounds like they all got inspired into a medical career

by their big sister.' Logan followed Ella as she unlocked the front door of the doctors' residence and went inside.

'I think it's more about what we all went through when Mum got sick. I was at university, doing my nursing training, so I wasn't around enough, but they were all still at home and it hit hard.'

'They don't sound like they're keen on settling down anywhere any time soon either.'

'They lost their dad not long after Mum died so it kind of felt like the family's roots got pulled out and there were only sad memories left. I'm not surprised they've all drifted away, looking for a new place to make a fresh start.'

'Wait a minute...' Logan was frowning. '*Their* dad?'

'He was my stepdad.' Ella paused at the bottom of the staircase. 'Mum and I were on our own till I was about five. He was more than happy to adopt me and be my dad but he desperately wanted a kid of his own as well, preferably a boy, so that's why Mum did the fertility treatment.'

'And you set out to be a nurse?'

'Then I decided I wanted to be a doctor.' Ella nodded. 'A paediatrician. But somewhere along the line I realised that you can have too much of a good thing. Obstetrics is perfect. I still adore babies but I prefer the mothers to be *my* patients. And there's no way I want any babies of my own. As I said, been there, done that. With bells on.'

She was heading upstairs now. 'I'm lucky,' she added. 'Most people don't get to appreciate real freedom until they're middle-aged.'

Freedom? So he'd been right in thinking that Ella's childhood had been overwhelmed by responsibilities?

Was that why she had a penchant for things that were a little childish now? And why she still got so much joy from being around babies and thought that the arrival of more than one at a time was magical?

Ella Grisham had a big heart, Logan decided, but there was an undercurrent to her story that struck him as being sad. She considered herself to be free now but...wasn't she also lonely? She was capable of meaningful emotional connection to others but if she kept flitting from place to place and never settling it was unlikely that she was going to find it. And maybe that was exactly why she was living her life as she was. It was really none of his business.

He didn't want to get involved and it was possible he'd heard too much of her life story already.

He felt in his pocket for his key as they walked towards the big arched window at the end of the hallway on the second floor. And then he felt his other pocket.

'Oh...no...'

'What's wrong?' Ella had her key in her hand and was about to unlock her own door.

'I have a horrible feeling I left my keys on the kitchen bench this morning. I remember thinking I'd better not forget them because it's too easy to just go out and shut the door and lock it automatically with that snib lock. But I was in a bit of a rush and then my phone rang...'

'Dougal can let you in. Oh...' Ella bit her lip. 'It was this time last week that he was out taking his mother grocery shopping, wasn't it?'

'I can't call him and make him rush back.' Logan sighed. 'It's not the first time this has happened. I have suggested they change the fitting so you have to use a key to lock them as well as open them.' He turned to pick up an envelope that had been on the hall table beside his door.

'That's a fat letter.'

'It'll be photos. I wanted prints of ones I took of my barn the other day. I'm planning to choose the best ones for marketing purposes.'

Ella had unlocked her door. 'Why don't you come in and show me while you wait for Dougal to get back? Returning the favour of not being left in the hallway is the least I can do.' She pushed her door open but stood back—an invitation for Logan to go in first.

He shrugged and accepted the invitation. And then he smiled. 'If you're hitting on me, Dr Grisham,' he said dryly, 'I need to warn you that it's doomed to failure. I'm already married—to my work—and I'm not about to get distracted.'

It was the first time he'd heard Ella laugh and the sound followed him as he walked into her apartment, as joyous as the sight of her dancing had been. There was something beneath the pleasure of that sound, however. This was a private joke, wasn't it?

A link that nobody else would understand that had the effect of creating a connection on a personal level that had come from nowhere. It had nothing to do with any attraction he'd been aware of with Ella but, despite Logan having dealt with and buried that unwanted reaction to his locum, the two things were mingling and somehow that alchemy was making them both bigger. Brighter...

* * *

There was nothing very personal about the apartment Ella had been inhabiting for a week now, apart from her laptop and a couple of books and a small framed photograph that she'd put on top of the almost empty bookshelf.

Logan paused as he went past the shelf. 'I'm guessing these are your brothers?'

'The babies.' Ella grinned as she nodded. 'None of them was over four pounds when they were born but they've kind of grown up now, haven't they? That was the last time we were all in the same place,' she added. 'Nearly three years ago now.'

She blew out a breath as a beat of missing her family came from left field. But staying in one place long enough to allow for a family reunion to be organised was getting more and more difficult with all of them chasing their own careers and personal freedom. And that was exactly what Ella loved so much about her life, wasn't it—that freedom?

'I think I'm still recovering from the overpowering dose of testosterone, to be honest,' she added lightly. 'It's much more manageable getting together with a group video call. Have a seat. I can make some coffee. Or tea? I've got some wine, even. I went to the supermarket yesterday.' It felt as if Ella was talking too much but she wanted to distract Logan. She'd said too much already about her family, which was probably why she'd found herself suddenly feeling…what…a bit lost?

'You choose.' Logan sat down at the table by the window that was right beside the small kitchen. He ripped the envelope open and was spreading photographs on the table by the time Ella had pulled the cork from the bottle of red wine and found two glasses in a cupboard.

'They're not real wine glasses, sorry. I'm guessing they didn't think it was appropriate to encourage visiting doctors to drink anything stronger than water but, hey... I'm celebrating. Here's to my first multiple birth in Aberdeen.'

Logan picked up the glass tumbler and touched it to the side of Ella's. 'May they all be as joyous as the first,' he said. 'And that you always have a corridor to dance in.'

His tone was so dry that it took a moment for Ella to process the odd toast and, when she did, she almost choked on her sip of wine. He'd seen her doing that happy dance on the way to the locker room? Just how often was she going to embarrass herself in front of this man who always seemed so in control? And serious.

Except...he'd made a joke, hadn't he? About her hitting on him. Twisting that warning she'd thrown at him when they'd first met, and it had been funny. A joke that nobody else would understand. She liked that. It gave them the kind of link that could be the spark of a genuine friendship.

She could only be grateful that Logan had no idea of how attracted she'd been to him that first evening. Ella was also grateful that the fact that he'd changed his mind about letting her work with him as part of the emergency response team had given them a professional connection that made it inappropriate to allow that attraction to be rekindled.

It had definitely helped that they'd both been so busy

that their paths hadn't crossed away from work. Until this evening. When Logan had seen her dancing. When he'd walked home with her and she'd shared far too much personal information about her background. At least he'd also seen her coping with what could have been a problem in that twin birth. What was needed now was to steer him away from anything more about her. It was Logan's turn to share.

'So…' Ella put her glass to one side and shifted some photographs to her side of the small table. 'This is the barn that was fabulous enough to make you pretty much live and work in the same place?'

'I had to sell the place I was in to buy the barn and to fund at least enough of a conversion to make it habitable.'

'Where is it? An easy commute to the city?'

'Thanks to Queen's being on the west side of the city, it's no more than twenty-five minutes if the traffic lights are in a good mood.'

'You'd spend a lot longer than that getting from one suburb to another in London.' Ella was arranging photos in front of her. She opened her mouth to say something about the property but found herself lost for words for a long moment.

The barn was stunning—a huge L-shaped stone and slate building that looked as if it had been there for hundreds of years. There was a crescent of forest behind it and a meadow in front that dipped over a bank to a picturesque pond with fronds of weeping willow reflected in perfectly still water.

'Oh…' Ella found a close-up picture of the pond and her awed silence was broken. 'There's a *duck*. A *Jemima*

Puddle-Duck sort of duck.' She sighed happily. 'My favourite.' She glanced up to find Logan smiling at her.

'I had a feeling you'd like that.'

It wasn't that lopsided, half-reluctant smile she'd seen on Logan's face before. This was almost a grin.

'It's gorgeous,' Ella admitted. 'And you're not going to have any trouble selling it. Especially if that duck is still there as the finishing touch.' She gave Logan a curious glance. 'Are you sure you don't want to turn it into your for ever home?'

Logan sidestepped the glance. 'Maybe I've discovered I'm not a "for ever home" sort of person. Kind of like not being a "settling down" kind of person except for the most important aspect of life.'

'Which is?' Ella was reaching for more photographs.

'A career,' Logan responded, as if the answer was obvious. 'Something that gives you a reason to get up in the morning and a reason to feel like you've done your best to make the world a slightly better place by the time you go to bed at night.'

Ella didn't dare try to catch his gaze as he finished speaking. She could feel an almost overwhelming shadow of something sad hanging over those words but she didn't want to try and analyse it because she knew it might make her question her own lifestyle choices and she didn't want to do that. She was happy.

Happy enough to have been dancing a very short time ago.

She picked up a photo. 'The interior of this barn is amazing.'

'Are you kidding? It hasn't got a floor. The windows

are just holes in the stonework and part of the roof has collapsed. There's actually a skeleton of a cow in one corner behind an internal division and a massive pile of musty straw and manure. I suspect the whole mess probably dates back to the eighteenth century.'

Ella waved a hand dismissively. 'You've got to use your imagination. You'd have to work around any limitations that will be in place given that it must have an historical listing, but I'm sure you could leave the stonework of that whole end as it is and build in an open fireplace. You could have stone floors or reclaimed Victorian pine maybe. I'd make a huge living, dining, kitchen area along the whole length from that end and put in a mezzanine floor at the other end that would lead to upstairs bedrooms in the L part of the footprint that would be right under those gorgeous beams.'

Ella was rearranging the photos in front of her, loving the ideas that were crowding her brain and different enough to anything she'd been thinking about all day to be complete recreation. 'It's a good thing that the roof needs repair because you could put in skylights. Solar panels, even. And this...' She tapped an image of a round stone structure with a pointed roof like a witch's hat not far from one end of the barn. 'What is it? A pixie's house?'

'The estate agent thought it might have been a grain silo.'

'You could make that a feature of an outdoor courtyard, with tables and a barbecue for entertaining. Open it up enough to make it like a summer house, with squashy old couches inside, or an antique day bed, so that you could just lie there and watch the ducks on the pond.' Ella laughed aloud. 'I'd find an old weathervane in the shape of a duck and put it on the tippy top of the roof.'

Aware of a sudden silence when she finally stopped talking, Ella looked up to find Logan staring at her.

'I *can* almost see it,' he said slowly. 'I think I saw maybe two percent of what you've described when I saw the property in the first place, but I could never have put it into words like you just have. And none of the architects I've spoken to in the last two years has ever made it sound like it would be worth the effort—and cost—of doing all the work.'

Ella couldn't look away from his eyes, even though she knew she shouldn't be holding eye contact like this. But while she'd noticed how intense a gaze they could deliver, she'd never really noticed their colour—a soft brown with notes of gold that made her think of autumn leaves or walnut shells. It was more than their colour that had captured her, however. It was an emotional note that looked like…hope? No…more like yearning. Something she'd said had touched a chord. It made her wonder if there was something that Logan Walsh wanted very much but he didn't know how to find it.

She dragged her gaze away, swallowing what felt like a lump in her throat. 'You never know,' she said as lightly as she could manage. 'You might change your mind about keeping the barn.'

But Logan shook his head. 'If I haven't found the time or motivation in the last two years, I'm not going to let it hang around my neck like a millstone.'

'What made you buy it in the first place?' Ella was genuinely curious. 'How did you find it?'

Logan shrugged. 'I was driving home from taking a seminar in Fort William and I'd always wanted to drive the Old Military Road through the Cairngorms National Park and it seemed the perfect time. I stopped for a break at one point and I saw a *For Sale* sign with an arrow pointing up a lane so I thought I'd stretch my legs and see what was hiding behind the hedges. There was no one there. It was just me and the barn. In an overgrown meadow with a pond that had ducks on it and...'

Ella wanted to hug herself. 'You fell in love with it,' she said softly.

Logan shook his head, giving Ella a glance that told her exactly how ridiculous that suggestion was. It was reminiscent of the glare he'd treated her to more than once now but Ella wasn't bothered. Maybe it was un-conscious—an unfortunate expression of being thought-ful in a professional environment. And quite possibly a warning not to get too close in a personal sense? Simply a defence mechanism?

What was he protecting? Ella wondered. And why?

'It was a pleasant spot, that's all,' Logan said. 'It seemed like a good investment.' He reached for his wine glass and took a long swallow. 'I should get you to help me with writing an advertisement for the place, though. You could inspire anyone to take on the conversion.'

'I could probably come up with more ideas if I actually walked around the place. I could do a few sketches, even.'

'Really? You'd do that?'

'It's a hobby.' Ella shrugged. 'Maybe it's because I

was desperate for a doll's house when I was a kid. It was always on the top of my list for Father Christmas but it never happened. I wouldn't have had time to play with it once the babies arrived, of course, and they would have destroyed it by the time they started moving. I'd draw pictures, though, when I needed some quiet time and then I discovered house hunting and renovation programmes on TV and that was when I fell in love with barns.'

Logan finished his wine. 'I'll take you out to see it as soon as we've both got a day off. Keep the photos in the meantime.' He was smiling as he got to his feet. 'I feel like I'm about to get a major weight lifted from my shoulders. When I've sold it, I can go looking for a property in the city. An apartment or house that I can move straight into that will feel like a real home.' Logan checked his watch. 'I expect Dougal will be back by now. I should be able to get back into my apartment now.'

Ella watched him turn away. Yeah…maybe that was what Logan was yearning for.

A 'real' home.

Maybe he needed to settle somewhere to feel grounded.

Ella needed to not have any ties in order to feel free.

They were so different. So why did it feel as if they had a connection that went a lot deeper than a passion for the same work?

It was something else Ella didn't want to try and analyse. And reminding herself of their shared work was the perfect escape route.

'There was something I've been wanting to ask you about,' she said.

'Shoot…' Logan was heading for the door. 'I'll owe you a huge favour if you can help me offload the barn.'

'It's about that course you teach on obstetric emergencies. The one-day seminar you take to ambulance stations and rural hospitals?'

'What about it?'

'Well… I've done locums in places where there's a huge lack of specialist backup for midwives and paramedics. I've done my best to do some training but I'd love to put something more structured together one day. Have you got an instruction manual I could have a look at?'

'Not exactly.' Logan made a face. 'That's something else on my to-do list. I've got notes. And lists. And some handouts for course attendees, but a lot of it's just in my head. I'll tell you about it when we've got a bit of time. Maybe when I take you out for that tour of the barn?'

'I'll look forward to it,' Ella said.

She meant it too. A period of time to talk about and to indulge in the two things she loved the most—her job and her favourite hobby. Put them together with the company of a very attractive man and there was nothing about the prospect not to love.

Ella didn't do one of those silly little dances when the door had closed behind Logan but that didn't mean she wasn't happy.

She was happier than she could remember being in a very long time, in fact. Excited even, and it didn't really matter which element of the expedition Logan had promised was responsible for this level of anticipation, whether it was an in-depth discussion of managing obstetric emergencies, playing with ideas for a barn conversion or enjoying the company of possibly the most attractive man Ella had ever met. Surely there was nothing wrong in simply enjoying this wonderful fizzy feeling without overthinking it?

CHAPTER FIVE

ELLA WASN'T AT all disappointed by the car Logan was driving when he pulled up in front of the doctors' residence where she was waiting, as arranged, in the early afternoon of her next day off nearly a week later. She had been wondering if he might turn up from where he rented a garage in either a flashy sports car or a luxury late-model sedan but his vehicle was a practical SUV—the kind that could be relied on to do whatever was needed but wouldn't stand out on the motorway. A bit scratched and dented in places but quietly capable. Perfect even, as far as traits that mattered were concerned.

A bit like Logan Walsh himself?

'Right on time,' she said as she opened the passenger door and climbed in. 'I like that.'

She also liked what Logan was wearing, although she certainly wasn't going to tell him that. He had well-worn jeans on and a plain black tee shirt but what took his outfit to a very different level was the ancient-looking leather jacket he had on top. Racer style, with a neck strap instead of a collar and no flashy metal to be seen. Even the zips were hidden. It was the kind of jacket a lot of men might wear to try and look cool but Ella had the impression that Logan would look just as comfortable and confident if he was wearing the most boring anorak on earth.

He waited for Ella to put her bag on the floor and reach for her safety belt. He clearly didn't have the same reticence about commenting on what someone was wearing.

'You've got the llamas on again,' he said.

'These are alpacas,' Ella corrected. 'Classic Peruvian design, probably because it's made out of alpaca wool.'

'What's the difference?' Logan was watching for a gap in the traffic to pull out.

'Llamas are much bigger, have a longer face and their ears are kind of banana-shaped. But you're right, there's not much difference from a distance. I don't think I'd like to wear something knitted from llama wool, though. It would be too scratchy.'

Logan's sideways glance was curious. 'You seem to know a lot about this. Are camelids another odd hobby of yours?'

Ella grinned at him. 'By "odd", I take it you mean "interesting"?'

He was smiling but busy watching the road ahead of them. 'Absolutely. And I'm very lucky you don't have normal hobbies. I'm looking forward to seeing what you think of the barn.'

'I'm not that into alpacas,' Ella confessed. 'They're not in the same league as dogs or ducks when it comes to rescuing them, but I did have a great time hiking the Incan trail to Machu Picchu a few years ago. This jumper was a souvenir and, I have to say, it's proving useful already in this Scottish climate.' She looked at a signpost they were passing. 'We're heading for Balmoral?'

'Well, we're going in that direction and following the River Dee but it's less than halfway to Balmoral. The closest town is Banchory so it's no more than thirty minutes away even if there's traffic in the city. Ideal for someone that doesn't mind a bit of a commute.'

'It's good.' Ella nodded happily. 'It gives you enough time to start telling me about the course. What's the scope of things that you cover?'

'Depends who I'm talking to,' Logan said. 'It's an intensive one-day seminar so it needs to deliver the information and practical training that is most likely to be of benefit and save lives. So, for example, if I'm talking to paramedics we might put more emphasis on emergencies that can evolve very rapidly, like a placental abruption following trauma or a cord prolapse at the start of labour. Unexpected out-of-hospital deliveries can mean that paramedics might need to manage a severe post-partum haemorrhage or neonatal life support too.'

'And something like complications from a breech delivery or shoulder dystocia are more likely to happen well into labour, which has given the mother more time to get to a hospital,' Ella observed. 'So that would be something that midwives or ED docs might want to brush up on.'

'Exactly. I've got great manikinsto practice the manoeuvres for correcting a shoulder dystocia.'

'I've got an excellent video tutorial that helped me when I was learning to deal with a nuchal arm breech birth complication scenario like the second twin the other day. I could send you a link?' Ella was enjoying the more rural views now they'd left the city behind them.

'That would be great. And I need to send you the draft of a paper I'm working on, because you'll be a co-author.'

'Oh…?' Ella turned a startled glance to Logan but he was focused on the road ahead so she allowed her gaze to rest on his profile a moment or two longer, taking in the strong angles of his face and lines that suggested he frowned more often than he smiled. The sombre tone didn't detract from his attractiveness, however. Quite the opposite…

'One of a few because I'm including everyone that made a significant contribution to the case, but it'll be directed to an obstetric publication so you'll be the first co-author.'

Ella blinked. That was quite an honour, considering Logan Walsh's prominence in the field and that she was only a locum colleague. 'Is it a case presentation?' she guessed. 'For the resuscitative hysterotomy?'

'Yeah… Success stories can be important. They may well contribute to someone making a decision to do a procedure that is, let's face it, more than a little daunting but making the decision in time might make the difference between life and death.'

'Mmm…' The sound Ella made was thoughtful. She turned to look at the countryside rolling past but, in reality, she was completely focused on the man sitting so close to her.

If Logan had been daunted when faced with that decision on performing such an invasive procedure when the odds were against it being successful, he hadn't shown it and that confidence and control of the situation had been pivotal to the entire team that day. How good was he at hiding his feelings? Ella wondered—a thought that was instantly followed by wondering why he was alone in life and whether anybody had ever got close enough to be allowed to know what was going on in his head. Or his heart?

He was several years older than Ella, which would make him close to being forty years old. Had he been married before—to something other than his work? It was unthinkable to ask such personal questions of this …what was the word that summed Logan up? Taciturn? Yeah… that was it. A good Scottish characteristic. Ella stole another glance in his direction, imagining Logan wearing a kilt, with all the traditional accessories like a sporran and socks and a hat and a fly plaid over his shoulder with maybe a brooch to pin it. Would he be traditional enough not to wear anything underneath his kilt?

And…there it was again. That spear of deliciousness deep in her belly that was undeniably sheer physical desire.

Stop it, Ella chided herself. *You're too close. He might notice and how embarrassing would that be?*

She needed to tap into the professional space that was more than acceptable to share but she couldn't think of anything to say. Thank goodness Logan could.

'I think the paper will create some interest,' he said. 'It's very unusual for both a mother and baby to survive an RH and in my discussion I've talked about how part of the success in a case like this can be due to the pre-hospital management by paramedics and that up-to-date training is vital to maintain.'

Ella was thoroughly back in a professional zone now. 'You don't mean having paramedics *doing* an RH, do you?'

'Why not? If a specialist paramedic in critical care can do a thoracotomy for a tension pneumothorax and associated cardiac arrest, why not an RH?' But then Logan shook his head a little. 'That wasn't what I meant, though.'

'What did you mean?'

'I suspect the course that the paramedics who brought Iona in had just done may have made a difference in this particular case. They knew to use a higher hand position on the sternum and to manually displace the uterus to take pressure off the IVD and aorta. A different crew in a different place might have still been using the old recommendation to have the mother in a thirty-degree, left lateral position that makes effective chest compressions almost impossible.'

This was good. Ella wasn't thinking of anything personal to do with Logan now. She was so back in that resuscitation room in the emergency department she could actually feel an echo of the calm control that had emanated from Logan.

'And you knew how fast you needed to make the decision to do the procedure,' she said quietly. 'You had the baby out in less than five minutes.'

'We did.'

Ella could allow herself a small glow of pride in his change of pronoun, even though it could be considered a grey area between professional and personal interaction. Like heading off to see Logan's personal possession of a barn, even though what they were talking about was purely professional?

'But those recommended time frames are also out-dated,' Logan added. 'There are reports of babies being delivered alive up to thirty minutes after CPR's been started and mothers have survived up to fifteen minutes.'

'It's still got to be a good thing to do it as early as possible.' Ella bit her lip. 'I know Iona's doing well but it's still going to be a long road to a complete recovery, isn't it?'

Logan nodded. 'I spent some time with her on my ward round this morning. She's probably going to be kept in as long as her baby's in NICU, for some intensive therapy and rehabilitation.'

He knew the baby's name was Finlay. Was he avoiding using it because he was deliberately creating distance? It couldn't be because he didn't like babies—he was an obstetrician, for heaven's sake.

'I was a bit shocked by her level of disability when she was first awake,' Ella confessed. 'She was having a lot of difficulty speaking and she was quite agitated. I could see how hard it was for her family.'

'She's making good progress. She's lost a lot of her vo-cabulary and has trouble naming things, but her husband tells me that as soon as he's told her the word it's back in her memory. She's frustrated and is fighting a fatigue that makes it hard to stay awake, but she's less emotionally labile and apparently determined to recover from the left-sided weakness. She wants to be able to hold her baby.'

He was doing it again. Creating distance by not using names and talking about people as if he was dictating clinical notes. It made Ella feel a little rebellious.

'I try and find time every day to go and visit Finlay,' she said. 'He's the most adorable baby ever. He's off CPAP now, although he's being carefully monitored for any apnoeic episodes, and he's starting to learn to suck from a bottle. Did you know that Iona's being helped to express breastmilk for him? The plan is to let her try breastfeeding soon. I'm so excited about that. I bet she and Gregor are too.'

Logan didn't appear to be listening. He had turned off the road and they were bumping down a rough narrow lane between hedgerows. She could hear the warning sounds of startled birds but wasn't going to take that as a warning to drop the subject.

'Have you been to see him?'

'No. I've been getting regular updates on his condition, of course. The data will be included in a table in the paper I'm writing on the RH.'

Maybe Logan could sense Ella's disapproval of his lack of excitement over Finlay's progress. He broke the silence as he slowed the car when they reached the end of the lane and had turned to see the barn and meadow and pond—as if one of those photographs, or maybe a landscape painting, had just come to life.

'NICU is not one of my favourite places,' he said quietly.

The undercurrent to his words suggested that Logan had seen too many newborn babies that hadn't survived—maybe from cases that haunted him—but still Ella said nothing. She could feel a compelling peacefulness of the scene in front of them inviting them in. She could also feel quite certain that Logan had just told her something that was intensely personal and private and, as much as she wanted to know more, this felt like a test. Could she be trusted not to pry into places he wasn't ready to show her, no matter how curious she might be?

Yes. She could.

And maybe Logan already knew that. He'd already invited her into a personal space, hadn't he? Ella had the feeling that she might be the first person he had confessed his preference to avoid the NICU. She was also possibly the first person, other than an architect perhaps, to set foot in this little patch of countryside since Logan had fallen in love with it enough to buy it.

Oops… Since he'd discovered an out of the way, 'pleasant spot' and convinced himself it might be a good financial investment.

She opened her door, hiding her smile. 'We'd better make the most of the sunshine,' she said. 'I'm not sure I like the look of those clouds rolling in.'

Logan hadn't been out here for months. Good grief…was it coming up to almost a year since his last visit?

He'd never been here with anyone else either, come to think of it. He'd been alone when he'd discovered it and he'd dealt with the estate agent and the purchase without feeling the need to see it again. He'd sent architects the directions to get there and told them where the key to the barn was hidden but he'd never managed to be available to be there at the same time.

Had he wanted to keep this place a purely personal retreat? Or had he, perhaps, been unconsciously worried that the spell it seemed to cast on him whenever he was here would be somehow tainted by sharing it with someone else?

If he had, he'd been very wrong.

Sharing it with Ella was...well, it was a bit of a revelation, to be honest.

He suspected that Ella had no idea just how much her changing expressions—and her eyes—revealed about how she was feeling. And if anyone was capable of something as ridiculous as falling head over heels in love with a property he might have known it would be Ella.

She was enchanted from the moment he reached into the hollow trunk of an ancient oak tree to find the old iron key that had probably been hand forged by the same blacksmith who'd created the heavy lock on the rustic wooden door. She caught her bottom lip between her teeth as he pushed that door open, as if she was holding her breath, and then she actually wrapped her arms around her body when she was standing inside the cavernous space with misty rays of sunshine pouring in through the small, high windows.

Those dark eyes of hers that were such a good match for her hair colour were shining just as brightly. Logan had become used to only seeing her hair tied back at work so it was a bit disconcerting to see it hanging in the long, loose waves that had caused that totally inappropriate thought about her riding a horse with nothing but her hair to cover her body. It was even more disconcerting to see the astonishing array of emotions in her reaction to this historic building.

'Those beams and the trusses...they're incredible. Hand-hewn. Maybe oak, or elm or chestnut wood? Oh...

can you imagine that mezzanine floor with the bedrooms having those beams on their ceilings? Close enough to see the marks that someone made with an axe or an adze? To be able to *touch* them?'

Logan was being sucked in again, like he had been the other night when Ella was full of ideas about a conversion project—until she'd accused him of falling in love with the property, which let him escape straight back to a safe distance. It felt more dangerous, somehow, hearing the passion in her voice while they were physically inside this building.

He needed to remember that he'd learned long ago not to play mental games with personal 'what ifs' or 'if onlys'. That it was so much safer to think about facts rather than fantasies. To push forward and focus on doing what mattered to the best of his ability.

His work.

The error of purchasing a project that would require too much of his time and money had taught Logan a good lesson. He hadn't realised the effect it would have to be forced into a space where you had to dream about the future and he'd quickly found that doing so could unlock doors he'd rather not go through, thanks very much. He needed a place to live that would help him do his work and live his life by *not* being a distraction or possibly even an ordeal.

'I still think it should be at the short end of the L shape,' Ella said. 'But I didn't see that stone partition in the photos. There's room for a stone staircase to lead up to the mezzanine level and that might be the perfect place to build in a gorgeous big open fireplace.'

Okay…he couldn't stop himself seeing that. Not when the solid stonework was right in front of him. He could actually imagine the roaring flames and a couple of super comfortable leather sofas in front of it. And Ella was sitting there, with a glass of wine in her hand. Smiling…

'I'm going to take some more photos.' Ella pulled her phone out of her shoulder bag. 'I've got a sketch pad too, but you probably don't want to hang around long enough for me to do any drawing here.'

'Do whatever you need,' Logan said.

'What would *you* need,' Ella asked, 'if you were going to be living here?'

'But I'm not going to be living here.'

Ella gave him a strange look. 'Help me out here, Logan. Play the game. It'll make it so much easier to make this real. Otherwise, you'll only get my ideas and I can probably make it appeal to a much wider market if I know what you'd want.'

Logan shrugged. If it was going to help get rid of this place, being temporarily uncomfortable would be a reasonable price to pay.

'What's important to you?' Ella asked. 'Outside of work, I mean.'

Logan was silent for a moment, genuinely at a loss to think of something that wasn't connected to his career that was important enough to need catering for in a dwelling.

'Do you love books?' Ella prompted. 'Would a library with a lovely old desk be attractive? It could be tucked behind the stone partition and the fire.'

Logan could see that too. Shelves and shelves of books,

with a whole section for the old medical textbooks he loved to collect that were sitting in boxes in storage. Maybe there were floorboards of the dark grainy wood of reclaimed pine Ella had mentioned, with an old Persian-style carpet square in a lovely deep shade of red.

Ella's voice broke into that glimmer of an indoor retreat Logan had never imagined having.

'Are you a secret gourmet cook? How 'bout a kitchen with an Aga and a butler's sink and a pantry built into the corner so it's got stone walls, which will make it a cool store as well. Or…even better—that space could be the wine cellar?'

No. A pantry would be better. Stocked with food that would simmer slowly in the Aga to make something delicious. He pulled in a deep breath through his nose, as if he could actually smell it cooking.

Ella didn't seem to mind that he wasn't saying anything aloud. She was turning in a circle, looking up at the too-small windows. 'What do you want to see as a view? The forest? Or, if we were allowed, we could put in huge windows or French doors and that way we could see the little pixie house and the pond from almost any corner of the house. I think…' Ella was frowning now. 'I've lost my sense of direction. Can we go outside and have a look?'

'Good idea…' Logan's head was starting to spin. It was getting far too easy to summon the images that Ella's words were creating and they came with a sting in their tail of doubts that were creeping in. Maybe he *did* want to live here after all. Maybe he'd forgotten what it was that had captured him that day he'd wandered in the direction of the 'For Sale' sign.

But, as perfect as Ella made it sound, would he want to be here? Alone? Was it the way she kept saying 'we'?

If we were allowed...

We could see the little pixie house...

Maybe it was being in Ella's company that was not only casting the spell again but bringing it to life in a way that was...disturbing, that was what it was. Logan was aware of an emotional response that was strong enough to be making it difficult to keep reined in with his usual ease. It would be easier outside, he decided. Especially with the chill of the breeze that had sprung up and the way dark clouds were swiftly moving to mask the sunshine.

They had to push through knee-high grass and weeds between the long wall of the barn and the pond. They walked past the small circular building to get closer to the pond and then both turned back. Logan could feel the first drops of rain starting to fall but Ella didn't seem to notice. She was taking photographs and then simply staring and Logan could almost see the ideas of that outdoor courtyard featuring the pixie house forming in her head.

He almost groaned aloud as he caught himself automatically referring to it as the 'pixie house' and he needed to shift his gaze so Ella didn't catch him watching the changing expressions on her face with such fascination. Turning his head, he gave a huff of laughter.

'There you go...' he said. 'Your duck's come to say hello. With a friend.'

'Oh…' Ella's face lit up. 'I wish I'd thought to bring some crusts of bread. I'll have to remember next time…'

Next time…?

Something like pleasure at the thought of being here again with Ella added itself to the strange mix of slightly out-of-control emotions Logan was grappling with but the distraction of the sudden, unexpected downpour of rain as the heavens opened was enough to kill the moment.

'Oh, my God…' Ella shoved her phone into her bag and wrapped her arms around it protectively as she turned to look towards the closest form of shelter, which was the pixie house. 'Has it got a doorway?'

It did. A narrow, low door space that they could just squeeze through, but there was plenty of room to stand up once they were inside. They could hear the heavy raindrops pelting the slates above their heads and they stood close together so they could both see out of the gap in the stone walls, through the veil of water falling outside to where the ducks were still floating on the now ruffled surface of the pond.

'I'm soaked,' Ella said. 'How did that happen so fast?' She pulled at the front of her jumper and drops of water flicked onto where Logan had his hand on the edge of the gap, which made him turn away from watching for a break in the downpour. Her hair looked almost as wet as the night Logan had found her unable to get into her apartment and she even had drops of water caught on the tangle of her dark eyelashes.

And there it was…

A blast of the sexual attraction he thought he'd dealt with more than a week ago and it was the straw that broke the camel's back as far as controlling his emotions went. Because Ella was staring back at him and he was quite certain that he was seeing a reflection of that attraction in her eyes.

He wanted to kiss her.

He was almost sure that that was what Ella wanted as well.

But that wanting was so powerful it felt dangerous. It might be the hardest thing Logan had done in a very long time but he managed to break that eye contact. He looked outside. There was no sign of the rain letting up but Logan knew what would happen if they stayed in this small space, and suddenly he wasn't at all sure that Ella wanted it as much as he did.

'It doesn't look like this rain is going to stop any time soon,' he said. 'Shall we make a run for it?'

He definitely needed to make a run for it—and not just to get out of the rain.

CHAPTER SIX

HAD SHE IMAGINED IT?

Or, by the power of wishful thinking, had Ella somehow seen how she had been feeling herself reflected in Logan's eyes?

She could have sworn he'd wanted to kiss her as much as she'd wanted him to, but now she was changing her mind.

It had been an awkward trip back from the property. They'd got even wetter by the time they'd locked up, put the key back in its hiding place in the hollow tree and reached the shelter of the car. With the heaters on the windows had steamed up and Logan had to focus on his driving. He also turned the radio on and Ella was treated to an exceedingly dull in-depth discussion about a recent football match and more than one controversial decision the referee had made so she kept her head down and scrolled through the photos she had taken in and outside the barn.

The rain had clearly set in for the rest of the day and, after having a long, hot shower and washing her hair, Ella couldn't see any point in getting properly dressed again, especially when it was already dark enough to need the lights on, so she put on her pyjamas and some fluffy socks even though it was only four p.m. The apartment was nice and warm and, having combed out her hair, she curled up on the couch with her sketchpad and pencils and quickly became lost in the pleasure of something creative that was the time out she loved the most.

The knock on her door just after six p.m. startled her enough to make her drop her pencil.

'Who is it?'

'Logan.'

'Oh...' For a moment Ella was tempted to say it wasn't a good time but it wasn't as though her pyjamas were something awful like flannelette with a kitten print or something. They were just leggings and an oversized tee shirt, and she could probably cover up the fact that she wasn't wearing a bra by just peering around the door to see what he wanted.

And...her heart rate had picked up quite noticeably and there was that knot of sensation that was getting ready to fire those spears of that very pleasant physical response to a man she was very much attracted to. Plus Ella was curious. Firstly as to why he was knocking at her door but also because she still had that question burning in the back of her mind.

Had she imagined that he'd been tempted to kiss her?

This was most likely the best chance she was going to get to find the answer to that question so she found herself walking to the door. She forgot to hide behind it, however, being instantly distracted by what she could smell.

'I thought you might be hungry,' Logan said. 'And... I was feeling bad that you got wet. Again.'

As if Ella needed reminding of when he'd found her,

soaked to the skin, unable to get into her new apartment. Or being in his apartment, using his towel to dry her hair. Or, most of all, discovering that she was attracted to him more than she had ever been attracted to anyone when she'd first met them, in fact. But maybe the reminder was why she was feeling it so strongly again right now. Enough to make her skin tingle right down to her toes.

'Do you fancy some Thai takeaway?' Logan's smile was an invitation all by itself.

Ella's toes were curling inside those fluffy socks as she took a deep, appreciative sniff. 'That smells *so* good.'

'Spring rolls, chicken satay, drunken noodles and green curry. I've been to this restaurant before and they make the best drunken noodles I've ever tasted…'

Logan's voice—and smile—were trailing away and his eyebrows were rising. Ella couldn't miss the way he deliberately shifted his gaze after it had drifted down to take in her attire. Or lack of it? Had he guessed she wasn't wearing any underwear at all?

It would be polite to acknowledge that she wasn't dressed for company and suggest that he came back in a few minutes but Ella could actually *feel* that Logan was struggling to keep a lid on his reaction.

That she hadn't been imagining a mutual level of attraction between them this afternoon and, dammit…she didn't want to give him the chance to put his barriers up again, the way he had when he'd made her listen to that boring dissection of a football match on their journey home.

'That's the best offer I've had in a very long time.'

Ignoring any flickers of doubt, Ella pulled the door open further. 'Do come in.'

This was a bad idea.

But he could hardly tell Ella that he'd made a mistake and he didn't think quickly enough to say he had other commitments, leave her the food and disappear.

And if he was honest…he didn't want to. He might have successfully taken control of the situation this afternoon by making a run for it but he hadn't been able to stop thinking about it ever since and the pull that had made him think up an excuse to knock on Ella's door had been, quite simply, irresistible.

So he followed her into her apartment. He tried—and failed—to think about the fact that she wasn't wearing a bra and her hair was a loose waterfall down her back and all that was in the way of that Lady Godiva fantasy was the thin fabric of a well-worn tee shirt.

Searching desperately for a distraction, he noticed the scattered pencils over sheets of paper on the coffee table.

'You've been sketching already?'

'Mmm…' Ella reached to take the paper carrier bag from Logan's hands. 'Why don't you have a look while I find some plates? And would you like a glass of wine?'

'Yes…but let me help.' Logan couldn't stop himself. Maybe it was the touch of Ella's fingers against his hand as she tried to take hold of the handles of the bag. He dismissed the escape route he'd just been offered and kept hold of it. 'You get the wine,' he said. 'I'll sort the food.'

He put the bag on the bench of the small kitchenette and took out the foil containers with their cardboard lids while Ella took a bottle of wine from the pantry cupboard. Logan had opened an overhead cupboard to find some plates and Ella reached for the glasses that were beside them.

Their hands touched again and they both pulled back to give the other a chance to get what they needed.

But neither of them moved.

There they were, standing so close that Logan wasn't sure if the warmth he was aware of was coming from the hot food on the bench or from Ella's skin and whether the aroma filling his nostrils was from the spices in his favourite cuisine or from Ella's hair. He could almost taste them.

He *wanted* to taste them.

And then he saw the look in Ella's eyes as she lifted her gaze to meet his and he completely forgot all about food. Or wine. Or the sketches on the table. Nothing existed apart from Ella Grisham and a deep, soul-scorching level of...need, that was what it was. It was too strong to be anywhere near the attraction point of a spectrum that included all shades of desire. And it was strong enough to stifle any warning that this might be a bad idea.

He could feel Ella getting closer, as if she was going onto her tiptoes. Or maybe it was because he was dipping his head. Just a little. Not enough to break that eye contact for a long, long moment. Because he needed to be sure that Ella wanted this as much as he did. If that was even possible...

Logan closed his eyes when they were close enough for Ella's face to have become a blur. Time seemed to be moving incredibly slowly. So slowly that he could take the time to let the tip of his nose touch the side of her nose for a heartbeat. For him to touch his lips to the corner of her mouth and then move, still in such slow motion that his bottom lip could feel the dent in her chin and then capture her bottom lip between his so that the tip of his tongue could touch…and taste…the unbelievable softness of her lip.

And then, without warning, time sped up. Perhaps it was the touch of Ella's tongue against *his* lips. Or the way she lifted her arms, lacing her fingers over the nape of his neck. Maybe it was because it felt as if she was losing her balance as she pressed closer, standing on those tippy toes, which made Logan instinctively reach to hold her steady and, as he did, the palm of one of his hands brushed her breast and beneath that thin fabric he could feel a nipple that was as hard as a tiny pebble.

It was most likely a combination of everything, combined with a rising level of a passion that promised to be as unrestrained and intense and joyful as Logan suspected Ella could be. Whatever the catalyst, something exploded so fast there was no time to make conscious decisions. Logan was being swept along in a tide that he'd never felt the like of. With one movement he bent and put an arm behind Ella's knees and scooped her into his arms. His lips found hers again as he turned, but he didn't need more than a glimpse of any obstacles in their way because he knew the layout of this apartment was the same as his own.

He knew where the bedroom was.

Oh…dear Lord…

Talk about being swept off your feet!

Not that Ella was about to try and slow this down. If anything, she wanted it to go faster so it was almost disappointing to find herself gently deposited on the side of her bed instead of being thrown onto her back on the mattress. But then she opened her eyes and found Logan looking down at her. And then he moved his hand to cup the back of her neck and bent down to start kissing her again and she just melted inside. She found the buttons of his shirt beneath her fingers and started undoing them one by one, without breaking those kisses for anything more than a snatch of air or a head tilt so that their lips— and tongues—could explore even more.

And then her fingers reached the band of his jeans so Ella lifted her arms into the air and Logan knew exactly what to do. He took handfuls of the hem of her tee shirt and pulled it up and over her head. He stripped off his own shirt and Ella unfastened the stud on his jeans. She didn't get the chance to slide his zip down, however, because Logan was lifting her to her feet, his hands sliding under the waistband of her leggings to push them down.

His soft oath was almost a huff of laughter.

'Do you often go around with no knickers on, Ella?'

'These are my PJs. You don't wear knickers to bed, do you?'

'I don't wear anything to bed,' Logan admitted.

A beat of silence and then he was shedding his jeans and Ella was kicking herself free of her leggings. She was still standing in front of him and he held her with one arm around her waist as he leaned in to cover her lips with his own. She could feel his other hand sliding down her back, cupping her buttock and then drifting into the gap between their bodies to touch her even more intimately.

Ella gasped, the astonishing flood of sensation taking her so much by surprise that she found herself sinking in to sit on the edge of the bed again, as if her knees were no longer useful. And then she was falling backwards, onto the bed, and Logan was still kissing her—following the movement of her body as if it was a dance and he needed to stay in contact. He was kneeling over her and it could have been all over far too soon except that they caught each other's gaze and the question was almost written in a bubble in the air between them.

'Bedside cabinet,' Ella said. 'Top drawer.'

Breaking the pace of the almost out-of-control passion to make sure they were both protected was a good thing, she decided. It had slowed things down again and Logan was kissing her with the same almost poignant intensity of that first kiss in the kitchen. Ella could have happily stayed in that space for as long as possible but, like it had during those first kisses, a switch seemed to get flicked and they were falling into a very different space where rational thought was overtaken by sensation.

The taste…

The touch…

The exquisite pleasure that built and built until there was no room left to contain it and it could only escape with all the drama this particular climax had promised. And then they were lying side by side, waiting to catch their breath and have their heart rates return to something like a normal level. Logan's arm was under Ella's neck and they were both looking at the ceiling. Until they weren't. Until, by some kind of telepathic signal, they rolled towards each other and kissed once more. A long, slow, delicious kiss...

'All right?' Logan asked softly.

Ella's smile started slowly but she couldn't help it continuing to grow. She wanted to say that she'd never been better. That she'd never had a first time with anyone that had been that good, but instinct told her not to make this into too much of a big deal or Logan would run and hide again. Like he had this afternoon. He'd even said it out loud, hadn't he?

Shall we make a run for it...?

So Ella held his face with both hands and gave him a gentle, short kiss on his lips. 'I'm still hungry,' she told him. 'I think I'm even hungrier than I was before.'

'That food will be stone cold,' Logan groaned.

Ella rolled away to reach for her tee shirt and leggings. 'Isn't that what they invented microwaves for?'

This was exactly the kind of situation that Logan had carefully avoided for more than a decade now. It wasn't that he didn't have a sex life—of course he did—but it was very carefully orchestrated to be a friendship with benefits that always ran its course when his partners either found that he was being totally honest about there being no chance of a permanent relationship and moved on or he needed to escape politely when they made it obvious they were hoping for more.

Any intimate encounters were somewhere that Logan was able to leave at a time of his choice. He never invited them into his home and he never stayed a whole night. He certainly didn't hang around to share a meal with anyone. He'd never chosen someone who lived close to his home, let alone merely a few steps away across a hallway and… oh, no…had he somehow forgotten that he had to *work* with Ella and, unless he actively avoided it, he might see her every day? Several times a day, even.

Logan expected this to be horribly awkward but it wasn't.

Ella was acting as if it was no big deal. As if they hadn't just shared the best sex he'd ever experienced in his life. Logan was still getting faint aftershocks of sensation deep in his belly—like when he watched her use chopsticks to start eating a mouthful of noodles but simply sucked in the ends that hadn't made it inside her mouth.

'Oh, wow…you were right. These are the best drunken noodles ever.'

'Have you tried the curry?' Logan reached for more rice to put in his bowl. 'I hope it's not too spicy for you. I wasn't sure what level of heat you might like.'

'Oh…?' Ella's eyes were dancing. 'I love a bit of heat…'

She reached over and helped herself to a mouthful of food from his dish—as if they were so comfortable in each other's company it was a given that they could share food without asking permission. 'Good guess,' she murmured. 'Why am I not surprised?'

It was obvious Ella was talking about Logan's ability to provide a level of heat that had nothing whatsoever to do with food but even that didn't make things awkward. Until he was helping clean up after their dinner and Logan could feel a clock beginning to tick. It was the logical time for him to excuse himself and go home. A day—and night—that he was never likely to forget was about to end.

Realising that he didn't *want* to go home was a gut feeling that was nothing like one of those pleasurable aftershocks.

'It's time I went home,' he said aloud, for his own benefit as much as Ella's.

Was he hoping that Ella would invite him to stay a bit longer? For a coffee or another glass of wine? Another session of sensational sex, even? If he was hoping for that he was instantly disappointed because Ella's response was a nod as she checked her watch.

'I've got to make a call to Australia soon,' she said. 'It might go on for a while.'

'Australia?'

'I've agreed to take on a six-month locum there for my next position and I think there are a few questions that need answering on both sides.'

'Australia…' It wasn't a question this time. A beat of dismay was the last thing Logan might have expected to feel. 'That's a world away from Aberdeen.'

'Last time I looked, yeah…' Ella was smiling at him. 'But Eddie makes it sound like it's the best place in the world so it's about time I went to see for myself. And if I'm there for long enough we might manage another family reunion. Somewhere amazing…like the Blue Mountains or Tasmania or one of those gorgeous islands on the Great Barrier Reef.'

Logan was completely caught by that smile. Or perhaps the sparkle in Ella's eyes and the excitement in her voice.

'You really love being free to go anywhere, don't you?' Was he impressed or envious of Ella's lifestyle? Or perhaps there was a bit of relief surfacing. It didn't matter how he felt about what had just happened between them because it wasn't a threat to either of their lifestyles.

'It's the best feeling in the world,' Ella said.

By tacit consent, they were both moving towards her door. In a few seconds Ella was going to open it and Logan could step back into his own world that had nothing like the kind of magic dust this woman seemed to be able to gather and scatter for others to share.

No wonder Logan had never found himself in a situation like this before.

He'd never met anyone like Ella before and he was quite sure he would never meet anyone like her ever again.

She was one of a kind and she wasn't going to be in his life for more than a few weeks so did it matter that he was breaking his own rules and boundaries? He didn't have to worry about a liaison that might not run its course in an amicable fashion because the end date was already built in. There was no need to be already planning a polite escape so there was also no need to take any notice of those faint alarm bells that were ringing in the back of his mind.

Logan paused when Ella opened her door.

'Thanks for dinner,' she said. 'I really enjoyed it.'

He was close enough to make it very easy to touch her cheek with his fingers.

'Thank *you*,' he said softly. 'It wasn't the food that I enjoyed the most.' He traced the line of Ella's jaw, caught her chin and bent his head to kiss her. Slowly. And thoroughly, because he could sense that she was in no hurry to say goodnight.

She looked slightly dazed when he finally lifted his head.

In that beat of silence Logan wondered who was going to be the first to suggest they did it again. Not him, he decided almost instantly. Ella had already made it clear that the sex had been no big deal. This was casual. It probably didn't matter that much to either of them whether or not it was going to happen again. If it did, great... If it didn't, well, that was fine too.

'You working tomorrow?' Ella's voice was a little rough. She cleared her throat. 'Maybe I'll see you then?'

'Maybe...' Logan moved through the door. Another step and he was almost halfway across the hallway. 'I am working, yes...'

But it did matter, he realised, when he reached his own door and looked over his shoulder to see that Ella was already closing hers, because how much he wanted it to happen again should really be a warning signal. He heard the click of her door lock and blew out a breath when he closed his own door a moment later. He was pretty sure that Ella would welcome another encounter just as much as he would but there was only one way to be sure.

He'd been the one to initiate things this evening by turning up with that food, so if there *was* going to be a next time it would have to be Ella's turn to hit on him.

CHAPTER SEVEN

WAS HE WAITING for her to make the next move?

Ella had fully expected not to have Logan acknowledge any difference due to their relationship becoming somewhat more than simply colleagues. Certainly not at work, anyway. She'd had the impression from the moment she'd met him that he kept his distance and his private life simply that—private. He'd also made it very clear that he wouldn't tolerate distractions of any kind so Ella would have been astonished if she'd been the recipient of meaningful glances across an operating table or patient's bed, or an obvious increase in time together like sharing a lunch break. A fantasy rendezvous involving a lot of kissing and inappropriate touching, in his office or a secluded corner on the hospital roof, perhaps, was the stuff of television soap operas, not real life.

And that was fine by her. She was just as passionate about her career as Logan was about his and this was, after all, only the second day back at work after their very private time together on their shared day off. Like the way Ella had backed off from asking personal questions to let Logan know he could trust her, she was more than happy to give him time to realise she wasn't going to be a distraction at work either.

She wasn't even thinking about him, in fact, when she got paged for a consult in the emergency department, other than a brief flash of realising that the last time she'd been in this part of the hospital had been when Logan had invited her to join him for that OERT response.

'Her name's Beth,' the registrar told her when she arrived. 'She's thirteen weeks pregnant and she's got severe abdominal pain—right lower quadrant. She's convinced she's miscarrying although we've found a healthy heartbeat on ultrasound and there's no blood loss. No fever, she's tachycardic at one forty bpm, has a respiration rate of twenty-four, but she's extremely upset. She lost her first baby at fourteen weeks.'

'Oh, no…' Ella's heart immediately went out to the patient she was about to see. 'She must be terrified.'

She was. Beth was sobbing when Ella entered the assessment. An older woman sat on a chair beside the bed, her face creased with anxiety.

'Hi, Beth… My name's Ella. I'm one of the obstetric consultants here at Queen's.' Ella grabbed a handful of tissues from a box on the bench and gave them to Beth. 'I know how scary this is,' she said softly. 'But we're going to take very good care of you, okay?'

Beth blew her nose. 'This is my fault. I shouldn't have come up to see Mum. But my GP said I was fine.'

'When did you see your GP?'

'A few days ago for the pain. He said it was probably just wind but he sent me to hospital for an ultrasound because I'd been spotting a bit before that and he knew… he knew…'

'He knew how worried she was,' Beth's mother put in.

'It's only a year ago that Beth lost her first baby. That's why I suggested she came to visit me for a few days while her husband's away for work—so that she wasn't by herself.'

Beth was sobbing again but her cry turned into an agonised groan. Ella turned to the registrar. 'What has Beth had for the pain?'

'Morphine. Five milligrams.'

'Let's top that up and get on top of this pain.' Ella could see the Luer plug taped to Beth's arm. 'Have you got any blood results back yet?'

'We should have got the full blood count back by now.' The registrar frowned. 'I'll go and check.'

'Thanks.' A high white count might be indicative of an infection and appendicitis was a common cause of lower right quadrant pain but a white count could be elevated in pregnant women anyway and there were many other potential causes, both associated with pregnancy and co-incidental. An acute abdomen in a pregnant woman was a challenge and overlapped specialties so Ella was already aware that a consult with a general surgeon could be needed. She asked the nurse to take another set of vital signs as she gave Beth a minute or two for the pain to settle before examining her.

She found Beth's abdomen to be rigid and still very tender despite the morphine and she was saying she felt sick, despite the antinausea medication that had been administered along with the opioid. The pain seemed to be spreading to the upper right quadrant as well, which only added to the differential diagnoses Ella needed to consider. Beth might have kidney stones or an infection, an ovarian cyst might have ruptured and the risk of an ovarian torsion in early pregnancy was already much greater than normal. It could be gallstones or pancreatitis and she wanted to see the blood test results on liver function. She also wanted to do her own ultrasound examination and she was in the process of doing that when both the ED registrar and another consultant came into the room.

The other consultant was Logan. He came up behind Ella to peer at what she was seeing on the screen of the portable ultrasound machine.

'I've got a meeting with ED management,' he said quietly. 'But I heard you were here and I got briefed on the history.'

Ella could feel a sudden tension in her body. It had nothing to do with the unexpected sound of Logan's voice, or the fact that he was standing close enough for her to be aware of the warmth of *his* body. It wasn't associated with any memory of the way Logan had taken over the management of a case she was assessing either— the way he had on the first day they'd met.

'See that?'

'Mmm...' It was a soft sound of agreement that disguised any underlying concern.

There was free fluid in Beth's abdomen. Not a huge amount but enough to be a real concern. Ella angled the transducer to try and get a clearer image.

'Appendicitis?' Logan suggested. His mouth was close enough to her ear for only Ella to hear what he was saying. 'Acute cholecystitis? Ovarian cyst rupture?'

'Can't rule any of them out yet,' she responded. She didn't say it aloud but she knew they were both thinking that urgent surgery might be necessary to both make the diagnosis and treat it. Changing the angle again, she picked up the baby's heartbeat and Logan smiled at the reassuring sound of a baby who wasn't in immediate distress.

'Can you hear that, Beth? That's your baby's heart.'

'I feel sick,' Beth moaned. 'And dizzy...'

'Blood pressure's ninety-five on sixty,' the nurse reported. 'Down from one-ten on seventy. That last recording was only five minutes ago.'

Ella looked up to catch Logan's gaze and she knew that his gut instinct was the same as her own. There was something potentially serious going on here. This abdominal pain might not be associated with the pregnancy but it still had the risk of affecting it and the sooner they could diagnose the problem the better. The best way to rule out the most serious possibilities was by an exploratory laparoscopic investigation.

'I think we're going to need to take a look at what's going on in your tummy,' she told Beth. 'We'll get a general surgeon to come and see you as well, because it might be something that has nothing to do with you being pregnant. The most likely cause is acute appendicitis.'

Beth was crying again. Her mother had gone almost as pale as her daughter. 'An operation? Isn't that dangerous for the baby?'

'The risk of not having surgery may be greater,' Ella said gently. 'I'll talk you both through any associated risks soon but you're actually at the safest stage of pregnancy to be having surgery. The risk of a miscarriage is higher in the first trimester and it gets technically a bit more complicated when the baby's bigger in the third trimester. We'll do the investigation laparoscopically and, if surgery is needed, we'll try and do that without having to open up your tummy, which means you'll have less likelihood of blood loss and a reduced need for medications, which is better for both of you.' Ella could see that Beth and her mother needed a bit of time to get over the shock of hearing that surgery might be needed. They also needed any reassurance she could give them at this point. 'You heard your baby's heartbeat, yes?'

Beth nodded, her face twisted with both pain and fear.

'He's not in any distress at the moment and that's a good sign.' Ella squeezed Beth's hand. 'We're going to look after you both, but we need to find out what's going on because you may be bleeding internally and we need to find out why and fix it.'

She caught Logan's gaze again then and she knew he would see a plea in her eyes. It wasn't that she wanted him to take over this case. What she wanted was for them to work together on it. The way they had for Lauren with her ruptured uterus and Iona with her dramatic surgery right here in this emergency department. They were a good team and Ella knew they were equally invested in keeping both a mother and her baby safe. More than a good team. Ella found this man inspirational in her professional arena and having his calm presence by her side gave her a confidence that was…empowering?

Together, they could tackle anything and Ella was far more likely to believe that they could win any medical battle. It was as simple as that.

He didn't need to nod. She could see that he understood. 'I'll let the guys here know I'm not going to make the meeting,' he told Ella. 'I'll also give Geoff, one of our general surgeons, an urgent call and get a theatre on standby while you go through the consent process with Beth.'

'Thank you.' Ella needed to get wide bore IV access in place for potential fluid resuscitation if Beth's blood pressure really crashed and she would also need a Foley catheter in preparation for surgery. They were going to be busy for the next little while but she gave no sign of being stressed as she gently wiped the ultrasound gel off Beth's distended abdomen. 'There you go,' she said. 'Dr Walsh is our head of department here at Queen's and he's on the case. You're in the best hands possible.'

Any doubts that he might have created difficulties in his working life by sleeping with Ella had been dispelled the moment Logan's path had crossed with Ella's on the ward yesterday.

Being in Theatre with her while she demonstrated her competence in manipulating laparoscopic instruments to try and discover the cause of their patient's abdominal pain made him very happy that he didn't need to avoid working closely with Ella because this was…impressive, that was what it was.

Logan had been more than happy to simply observe Ella's work, right from the first small incision below Beth's belly button to allow insertion of the first trochar that was used to infuse the gas to inflate the abdomen and the insertion of the laparascope with its bright light and video camera that sent the images onto the screen for the surgeons.

He could see what Ella could see and when her gaze flicked up to catch his for a heartbeat he knew exactly what she was thinking. While this wasn't an unheard-of complication in pregnancy, it was rare enough to qualify as a zebra and not a horse. This wasn't acute appendicitis or any of the other differential diagnoses that had sprung to mind initially.

'It's a heterotopic pregnancy with a ruptured ectopic,' Ella said for the benefit of the rest of the surgical team. 'It looks as though we'll need to do a total salpingectomy and remove this fallopian tube.'

Logan agreed. Beth had, in fact, become pregnant with twins and it was a heterotopic pregnancy because one of the implantations had happened where it should, in the uterus, but the other had become stuck and implanted itself in one of the fallopian tubes. The gestation of the healthy baby in the womb shouldn't be affected but the ectopic pregnancy was not viable and had to be removed before it endangered the mother's life. It was obstetric surgery and Logan was quite confident that Ella was more than capable to be the person performing it.

He assisted Ella to insert more trochars for both a left and right port on the side of Beth's abdomen. He watched the screen as she suctioned blood from the area around the affected fallopian tube.

'That's a litre of blood loss so far,' he noted. 'Do you want to start some blood products? Packed red cells?'

'Yes. Thank you.' Ella took a moment to glance at the screen with the display of the continuous monitoring of their patient's blood pressure, oxygen saturation and heart rate and rhythm. The anaesthetist gave her a reassuring nod.

'All good.'

Logan could see, on screen, the deft way Ella manipulated her instruments—graspers to hold tissue and to cauterise and cut the fallopian tube to stop the bleeding and remove the mass and a bag with purse strings to contain and then remove it. And he could see by looking at her face how intense her focus was. Somewhere in the back of his mind any doubts he might have had about it ever being difficult to work with Ella due to anything related to their personal lives evaporated. She might be far more involved with her patients on an emotional level than he ever became but she was as capable as he was himself of keeping enough distance not to let it affect her professional judgement.

Her patients were safe.

He was safe...

They did an intraoperative ultrasound to check on the condition of the baby in Beth's uterus and they checked again at the end of the procedure. Logan excused himself as Beth was transferred to the recovery suite.

'Everything's looking great,' he said to Ella quietly. 'Good job.'

'Thanks for being here,' she responded. 'I wasn't at all sure what we were going to find.'

'It was a pleasure,' Logan said. And he meant it. 'But I'd better get on with my day. I'm two meetings behind already and I've got my own theatre list. It might be a long day.'

'In that case, I think it must be my turn to provide dinner.' Ella's voice was quiet enough not be overheard but, even if it had been, it was casual enough for any hidden meaning to be missed unless you knew what had happened the last time they had had dinner together.

Ella knew.

Logan knew.

And the flick of a glance they shared as Ella stripped off her gloves and followed her patient out of Theatre made it crystal-clear that they both knew it was going to happen again.

Ella chose Mexican takeaway for their dinner and she had extra spice added to their tacos and burritos and quesadillas but it was never going to be able to compete with the heat that seemed to ignite in an instant between herself and Logan Walsh.

The food had been waiting on Ella's kitchen bench to be reheated because she had no idea what time Logan would get away from work and all it took for that meal to be totally forgotten was the knock on her door just after nine p.m. When she opened the door to see the look in Logan's eyes Ella was already lost in the moment.

He was kissing her even as he dropped his bag by the door and pushed it shut. Off balance, Ella needed the support of the wall at her back so that she could raise her arms to wrap them around Logan's neck but he caught her hands and held them above her head and kissed her so thoroughly that her head was spinning by the time she had a chance to catch her breath.

'I should go home,' he said, sounding out of breath himself. 'It's been a long day and I need a shower.'

'Don't go…' When she ran her tongue over her bottom lip Ella could still taste him. 'I've got a shower…'

He was watching her mouth. And then he lifted his gaze and Ella had never felt less hungry for food in her life. Seconds later, they were in the small bathroom of her apartment, which wasn't built for two people using it at the same time so it meant getting really close as they undressed each other, and they were skin to skin when they got in under the rain of hot water. And then there was a slippery bar of soap and the foam of shampoo and more kissing. There was laughter and murmurs of pleasure and encouragement and…and it was the best sex Ella had ever experienced in her life.

Until they wrapped themselves in towels and went to her bed and did it all over again and that was slow and tender and…

…and Ella knew she was beginning to fall in love with a man who could be so distant and calmly professional on one hand and have the ability to make love like *this* on the other. He was an intense, super intelligent and passionate man but he was also more controlled than anyone she'd ever met and that gave him an air of mystery that was more than simply intriguing. It was compelling…

She could feel his heart beating strongly and swiftly under her cheek as she nestled in his arms.

'Where did you learn to be this good in bed?' she asked.

Logan gave a grunt of laughter. 'I could ask you the same thing.'

'Hey... I'm well out of practice. It's been quite a while for me.'

'Same...' But there was a gleam in Logan's eyes. 'I'll look forward to you getting your mojo back,' he said. 'I'll just have to hope I can keep up.'

Ella lifted herself onto one elbow so that she could reach his lips with her own. 'I have every confidence in your ability,' she told him. 'And, seeing as we've got a limited shelf life, we should probably make the most of it, don't you think?'

For a long, long moment, Logan held her gaze silently and Ella's heart skipped a beat. Was he going to tell her that this couldn't happen again? That he never let people into his life far enough to throw caution to the winds and indulge in a passionate affair?

This wasn't something Ella had ever done before in her life either, but it was in this moment that she realised just how much she wanted to spend the remainder of her time in Aberdeen with Logan. It wasn't only because of the amazing sexual connection they'd discovered with each other. She really wanted to get to know him. To understand what had made him into the person he was today—a man who was capable of so much passion and yet he'd chosen to funnel it almost entirely into his career. Wasn't he lonely, at least sometimes?

She didn't believe that he lived alone and had no significant relationships outside of work purely in order not to dilute that focus because she could sense something much bigger had been responsible for shaping his ability to distance himself and be content to be alone. Something traumatic enough to make Logan hide a significant part of who he was. Enough to create a barrier that Ella knew she might never be able to breach, but that wasn't enough to push her away. If anything, it was making her feel even more drawn to him.

You couldn't fall in love with someone unless the connection was on a much deeper level than just sex. You had to care about them. A lot. And if you cared about someone that much it was only to be expected that you would want to understand what might be holding them back from being as happy as they deserved to be.

Ella had just reminded them both that they only had a limited amount of time to be together and that they should make the most of it, but now she was holding her breath, wondering if she'd pushed a little too hard against that barrier and she'd never get an opportunity to understand why it was there in the first place—or think about whether she might be able to contribute more than just a memorable physical fling to Logan's life.

What if she could help him loosen that hold he had on his emotions and he realised that there was more to life than work? If he not only got persuaded to live in that bit of rural paradise he'd been inspired to purchase but shared it with someone he could love as much as they loved him?

It seemed as if Logan might be reading her thoughts because he was smiling, but when he spoke she realised that he had backed off into a safely distant place because he was speaking in the same tone he might have used to tell her about an interesting case he'd seen recently.

'I'm going up to Inverness in a week or so,' he said. 'To present an obstetric emergencies seminar. I'll leave

Friday afternoon, do the seminar on Saturday and be back here by about eight p.m. Maybe you'd like to come with me if it fits in with your roster? It might be a good chance for you to find out everything you want to know about the course with a bit of sightseeing thrown in? We could come back over the Old Military Road, which is worth seeing if you've never driven it. Some people say it's one of the best roads in the UK.'

Ella drew in a breath. While it was disappointing that Logan had retreated from the closeness that had been there while they'd been making love, she was relieved to discover she hadn't pushed too hard on that barrier after all. Logan wasn't running. Or, if he was, he was inviting her to go with him and she liked that. He was making it sound as if he wanted her company too, by throwing in the bonus of some sightseeing. It was possible she might be able to find out as much about Logan as the course's clinical content but, if not, it would be a longer time in his company than she had had so far and there was no way she could turn that down. Not with the strength of that pull she could feel towards him.

But she kept her response light. Affirmative but casual. No big deal. No pushing of any boundaries involved.

'Sure,' she said. 'Sounds great... I'm in.'

CHAPTER EIGHT

LOGAN COULDN'T REMEMBER exactly when he'd started his programme of advanced training and refresher courses for medical professionals who were likely to have anything to do with pregnant women and childbirth but it was quite a few years ago now.

Initially, he'd worked with the local ambulance service, midwives and general practitioners who still offered obstetric services, but word had spread and he'd started getting invitations to work with other centres that offered a convenient hub for remote areas and he'd been more than happy to fit those commitments into his schedule. He sometimes got flown to cities all over the United Kingdom, but he particularly enjoyed being able to pack what he needed into the spacious hatch of his vehicle and drive off to explore his own backyard. His roots were very firmly in Scottish soil and he appreciated the often breathtaking landscape it offered.

He liked the break in his normal routine too. Ella might lose herself in dreaming up and sketching house restorations and renovations but this was his 'time out', even though it was still so closely related to his day-to-day work. And meeting new like-minded people who shared his vision in making childbirth as safe as possible was the closest thing Logan had to a social life, in fact. It was never a hardship travelling to parts of Scotland that he didn't know so well, but these days he was starting to revisit many of them. He knew they were heading into Forres now without needing any signposts.

'That's Nelson's Tower you can see on the hill over there. And there's the Witches Stone I stopped to have a look at once. I won't horrify you with the gory details of that grim bit of history.'

'I'll look it up myself,' Ella warned. 'I love everything about Scotland. The history and some of the countryside might be grim but it's got a wildness that's unique.'

Logan loved his homeland too, but enjoying its scenery and people and the snippets of history that he discovered was a bonus. He wasn't travelling around to have fun, after all. This was what he was most passionate about and what had become his personal mission in life. Teaching skills and giving people the confidence to handle emergencies because, even if it helped to save one life, it was worth putting all this time and effort into. As he'd said to Ella, the fact that the paramedics who'd been called to that cardiac arrest case they'd done the resuscitative hysterotomy on had recently done a course and were up-to-date with how to modify CPR for a pregnant patient could have made the crucial difference to the outcome for both mother and baby.

And that reminded him…

'She's doing really well,' he told Ella. 'Our mother who had the cardiac arrest.'

'Iona?' Ella looked up from the sketch pad on her lap that she'd gone back to working on as they left the town behind. 'I know… I went to visit her this morning and she and Finlay were having their first go at breastfeeding.'

'Successful?'

'He didn't quite manage to latch on properly but it's early days and it's a big step forward. He's doing well with bottle feeding and it was just wonderful to see him being held by his mum. Iona was crying happy tears. Oh, and he passed his hearing test this week too, and he's started to track things visually. I'm sure he's watching me when I go to visit him now.'

Logan was starting to regret mentioning the case. Ella didn't care that she got too involved with patients, did she? She made it sound as if it was quite okay for her to still be visiting a baby every day whose mother wasn't even her patient. She was clearly revelling in every positive step of the journey Iona and her family were embarked on. Logan shook his head.

'Are you still visiting him every day?'

'If I can. I love seeing his progress.'

Logan didn't need to turn his head. He could hear the smile in Ella's voice.

'I told him I'd try and find a toy Loch Ness monster for him while I'm away this weekend,' she said.

Logan did turn his head this time. 'I don't know how you do it,' he said.

'Do what?'

'Get so involved with the patients you treat—and their families. I mean, it's fine if a case goes well but how do you cope with the ones that don't go well when you get that close? I've seen people having to walk away from the careers they loved because they can't protect them-

selves from the downside of a tragedy they feel too connected with.'

'I guess it's a matter of balance,' Ella said thoughtfully,
after a short silence. 'Protecting yourself from not feeling the pain of a distressing case means that you're not
feeling the joy of the majority of our cases and isn't that
what makes this the best career in the world? Helping
babies get born...helping families get created?'

'I agree that it's a matter of balance.' Logan nodded.
'But you can't let the pendulum swing too far in either
direction—whether it's the happy side or the painful one.
If it swings too far, that's when things can get out of control. And when you can make bad decisions.'

'My pendulum probably does swing a bit more than
yours,' Ella admitted. 'But I never get *too* involved. I
can't, because I'm never in one place for long enough so
there's no danger of getting too attached—to people or
places. That would definitely do my head in when I had
to move on.'

'Because your freedom is everything.' Logan's words
were no more than a thinking aloud kind of murmur but
Ella obviously heard him.

'And adventures,' she said firmly. 'I do love an adventure.' She was peering ahead at a signpost they were approaching. 'I've never been to Nairn,' she said. 'Do you
know anything about it?'

'I believe it's an old fishing port and a seaside resort.
We've got time for a quick look if you like.'

'Ooh, yes, please. I haven't been near a beach since I
was in California. I'm missing waves.'

If Ella was trying to change the subject of their conversation, that smile was an encouragement that Logan couldn't refuse. Maybe these courses weren't intended to be fun, but he'd known deep down that having Ella's company would make things very different and mixing fun with work wasn't necessarily a bad thing, was it?

He smiled back. 'I might even buy you an ice cream if you behave yourself.'

It was like being on a real date with Logan Walsh for the first time.

They found ice creams at a beach café that advertised interesting flavours like cinnamon basil and Ella's choice of chocolate liquorice. She rolled her eyes when Logan went for a boringly safe vanilla but refrained from teasing him. They wandered off to admire the ornate Victorian era bandstand with its cast-iron finials and steeply curved roof while they ate them and then walked hand in hand on the beach and let the fresh sea breeze ruffle their hair and the waves break and roll so close they had to jump out of the way to keep their feet dry. It wasn't far to Inverness after that and daylight was fading so they stopped by a fish and chip shop near the river and sat on the bench in the shadow of the castle eating fish dinners with little wooden forks.

Ella wanted to keep the feeling of being on a date, even though she knew this was a work-related trip, so she did her best to entertain Logan with stories that had nothing to do with work and counted it a win when he snorted with amusement hearing about the alpacas that spat all over her in Peru and then laughed out loud at her description of what her triplet brothers looked like when they'd stolen their mother's nail scissors and given each other haircuts when they were about three years old.

It was the first time she'd heard Logan really laugh and it gave Ella a squeeze in her chest that was pure happiness.

She realised it would be the first time they would actually sleep in the same bed too, when they checked into a bed and breakfast establishment in the attic of a lovely old sandstone villa. Even though Ella knew they had a very early start the next morning, to set up the training room in a local hospital for the seminar, she wanted to stay awake and enjoy the prospect of drifting off to sleep in Logan's arms after their lovemaking, knowing that he would still be there beside her when she woke up in the morning.

And in that final moment, hanging in that misty space between thinking and dreaming, Ella remembered what she'd said to Logan in the car about being in no danger of getting too involved with any person or place because she never stayed anywhere long enough for it to become an issue. She couldn't have been in control of where her thoughts were drifting, however, because for a distinct moment she could imagine being with just one person. Settling down in just one place, even. Being so much in love with someone that it would be worthwhile giving up the freedom to go wherever she wanted to go in the world and have whatever adventures took her fancy.

Was she more than halfway towards being that much in love with Logan?

If she was, there was no point in worrying about giving up her freedom yet or starting to think about what it might be like to put down roots in one place because Logan was just as determined to protect his own version of freedom as she'd been over the last few years. He was never going to let his emotional pendulum swing far enough to distract him from his work and he wasn't about to include anyone else in his personal life.

And that was a good thing, even if it meant that Logan was sacrificing what many would think of as being one of the most important aspects of life. Ella had experienced the calm confidence that Logan's ability to keep his distance could bring to the way he handled an emergency and if she was a patient she would want someone exactly like that to be in charge.

Her thoughts circled back once more to that small epiphany as she finally fell asleep—that maybe she would consider settling down one day if she met the 'right' person—but this time she let the thought evaporate without taking any further notice. 'One day' was too far in the future to see and there was no reason at all to let it interfere with the present. It was rather nice, though, to think that she might find a partner who could add a permanent extra dimension to her personal life. The way Logan could when it came to her professional life?

She snuggled closer to the person she was with. While it wasn't an unpleasant idea that she might find that perfect partner in the future, she didn't need the 'right' one yet. She could enjoy the 'right now' person she had been lucky enough to meet.

This had to be the best group of medical professionals that Logan had ever had the pleasure of teaching. There were twenty people ranging in age from mid-twenties to late-fifties and they had come from all over some of the most northern areas of Scotland and as far east as Skye. They were engaged with the subject matter and eager to either learn new skills or practise the ones they already had because they might only have to deal with an obstetric emergency once in a blue moon and it was easy to forget how to do something you didn't do on a regular basis.

It wasn't the first time Logan had brought an assistant with him to help run the seminar, but this was Ella and he might have known it would be different.

The first session of this intense one-day course, after introductions and an icebreaker, was the subject of breech births.

'Because they account for three to four percent of all full-term pregnancies so you're likely to encounter one at some point. They can happen suddenly, especially if the baby is premature and it hasn't had the chance to turn itself around, and that can also mean it's quite likely to happen away from a nice, controlled hospital setting.'

Logan had one hip perched on the corner of the desk at the front of the room, with a laser pointer in his hand as he opened up an audio-visual presentation on the big screen that had been lowered over a blackboard. Ella was standing on the other side of the classroom and was holding one of the infant manikins that went with the lower torso models used to practise delivery techniques.

The first slide had images of babies in various breech positions within the uterus.

'A frank breech is what we prefer to deal with, where

the baby's bottom presents first with the legs straight up in front of the body and the feet near the head.'

Ella held the soft manikin baby in front of her and bent its legs straight up.

'A complete breech is where both the hips and knees are flexed so that it looks as though the baby is sitting cross-legged and a footling breech is where one or both feet will deliver first.'

Maybe it was the look of dismay on Ella's face as she let one of the manikin's legs dangle that led to the ripple of laughter that ran through the classroom. It could have been a distraction from what was actually a very serious topic to cover but Logan could feel a corner of his own mouth curling upwards.

Perhaps this was why it felt like the best group of participants he'd ever had? Because there was a hint of something lighter in the atmosphere than Logan had encountered before? It felt like a good thing. Surely if people were relaxed and comfortable they would learn more easily and wouldn't hesitate to ask questions if there was something they needed more clarification on?

It wasn't until he'd divided the room up into five groups of four people, each with a table and manikins and a work sheet to practise delivery techniques for type of breech presentation, that Logan could pinpoint what was so different about today's course.

He'd seen the way Ella could connect with people. He could remember the very first patient she had seen at Queen's as they'd rushed her off to Theatre. The young mother was in trouble. Despite being in agonising pain and frightened, she had made a heartfelt plea.

'But I want Ella to look after me...'

And then there'd been Iona's husband and the way he'd bonded with Ella as the doctor who understood exactly the overwhelming emotions he was dealing with as his wife was still fighting for her life and his tiny baby was doing the same thing in a very different part of the hospital.

Somehow, Ella had connected with twenty people she'd never met before without even trying and there was a buzz in the room that was energising for both the instructor and the people here to learn. Having Ella with him not only made everything different, Logan thought, it made it a whole lot better.

And how much more fun had the journey been to get here in the first place? He might have been tempted enough in the past to visit the intriguing Witches Stone but he would never have stopped to eat ice cream and walk on a beach. Or eat fish and chips sitting by a river with a castle as a backdrop. It was, quite frankly, life-changing to be around Ella Grisham and she was right—it wasn't going to be for very long so they needed to make the most of it.

'When you've got Ella at your station...' Logan raised his voice so that everybody could hear him. 'Get her to show you how to deal with entrapment. I watched her deliver a breech baby with a nuchal arm very recently and I'm sure she'll walk you through it better than I can.'

She was smiling at him as he turned back to the group he was working with and, for a fleeting moment, he held that eye contact. Because it felt good. Because he was really enjoying himself? A young paramedic was halfway through a practice run of a breech delivery, with both legs of the baby already born.

'Grasp the baby so that your thumbs are over the baby's hips,' Logan advised. 'If you hold any higher than that, there's some risk of injury to the kidneys and abdominal organs. Wrapping a towel around the baby will improve your grip and lessen the need for too much pressure. If you've got someone to help, get them to apply suprapubic pressure to keep the head flexed.'

He glanced back at the table where Ella was a minute or two later and he could hear her answering a question about freeing a trapped arm.

'I'm not going to hurt the baby, am I?'

'There are some risks,' Ella told them. 'It's possible to cause fractures or dislocations to the shoulder, collarbone or humerus so be as gentle as you can, but remember…broken bones will heal. If the baby stays trapped it will end in a fatality and that's exactly why you're here today, isn't it? To try and make sure you can avoid having a case that might haunt you for the rest of your life?'

Logan turned back to his own student. 'That's great,' he encouraged the paramedic. 'Don't raise the baby above the horizontal axis until you can see the mouth and nose,' he added. 'That way, you'll avoid hyperextension and the risk of a spinal injury. Okay…who's next?'

He needed to move things along because they still had a lot to cover before the lunch break, including cord prolapse and shoulder dystocia, but there was something else vying for attention at the back of Logan's head.

Something Ella had said about this being the best career in the world. About letting yourself experience the joy of it going well. Had he ever done that? Or was relief the only emotion he allowed himself to feel at the end of a well-managed birth?

He envied that easy connection she could find with people. He also envied the way she could feel joy to such an extent that it overflowed and made her dance in a corridor. Was he even capable of letting his emotional pendulum swing a little further on that spectrum? And, if he did, would he feel joy again?

Maybe the real question was whether he was brave enough to try...

They packed up all the manikins and other teaching aids, collected leftover handouts and tidied the seminar room with participants still lingering to say how much they'd enjoyed the course and how much they'd learned.

'Can you guys stay for a while?' The young paramedic Logan had worked with on the breech delivery practical work seemed the most reluctant to leave but it was Ella he was speaking to. 'Some of us are going out to dinner together and there's a great bar not far away which always has a live band and good music on a Saturday night. Do you like dancing, Ella?'

Ella caught a glance from Logan, who was shutting down his laptop at the desk. She knew perfectly well that he was thinking about seeing her dancing in the hospital corridor that evening and she felt a flush of warmth reach her cheeks. Because it was still a slightly embarrassing thing for him to have witnessed? Or was it that she liked the fact that he was thinking about it at all? It was another personal secret—like the joke about hitting on each other...

'I do...' Ella hurriedly stuffed a silicone pelvis and abdomen into its protective cover. 'But we have to head straight back to Aberdeen, don't we, Logan?'

'We do. Sorry, mate.' Logan didn't sound sorry. 'Ella's working tomorrow and I'm on first call so we need to be back in Aberdeen tonight. And we're going to drive back over the Old Military Road so we need what's left of the daylight for that. There wouldn't be much point in going that way if we can't see the views.'

'No worries.' The paramedic shrugged and then winked at Ella. 'It was worth a try. Let me help you carry some of this gear out to your car.'

If Ella had wanted immersion in some of the wildest and most beautiful of Scottish landscapes, this road through the Cairngorms would have been her first choice. They passed isolated farmhouses—one even advertising that it was a B&B—along a rollercoaster of hills and dips, twisty curves and stunning views across farmland and mountains. Startled deer ran away from them across endless bare stretches of grassland and there was even a touch of snow on the highest pass.

'I can imagine people loving a stay at that B&B to get totally away from it all,' Ella said. 'And it must be gorgeous up here when it really snows, but the road probably has to close, yes?'

'Not often,' Logan responded. 'But it is one of the first British roads that will close during a snowstorm. It gets a bit dangerous.'

'I'll bet. I'm glad we can keep going. I love it, but I'll be happy to be a bit closer to home before it gets dark.'

'Speaking of which, if there's still any light when we're going past the barn, do you mind if we stop for a few minutes?'

'Not at all. I'd love to see it again. It's all very well doing sketches from photos but the feeling of the place isn't the same.'

'I'd love a copy of some of your sketches, if that's okay. I spoke to the estate agent that sold me the place and told him what you were doing and he thought it might really help to get a fast sale. He also wants me to get a bit of a tidy-up done, so I want to have a look and see how much work it would be. It might be a lot quicker to hire some grass-cutting equipment and do it myself on my next day off.'

Ella could feel her heart sinking. She didn't want Logan to sell that magical old barn with its pixie house and pond and resident ducks. She had been enjoying working on her sketches because she was hoping he might change his mind. That she might be sketching a vision of his own—happy—future.

But he was still intent on selling it.

And it wasn't any of her business anyway. Because she wouldn't be here.

Her heart sank a little further. Ella leaned her head back and closed her eyes.

'You okay, El?'

It wasn't just that he'd used a diminutive of her name that no one else ever had. It was the very genuine concern in Logan's voice that was threatening to undo Ella. The idea that he really *cared* about her?

Even if he did, it wouldn't change anything. He was going to sell the barn and make sure that nothing distracted him from the only focus he wanted in his life, which had nothing to do with property or personal relationships. And a meaningful relationship wasn't something that Ella wanted anyway, so why on earth was she feeling this odd sense of, what was it…disappointment?

A hint of heartbreak, even?

Random thoughts that she might be ready to settle in one place, with one person, needed squashing. A relationship would tie her down and there would be the expectation of starting a family and she'd already spent too much of her life being a surrogate mother.

Ella was all too aware of how easy it was to sacrifice—or be *expected* to sacrifice—personal desires or even needs because of how much you loved the babies in your life. This was *her* time now. She got all the time with babies anyone could wish for in her working life and, best of all, she got to hand them to their mothers for all the hard work. Given how popular all her brothers were with women, no doubt they'd be producing their own offspring before long too. Ella could imagine herself as the fun auntie who was a part of all their lives but had an important job she was very, very good at as well.

She could be exactly the person she wanted to be.

But who was that again? The confidence with which Ella had always imagined her future self seemed to have become blurry around the edges—as if she wasn't quite so sure about the outline of that image any longer.

'I'm fine,' she said without opening her eyes. 'Just a bit tired.'

She did look a bit tired.

Logan only stopped briefly at the barn.

'Where on earth would I start?' he wondered aloud. 'The grass is probably high enough to stop someone wanting to even get out of their car and this isn't the best side of the barn to be looking at, is it?'

'You could cut a path through the grass, leading around to the other side. It would be an invitation that most people wouldn't be able to resist.'

'That's a great idea.'

'I'm full of them.' Ella smiled but didn't get out of the car to follow Logan as he went to see if there were any obstacles to creating that path.

There didn't seem to be. And if he focused on clearing the area between the ancient building and the pond at the end of the path from the lane, it should be enough to encourage any potential buyers to stand in the perfect spot to imagine the outdoor courtyard in Ella's sketches, with the big windows in the wall of the barn and the pixie house opened up enough to make a romantic little summer house. He was going to need to hire a commercial grade grass trimmer and lawnmower and some loppers, hedge clippers and a pruning saw might be a good idea as well, to trim back some of the ivy scrambling over stone walls and to shape the trailing branches of the weeping willow beside the pond.

'Doable.' He nodded as he got back into his car. 'But still a big day's work.' He glanced at Ella's face as he started the engine again. Was she okay? Was it his imagination or did she look a bit pale? Sad, even…?

'Are you any good with a grass trimmer or lawnmower?' he asked lightly. He lowered his voice into a deliberately OTT sexy drawl. 'If you came to help me, I promise I'd make it worth your while.'

That made her laugh. 'Might be good practice,' she said. 'Being good with machinery might look good on my CV, and who knows what extra skills I'll need in Australia? Apparently the hospital I'm going to works with the flying doctor service for anything to do with obs and gynae. I might need to learn something about planes as well. Imagine if we break down somewhere in the outback?'

Logan could imagine Ella in the Australian outback. She was wearing a ripped pair of jeans, cowboy boots and a loose white shirt with the sleeves rolled up. Her long hair was hanging down her back in a braid from beneath one of those hats with the corks dangling around the brim. She looked…ultimately desirable… Not purely in a sexual way either. She was great company—as sharp as a tack and as warm and generous as anybody you could hope to meet. A friend as well as an amazing lover.

He was going to miss her when she moved on, that was for sure.

'That sounds like something that will be right up your alley,' he told her. 'An exciting job, a country that's renowned for the freedom it offers and so many adventures you won't be able to keep up with them all. What more could you possibly want?'

Ella laughed again, and this time it seemed to dispel some of that weariness. 'Nothing,' she agreed. She sounded almost cheerful now. 'Nothing at all.'

CHAPTER NINE

WHEN ELLA HAD applied for this locum position at the Queen Mother's Maternity Hospital in Aberdeen she had been hoping she would be able to become a part of the team headed by Logan Walsh that provided education and responded to emergency obstetric cases.

It had never occurred to her that she might need to activate a call to the response team herself but here she was, in the car park of the closest shopping centre to the hospital that had a supermarket, beside a car with an obviously pregnant woman sitting sideways behind the steering wheel with her legs hanging outside. A woman who was crying in agony and currently vomiting uncontrollably.

'Are you having contractions?' Ella asked. 'Have your waters broken? Are you bleeding?'

'No-o.' The woman shook her head. 'Oh, God...it really hurts. And I feel *so* sick...'

'How far along are you?'

'Almost thirty-three weeks.'

Ella was trying to take her pulse but she couldn't feel one in the woman's wrist, which meant that her blood pressure might be way too low.

'My name's Ella,' she said. 'I'm an obstetrician at Queen's.'

'That's where I'm supposed to go for my Caesarean.'

'You're having an elective Caesarean?' Ella knew this meant there had to be known complications of some kind with this pregnancy. 'Okay…hang on. I'm going to get an ambulance on the way for you and then I'll ask you some more questions.'

She dialled the emergency phone number and gave her location. When she told the call taker that she was a doctor and this was an obstetric emergency the dispatcher said she was giving the call the highest priority.

'I'll activate the Obstetric Emergency Response Team as well. They'll be with you as soon as possible.'

It took long enough for the ambulance to arrive for Ella to have acquired a lot more information. It wasn't really a surprise that Logan had been available to join the ambulance crew—this was the kind of thing he lived for, wasn't it? Logan, however, was very surprised when he jumped out of the back of the ambulance.

'Ella? What on earth are you doing here?'

It was Ella's day off. She had come, by bus, to this supermarket with a list of the things she needed because she wanted to cook dinner for Logan instead of sharing a takeaway meal like they usually did. Her list included fillet steak and mushrooms, the ingredients to make a potato gratin and a reminder to choose all her favourite salad items. She had been intending to impress him. And then seduce him. Or let him seduce her—whichever came first… But any explanation of what she was doing here and why merely flashed through the back of her head with a whiff of wry amusement and then vanished into thin air.

'This is Gemma McKay,' she told him. 'Thirty-three weeks pregnant. Sudden onset of severe, ten out of ten, abdominal pain about half an hour ago. She's unable to move and her abdomen is rigid and extremely tender. No contractions and no observable bleeding but her radial pulse is absent. She's been vomiting frequently.'

'I know Gemma.' Logan was still sounding surprised as he crouched down in front of the woman. 'I'm Logan Walsh. I think I did your first Caesarean, didn't I? When you'd gone a couple of weeks over your due date and the baby wasn't happy?'

'Oh…' Gemma raised her face. 'Yes… I'm so happy to see you, Dr Walsh.' Her face crumpled into lines of pain. 'Something's going really horribly wrong this time…'

'Let's get you into the ambulance and take you into hospital. We'll be able to take much better care of you when we're not in a car park.'

The ambulance crew helped get Gemma onto a stretcher and into the back of the ambulance. Ella shut the door of her car and locked it, climbing into the ambulance to put Gemma's handbag somewhere safe.

'I've put your car keys in your bag,' she said. 'Your phone's in there too.'

'I need to call my mum.' Gemma was having a blood pressure cuff wrapped around her arm, an oxygen saturation probe clipped to her finger and Logan had his hands very gently on her abdomen but it was still making her grimace. She kept her gaze on Ella, however. 'Mum'll need to pick Timmy up from childcare for me.

His dad doesn't finish work till six o'clock and he'll be on the road anyway.'

'Maybe I can do that for you.' Ella found Gemma's phone.

'BP's fifty-six over forty,' the paramedic in the back with Logan reported. 'Heart rate one-one-four. Her temperature's normal. Oxygen saturation a hundred percent on air.'

Logan sounded remarkably calm given that Gemma's blood pressure was dangerously low. No wonder she was feeling so sick.

'Let's get an IV in and some fluids up,' was all he said. 'And I think we should get moving very soon. Ella, could you ride with us? I might need you...'

Of course she could. If Logan thought he might need assistance he must be worried that Gemma's condition was serious and Ella was prepared for anything. She made a quick call to Gemma's mother, who was happy to pick up her grandson, as Logan unrolled an IV kit and put a tourniquet around Gemma's arm.

'Try and keep really still for me,' he said. 'We need to get a line in and give you some fluids but your blood pressure's very low so your veins might not want to cooperate.'

The paramedic in the driver's seat of the ambulance was leaning to look into the cabin. 'Want to get moving, Doc?'

'No. Wait a sec.' Logan was carefully inserting a needle under the skin, clearly searching for the antecubital vein which would be much easier to access than anything smaller but Ella could see how difficult it was, which suggested that Gemma's veins were on the point of collapsing.

A tiny flash of blood in the cannula chamber showed that Logan had found the vein but it was at that moment that Gemma suddenly moved.

'I'm going to be sick...'

Logan shook his head and took the needle out of her arm as she jerked. The paramedic held a container for Gemma and supported her head. Logan straightened to meet Ella's gaze.

'Blood pressure this low with no evidence of bleeding and vomiting that could be due to vagal stimulation makes me think this is neurogenic rather than hypovolaemic shock.'

Any shock, with the subsequent shutdown of organs due to insufficient oxygen, was dangerous. Fluid resuscitation was the first response and it was needed urgently.

'Intraosseous access?'

Logan nodded. 'We need to get moving and it'll be quicker than anything else. Could you set up the fluids and giving set?'

'Sure.' Ella opened a glass-fronted overhead cupboard where she could see the units of saline were stored. As she opened packs to hang the bag and attach the tubing set before running some fluid through the line to get rid of any air bubbles, she could see how swiftly Logan was working beside her.

Gemma was still in the throes of vomiting and barely heard Logan explaining what was happening as he opened the IO kit. He felt for the markers below her knee, attached the needle to the drill and it was through the skin and into the bone marrow space of her tibia within seconds. Ella could see the concentration on his face and for a split second she remembered how intimidated she'd been on that first meeting, when he'd burst into the delivery room and stood there glaring at her. She knew now that it was simply an expression of how important what he was doing was.

How much he cared.

And she loved him for that. She trusted him completely as well. There was no one she would rather be working with.

Logan secured the port with a dressing and attached tubing with a syringe on the end that he used to flush the line. Ella could hand him the end of the tubing in her hand to replace the syringe and adjusted the drip rate to increase the speed of the infusion.

'We're good to go,' Logan said. 'We'll get some pain relief on board while we travel.'

The engine was already running and lights and the siren were activated to get them to the hospital as quickly as possible, but Ella was happy to see that Gemma's blood pressure had already risen a little with the fluids she was receiving. Logan called ahead to alert the emergency department of their arrival and to request Gemma's medical records. She was under the care of another obstetrician for this pregnancy so he hadn't had anything to do with her since her Caesarean more than three years ago.

A resuscitation area had been cleared for them and one of the ED consultants had been busy getting ready for their arrival.

'We've got a CTG machine here and portable ultrasound. We've tried to contact her obstetrician but he's unavailable. We have got her records and she had an antenatal visit last week.'

'And...?'

'Nothing of concern noted. She'd been getting some pain during the night and when she rested in the afternoons but it stopped when she changed position and moved. She has a low lying anterior placenta but an elective C-section without a trial of labour had been the preferred option from the start after the problems Gemma had last time.'

Ella was getting ready to place the foetal monitoring electrodes on Gemma's abdomen as soon as Logan finished the ultrasound examination. He squeezed gel onto her skin and then touched the transducer to her skin.

'Ow...' Gemma burst into tears. 'That hurts...'

Ella took hold of her hand. 'Sorry, sweetheart, I know it's painful. We'll be able to give you something more for that pain as soon as we get an idea of what's going on.'

'I'm scared...' Gemma sobbed.

Logan moved the transducer, his gaze fixed on the screen. 'I can see your baby's heart,' he told Gemma. 'It's moving well. He's not too bothered by whatever's going on in there.'

'It's a girl...'

'Is it?' Ella squeezed her hand again. 'Timmy must be excited about getting a little sister.'

'I can't see any evidence of bleeding,' Logan said. 'And the previous scar tissue is intact. Baby's in a transverse lie. And there's the placenta.' He turned to the ED consultant. 'It's posterior. Didn't the notes say it was anterior?'

'They did. Probably a typo.'

'Hmm...'

Logan had finished the ultrasound examination and Ella wiped the gel off Gemma's skin and then attached the transducers for the CTG. The trace of uterine activity suggested an irritability, with low level contractions that weren't likely to be affecting the cervix. The baby's heart rate was initially a good rate of one hundred and forty but, even as Ella started printing a recording, it dropped to just over a hundred. It picked up and then dropped again, with no cessation of the uterine irritability, and the decision was made to take Gemma to Theatre for an emergency Caesarean.

Ella could have excused herself at that point because she wasn't actually on duty today. Except she couldn't, could she? She'd been the person who'd found Gemma in trouble and had been by her side ever since. There were no family members here to comfort and reassure her as she was taken to Theatre and Ella knew how frightened she had to be. She wasn't about to leave.

Besides... Logan had wanted her to come back to the hospital with him. Because he might need her. And just the possibility of being needed by Logan was an even more powerful reason to stay.

'There's something about you, Ella...' Logan was standing beside the wall of stainless-steel scrub sinks adjacent to the operating theatre they were preparing to enter. His hands and arms were soapy and he was using the nail brush to clean each fingernail, one at a time. 'You and zebras.'

'Oh?'

Ella had just begun to soap her skin. Her hair was tucked away under the disposable hat and her mouth and nose were covered with a mask so it was only her eyes that Logan could see—along with the movement of the tiny muscles around them that let him know she was smiling beneath that mask. It was more than just a smile, though. There was a warmth in her eyes that was only there because they'd become so close. A look that was for him alone?

Whatever... It kind of felt like they were holding hands...

Oh, man...he really was going to miss Ella when she moved on.

But what if she didn't?

'I forgot to tell you,' he said. 'Kirsty—the O&G consultant you're filling in for—has just put in her resignation. She's not coming back.'

Ella was opening the pack that contained the soap-impregnated nail brush. 'Really? Is she enjoying being a mother too much?'

'I suspect that's part of it, but her husband's got a new job. They'll be moving to Ireland before her maternity leave is finished.' He deliberately kept his tone light so that it wouldn't seem as if he was putting any pressure on Ella. 'I'll be advertising the permanent position straight away. I just thought I'd let you know in case...' he pulled in a breath as he put his hand under the tap, letting water stream down his arm to his elbow '...in case you're finding it good enough here to want to stay a bit longer?'

Ella seemed to be avoiding his gaze now, focused on

finishing her nails. 'A permanent position is a whole different ball game to staying a bit longer,' she said. 'And I think Australia might have more adventures on offer.' There was a moment's silence and then Ella's tone changed to one of amusement. Or was she trying to change the subject?

'No zebras at the bottom of the world, though. What did you mean when you said "you and zebras"?'

Logan was drying his hands. 'There are some cases that are so rare they're once-in-a-lifetime scenarios. I'm starting to think that Gemma might be one of them.'

There was nothing soft or personal about the eye contact this time. Ella was thinking only of their patient, who was currently in the hands of the anaesthetist and theatre team, being prepped for the emergency Caesarean. It eliminated any thoughts about trying to talk Ella into staying in Aberdeen as Logan also focused completely and…he was aware of a faint wash of relief as he did so. He didn't want to think about how much he was going to miss having Ella in his life. He didn't want to think about any implications of why he'd just encouraged her to stay either.

'What if that discrepancy in the position of the placenta wasn't a typo?' he continued. 'And that was the piece of the puzzle to add to what looks like hypovolaemic shock when there's no evidence of bleeding?'

Ella had just rinsed her arms and hands. She was holding them in front of her and they were dripping but she wasn't reaching for her sterile towel. 'A uterine torsion?' she breathed. 'I've never seen one.'

'Neither have I, but the early symptoms could fit.'

Logan was thinking aloud as he put his gown on. 'She's had episodes of pain on rest that went away when she changed position and moved around. What if she was getting a partial torsion that resolved itself, until the gestation reached a point where it was too big for that to happen?'

'And if the uterus had turned to a hundred and eighty degrees, then the placenta would seem to be on the opposite side on ultrasound. Maybe there was no typo in the notes.'

'Exactly.' Logan was putting his gloves on now. Then he turned to let a theatre technician tie his gown.

Ella was catching up in her prep. She'd dried her hands and put her arms into the sleeves of her gown. It would only be seconds before she was also gloved and ready to enter Theatre. They were possibly about to face a surgical case that neither of them had any experience with and Logan was very happy that he had Ella as his assistant. He knew how good she was at her job and how well they worked together.

He led the way into Theatre, aware that, as a team, they were better than either of them would be on their own and that gave him a confidence that let him focus even more sharply. He was also aware of how rare it was to find a colleague like this.

It was a kind of zebra instead of a horse all by itself.

Ella knew Logan's suspicion was confirmed the moment they opened Gemma's abdomen and found the pelvic anatomy so distorted they couldn't find her bladder and they could see that her left fallopian tube and ovary had been pulled across the uterus to lie on the opposite side.

'It has turned a full one eighty degrees,' Ella said. 'It's extraordinary.'

'A slight rotation of the uterus is common in pregnancy.' Logan had raised his voice to include the whole team. 'It rarely exceeds forty-five degrees and it happens most often to the right. It's associated with foetal compromise and significant maternal morbidity so we need to get this baby out stat. We can't correct the torsion in a gravid uterus so we'll have to go in posteriorly. Scalpel, thanks…'

The baby girl came out completely limp and it was Ella who handed her over to the neonatal paediatric team. It was Ella who delivered the placenta by controlled cord traction under Logan's supervision and then closed the uterus in two layers. The baby's Apgar score had picked up by then and she was taken away to the NICU.

With Logan's calm instructions that were quiet enough to be just for her to hear, Ella then turned the uterus back to its correct anatomical position. Together they checked that everything in Gemma's abdomen—including the bladder that was now visible—was not a cause for concern and then it was time to close up.

'I can do this if you want to get away,' Logan offered. 'It is your day off, after all.'

'I'll see this through,' Ella responded. 'It's a once-in-a-lifetime case and I was there right from the start of it. I think this qualifies as a bit of an adventure so I don't want to miss anything.'

The closure of the abdominal wound was routine. So

routine that Ella could let her thoughts wander a little as she watched Logan's deft suturing.

Why had Logan told her about her locum position becoming available as a permanent job? Did he want her to apply for it?

Maybe he did. Because they worked so well together? His work was, after all, the most important thing in his life. Something that he had no intention of being distracted from.

But if she stayed would their personal relationship continue? Would Ella want it to when she knew she was falling more and more in love with Logan? That could end up being even more heartbreaking than leaving him to go and be almost literally a world away from him.

There was an ache somewhere below Ella's ribs that she hadn't felt for so long it took a moment or two to realise what it was. It made her remember the time when she was far away from home and got the news that her mother was so ill.

It was grief, wasn't it? The kind of grief that could start even before you were actually missing having a particular person in your life. Because you knew with every fibre of your being just how much of a hole they were going to leave in your life when they were gone.

Ella couldn't possibly stay here permanently. Because that hole might become big enough to swallow her up completely.

She put a dressing in place over the wound in Gemma's belly. 'You know what? I might go and see how the baby's doing in NICU.'

And Logan nodded but he was turning away to look

at the monitor screens as Gemma was being brought out from under the general anaesthetic and Ella could feel distance being deliberately created between them. Because she'd mentioned the NICU? She'd never discovered why it was not one of his favourite places because she had respected his privacy, but feeling that distance—that barrier—was another warning that she'd got herself in too deep this time.

And it was another reason she could never stay.

Ella spent more time in NICU than she had intended but it was so good to see how well Gemma's baby daughter was doing and to hear that Gemma's husband had been contacted and was on his way to be with his wife and new baby. And then, of course, it would have been unthinkable to leave without seeing Finlay and she found Iona there in a wheelchair, having skin-to-skin time with her son, tears of joy streaming down her face.

That joy was still with Ella after she'd been to the locker rooms and changed out of her scrubs and back into civvies. She hadn't seen Logan since she'd left the theatre suite and she wasn't sure she even wanted to see him this evening, given the fear of how deeply involved she had somehow let herself get. She did, however, see someone who looked familiar as she was walking through the hospital foyer.

A pregnant woman who was holding hands with a man. And they both looked pale. Frightened…?

Ella stopped as they got closer. 'It's Margaret, isn't it? Didn't I see you at antenatal clinic last week?'

The woman nodded. 'This is my husband, Tom.'

The couple had stopped as well. They were an island of three people in the middle of a still-busy foyer, but instinct told Ella that help was needed here.

'Is everything okay?' she asked. 'Can I help?'

Margaret's eyes filled with tears. 'I can't feel my baby moving.'

Ella caught her breath. 'How long since you felt anything?'

'A couple of hours.' It was Tom who answered, as he put his arm around his wife's shoulders. 'She rang me at work when she started getting worried. I came home after that and I didn't know what to do, so I've brought her here.'

'You've done exactly the right thing,' Ella told him. 'Come with me.'

She was holding her breath as she pushed the lift button to take them to the radiology department where she knew an ultrasound room would be available.

'I looked it up online,' Margaret told Ella as she climbed onto the bed in the dim room. 'I'm thirty-seven weeks now so I know there's less room in there and there won't be so much kicking or anything. And I'd been busy doing some housework so I thought I might have missed feeling any movements and that was when I was going to start counting.'

'When was the last time you can definitely remember feeling anything?' Ella helped Margaret pull the waistband of her skirt down to expose her well-rounded belly and tucked a paper towel in to prevent gel getting onto the clothing.

'At lunchtime. I had started to think he'd been asleep

for a long time so I had something sugary. And I patted my tummy to try and wake him up and I did feel something then, but that's…' Margaret caught tears with her fingertips. 'That's hours ago…'

Ella was scanning already. She could see the outline of the baby's head and body. She could see limbs that were completely still. She changed the direction of the transducer and did a slow sweep across the lower abdomen. And then she stopped. She stared at the screen for a long, long moment, desperately wishing she didn't have to tell these parents what she could see. But she did.

'I can see the whole of baby's heart,' she told them quietly. 'And it's not moving. I'm so, so sorry but…your baby has died.'

CHAPTER TEN

LOGAN WALSH HESITATED before he was close enough to knock on the door of a very private delivery room.

He needed to gather the strength he knew he had to deal with this most difficult situation and it required a mental tightrope that allowed him the distance he needed to protect himself and the compassion that was naturally there as a doctor, as a head of department. As a fellow human being. Logan had learned long ago how to do this, but it was so much harder this time.

Because Ella was part of this.

And he knew that she hadn't hesitated to involve herself emotionally in this case and share the grief of a mother who had already lost her baby but still had to go through the birthing process.

He'd been there for a meeting with Margaret and Tom when they'd had time to process the devastating news of their baby's death. He'd talked them through the options, including waiting to go into a natural labour, which could take up to three weeks, and Margaret had chosen to be induced before being allowed to go home and prepare for the labour and birth that might not start for another forty-eight hours.

'We'll do whatever we can to help you through this,'

Logan had promised. *'I'll come and see you as soon as you're admitted and make sure you're getting everything you need.'*

So, here he was. He knew that Margaret and Tom were in this room, along with Judy as midwife and Ella, who had promised she would be with Margaret throughout her labour. Again, Logan had seen the way Ella could connect with people so easily and he could see the bond that was already there. He also knew that Ella would be the best person that these grieving parents could have with them at this time. He probably wasn't even needed here.

He hadn't been needed by Ella in the last couple of days either. He'd tried to see her. She hadn't answered his knock on her door the night before last, and when he'd turned up last night with a takeaway meal she'd thanked him with a smile that was heartbreaking but said she wasn't hungry and that she needed to be on her own right now.

Logan understood that better than anybody and he respected Ella enough not to push into the space she wanted—or needed—to deal with alone.

But he'd promised Margaret that he would come to see her and he wasn't about to break that promise. Logan tapped lightly on the door and slipped into the room.

A lot of effort had clearly gone into the planning and preparation for this time. Margaret had her own linen and a soft woollen blanket on the bed. There were aromatherapy candles burning and soft soulful music playing in the background. Margaret was standing beside the bed, leaning forward with her hands clutching the blanket and Tom was standing beside her, rubbing her lower back.

Judy was quietly in the background, like the music, but Ella was in the thick of it, leaning over the other side of the bed, her hands on top of Margaret's, her focus completely on her patient.

'Keep going, Margaret. Faster, lighter breathing as your contraction peaks—that's it… Now you can slow it down again. That's brilliant…'

Logan waited until the contraction had passed and Margaret straightened to lean back against Tom. She noticed him standing near the door.

'I won't disturb you,' Logan said. 'Is there anything else you need? Are things okay with your pain relief?' He glanced at Ella. 'Is there still time for an epidural?'

'I don't want one,' Margaret said. 'I need to feel this.'

'We've got a Luer in,' Ella said. 'We can give as much pain relief as Margaret wants.'

'You know what I really want?'

'What's that?'

'I didn't ask… I wasn't really thinking of it as the birth I planned and I didn't think it would be possible but… I really wanted to have a water birth for Tayla…'

Oh… *God*… Hearing the name of the baby was almost Logan's undoing. He could feel his protective casing cracking. It wasn't helping that he'd never seen Ella looking so sombre. Her eyes were so dark they looked black and there was a stillness to her features that was a complete contrast to the way he had become so used to seeing emotions play out on her face.

He felt a bit lost, not being able to read how Ella was feeling as easily as he'd been able to before, but maybe this was an occasion when she needed to tap into some professional distance herself, even if it was only to gather her own strength at times?

She sounded completely in control. 'We can do that for you, Margaret. I think it's a great idea.'

Judy was already turning on the taps for the birthing pool in the room. As Margaret groaned with another contraction starting, Logan caught sight of what was to one side of this space—a Moses basket with tiny clothes folded into a pile on top of the mattress. Would Ella still be here when the birth was over and the baby was gently cleaned and dressed to be given to the parents to be with for as long as they needed?

Logan was quite sure she would be.

He could be too, if it would help Ella. She didn't need to know how hard it would be for him. But when she saw the silent question in his eyes she gave a tiny shake of her head. A hint of a smile even, to let him know that she was fine.

That she didn't need him.

The sadness stayed with Ella for days.

She would never forget delivering that perfect baby girl who had suffocated in the womb because the umbilical cord had wrapped itself around her neck, or the courage of her parents as they both welcomed and prepared to say goodbye to an already much-loved infant. It had to be one of the most profound silences you could ever hear in that space of time after the birth, when no baby's cry was going to be heard.

Margaret and Tom were left in privacy with their baby for much of the next twelve or so hours that they chose to spend with Tayla, but Ella had made herself available at all times and paid brief visits to check on how they were doing. Precious memories were being collected. A lock of hair, prints of tiny hands and feet. Visits from other family members including Tayla's big brother, Lachlan There were some hauntingly beautiful photographs taken by a studio that was experienced in handling a session like this with compassion and sensitivity.

Logan was being very sensitive as well. Ella knew there was an open invitation to talk to him or share a meal after work but she found herself pulling back. Because she knew she would probably fall apart in his arms and might even confess how she felt about him, and that would change everything. Any remaining time in her locum position here might become unbearable. And it had been her idea right from the start to make the most of the time they could be together, hadn't it? It would be a bit unfair to ruin it for both of them. She just needed a day or two to pull herself together and find the kind of optimism that had always kept her moving forward and making her life as good as it could possibly be.

She was trying to remind herself of what she'd told Logan. That protecting yourself from not feeling the pain of a distressing case meant missing out on feeling the joy of the best cases, but this was hard enough to make her wonder if Logan actually had the right idea. That the way to protect yourself and be the best doctor you could be was to keep a professional distance.

Maybe she could adjust her balance and learn to not let her emotional pendulum swing quite so far.

She was going to give it a go. Starting from now…

Mind you, even Logan looked as though this case had got to him, despite his ability to keep that distance. He'd looked kind of tired at work over the last couple of days. A bit paler than normal, even? Perhaps it wasn't as easy as he'd made it look up till now to maintain a purely professional relationship in some cases?

Ella finished the sketches she'd made of her ideas for converting Logan's barn and put them in an envelope to leave quietly by his door before she headed out for a walk on her next day off. He must have heard her door closing or something, however, because his door opened.

'Hey…you've got a day off too?'

'Yeah… I'm just heading out for a walk. I was just leaving this for you. They're the sketches I've been doing for the barn.'

Logan slipped them out of the envelope and scanned them in silence.

'These are amazing,' he said. 'I can't thank you enough.' He caught her gaze. 'You're very talented. You know that, don't you?'

Ella shrugged. She could feel another question beneath that one.

Are you okay? Is there anything I can do to help…?

She wanted to ask the same thing of him, but it felt as if she could be treading on an emotional minefield and what she really needed was a break.

So Ella gave her head a tiny shake as a response to both Logan's questions, spoken and silent. 'You could take a photo of your favourite sketches,' she said brightly. 'And send them to your estate agent. Have you put the property on the market yet?'

'I'm about to go out there and cut the grass. I've been to the hire place this morning and got all the gear I need in my car. I just came back for a bite of lunch.' Logan's eyebrows rose. 'Would you like to come out with me? Get some fresh air?' His smile was completely crooked. 'I seem to remember you wanted some experience with grass cutting machinery to put on your CV?'

That made Ella smile, and just the act of smiling somehow made things a little bit better.

'That's true. I did say that.'

Ella could remember what Logan had said too. About the way he'd promised to make it worth her while in that raspy, sexy voice. And maybe that was exactly what was needed here. A reset? Getting back to where they'd been, content with making the most of a temporary relationship.

'And I meant it,' Ella added. She smiled at Logan. 'Just give me a minute to put on some old clothes?'

'Take your time. I'm going to have another look at these amazing drawings of yours.'

This was just what the doctor ordered as far as Ella was concerned.

Some hard physical work outside. A world away from work and such a painful reminder of the downside of being emotionally involved with her patients. Logan seemed to sense that she didn't want to talk about anything work-related so he only talked about what they were doing. How short the grass needed to be. What branches needed to be pruned off the trees and did the ivy on the pixie house need to be trimmed?

'Yes,' Ella decreed, her arms full of pruned branches

from the willow tree that she was taking to the heap, out of sight around the corner of the barn. 'But try not to cut that daisy bush that's growing near the door. That's really pretty.'

The sun came out and gave them a hint of what this garden—when it became a garden and not just an overgrown patch of meadow—would be like in summer. Both Logan and Ella took off their warm layers of clothing and got their arms scratched by branches and prickles in the grass that needed to be trimmed and raked before the mower could be used to make it look something like a lawn. They got hot and dirty and tired but it was one of the best afternoons Ella had had in a very long time.

'I think we're done,' Logan finally declared.

'Thank goodness.' Ella sat on the bank beside the pond and then dropped backwards to lie flat, closing her eyes from the low angle of the sun in the late afternoon and stretching her arms out sideways. She knew Logan had sat down beside her because his leg brushed her fingertips. He didn't say anything and as the seconds ticked by and she breathed in the delicious smell of freshly cut grass she began to hear the faint birdsong from the hedgerows and the sound of sheep in the distance. A bee buzzed overhead and something splashed in the pond. And then she heard something unexpected. An insistent peeping sound that was loud enough to make her sit up.

'Is that...?'

'It's your duck.' Logan nodded. 'Look...'

Ella shaded her eyes. The lovely big white duck with the yellow beak was swimming towards them on the pond, and behind her was a string of fluffy yellow ducklings. They came closer and closer and then climbed out of the pond to inspect the newly mown grass.

'Oh…*oh*…' Ella found her eyes suddenly filling with tears. 'They're so adorable…' She swiped a tear away. 'This is exactly what I needed after such a horrible week at work. Thank you, Logan.' She turned to smile at him, wanting to kiss him perhaps, but as soon as she saw his face she froze.

She wasn't the only one crying.

Logan was staring at the ducklings. And he had tears rolling down the side of his nose.

And Ella's heart was breaking.

'What is it?' she asked softly. 'What's wrong?'

She could see the effort that Logan was making to control himself. To push things away. Whatever it was, he didn't want to talk about it, but this time Ella wasn't going to let him run away. She wanted to understand. There was something hurting the man she loved and she desperately needed to know what it was.

'Tell me,' she whispered. 'Does it have something to do with Tayla?'

Logan closed his eyes. 'I met them,' he said, his voice catching. 'Margaret and Tom. When they were leaving the hospital. They were taking Tayla to the funeral home themselves and they had her in that Moses basket. Anyone who'd seen her would have thought she was just a perfect sleeping baby but…'

'…but you knew,' Ella finished for him. 'And it broke your heart.' She reached for his hand and held it.

'She looked so like another baby I knew,' Logan said,

and it was the pain in his voice that made Ella guess what he wasn't saying.

'*Your* baby? Oh, my God, Logan… Did you lose a baby?'

He was silent for such a long time that Ella thought he wasn't going to answer her, but then he nodded. He opened his eyes but he was still looking in front of him, at where the ducklings were pecking the ground, searching for bugs.

'I'd just graduated from medical school and was about to start my first Foundation Year,' he said slowly. 'Katie and I had been married for a couple of years by then and we were expecting our first baby in a few weeks. We were moving into a new flat and she suddenly got terrible abdominal pain. And she was bleeding. I called an ambulance and went into Emergency with her, but everything took far too long and I didn't know enough to realise how much trouble Katie was in. All I could do was trust the people involved and I'd never felt so helpless in my life. By the time they got to Theatre and found she'd had a uterine rupture it was too late. She'd lost too much blood. She arrested in Theatre and they couldn't get her back.'

Ella swallowed the painful lump in her throat. So this was why Logan had made it his mission in life to train people to recognise obstetric emergencies early enough to make it more likely that lives could be saved. It also explained why he considered himself 'married' to his work. He'd gone through the agony of losing the woman he'd loved enough to marry and it was easy to understand why he never wanted to risk his heart like that again.

But it was so sad… Logan had so much love, so much

tenderness that he *could* give if he could bring himself to take that risk. And he could get it back and…and find that special kind of joy in life.

Logan cleared his throat. 'Our baby—Sam—survived the surgery, but only just. He'd been without oxygen for too long and we knew he wasn't going to survive, but somehow he held on. For weeks. I was given special leave and I sat with him in NICU every day for hours and hours. I got to hold him.' There were tears on Logan's face again. 'Until I couldn't. Until the day I buried him in Katie's arms.'

Ella had tears on her own cheeks. The final pieces of the puzzle were coming together and she now knew exactly why the NICU was not one of Logan's favourite places. She could imagine him sitting there beside an incubator with a tiny, fragile infant struggling to survive. A struggle that had been tragically lost after a valiant fight lasting so long when even a day would feel like a week. And she remembered that day when she'd been sitting beside Finlay in the NICU and the baby boy had opened his eyes and looked at her and she had been so sure he was going to make it that she couldn't help shedding a happy tear or two. And she'd looked up to see Logan watching her through the window and thought he was clearly disapproving of her involvement in that case.

But how badly had he been hurting in that moment?

Logan Walsh had buried his son in his wife's arms. It couldn't be any more tragic than that. Ella could understand completely that any desire to be that involved with anyone ever again had been buried along with them.

She had no words to tell him how her own heart was

breaking on his behalf, but she moved so that she was on her knees beside Logan and she put her arms around him. He buried his face against her shoulder and neck and she bent her head to touch his. She could hold him for as long as he wanted.

And they could cry together. Because Ella suspected that it might have been far too long since Logan had let himself feel this grief at all, let alone to share it with someone else.

You never knew. This might be what he remembered about her for the rest of his life and it was a gift she was only too happy to give. Because she knew now, beyond a shadow of doubt, that she was totally and utterly in love with Logan.

And what she really wanted to give were the words that were scrambling to get out of her head—and her heart.

She desperately wanted to tell him that he was loved. That *she* loved him. As much as it was possible to love another human being. Enough to want to spend the rest of her life with him.

But how could she?

Especially knowing what she now knew about him. That he'd not only lost the woman he'd loved but his baby son as well. She knew how much love he was capable of giving because she had been able to feel the edges of it from the very first time he'd made love to her, so she knew just how devastating that must have been. That Logan might never want to risk living through that kind of pain again.

She also couldn't tell him because she knew he cared about her enough to not want to hurt her and, if he knew how she felt, he might be unable to stop himself responding by saying he loved her back. Asking her to stay for more reasons than to simply fill a consultant vacancy on his staff. To offer her something that he might think was genuine even, but if it wasn't offered freely—without any kind of pressure—she would never know if it was real. To offer herself and potentially give up the freedom that had been the best part of her life for so many years now could turn out to be a soul-destroying mistake that she might never recover from.

So Ella held in those words as tightly as she was holding Logan.

Both physical and emotional weariness wrapped them both in a sombre silence as they travelled back to the city a while later. They both knew that something huge had changed between them and it seemed that neither of them wanted to talk about it.

Because they both knew it marked the end of the road?

They'd both known that what they had was supposed to be temporary, but Ella was feeling more miserable than ever now. Because it wasn't supposed to end quite this soon.

CHAPTER ELEVEN

BY TACIT AGREEMENT, both Ella and Logan gave each other space over the next couple of weeks, perhaps because they were both waiting for any sign that the other was wanting something closer than being friendly colleagues. Or maybe it was because they had got too close the day of the grass cutting and it was instinctive to retreat to a safer place.

Ella hated it to begin with but she soon realised how helpful it was in her new mission to learn how to keep a safe emotional distance. She focused on her work, on keeping a smile on her face and a cheerful rapport with her patients as she reassured them in antenatal clinics, supported them through any investigations or interventions they needed and shared the challenge and triumph of bringing their babies into the world.

She was happy to let Logan retreat into his own space because she recognised that he might need to do that for his own peace of mind. His own dignity, even? And she suspected early on that maybe he was doing his best to avoid meeting her in the hallways of the doctors' residence in the same way she was avoiding him—by listening for the sound of his door closing and then waiting long enough for the coast to be clear before she went out of her apartment.

When they did see each other, on the way to or from work and when they were working together, they were ultimately professional. And friendly. And, okay...if they made eye contact with each other, there was always a frisson of just how well they knew each other but also an agreement that it was over. Ella wondered if it was like this now because they knew each other *too* well. That perhaps Logan was quite well aware of how she felt about him and he was trying to be kind in escaping something he didn't want in his life.

He had the right to be alone if that was his choice and Ella couldn't hold it against him. He'd made it perfectly clear from the start that he didn't want a significant relationship. He hadn't even wanted anyone 'hitting on him'. That private joke had a very poignant note to it now, which meant it was probably already being consigned to being no more than a memory that would resurface every time she heard the phrase in the future. Like remembering that Logan had seen her doing her stupid happy dance in the hospital corridor if she ever felt like dancing again. Or the significance that zebras versus horses would always have whenever she was listing differential diagnoses for any medical challenge.

As she neared the end of the second week of being simply colleagues again, Ella knocked on the door of Logan's office.

'Have you got a minute?'

'For you? Of course.' Logan closed the lid of the laptop he was working on. 'What's up?'

'I wondered whether you've had applicants for the consultant position here yet?'

There was a flash in Logan's eyes that Ella couldn't interpret. Did he think she'd changed her mind about applying for the job? Was he hoping that she wouldn't?

'A few,' he said cautiously. 'Why?'

'How soon do you think you could appoint someone?'

'Ah…that would depend on a few factors. Like whether they needed to give notice from their current position or shift from another city or country, even.' Logan was frowning now. 'Why do you ask?'

'I've been contacted by the hospital in Australia that I'm heading for next. They're desperate to fill their gap and have asked me if there's any possibility of getting there a bit earlier than planned. I don't want to leave you in the lurch but…' Ella's gaze slid away from Logan's. 'It feels like it might be a good time to move on…'

The silence grew in the small room until it started to feel awkward. And then Logan cleared his throat.

'I'll see what I can do,' he said. 'And I understand. Moving on is a good thing. I've got an offer on the barn that's just come in.'

He was smiling as Ella lifted her gaze in surprise. That crooked smile that caught her heart like a hook, every time. More now, in fact, because she could feel the undercurrents for Logan. Everything that had happened to make him the man he was today. How much his smiles actually meant.

'The estate agent told me it was your sketches that sealed the deal.' Was there a tone of forced brightness in Logan's voice? 'The buyers could apparently see themselves on a summer evening, outside on that courtyard, having a barbecue. Or sitting in the pixie house, watching the ducks on the pond.'

Oh…that would be a dream of her own for ever, Ella realised. It would be…home, that was what it would be. But only if Logan was there.

'Are you going to accept the offer?'

'It's a good offer. I'd be silly not to accept it. I've got the contract right here. I just need to sign it and send it back.'

Ella nodded, swallowing hard at the same time. She excused herself then, desperately needing to escape Logan's office and try and walk away from the idea of other people doing the barn conversion she had put her heart and soul into creating. Even worse was the thought of other people in that pixie house where Logan had very nearly kissed her for the first time.

In the rain.

It had been raining that first day when she'd got soaked walking to her new accommodation and found herself locked out.

It was raining again today. More than raining, in fact. It might be well into spring in Scotland but there was snow mixed in with that relentless rain. It was sleeting and freezing and about as miserable outside as Ella was feeling at the thought of Logan walking away from the barn or that she could be packing up to move to the other side of the world in a matter of days.

Ella wasn't in any hurry to get home. Because it didn't feel like home any longer? It was just an apartment. Temporary lodging. For a place to feel like a home it needed to be somewhere she wanted to be. Or with someone she wanted to be with?

Logan's barn felt like a home. Even though it was completely uninhabitable at the moment.

It was going to get dark early, though, thanks to this horrible weather so as soon as Ella noticed a break in the precipitation she headed for the locker room to change out of her scrubs. She'd known it would be cold and miserable today, so she'd come to work wearing jeans tucked into her boots and a tee shirt beneath her favourite alpaca jumper. She was reaching for her anorak when Logan burst into the room. He headed straight for his locker.

'There's a call-out,' he told Ella. 'For OERT.'

'Oh, no… In this weather?'

'It's because of the weather that the call's been made.' Logan stripped off the tunic of his scrub suit and Ella found herself staring at his naked back as he kept talking. 'Do you remember that B&B we passed up on the Old Military Road, when we were coming back from Inverness?'

'Yes…' Suddenly it was easy to focus on what Logan was saying and not what she was watching as he pulled a tee shirt over his head and then reached for the dark fisherman's rib jumper hanging on the hook inside his locker. 'Is that where you're going?'

'Aye. There's a woman alone in the house. And she's been in labour for hours now.' Logan pulled the jumper on. 'Her midwife can't get to her. The helicopter can't go up in this weather. We can't even send an ambulance because they don't have chains and it's already snowing heavily and beginning to settle.'

'Is she at risk of complications?' Ella was already imagining how frightened the mother would be. She barely noticed that Logan was taking off the trousers of his scrub suit to pull on a pair of chinos. 'Is it her first baby?'

'It's not only her first baby, she lost her husband just before she knew she was pregnant. Her midwife said that this pregnancy has been the only thing that's kept her going.' Logan took his shoes and socks to the bench that ran down the centre of the room and sat down to put them on. 'She hasn't got any known risk factors but...'

He lifted his gaze to catch Ella's and there was far more than a frisson of intimacy there. She understood instantly why he wasn't going to let this woman deliver a baby alone when her whole future might depend on the outcome.

'I'm going to take my SUV,' Logan said. 'I've got a set of chains so it should be fine as long as I head off ASAP. I've got the usual OERT gear good to go. He held the gaze a heartbeat longer. 'Will you come with me?' he asked quietly. 'I think we make a team where the sum is greater than the parts.'

A part of Ella's heart was melting at those quiet words. She understood exactly what Logan meant because she knew she was a better doctor when he was by her side. She was more confident. More courageous. Just...more of everything she wanted to be in her life, really. She just hadn't imagined that Logan might feel the same way.

'Of course I will,' she said.

They barely spoke on the drive.

Logan was completely focused on the road conditions

and the deteriorating weather. Ella was almost hypno-
tised by the swirl of snowflakes rushing towards them
in the muted glare of the vehicle's headlights. The road
was white by the time they got to the high altitude of the
mountain pass but the rugged tyres of the SUV were able
to cope and they didn't need to stop to put the chains on.

'We're going to be stuck up here overnight at least,'
Logan warned. 'But the forecast for tomorrow is much
better. They're saying this low pressure will be short but
sharp. I'm sure they'll be able to clear the road in daylight.'

'I'm not bothered,' Ella told him. 'I just hope we get
there in time.'

They arrived in plenty of time. The mother, Maureen,
was already worn out by the hours of painful contractions
and terrified of giving birth alone and she was so happy
to see Logan and Ella arrive that she burst into floods
of tears and, dammit, but Ella was crying already too.

Just a bit. A single tear that she swiped away very fast
and Maureen didn't seem to notice. If Logan had noticed
he didn't seem to mind, but then he was looking a lot less
calm and controlled than usual himself.

'It's a wee bit bleak out there,' he told Maureen after
they'd introduced themselves properly and it was obvious
that a birth was not imminent. 'But we're here and we're
not going anywhere any time soon. How 'bout I get your
fire going and get the rest of our gear inside while Ella
has a look to see what's going on for you?'

The back of Logan's car had been stacked with all
sorts of equipment. They had a portable CTG machine,

a portable ultrasound machine, a cylinder of Entonox as one form of pain relief, along with a raft of drugs and IV supplies. They also had a kit for assisted delivery with forceps and a disposal ventouse suction cup and pump.

'You've done a brilliant job so far,' Ella told Maureen. 'You're about six centimetres dilated already and baby's doing well. I'm more than happy with the heart rate and the response to your contractions. Let's see how comfortable we can get you before you transition into second stage of labour. Would you like a nice warm shower or bath and then we can find something really comfortable for you to wear?'

'I'd like that,' Maureen said. 'I've got a cotton knit nightdress in my hospital bag. It's in the bedroom upstairs.' Then she bit her lip. 'I don't want to go up there to have my baby, though... I'd rather do it here.'

'I could bring the mattress from your bed down here into the living room,' Logan offered. 'It's lovely and warm in here now with the fire going and you may want to deliver lying down.'

'We'll pop a line in your hand too,' Ella said. 'After you've had your shower. That way we'll be able to give you some stronger pain relief if you need it.'

'It's a boy,' Maureen told them when Ella slipped a cannula into a vein on the back of her hand a while later and secured it with tape. 'I'm going to call him Dougal... after his dadda.' She pressed her other hand against her mouth to stifle a sob. 'I'm sorry... It's just been so hard to be doing this without him. I miss him *so* much...'

'I know you do.' It was Logan who put his hand over

Maureen's. 'And I'm so sorry for your loss. He'd be very proud of you right now.'

Maureen was smiling through her tears. 'Do you really think so?'

'Absolutely I do.'

Logan's smile was gentle. He was still holding Maureen's hand as her next contraction started and Ella watched in amazement as she saw lines on Logan's face that looked as though he was actually feeling some of the pain Maureen was in. He was emotionally connected, she realised. He didn't seem to have any of the professional distance she'd come to expect of this doctor. What had made the change? Tapping into his own traumatic past?

And would that mean the calm confidence he displayed in coping with any problems would be inaccessible?

In the next hour they kept a close watch on the baby's heart rate during contractions and helped Maureen change position and walk around a little. They gave her sips of water and had snacks available, although they weren't wanted. As the end of her first stage of labour approached, Maureen got a little anxious.

'What time is it?' she asked.

'Nearly eleven p.m.'

'Is it still snowing?'

'It looks like a Christmas card outside.'

'Oh, no… You're not going to be able to get home after this.'

'We weren't planning to go anywhere until it's clear enough to get transport for you to get to hospital.'

Maureen nodded, pushing her hair back from her face. 'It's no worry. The bedroom we use for guests is always made up with clean sheets. It's out in the barn so it might be far too cold, though. But there's a spare bedroom upstairs, next to ours, and it's always warm when the fire's going because the chimney's part of the wall.' She was pacing now, bent over and rubbing her own back.

'This was our dream, you know… To be on the family farm but run a B&B as well and share the countryside that we both loved. We wanted a whole bunch of bairns to be running around out there…'

She walked towards the fireplace and then stopped. 'It was so sudden,' she told them. 'Dougal got sick and we found out he had pancreatic cancer and…and he died only six weeks later. He didn't even know he was going to be a daddy.' Maureen's face twisted into lines of renewed pain, both emotional and physical. When she cried out with an agonised groan, Logan and Ella both helped her back to the mattress, where she crumpled and knelt down to ride out what seemed to be a noticeably longer and stronger contraction than any earlier ones.

'You're fully dilated,' Ella was able to confirm moments later. 'It's time to start pushing. I think we're going to be meeting wee Dougal soon.'

Except they didn't. Fifteen minutes of regular contractions and hard pushing from Maureen turned into thirty minutes.

Thirty minutes became an hour and then an hour and a half. Maureen was exhausted and Logan and Ella began exchanging concerned glances. When they began to see changes in the baby's heart rate during contractions, Logan crouched beside Maureen, who was on all fours.

'I can see his head, Maureen. You're almost there. Big push...'

'Keep it going,' Ella encouraged when the next contraction started. 'Keep pushing. Push, push...push.'

Maureen had her head bowed and her groan sounded desperate. 'I can't do this... It's too hard...'

The baby's head hadn't moved during the last contraction.

'I need to examine you,' Logan said. 'And see what's going on. I'm sorry, it won't be very comfortable.'

Ella held her breath. She watched Logan's face as he gave her an internal examination and she saw the moment he realised what was going on.

'Your baby's shoulders are a wee bit stuck,' he told Maureen. 'He's going to need some help to come out. Stay where you are for the moment. I'm going to need to give you an episiotomy to make a bit more room. Are you okay with that?'

Maureen nodded. She sounded frightened now. 'Just help...please...get my baby out safely...'

Logan's gaze met Ella's as he looked up to take the syringe of local anaesthetic she had drawn up and then the sterile scissors from the pack she'd opened to hold out for him.

Shoulder dystocia. The baby's head was delivered but his shoulders were stuck inside the pelvis. They had only a few minutes to get him out before there was a significant risk to the baby.

'My hands are smaller than yours,' Ella said quietly. 'Shall I try a Rubin's manoeuvre?'

Logan nodded. 'Let's get you lying down on the mattress,' he told Maureen. 'You're going to feel Ella trying to rotate the baby a little to help his shoulders come out.'

Ella slipped her hand in to find the posterior shoulder of the baby to rotate it to an oblique position.

'Can you give me some suprapubic pressure, please, Logan?'

'I need to push,' Maureen gasped.

'Not yet.' Logan sounded just as calm as he always had in any emergency situation Ella had shared with him. 'Just wait, Maureen. You'll be able to push as soon as we get a shoulder free.'

Ella was still trying to get her fingers into the right position to push the underneath shoulder around. Logan was waiting to help by pressing on the upper shoulder. They both knew that if this failed they'd have to work very fast with another manoeuvre and if *that* didn't work they might have to break the baby's clavicle. Ella really, really didn't want to have to do that, but if that was what it took to save Maureen's baby, of course she would do it.

But…this was working. She could feel the baby rotating under her hand, with the shoulder moving away from her fingers and his face turning upwards into her other hand. She cupped the chin with that hand and the back of his head with her other hand and helped him rotate further, easing first one shoulder and then the other through the pelvis.

'You can push now, Maureen,' she said. 'He's coming….and…here he is.' Ella lifted the newborn and, to her enormous relief, he was already taking his first breath and getting ready to give his first cry, which startled them all with how loud it was.

'Good set of lungs.' Logan was grinning.

'Oh…*oh*…' Maureen was trying to sit up, reaching for her baby.

Logan helped. With the umbilical cord still attached, he got the baby settled against his mother's chest, skin to skin, with pillows supporting her and a warm blanket over them both.

And then, after the maelstrom of extreme tension and pain and effort and the relief of the baby arriving safely, there was suddenly a silence in this room.

Baby Dougal was lying on his mother's bare skin, looking up at her, and he was completely silent. Ella was simply soaking in the joy of the moment before starting to think about the third stage of labour and watching for anything of concern like excessive post-partum bleeding. Logan seemed equally stunned. He still had his hand on the pillows behind Maureen that he'd been adjusting but he stopped moving.

It felt as if they were all holding their breath and the only sound was the soft crackle of the fire that was warming this room so well and creating soft flickers of light.

It was Maureen who broke the silence.

'He's so perfect,' she whispered. 'Welcome to the world, Dougal…' She lifted her gaze then, staring at the doorway of the room that led to the stairs. 'He's here,' she said softly. 'Your dadda, Dougal. I can feel that he's here.'

'He is…' Ella's tears were really falling this time. 'He'll always be here. In your home and in your heart. And wee Dougal will grow up knowing who he is because of how much you loved his dadda. How much you loved each other…'

She looked up to catch Logan's gaze when she finished speaking and it felt like she'd just told him how much she loved *him*. To her amazement, his gaze held hers with a softness that suggested he understood and it wasn't something he was about to run away from.

It almost felt like he wanted to echo her own words.

It was in the early hours of the morning by the time Maureen had finished her labour and was tucked up into her warm makeshift bed with Dougal beside her in a Moses basket, so close that she could press a featherlight kiss to the whorls of hair on her baby's head before snuggling beneath the feather duvet Logan had brought downstairs.

'Try and sleep,' he suggested. 'Goodness knows you deserve a rest.'

'I can't tell you how happy I am you were here with me.' Maureen lay back on her pillows, her eyes drifting closed. 'I can't believe how happy *I* am, to be honest.' She opened her eyes again, looking straight at Logan. 'Do you know, I hated it when I knew I was pregnant. I thought I couldn't do this without Dougal. I wanted to just curl up and hide from the world for ever.'

Her words were gripping Logan's heart so hard it was difficult to take a breath. He'd never let himself become this emotionally involved with a patient but there was no way he could have prevented it this time. He wouldn't have wanted to.

'I know,' he said softly. And he did. He knew how that felt. It was his work that had forced him to keep going. Maureen's pregnancy must have become the same kind of escape from the depths of grief.

'This is a new life for me,' Maureen whispered. 'And it's going to be wonderful. I have someone to love again.' She reached out to touch baby Dougal's head with her fingertips and she might have been talking to him rather than Logan. 'You've got to take the risk of loving some-one this much again.' Her words were fading now. Maybe she was just thinking aloud. 'Otherwise you're not really living at all...'

Within seconds, Maureen was as soundly asleep as her baby.

'I don't know about you,' Ella said. 'But I'm desperate for a cup of tea. Maybe something to eat too. I'm sure Maureen won't mind if I poke around in her kitchen for a bit.'

He watched Ella go through the open archway that led to a big kitchen dining room in this old farmhouse but he stayed watching Maureen and the baby, even though it was for purely emotional reasons. His pendulum re-ally had swung far too far on this call-out but the fear that it could lead to him making bad decisions had been unfounded, hadn't it?

Maybe it was because he was isolated so far from any hospital. Or, more likely, it was because he'd been work-ing with Ella by his side, but he felt as though he'd made *better* decisions.

And he knew that Ella had been right and he could understand why and how she connected so well with people—because there was so much more joy that could be found in the work they did if they let it touch their hearts. There was no medical reason that made it neces-sary for him to sit there any longer. Their patients were both doing very well. No doubt they would clear the roads in the morning and an ambulance would be able to come and take this mother and infant in for more extensive checks in hospital but, for now, all they needed to do was rest.

Logan had something he needed to do before dawn broke, however, before any part of the rest of the world intruded into this time and space he would remember for the rest of his life. He went into the kitchen.

'I've made cheese on toast,' Ella told him. 'But it's too hot to eat just yet.' She was smiling at him. 'I don't want you to burn your tongue.'

Logan couldn't smile back. 'I don't want you to go to Australia,' he said. 'I love you, Ella Grisham.'

He saw the way her eyes widened and then she became so very, very still.

'I love you too, Logan Walsh,' she whispered. 'But I do really understand why you can't go there. Why you can't risk your heart again.'

Logan took a step closer. He reached to take and hold both of Ella's hands.

'Maureen's a wise woman,' he said slowly. 'I think I already knew what she said about not really being alive unless you loved someone, but it was so much easier to ignore it. To not take that risk and just pretend that everything was fine the way it was. To not even think that there might be a zebra amongst that herd of horses going past in your life.'

How weird was it that Ella felt as if she completely understood what Logan was saying? That she was the person he wanted to be with. Because she was different. This—what they'd found together—was different. Incredibly rare.

Worth risking your heart for, because if you didn't take that risk you weren't truly living.

More than worth giving up what she had perceived as freedom for as well.

'I've been travelling for so long,' she said aloud. 'Moving from place to place and meeting so many people.'

'Because you need your freedom.' Logan nodded. 'I get that. I understand why you don't want to stay still.'

But Ella shook her head. 'I think I knew it was time to stay still the day you took me to see your barn. I think I had to do all that travelling to find you. To find the home I've been searching for.'

'I didn't sign that contract,' Logan told her. 'I couldn't. I kept thinking of you in the pixie house and your ducks and… I didn't want anyone else to be living in *our* barn.'

'*Our* barn…' Ella breathed. 'Oh… I love that idea… almost as much as I love you, Logan.'

'You mean…you'll stay?' Logan's gaze was fixed on Ella's. 'Here, in Aberdeen? Here…with me?'

Ella dropped her hands and stood on tiptoes so that she could put her arms around his neck. 'I should warn you,' she said solemnly, 'I'm hitting on you, Logan.'

The side of his mouth lifted in that quirky smile of his. 'I should warn you. It's doomed to succeed.' He was dipping his head to kiss her. 'But I think I should warn *you* because I think it's actually me that's hitting on you. Because I love you. I may well be hitting on you for as long as you'll let me. A lifetime, I hope…'

'Mutual hitting,' Ella murmured in the blink of time before his lips touched her own. 'For ever. The very best kind...'

EPILOGUE

Four years later...

ELLA'S BELOVED ALPACA jumper had a few holes in it these days, but she was still wearing it because it was unlikely she was ever going to be able to choose a replacement for it on a trip to Peru.

And she could not be happier about that.

She needed to wear it this evening because there was a hint of snow in the air and she was outside, standing beside the pond, armed with the ducks' favourite food, which was a mixture of bought duck 'crumble', vegetable peelings and suitable leftovers. Today it was green peas from last night's dinner which the expanding flock of ducks were snapping up first from the grass as Ella scattered handfuls of the mix.

'El…' Logan was calling from one of the French doors on this side of the barn that he'd opened just a little. 'Come into the warm, darling. The boys will be here any minute.'

'Coming…'

Ella turned back to the house with a grin. The 'boys' were turning thirty years old today and it was going to be the first time in years that they'd all been in the same place at the same time. The first time they would be seeing the home that she and Logan had so painstakingly designed for their barn conversion. It had taken a long time to get planning permission, find the right craftsmen to do the work and source every material and feature needed from architectural antiques and recycled treasures.

Logan had a roaring fire going in the stone-built fireplace and the huge dining table was set, ready for the feast both she and Logan had been preparing all day.

'We could have done takeaway, you know,' Ella had told him. 'My brothers are not the least bit fussy about what they eat. The odd horse has probably gone missing here and there because they got hungry enough.'

It just took a glance.

Or was it the mention of a horse?

Whatever. They'd not only developed a kind of telepathy over the years but they had so much shared history now. So many private jokes or significant memories. Takeaway food would always remind them both of the meal that had been stone cold thanks to the first time they'd ever made love. And neither of them could ever forget that they were each other's 'zebra'. And, like zebras, they had very different patterns in their stripes but that didn't mean that they didn't belong together.

They both knew they were perfect for each other.

Ella's triplet brothers arrived en masse, having shared the same rental car from the airport. None of them had brought anyone else with them.

'What is wrong with you all?' Ella demanded when they all had drinks in their hands and were thawing out in front of the fire. 'Where are the girlfriends? Wives, even?'

There was a shout of male laughter. It was Mick who turned the table, however. 'Where are the babies, Ella? You guys have been married for...what it is...three years now?'

'Three and a half. And the babies are all at work.' Ella looked up at Logan, who was standing right beside her, his arm around her waist. 'We're very happy the way we are, thanks. I suspect you lot put me off having babies for ever.'

Except...she and Logan had been invited to wee Dougal's fourth birthday party not so long ago and seeing Logan with the little boy had made her wonder whether he might be hiding a secret desire to have a child of his own. Because he thought it would be the last thing Ella would want?

She could feel her gaze softening into something that felt like pure love as she held Logan's gaze a heartbeat longer. She might have to let him know that it might be easy to persuade her to change her mind if it was something he wanted. As long as it wasn't triplets.

And if Logan was their daddy.

The shout of male laughter after Ella's jibe at her brothers was fading.

'And you've put us off finding girlfriends to bring home,' Jimmysaid. 'Let alone marry. You set the bar too high, Ella.'

Eddie was gazing around the huge space that was the long side of the barn. 'This was a wreck the last time I was here. Wasn't there even a cow skeleton in the corner?'

'There was,' Logan told him. 'Wow...has it been that long since you visited?'

'Australia's a long way away,' Eddie said. 'That's why I couldn't come to your wedding. Oh, wait…we didn't get invited, did we?'

There was more laughter but it was totally good-natured.

'We didn't invite anyone,' Ella said. 'You know that. We went off to the most amazing island and had a ceremony just for us in the ruins of an old church. If you ever get a chance to visit Iona, you really should.'

'There are forty-eight Scottish kings buried there,' Logan added. 'And it really is a magical place.'

'I won't get there on this visit.' Eddieshook his head. 'I've got to get back to my uni course and exams aren't that far off.'

'Are you still working towards your critical care paramedic qualifications?' Ella asked.

'Nope. They're done and dusted. I'm getting some helicopter credentials now that'll take me anywhere I want to go.'

'Where *do* you want to go?'

'Dunno. I think I'll stay in Australasia for a while. It's beginning to feel like home.'

'And I'm thinking of taking a break,' Mick put in. 'I might go and join Médecins Sans Frontières and see if I can do some good in the world.'

'What about you, Jimmy?' Logan asked. 'Are you happy where you are? You've just finished a surgical rotation, haven't you? How was that?'

'Loved the surgery.' James nodded. 'But now that I'm in the emergency department I think I might have found

the place I'm meant to be. It just feels like what I could
be happy doing for the rest of my life.'

'When you know, you know,' Logan agreed.

'Same goes for people,' Ella added. 'One of these days,
you boys will find that out. You'll find your person and
you'll just know. Like I did with Logan.'

'Yeah, yeah…' Mick was looking around as if he
wanted to find a way to change the subject and his eyebrows were rising. 'This might be a silly question,' he
said, 'but why do you guys have a picture of zebras on
your wall?'

Logan and Ella shared another glance. And a smile…

'We just like them,' Ella said. She raised her glass.
'Hey… Happy Birthday again, by the way. Here's to the
next thirty years and an amazing future for you all.'

'You too,' they chorused.

'We've already got ours sorted.' Ella leaned her head
against Logan's arm and he bent his head to place a kiss
on her hair. 'It's your turn now.'

* * * * *

SOUTH AFRICAN ESCAPE TO HEAL HER

BECKY WICKS

MILLS & BOON

Dedicated to *The One Who Took Me To Cape Town*
and all the sunsets we shared.

CHAPTER ONE

ARNO NKOSI KEPT one hand on the wheel of the Jeep and ran the other lovingly through the thick, coarse fur around Tande's neck. A night drive across the expansive game reserve with all its bullfrog songs and wildlife surprises was an experience his lioness had loved, ever since he'd found her as a lost cub on a sandy roadside, four years ago. Arno assumed Tande's mother had been shot. Or maybe she'd perished in the blade-sharp jaws of a crocodile—who could say?

In this part of the Limpopo Province, in what they called the Safari Capital of South Africa, anything could happen. Which was precisely why he was driving faster than he normally would towards his new volunteer recruit.

A certain Kaya Van der Bijl had flown in from her native Netherlands to work for him and *with* him, but she'd somehow managed to take the wrong bus from Cape Town. Luckily she was waiting for him right now at his friend Rai's small guest resort, which was the closest place he could think of to send her from the bus stop in a pinch. Rai had gone to get her, being the great family friend he was, and had been for a long time, since even *before* the fire...

Arno let a gush of air from his nostrils, turning off all thoughts of the fire before they could burn him, as usual, and sped up towards the game reserve gates. Dutch-born doctor Kaya was out of harm's way, but it did not sit well with Arno that a woman was waiting for him alone in a strange new place, when she should be unpacking with the other volunteers already.

He hoped the staff quarters would be comfy enough. He'd had the basic huts built at the Thabisa Game Reserve to host the steady stream of medical professionals who came to volunteer for six months, sometimes more, with the pioneering healthcare infrastructure project he'd also built—so to speak—from the ground up. He swelled with pride every time someone praised the Lindiwe Health Foundation but in no way could he take *all* the credit. These volunteers made it the success it had been for the last decade, and he needed them safe, comfortable, well fed and well rested, alert and ready to help people in the surrounding communities. Not stranded fifty miles away.

Arno slowed the vehicle, noting Tande's ears flatten. If a lioness cohort was good for anything, it was for sensing people and animals way before they hit the glare of a handheld spotlight, or his headlights. He watched her long whiskers twitch, and the way she held her nose to the wind. She could be sensing a jackal. It could even be a giraffe. The Thabisa Game Reserve was more alive at night than in the day; you never knew what you might come across, chomping away on a nocturnal feast.

Arno squinted, scanned the darkness ahead for the gleaming green eyes of an impala or a skittish rhino, either of which they would do best to avoid. His mouth flickered with a smile as two snuffling bush pigs looked up in alarm, then darted out of the spotlights.

'Hey, guys,' he muttered at them, drawing to a stop at the gates and turning to Tande.

'They're lucky you've eaten already, huh, girl?' he muttered, and Tande, as if on cue, excused herself from the Jeep by way of leaping gracefully over the door, and padded off into the night. Somehow, she always knew when to make her exit; when Arno was safe from all other wildlife in the reserve, and when *she* could remain well out of sight and reach from whatever might lurk outside.

Of course, he had a gun at hand always, plus a tranquilliser kit and enough antivenom to kill a superhero's arch-enemy, but still. Sometimes it wasn't even the animals you had to be afraid of, he thought ruefully, and the flames roared back into his memory, as bright and loud and ferocious as they were when they tore through the restaurant, twenty years ago.

Back when he was too busy pouring liquor down his throat with his buddies to be home, where he should have been.

He should really call Mama back, he thought suddenly. *Maybe later.*

Arno bobbed his head at Mikal, who opened the gate from his protective booth, ushering him on through to the main road. His rammed schedule was just an excuse. It just made his guts squirm, knowing the conversation he'd been putting off for years was always lingering unspoken between them.

Mama never talked about the miscarriage, caused by the carbon monoxide in the smoke, but he still thought about it, every single day. A little brother for Arno she'd never seen coming! A miracle, she'd said. Mama got labelled a geriatric, because she'd had Arno at twenty-two, then fallen pregnant again aged forty. She'd even named her little miracle—Kung, short for Kungawo.

The day he learned they'd lost Kung was still one of the most vivid memories of his life so far. Mama would be a proud mother of two right now, if he'd only been there when the fire broke out, woken her up from her nap, as he had said he would…

Damn, Arno, focus.

It was twenty goddam years ago, he'd done so much since then. Started a foundation, launched a medical centre, helped to save a thousand lives in the surrounding villages. Reared a frightened little animal from a lion cub to a full-grown lioness, refused even a drop of alcohol…which most people thought strange, considering the family wine empire. But his father's voice was still clear as day, even two whole decades later, blaming him in a moment of rage. Calling him out for not being there; which he'd had every right to. The whole thing had been stalking him like a lion all these years.

He only hoped his waiting volunteer wasn't some frightened little animal; this wasn't exactly work for the weak. Kaya Van der Bijl had seemed pretty tough on the voice call, he mused. She'd talked about her qualifications a lot. Her long years of studying to become a doctor, and the requisite year of training in a Dutch hospital—that was all certainly impressive. As if all that meant a damn thing if she wound up freezing in the face of a flesh wound inflicted on a human by an angry animal.

Or showed up ten minutes too late to a fire.

Arno forged ahead into the night, praying there wouldn't be anything too dramatic to scare Kaya and the other volunteers off. At least not *this* week.

Kaya Van der Bijl had to do a double take. The man jumping out of the orange and black safari vehicle in a cloud of dust and striding towards her now had an air about him that she certainly hadn't witnessed before, not least because of the military-style boots, and the off-white safari trousers tucked into them, and the black T-shirt stretched across a broad muscled chest. This was not Amsterdam attire, not by any stretch of the imagination.

This was pure South African magnificence.

He took her overstuffed suitcase in one big hand and extended the other to greet her, and she noticed the way his shaved head gleamed in the headlights below a trace of jet-black regrowth; the way his sharp cheekbones and strong jawline served to turn him into some kind of living, breathing sculpture. The moonlight just made him seem like a magical creature, born from the wild plains all around them.

'Kaya?' he said, interrupting her thoughts.

It wasn't often she was thrown off her usual course of thoughts around new men—which usually went something like, *Yes, brain, he's very good-looking, but he probably can't be trusted.*

'Hey, Kaya? Good to meet you, I'm Arno. Took the wrong bus, did you?'

Kaya stared. This was Arno Nkosi? The chief medical manager and founder of the volunteer programme at the Lindiwe Health Foundation, which was set to be her place of employment for the next six months? She'd seen a couple of photos of him on the website, but nothing up close...as he was now.

He was partly amused, partly annoyed and trying not to let it show, she observed, forcing her shoulders back and telling her eyes not to rove over his bulging forearms as she smoothed down her white linen dress. Being astute was her speciality, she'd made it that way after everything she was trying to leave far behind her in Amsterdam. Her instincts were primed, all ready to mistrust this strapping man, who was leading her towards the safari four-by-four with the name of the resort they were headed for on the side of it—*Thabisa Game Reserve.*

She was already late for unpacking hour in the promised 'rustic yet scenic' staff quarters she'd be staying at on a self-catering basis. Suddenly she thought less about not trusting him, and hoped he didn't think less of her for missing the bus. They'd be working closely together.

Lifting her bag effortlessly over the side of the Jeep, despite the array of vacuum-sealed bags she'd stuffed inside to hide the actual bulk of her belongings, Arno nodded in the direction of the three steps she had to climb to take her seat. She was careful to jump up without letting her dress rise too high.

The leather seat felt thin and she wasn't entirely sure it had much in the way of suspension, but hey, she was here in South Africa, the place of her mother's birth. And where she was headed, she wasn't exactly expecting luxury.

'Sorry I missed the bus,' she heard herself saying when Arno had exchanged a quick goodbye with the guy he'd apparently sent to rescue her from the bus stop. He must know everyone around here.

'It happens,' Arno replied in a manner that suggested it didn't usually happen and should not have happened tonight. She cringed internally as they swung out of the quaint guest house's driveway. His hands looked big and strong on the steering wheel.

'Did you have to drive very far to come and get me?' she asked, wondering how many lives he'd saved with those two big hands. 'I know we're surrounded by game parks so I wasn't sure if there's a shortcut you might have.'

'The only shortcut is through the game park,' he said. 'The one where you'll be staying. It's gated and guarded like they all are, but you wouldn't want to walk it. Not unless you want a face-off with a wild pig. Or a rhino.'

'How often does that happen?'

'More often than you'd think.'

She caught his lips curl slightly and wondered if he was joking, and also if she'd sounded naive talking about shortcuts. She had been quite distracted at the airport, noticing all the things her mother had been talking about for years—the wide welcoming smiles, the colourful clothes, the African trinkets shining from the tourist stalls. No wonder she'd taken the wrong bus. She'd finally made it to her mother's birthplace. She'd always been curious about this side of her family but never enough to actually come here. Scrap that, had she just made herself too busy, or been too afraid? Since the attack, she hadn't exactly been chomping at the bit to leap out of her comfort zone. She was only just now realising she'd probably wasted some of the best years of her life—well, no more!

'So, this is your first time here?' Arno was looking at her sideways, as if he'd read her mind.

'To South Africa? Yes. But I've been dreaming about it for years,' she replied, unable to hide the excitement in her voice, or the urge to study him closer while he was driving. The contrast between her mocha skin and his sun-kissed whiteness was striking, even in the low light. They didn't make male specimens like Arno where she'd grown up in the Netherlands—the men were tall enough but, to her, they all looked kind of the same. Not that she'd noticed any of them with romance in mind since the attack, or since Pieter...

Nope. He was not allowed into her thoughts any more, not here, the cheater.

'It's not a vacation,' Arno replied, coolly, watching the road. Kaya straightened her back in the bumpy seat and gripped the side handlebar. They were speeding down a dirt track now. The lights from the guest house were a mere glow behind them.

'I'm not expecting a holiday. I just meant my mother is from Cape Town, and I've always wanted to see the country she left when she moved to the Netherlands. That's where my dad's from, but they met here.'

'Do you have siblings?' he asked, seemingly interested.

'I have one younger brother,' she replied. 'Daan is three years younger than me, he's twenty-four. He's studying architecture.'

'Younger brother, huh?'

She nodded. 'We're quite close. Do *you* have siblings?'

A furrow appeared between Arno's eyebrows as he looked dead ahead over the steering wheel. 'Nope. Just me.'

The inkling of something like anger lingering beneath his words caught her off guard. On instinct she searched the road ahead for something blocking their path, or anything that might have caused 'that look', but there was nothing.

Was she talking too much? Kaya smoothed her dress hoping it wasn't sweaty, and wondered if her English was as good as everyone said it was. Everyone spoke English at home, as much as they did Dutch, but she was aware of her own accent now, as much as she was aware of Arno's.

His South African lilt sent his words up at the ends in little sing-song flourishes. She quite enjoyed it. But now he was simply frowning at the windshield.

What was he—late thirties? He looked at least a decade older than her. He'd done some pretty incredible things in Limpopo, she thought, starting with founding and recruiting new volunteers every six months to assist with important medical rounds and much-needed treatments in the local communities. The nearest town of Hoedspruit was surrounded by game reserves, and therefore called the Safari Capital of South Africa. This position, for the next six months, could mean some difficult tasks, out in potentially dangerous places. She wondered if he was concerned that she wouldn't be up for the task.

Usually she'd be wary of all this herself. Not because she felt she was lacking in qualifications or experience—she most certainly was not. But because…well…

Kaya glanced his way; the old nemesis of distrust flaring up against her will. Was this Arno a man she could be alone with? He might be a man of few words, but then, he *was* someone everyone knew, she reminded herself. He'd done more in his years as a doctor and surgeon than most people half his age—if he was indeed in his late thirties, as opposed to her twenty-seven years.

That didn't mean she hadn't conquered enough on her own since dragging herself up from rock bottom, she mused, watching the row of thick bushes spike towards the sky along the roadside. Her poor parents, while happy she was here doing something to help put the past behind her, were apprehensive. Close as they were, they knew she wasn't totally over the assault, not by a long shot. The man still pounced on her in her dreams every now and then; sometimes they were back in the park where it happened three years ago. Sometimes they were in a darkened vault or, worse, her bedroom, where she'd holed up for months afterwards at her parents' house.

Inhaling a lungful of dusty air, she reminded herself in the side mirror that this was a chance at a new start, a new beginning.

'I noticed your name, Kaya, means *restful place* in Zulu,' Arno said now, thoughtfully. 'Interesting, considering you chose a profession that doesn't offer much rest.'

'What?' His observation broke into her daydream.

'Still, I can't see you in a library,' he continued, 'or an ashram. Not if your résumé is anything to go by.'

Kaya laughed nervously. Having someone she barely knew admitting to thinking about her and her history felt a little uncomfortable. But he was her mentor and employer, so, of course, he'd have some questions. And she'd do well to try and at least seem open. Something in his eyes as he looked at her sideways had her nerves rewiring the whole way up her arms.

'What do you do for fun?' he asked now.

That was an interesting question she didn't quite know how to answer. There hadn't been much fun for her, for a while.

'I've done Pilates for a while. Kickboxing too,' she replied carefully. 'And you know how the Dutch love a peaceful bike ride.'

Arno laughed. A nice laugh. A laugh she wanted to hear more of, even though it administered a sharp shot of self-loathing that calmed her hummingbird heartbeat in a flash. How was Arno to know she still took the bus everywhere at night, instead of hopping back on her bike, as the Dutch did by default?

The ability to go anywhere alone after dark had abandoned her long ago. What if another faceless male vulture tried to steal her dignity, along with her belongings, like *that* guy… the one who got away? The one who had never been caught.

She hadn't been able to prove a thing. The assault and the injustice had ruled everything for years, ruined her relationship. Pieter wound up cheating, saying he was forced to, because she wouldn't let him near her, but could he really blame her after having a stranger almost rape her in a park? Just the smallest touch, or brush against her arm in a crowd, by anyone, not just him, had flooded her with panic and self-loathing.

She only hoped no one else came along and tried the same thing with her. Maybe this time they'd succeed in getting further than a handful of her breasts and a feel of her…

No, God, no…

'You OK?' Arno was looking at her in concern now and

she drew her chin to her chest. 'I know it all probably looks a little different from what you're used to, and getting the wrong bus might have thrown you, but no harm will come to you on my watch. I can *promise* you that.'

Kaya turned to look at him. His last statement...that had sounded serious. As if he knew what she'd been through to get here—as if he *possibly* could.

'That's good to know. And thanks, I'm fine,' she replied, noting how her heart was thudding wildly again in her chest, like a satellite that for years had been floating silently in space, and was finally now picking up a signal.

CHAPTER TWO

Arno waved at Mikal again as the guard opened the gates to Thabisa Game Reserve. He saw him take a long look at Kaya, before peering through the window and resting his arms on the frame with his usual wide, toothy grin. 'Welcome to Thabisa, young lady. I see you're getting the special treatment already, being collected by the boss.'

'You came out of nowhere!'

Kaya sounded panicked. She drew a sharp breath and recoiled in her seat, as if she couldn't get away from Mikal fast enough. Quickly, sensing her discomfort, Arno left Mikal behind in a cloud of dust, almost as fast as poor Mikal could pull his head back out of the Jeep.

'Mikal is a big guy but he wouldn't hurt a sandfly,' he told her as he rumbled back the way he'd come, towards the resort and its staff quarters. 'Did you see his gun, in the holster? Everyone has one here.'

Kaya looked embarrassed now. His forehead wrinkled with a frown as she released her own forearms from the knot she'd tied herself up in. 'Oh, no, I didn't even see the gun. Sorry, Arno, he just came out of nowhere...sorry.'

'Don't apologise,' he said, feeling a little bad for the way he'd almost reprimanded her before, when he said this wasn't a vacation. He realised now that maybe his tone had been a little harsh, and that his defences were up because she was undeniably attractive, and he didn't quite know what to do with that. He wasn't prepared to spend the next six months fighting some attraction to someone he couldn't touch—he was meant to be a professional, a mentor. Not some Romeo, following her with his eyes through every emergency. And there would be emergencies. Distractions weren't welcome, not here.

Then the whole sibling thing had struck a nerve, too...

But really, she hadn't seen the gun? What on earth was so frightening about big, goofy Mikal? Maybe she was just exhausted from the journey.

'You're in a new place,' he offered. 'You're probably also jet-lagged. Let's get you to your new home, shall we?'

Kaya forced a smile verging on wary and kept her eyes on the road ahead. She kept her right hand clasped like a steel vice around the overhead handle, as if she didn't trust his driving either. He always drove safely, but if he didn't go fast he'd never get anywhere; at least, not before it was too late.

Arno slowed the Jeep a little anyway, glancing in her direction, instincts primed. That had been some reaction. What on earth...was she going to be visibly frightened of new people out here, new experiences? That wouldn't get her very far. A muscle in his jaw ticked. A pretty woman like this, with eyes like hers, and flawless, caramel skin like hers, and full heart-shaped movie star lips...she'd do well to keep her wits about her, and not let any ruffled feathers show. Plenty of people could take advantage of that.

He felt his hands clamp harder around the wheel. Kaya was his responsibility now.

'What is that?' Kaya's eyes had popped beside him. Her look drew him from his reverie, which had strangely and rather irritatingly been veering on admitting to himself that she was possibly the prettiest volunteer who'd shown up here in a long time.

'What is what?' he followed, clearing his throat, but no sooner had the words left his mouth than the shadow of a figure he knew well drew up alongside the Jeep. *Tande*.

Her fur was a blaze of white in the moonlight. The glint of her cat eyes as she streaked across their path just ahead made Kaya let out a shriek. 'A lion! Arno, it's a lion, hurry up, we need to…'

He stopped the Jeep. 'It's OK.' Arno put a hand to Kaya's shoulder, looked towards Tande, who'd stopped to eye them both up through the windshield. 'You're about to meet a friend of mine. Just stay calm.'

'A…friend of yours?'

He pressed a finger to his lips. 'Calm. OK? Trust me. Do you trust me?'

A moment passed between them. Kaya's obsidian eyes burned into his as she nodded mutely, her expression flickering between hope and caution. Trusting him wasn't coming easily, he could tell. Basic instinct told him it went beyond Mikal and the lioness just outside, and his mind spun suddenly—who was this woman and why was she really here?

He removed his hand from her arm, just as Tande leaped gracefully onto the bonnet of the Jeep and started licking her paws like a giant house cat who'd been looking for a warm place to sit. He could tell Kaya was biting her cheeks, trying not to make a sound. This time he definitely did not blame her for startling, but they were going to meet eventually, so now was as good a time as any.

'Tande is a rescue,' he explained, opening the door slightly. 'I found her as a cub. She just likes to hang out, that's all.' He jumped to the dusty ground, shutting the door behind him, protecting Kaya. Tande had never hurt anyone, but she was still a wild creature and she could sense fear in strangers.

His boots shook up more dust on the dry moonlit ground. Every stride echoed through the night, and he felt Kaya watching him as Tande jumped from the Jeep to greet him. He ran his hands across her head and ears, letting her nuzzle him, showing Kaya she could be trusted. Then he held out his hand to her.

He half expected her to flat-out refuse to participate in this introduction, but Kaya obliged, if tentatively, crossing to him slowly and taking his outstretched hand. He used his other hand to rub Tande's ears, then gently placed Kaya's palm to her fur, encouraging her to take over, noting the fuzzy sensation that took over and blurred the world around them at her touch.

'I wouldn't let you, if it wasn't safe,' he said, looking into her eyes, and relief washed over her features as she started to run a hand lightly over the lioness's head.

Pure elation crossed her face in the headlights and Arno found himself lost a second, dazzled by the broad smile—this was the first he'd seen of it, and she was truly stunning. South African and Dutch, huh, he mused. The two made for a good mix.

As if watching the moment from above, he observed the fact that he was actually sharing the magic that was Tande under the moon with a woman he'd just met, and how weirdly calm he felt about that. This had never happened before.

'She's beautiful,' Kaya breathed, and he studied the smoothness of her mocha skin up close, the depths in her eyes. The way her dress nipped in around her middle, enhancing her small waist and toned upper arms.

'She is,' he agreed.

'Tande…that means teeth, in Dutch,' Kaya observed as

Tande decided she'd had enough petting for one night and turned her back on them slowly, her attention switching to some distant noise that they as mere humans couldn't hear. 'I suppose that fits. Aren't you ever scared?'

'Of Tande?' he answered.

'No, of the dentist. Of course, Tande!'

He shrugged. 'I've known fear,' he admitted, picturing the moment he had arrived on the driveway to find the flames licking the stone walls of the villa, shattering windows; people screaming, no sight of his pregnant mama. 'It's never been related to my lion.'

Kaya cocked a head at him. 'What kind of fear are we talking about?'

Arno shook his head at the floor. He *could* elaborate on how that fire had taken three of his parents' beloved staff members, and, later, his unborn baby brother. It had dominated the news for a long time, back when the prized family business and the longest running winery in Stellenbosch went up in flames, but they'd only just met. Anyway, he never really talked about it with anyone, let alone a stranger. If he did, he'd have to mention how the miscarriage was *his* fault.

He'd abandoned therapy because not even the long-faced lady with the big, beguiling eyes and irritatingly soft voice could get him to talk about it. It was stuffed down deep under the daily grind where it couldn't get to him. Apart from Bea, the one woman he'd opened his heart to about it all, no one had met Mama Annika. There hadn't been anyone since, but he'd never take another woman home.

What if someone asked the same things Bea had, like why they hadn't redecorated and reopened the restaurant? He'd have to say it was because Mama wanted to keep the memories alive through the blackened walls and fire-tinged beams.

Memories of his brother, who had died because of him.

Bea had left him shortly after learning the truth, five years ago now. She'd wanted to explore other places, and other relationships. He had never found out for sure if she just thought less of him, after learning how he'd let his family down, but he had clearly let Bea down too, somewhere along the way. A year-long relationship, his longest one ever, had just gone up in flames, like everything else. His biggest dread was letting people down, the way he'd let his parents down. God, his father had been so damn angry. The family had never been the same since.

'What kind of fear?' Kaya asked again, eyes narrowed.

'The debilitating kind,' he replied darkly.

'Well, that makes two of us.' Kaya sighed, and Arno detected a deep sadness, at the same time as he became acutely aware that her hand was still in his, even with no lioness to pet or protect her from.

As if realising the same thing, she pulled away and busied her hands with smoothing her hair, eyeing him sideways as Tande padded off. 'But if you say your lion has never eaten anyone…'

'Not that I know of.' He motioned her back to the Jeep, forcing himself not to look at her. They'd be working together; in some tricky situations, no doubt. The last thing he needed was a distraction, but he could have sworn they had just had some kind of *moment*. And what kind of fear was *she* talking about, exactly?

'Do you have many animal friends?' she asked as they bumped along the dirt track. The lights from the resort were just ahead, which for some reason was a relief to him now. 'I mean, should I expect a friendly elephant to climb in next?'

'Maybe just a rhino or two,' he replied, deadpan, and she huffed a small laugh, looking around her warily. 'I'm kidding, of course,' he continued. 'No one's friends with the rhinos.

They love to charge off in the direction you least expect, just to relieve their own boredom and stress. They're unpredictable. Never approach one, ever.'

'I wasn't planning on it.'

His turn to smirk now.

By the time he pulled up outside the staff huts and carried her suitcase diligently to her door, he'd decided there was something dangerously interesting about Kaya Van der Bijl. He'd do best to keep away from her, outside their professional duties. Already she stirred something up in him that reminded him of Bea. Bea had tornadoed into his life, a PR for a wine company who'd come for a safari and slashed her leg on a wire fence. Their romance had been the best year of his life, until it became the worst.

The moment he'd finally opened up about the fire, and told her why it had taken him almost a year to take her home to meet his mother, no thanks to his debilitating guilt over ruining her life, she'd all but disappeared. She was thriving with a new man now, somewhere in Spain, that much he knew. And here he was, single, which was maybe the only way he couldn't disappoint anyone else.

Sometimes he wondered if it had been the wine estate Bea was interested in that whole time, more than him. But either way, no one since had got close enough to break him and they never would if he could help it. Especially not someone he was supposed to be working with!

CHAPTER THREE

'THIS IS BETSY, named by the British volunteer who first drove her out through the gates,' Arno explained, and Kaya watched his bicep rise like a boulder in his white T-shirt as he slapped a hand to the side of the huge truck that was their mobile medical clinic. The bus-sized vehicle had been designed to be driven through the townships around Cape Town, and the local communities in between.

The sunlight streaked across his arms, and she noted the faint line where a watch might have been; the black snake tattoo that curled like some family emblem on his bicep. She didn't usually like tattoos on anyone, not even Pieter when he'd had the initials of his late grandfather inked on his upper arm in memory. But Arno's was hot, she decided, while allowing the fact to sink in that she was literally admiring a man, rather than wanting to run a mile. So strange. But not entirely unwelcome. Maybe it was being so far away from home, away from triggers. The old 'out of sight, out of mind' thing?

'Every doctor that's here is making a huge impact on the health of the surrounding community and to individuals themselves,' Arno was saying now, arms crossed. He was wearing the black military boots again, the same cargo trousers, and a blue T-shirt with the foundation's logo on it—the same as the one she was in, only hers was slim fit.

'As you all know, the Lindiwe Health Foundation's services are varied. There's not one emergency we haven't already dealt with. You're all here because of your individual skills, and because I saw something in each of you during the application process...'

Arno caught her eye then, mid-speech, and dashed his shaved head with one hand. As he continued talking about the last few surgeries he'd done in the well-stocked mobile clinic to the group of five other volunteers she was standing amongst, Kaya realised she was mirroring him, scraping her wild curls back on her hot head, wondering why he made her nervous.

It wasn't the usual nerves she felt around men; as in, it wasn't general disdain or mistrust occupying her brain whenever Arno was near. It was a kind of natural attraction that had fizzled into her conscience in the Jeep last night. Who wouldn't admire this brooding surgeon's looks?

But looks were just surface distractions. She'd been awed speechless by the fact that he'd tamed a lion.

Tande. Wow!

She'd never had a moment like that before, and probably never would again. Not just meeting a real lioness, but letting a guy she'd just met hold her hand throughout the whole experience. It would never have happened normally, but she'd been thrown, numbed almost by the creature's magnificence. And Arno's. What kind of man tamed a wild lion from a cub to the creature she'd met last night? Someone special, for sure.

Not that she was here to pet the wildlife...or wonder what made Arno Nkosi tick. She was here to work.

Except, she couldn't *help* wondering what made him tick. There had been a moment between them, she was certain, because she never had 'moments' with men. What debilitating fear had *he* known? Whatever it was, she recognised a kindred spirit when she saw one.

Obviously, she had no desire at all to elaborate further on her own experience, spending three whole years being afraid to cycle through a stupid park thanks to one drunk, entitled arsehole. But how could she not want to know what he'd gone through himself, what caused that look on his face— so distant, as though he'd gone someplace else in his head, somewhere bad?

Was he attacked by the rhinos he'd warned her about? Did he fight a snake after it bit him, thus inciting his desire for the tattoo? Maybe she shouldn't be thinking about it so much…

'He's so sexy, don't you think?'

Kaya was pulled from her reverie by the whisper of a volunteer next to her; a short, pale-skinned lady from Australia in a red hat called Kimberley. Kaya kept a straight face, refused to turn to her. Instead, she shrugged as her cheeks flushed.

'You couldn't keep your eyes off him at breakfast. I saw you.' Kimberley grinned and nudged her. 'Don't worry, who wouldn't think that?'

Kaya flinched. Touching her was unnecessary—no one touched her if she could help it. Well, no one but Arno last night, which she was still processing. The fact that she'd let him was still a surprise, lioness or no lioness. And anyway, she hadn't been staring at Arno over breakfast.

Had she?

Arno was still talking. 'You'll be getting plenty of hands-on and practical experience, all of you. A lot of our rural doctors who do come and work here end up leaving a lot more confident in their skills, and in their training…'

Her eyes caught his again. *Hands-on* didn't sound so bad. She straightened up, feigning a confidence she didn't feel in his line of vision. *He* wasn't to know she'd lacked confidence of sorts since the assault, or that she was here to try and prove to herself that she could face life without fear again, explore new places without being afraid of her own shadow, and gain back some of the confidence that had pretty much defined her before that night in the park.

Kimberley nudged her again and she frowned, moving away. OK, so maybe she had been watching Arno at breakfast, regretting the way she'd recoiled from that guy at the gate on the way into the resort in front of him—the one who'd stuck his head in the window out of nowhere and given her a fright. She hadn't even noticed the gun. He'd just shown up out of nowhere; something that was bound to trigger her.

While wishing—again—that she hadn't made quite such a scene in the Jeep, she'd counted two slices of toast at breakfast, two hard-boiled eggs and three rings of pineapple on his plate. Then, when he'd sat down opposite her and eaten in silence, she'd counted the freckles that formed a jagged constellation on his left forearm—seven—and the tiny scales on the snake tattoo—twenty-eight—and allowed herself to ask him if he had any more tattoos.

He'd replied no, and that had been the extent of their exchange, although his piercing slate-blue gaze had lingered on hers until she'd pulled her eyes away.

He'd sprung up after that, as if he was far too busy to be eating breakfast, let alone discussing tattoos with her, and she'd found herself watching him stride purposefully towards the mesh mosquito-proof door, until he'd disappeared from view.

'I need a volunteer,' he said now. Without missing a beat, Kaya shot up her hand. What she was volunteering for, she had no idea, but she was going to at least come across as a professional, starting now.

Arno beckoned her towards him. 'Great, Kaya,' he said. 'You'll be coming with me on our first round—we only need the two of us where we're going. The rest of you five can go with Dr Zula in Betsy here and start on the PLH Project.'

He turned to her and scanned her eyes. 'That's the Positive Lifestyle Habits Project—volunteers can work with small groups to deliver information on basic health, lifestyle and nutrition. I think you missed that intro yesterday, because you got here late, but don't worry. You'll catch up.'

Was that a dig for the fact she got on the wrong bus? Kaya wasn't sure, but she stood taller anyway. 'I read up on this before I came,' she told him, while the others were chatting amongst themselves, boarding the mobile clinic. 'I was thinking maybe we could start a small vegetable garden somewhere that the community can help look after. We can use the harvest for malnourished patients too.'

Arno ran a hand across his chin this time, seemingly running her idea around in his head. 'I love it,' he replied after a moment, and her heart did a little leapfrog.

Before she knew it, Kaya was back in the Jeep and Arno was bumping them back across the reserve, this time in the midday sun.

She squinted through her sunglasses as he explained they were heading to visit some patients who were too sick or impoverished to get to their nearest clinic. They were in a tiny village that not even the mobile clinic could reach, which already made her heart pang with sympathy.

'You'll be helping me with the new TB antigen tests today. There was a recent outbreak in the village where we're going.' He paused and slowed as a zebra wandered into the path and trotted off again. 'All children are supposed to get the BCG vaccine at birth in South Africa, but some slip the net. A high

HIV co-infection rate means that in some of these rural, re-source-poor areas...'

'I read about it. It's terrible.' She sighed.

'Yes. It is.' He pulled the visor down, shading his face. 'Some of these people already have both tuberculosis and HIV,' he followed. 'It might be a little confronting at first...'

'I can handle it,' she assured him, hoping she could. 'I'm willing to do whatever is needed, Dr...'

'Just Arno is fine,' he asserted, and she noticed how his face softened slightly. 'I'm sure you're up to this. You wouldn't have come here if you weren't, right?'

'Right,' she said, forcing conviction, hoping this wasn't another test of her abilities and confidence.

'I appreciate your idea too, about the garden. Are you green-fingered back home too?'

She shrugged, picturing the patch of tomatoes, courgettes and lettuces she'd tended over the last three years. It had all started as an excuse to disappear from society after the attack.

'I got a little something going on my rooftop in Amsterdam,' she ventured. 'I didn't know how much I would grow to enjoy it. Something about putting your hands in the dirt, in the earth, growing something tangible from nothing under the sun.'

'You get sun there?' He cocked an eyebrow.

'Sometimes.'

He nodded, a rueful smile hovering on his lips. 'Growing something tangible from nothing under the sun. Sounds like something my mama would say, Kaya.'

'Why did you start the foundation?' she asked him now, keen to continue the conversation, and also registering the way her name sounded from his mouth, how it made her feel as if he'd grabbed her insides with his big hands and twisted them ever so slightly into brand-new positions, every single one attuned to his intonations.

'It's a good feeling, knowing you're making a difference to someone's life,' he replied. 'Besides, I didn't think the wine business was for me.'

Kaya studied his taut jawline. 'Wine business?'

'My whole family is in the wine business,' he said. 'You hadn't heard?'

'*Should* I have heard?'

The moment she said it, the faintest recollection of a gold-embossed wine label flashed to the front of her memory bank. 'Oh… Nkosi Valley wine… I don't drink, haven't for years but, now that you mention it, I've seen it. That's your family?'

He nodded sagely. 'I don't drink either,' he told her, as visions of a family-run vineyard enchanted her suddenly. She didn't know much about the world of wine but surely wine producers around this region were rich, so Arno must have come from money. He could have done anything, but he'd chosen to help others. Her admiration for him ratcheted up another notch.

'When was the last time you had a drink?' she asked, wondering if it was as long ago as her. She hadn't touched a drop since the assault three years ago. Maybe if she hadn't been tipsy following her expat friend's birthday shenanigans at an Irish pub in the Red Light District she would've been more aware of her surroundings, maybe veered left at the lights instead of right into the park and into the hands of…him.

'Haven't touched a drop since I was eighteen years old,' Arno answered.

'Most people don't start till then,' she observed.

'I started too early. *Big* mistake.'

'Too early? How early is too early?'

'Early enough to make me late for something way more

important. So tell me, what kind of music are you into, over in the Netherlands?'

Without leaving room for her answer, he reached for the dial on the dash and, in seconds, music blasted through the vehicle, signalling the end of their conversation. Kaya set her gaze upon the jagged trees outside the window. It felt a lot as if he'd been about to tell her something he deemed incredibly important, and then decided not to.

Oh, well, everyone had their secrets, she supposed. Especially her. Except the most puzzling thing was happening to her now. The more Arno talked, the more she was finding herself drawn to him...wondering things about him. She'd do well not to get too personal in any further discussions.

Gosh, she'd die if he knew some of the things *she* kept hidden...like the fact that Pieter started seeing someone else behind her back because she was, in his words, 'frigid and cold', but he 'didn't want to hurt her more by breaking things off'—coward.

Last night was the first time since that awful night when she'd actually let a man she didn't know take her hand. Why she had let Arno, why he was getting to her after so long of trying to forget all men existed, was not only interesting, it was a little jarring too. The thought of letting anyone get that close again, close enough to hurt her, was...well, terrifying.

CHAPTER FOUR

THE CHILDREN DESCENDED on them, the moment they pulled up in the Jeep. They always did. The little ones especially expected crayons and sweets, although Arno never brought the sweets. 'Dentistry is not what it is in the western world,' he explained, when Kaya asked why he hadn't brought the candy hearts they were asking for.

Arno watched her eyes widen and narrow in shock and despair as she took in the full extent of life in this tiny community, hidden from the world, an hour's drive from the resort in a remote valley. The mountainous backdrop promised safaris and breweries and wineries beyond, a plethora of luxurious modern charms, none of which existed here.

'This is where they live?' Kaya whispered to him, gesturing to the row of bleak-looking thatch-roofed huts stitched together with woven branches, mud and dried cow dung. Two pigs that looked far too skinny were snuffling around a wire-fence enclosure, where several chickens pecked at the ground.

He nodded sagely. 'They're pretty self-sufficient, and they share what they have,' he said. 'But I know they'll get a lot out of your garden.'

'Where should we build the structure for that?' Kaya swung around, bumping into him, making him drop the box of tests he'd just pulled from the back seat. His heart slammed into top gear at her proximity as her scent washed over him. 'Sorry, sorry,' she said quickly as she sprang away from him, then immediately bumped into his arm again as she tried to help pick it up.

'It's OK,' he assured her, collecting the fallen box and brushing the mud off the bottom with his hand. 'It's dirty work out here; as long as what's inside it is kept clean, we're good.'

Kaya rubbed her arm self-consciously where she'd knocked him, and he caught the same haunted look in her eyes that he'd seen yesterday, when she'd admitted she knew fear, as he did. Things were falling into place, he thought to himself. Kaya had a thing about physical contact. The way she'd re-acted with Mikal at the gates to Thabisa was one thing, but what about this morning? He wasn't born yesterday. That Australian volunteer, Kimberley, had been whispering about him, but Kaya was having none of it. Not only did she keep her mouth shut, which he respected, she'd practically built a wall between them when Kimberley prodded and nudged her.

His animal instincts were primed; something must have happened to make her so guarded. Probably something bad.

A strange kind of need to protect her took a hold of him, more powerful than yesterday. And instantly jarring—he hadn't felt this way since he'd seen Bea lying bloodied by that fence and raced to help her, determined, as he had been every day since that fire, not to let a person who needed him down. Why Kaya was summoning those same feelings he almost didn't want to contemplate; she'd be leaving soon, as Bea had, whether she knew his family secrets or not.

A burst of laughter made them turn. Two little girls were climbing into the Jeep, pretending to steer it, and he let them. 'They're always so grateful for everything they have,' he said to Kaya, retrieving another box from the back seat and side-stepping around her, wary now of getting too close to her.

He opened the back to retrieve a trellis table and foldable chairs and set them apart. This was the extent of their 'clinic' out here, but they had the new batch of antigen tests they needed and now he had Kaya, and that was all that mattered.

Two barefooted kids dressed in scruffy football shirts and shorts were digging ferociously with plastic shovels over by a makeshift cowshed. He watched Kaya wander over to them.

'What are you digging?' he heard her ask as he stuck the table legs firmly into the mud in front of the Jeep.

'Fossils,' they told her in unison.

'Fossils? Out here?' she replied, getting to her haunches to inspect something they'd dug up.

'You'd be surprised,' he called over, admiring the curve of her hips in her khaki shorts, and the way that the simple white T-shirt rendered the whole of Kaya the kind of untouchable that could cause a sleepless night if he dwelled on it too long. 'Indigenous habitants left a lot for these guys to unearth. They can sell what they find, so they never stop looking.'

Kaya smiled, touched a hand to the head of one of the boys, and then crossed her arms as she walked back to help him set up, giving him the chance to admire her again with the sun glinting off her mocha skin and wild raven curls.

It wasn't just her looks, though, he considered again as she fetched a box of vials and made small talk with another curious child.

He hadn't been able to stop thinking about that moment with Tande yesterday. Maybe that was what had led him to sit opposite her at breakfast. He'd thought better of it and left the dining hall shortly after, biting back his questions; what was the point of getting personal with a volunteer? That would lead nowhere and, besides, he wasn't exactly the type to invite intimacy in. That always led to questions about…everything…

No, thanks. He had enough on his plate without twisting knives into old wounds.

But never had he allowed a stranger that close to his lioness so soon—not because he didn't trust Tande, of course. He just didn't want to freak anyone out by initiating contact. Kaya had been calm and gentle and Tande had responded. She hadn't padded off straight away as she usually would. He admired a woman who could admire his lioness, but there was something about her.

Maybe it was the haunted look in her eyes he caught every now and then, the hint of a troubled past that made her so... attractive. Now *that* he could relate to, he thought disparagingly, along with the need to escape every now and then.

A little boy no older than four or five was tugging at Kaya's sleeve already and to her credit she didn't even wince at the muddy streak that was left behind. 'Can I go first?' the child asked her, placing his forearm flat on the table, even before she'd sat down.

'You want to be the first to be tested?' She smiled. 'You're one brave boy.'

'I'm not scared of blood,' he told her proudly, and she laughed, right before the kid regaled a story about helping his father catch, then carve up one of the chickens. Then he said, 'I think I have TB. I'm very tired all the time. I sweat in the night.'

Kaya shot him a sideways look and Arno felt his brows meet in the middle. It wasn't uncommon for kids to diagnose themselves; they saw enough cases to know the signs.

'We'll get you tested, buddy, and if you do have it, we'll get you treatment, don't worry.'

Arno ripped the tape off one of the boxes he'd put on the trellis table. 'These tests are a new alternative to the regular tuberculin skin test,' he told her, sliding a box her way, and placing a box of vials in between them as she took a seat. 'More cost-effective for the foundation, and more accurate.'

'Well, that's always a good thing,' she replied, pushing her hair from her face and eyeing the giant grey resident elephant who'd just plodded into view, led by her keeper.

'That's Alma,' he told her as the huge creature flapped her ears free of pesky flies and sent fresh dust swirling their way. 'One of the guys here rescued her years ago. She pays her way now, pulling timber, giving kids a ride to school. Been through the wars, but I think she's happy here.'

It was getting hotter by the minute, and as Kaya watched the elephant plod past out of view again, with a look of total enchantment on her face, he found himself wondering if she'd applied sunscreen—the last thing he needed was for her to burn on day one. It was disconcerting how much he was thinking about her already, he realised.

He watched as she rubbed the boy's arm with alcohol and pushed the needle bevel into his skin. Sure enough, the boy didn't even flinch, though an interested circle of faces had gathered, and some of the girls were squealing, not sure what to think.

Arno filled in the labels on the vials, and, along with Kaya, instructed those just tested to avoid scratching or rubbing their arms. The first young boy, who seemed to take a liking to Kaya, lingered as she tested his friends. Worryingly, he'd started to cough, and Arno hoped it wasn't another case of TB, rather another case of a kid breathing in too much dirt, and not eating enough vegetables. He caught Kaya's concerned glance and lowered his voice again, reading her mind. 'We'll have all the results back from the lab in a few days,' he told her.

Within thirty minutes they'd effectively tested everyone who hadn't been tested last time he visited this village, but their mission wasn't over.

* * *

Kaya *was* a little conflicted, if she was honest. The little mud hut they were standing in now wouldn't have even held up as a garden shed where she was from, but the little bony lady Arno called Mama Imka, lying on the thin mattress on the ground was still looking up at her with a sparkle in her eyes.

And what was in all these jars? she thought, noting the haphazard array of glass containers along the cake-like brown walls. So many jars and candles, stacked up in the subdued light bleeding in from the doorway.

'She's a Sangoma. A fortune teller,' Arno explained, seeing her puzzled stare.

'Really?' Kaya felt her eyes widen. She half expected Arno to laugh or roll his eyes her way on the sly—a man of science and medicine didn't believe in all that, did he? But he seemed deadly serious.

'Those are Mama Imka's tools,' he told her, signalling for her to pass him the medical box she'd carried inside. 'Two different worlds, huh?'

The children from outside were crowded around the door, as if they couldn't get enough of watching her and Arno. Or maybe they were wishing their village fortune teller better? She held up a hand at them, noting their muddy feet in the dirt. Different worlds indeed.

'How are you feeling today?' Arno asked the sixty-something lady kindly, crouching to her side. Kaya watched how gentle he was as he rested a hand on her thin, brittle fingers.

'I'm grateful you're here for the others,' she responded, sucking in a breath and flicking her gaze to her again. 'Although you know, and *I* know, what will come for me.'

'Do we?' He smirked, squeezing her fingers. 'I wish you'd accept that your meds are helping, Mama. You're looking better than last week.'

'My dear boy, medicine can only do so much when fate has dealt its cards.'

'Well, let's just keep following doctor's orders anyway, OK?' he said sternly, yet with a stroke of fondness for her that melted Kaya's heart.

Mama Imka sighed and dropped her head against a lumpy-looking pillow. 'As you wish.'

Kaya crouched beside Arno, brushing his arm again accidentally, noting how her body didn't bristle like a frightened cat's at his closeness. Why did even touching him by accident feel different from when she'd brushed anyone else by accident over the last few years? Instead of shooting flashbacks of the assault through her, she felt something like…adrenaline? Excitement?

Maybe it was just being here, with this intriguing woman, she told herself. It wouldn't do to develop a crush on her mentor; besides, it was likely he was around ten years older than her. Completely out of her league in all respects. She hadn't been herself enough to like a guy for years, and she was damned if she'd start now with someone she couldn't even have!

'I'm Kaya. We're here to do your monthly blood test,' she said, noting how the woman's arm was adorned with more beaded bracelets than she could count. Her lips were stained red from some kind of plant or natural dye, she could tell. In fact, she did look quite well considering she was suffering both TB and HIV.

Arno had explained outside how the NGO the foundation worked with provided all TB medications, laboratory testing, X-rays and in-patient care, but it was their job to visit these infected patients weekly and provide injections and support, monitor adverse events, and educate them and their family members in how best to control infection. She hoped the education made as much of a difference as the medications. Already the stench of dirt and animals was making her eyes water.

She watched Arno take the blood test, and then he allowed her to do the sputum culture—testing for infection in the lady's lungs. Mama Imka watched them both intently as they worked, adjusting her bright red headscarf and beaded necklaces as if her appearance to them mattered. Then, just as they were getting ready to leave, she grabbed for Kaya's hand with a strength that defied her size, sat bolt upright and urged Kaya back.

'Come, come here.'

'Everything OK?' Arno was back at her side in a heartbeat.

'I'm fine,' Kaya told him, registering the way he was studying her, as if he was afraid she might cower in fear of this poor patient, the way she had with Mikal yesterday on her way into the resort. She was already regretting that reaction, as if she could've helped it!

Arno prised the lady's hand gently from hers and she felt the sparks shoot up her arm at the gesture, his fingers brushing hers again. He cleared his throat and stepped away, dashing his head with the same hand. Did he feel some need to protect her now, because of the way she'd been yesterday, and today too, when she'd knocked the box of tests to the ground? That would be mortifying.

She was sure her cheeks were flaming red, but Mama Imka was still looking at her imploringly. Her eyes flickered to Arno. Then back to her.

'Let me read for you,' she croaked, pointing a finger her way. She gestured to another woman, younger—her daughter maybe—hovering in the doorway. 'Get me my shells.'

Arno busied himself with clearing away their equipment

while Kaya was ordered to sit cross-legged on a woven mat on the mud floor. So, he wasn't going to save her from this, then?

Her heart was a lion, begging for release inside her chest. She had most definitely not come here to have her fortune told, but how was she supposed to get away now? The woman was already shuffling around from the makeshift bed and sliding to the floor opposite her, her skirts billowing around her.

A jar of what looked like seashells, bones, shiny stones and sticks was promptly opened and spilled in front of her. Mama Imka seemed to study the array of items for what felt like an eternity, frowning and chanting something under her breath, garnering some kind of message, she supposed.

'My dear, you have been through some hardships...' she started huskily. 'I see your past through a veil of tears, but your future is...'

She tailed off thoughtfully, glancing up at Arno conspicuously. Kaya's heart leapt to her throat. Why was she so nervous when she didn't even believe in all this stuff? *Everyone* had cried at some point in their past. OK, so maybe she'd shed a few more tears than most while she was putting the pieces of her life back together but, still, that was a pretty generic statement, taken from a bunch of shells, no less!

Arno stood somewhat awkwardly behind her, as if he too wished this would be over. Thankfully he left the hut, distracted by one of the children, before he could hear what the woman said next, because what Mama Imka went on to tell Kaya about life, and even potential *love* made her heart stop altogether, then slam like a bullet against her ribs.

She'd stew on these words in secret for the next two weeks.

CHAPTER FIVE

ON THE ROOF of the Jeep, Arno swigged from his coffee flask and studied the mountains across the reserve. This new birth of a day in all of its colourful motion was something he wished he could transfer to a canvas...but his mother was the painter, not him.

He sighed at the grass. He'd have to go home today, after his rounds. Dad had called yesterday, which sent the usual icy blast through his bones—they had never been close. Not since that night when they lost the baby and he told him, his only son, that he should've been there to protect Mama.

Going home was awkward to say the least. Arno still didn't enjoy the thought that he might see that blame in his father's eyes again one day...or in Mama's eyes. He could barely talk to Mama in case she confirmed she too blamed him for the miscarriage. Instead he did nice things when they asked him to, and made his polite exit soon after.

This time Dad had asked if he could come and oversee the removal of an old piece of furniture someone was coming to buy from the villa. He was heading overseas for a wine convention—and secretly didn't trust his wife not to sell the antique sideboard off cheap.

'No Tande this morning?'

A voice behind him made him start and he swung his legs over the side of the Jeep to address Kaya, walking towards him, a vision in the half-light. She was clutching a book to her chest.

'She doesn't get to come past the fence to the staff buildings…and good morning,' he said, taking in the sleepy yawn she failed to hide behind her hand, the loose cotton trousers with the zebra patterns on the sides that she might or might not have slept in. To his chagrin, he had thought a little too much about what Kaya might sleep in lately.

They hadn't really spoken much since that first day in the village, over two weeks ago now, not on a personal level anyway. But he'd found himself watching her, how poised she was, how hard-working and determined. She stood out in the group. She wasn't the chattiest, or the most social, so every time she laughed it was like a light coming on, and he was drawn to her undeniably, a bee to a honey tree. He'd been reminding himself it would do him no good to actually get her alone, or ask her what he wanted to ask—what had Mama Imka said?

'You're up early,' he said, motioning her over and pulling a tin cup from his backpack. 'Coffee?'

'You read my mind,' she said, placing her book on the roof and taking the cup of hot black liquid gratefully. She breathed a happy sigh over the rim. 'I thought I'd find a spot to read before breakfast. Then I saw you here, looking at the sky.'

'Another masterpiece, isn't it?' He gestured upwards with his cup and studied the angles of her face as she gazed in wonder at the screaming pink, now blazing a trail through the purple, and the mountain range beyond.

He was itching to ask her now. What did Mama Imka say? It shouldn't bother him so much, but she'd looked so shocked at the time, and he knew from experience that Mama Imka had hit a few nails on the head in the past, despite his scepticism in general.

Kaya had clammed up right after, spoken only about the garden and what she'd need to plant before the rains came— usually they arrived just a few weeks from now. The mystery made her ever more intriguing. He got the distinct impression she'd been told something she deemed to be life-changing, if indeed *she* even believed it.

'So, how are you doing?' he asked her now, as she sipped from her coffee cup on the ground below. She frowned as the cry of a rooster broke the silence and a passing zebra gave a dog-like bark in response.

'This is something I'm still getting used to,' she admitted, gesturing to the zebra now peering through the window to the mess hall, where breakfast would soon be served. There was a herd on the property, protected from the rest of the re- serve and the hunters in it, like Tande.

'All these animals roaming freely. I mean, not too freely, I do feel quite safe here at the resort. And out there too, thanks to you.' She glanced at him quickly, then looked away too fast, and he caught something in her eyes that spoke loudly of what was clearly a mutual appreciation of the other. He cleared his throat, felt his hand dash his head of its own ac- cord.

'I'm happy to hear that. I was hoping we could go check out the plot for the garden at some point. Maybe today? My guy in Cape Town has some timber up for grabs, he just needs to know how much to bring over.'

'I'm scheduled to be out in the mobile clinic till four,' she said quickly. 'With you…and some of the others.'

He nodded, noting her chewing her lip. Of course he knew the schedule. Didn't she want to be alone with him at all? He was not imagining this tension; he could feel it rising up be- tween them like a hissing cobra. It wasn't as if he were sug- gesting a date though.

'We can go after,' he found himself saying. 'I know all the antigen tests came back negative but I need to check up on Mama Imka anyway.'

Kaya took a deep breath and closed her eyes, gripping her coffee cup tightly. 'Mama…right.'

'She got to you, huh?' He couldn't help it now. Her face after leaving that hut had said it all, but it wasn't as if he'd believed Mama Imka's predictions last time he'd let her read for *him*. When she'd said he had a big life ahead of him, and that a great love would bloom with the sunflowers.

There weren't any sunflowers growing anywhere in these parts, not that he knew of, and the thought of a big love coming his way was like expecting a spacecraft to land on the property—never going to happen. He hadn't so much as been on a date since Bea. Mostly because he cut them all off when they started asking if they could visit the winery. They were all only in it for the winery.

Or maybe he just didn't want to invite the kind of heartache that had knotted him up when he'd finally told Bea about how they'd lost his brother, and she'd gone on to ditch him not long after.

Kaya still hadn't spoken. When she realised he was watching her she laughed to herself, shrugged and leaned back against the door of the Jeep, right by his legs. 'I don't know. I shouldn't have let her get to me, it's just that she was very… *specific* about some things and I'm still not sure what to think.'

'I wouldn't worry. I heard her say she saw your past through a veil of tears and people like you don't have time for tears.'

Kaya studied his boots a moment, then looked back up to the sky. 'People like me?'

'You've been so busy, becoming a qualified doctor, living your full fun life in a privileged first-world society...'

'Busy, privileged people can suffer hardships too, you know,' she bit back haughtily.

Damn, that clearly hadn't come out how he'd intended. He dropped to the floor with a dusty thud, went to refill her cup but she put a hand over it.

He shoved his flask into his backpack. 'I know that. I've been through my share of it too. I just meant...well.' He paused, rubbed his chin. What had he meant exactly? He'd been fishing for information on her and dug himself into a hole by insulting her instead.

'Sorry,' he offered. 'Maybe I was just curious. She gave my father a reading once, a long time ago. Me too, about a year ago, just after she fell sick.'

'What did she say?' Kaya's dark stare was flecked with the amber of the sunrise as she studied him. His thoughts whirled around in the depths of her eyes.

Mama Imka had seen the fire coming. She'd warned his father. He thought for one split second about telling Kaya this and didn't. Because then he'd have to tell her how he was out drinking instead of watching his mother when the fire broke out, how the three guys in the restaurant lost their lives; it was all too bleak for such a beautiful morning, and woman. And anyway, he was her mentor; he was supposed to be someone she could trust.

'You tell me yours, and I'll tell you mine,' he said instead, stepping closer on impulse and reaching out to brush a mosquito away from her arm.

Kaya stepped backwards immediately as if he'd drawn a gun on her, crossing her arms around herself.

'I can't...' she mumbled, eyeing him warily, then shaking her head. 'Sorry, it's not you, it's...'

'What's wrong?' he said now, concerned. 'I've noticed you're a little…tetchy when people get too close to you, even by accident.'

Kaya bristled and looked at him sideways before squaring her shoulders. 'Sorry.'

'Don't apologise,' he said, surprised at the softness in his own voice. There was nothing like a vulnerable woman to propel him into protector mode. Something about making up for what he did to Mama, he supposed. Dad had told him clearly before he left, just days before the fire: 'You need to look after your mama, son,' and he'd chosen to go out with his friends instead.

'Did something happen to you?' He frowned at her. He had to know.

'I'm totally fine.' Kaya's words were clipped, and she didn't meet his eyes. Then, before he could utter another word, she made an excuse to go back to her room.

Arno kicked himself. He'd gone too far.

He snatched up the book she'd left behind and put it on the back seat. She was harder to read than the Dutch text on the jacket. He'd have to return it later. Something told him he might get his marching orders if he followed her to her room and, besides, he'd been about to invite in questions he wouldn't know quite how to answer himself.

The village demanding their attention today was once again echoing with the sound of children laughing and playing. This time they were on a break from classes at the little school they'd parked Betsy, the mobile clinic, outside.

'They're so adorable and cheerful,' Kaya observed aloud to Arno, before she could think. She still felt pretty bad for scuttling off this morning mid-conversation, but her reflexes simply would not be retrained as easily as she hoped they might be.

'When you don't know what you're missing, I guess there's not much to be sad about,' he replied, opening a drawer and pulling out a stethoscope, then turning to the young woman who'd taken a seat, who was complaining of a sore throat.

Kaya worried she'd scared him off for good now. All he'd done was try to wave off a bug and she'd reacted as though he'd been about to assault her. Then, when he'd pretty much given her the opportunity to admit that yes, something terrible did happen to her once, and get it all out in the open— at least, with her mentor—she'd brushed him off instead. He probably thought she was cold as ice. Or frigid, as Pieter had said. But he wasn't Pieter. And enough time had passed since all that—she should have just said *something*.

It wasn't even that she didn't trust him. Look at the man, she thought, sneaking a quick glance at him in action, his muscles struggling to escape the short sleeves of his T-shirt as he monitored a woman's heartbeat, a look of consternation on his face that always made her wonder what selfless thought was running around in his head.

He'd been nothing but a muse, a teacher, and a... OK, yes, a gentleman tough to look away from. To her and everyone here over the last couple of weeks. So much so that she'd tried to keep her distance. Crushing on him was not a good idea, and would surely go nowhere for multiple reasons, but on top of all that, Mama Imka's cryptic words wouldn't leave her head:

'Pay attention, dear. If you see a snake as nothing but poison, poison is all it will be. You can learn from snakes, you see. They show us how you don't have to always move quickly. You can still get where you want to be, by crawling.'

There had been more, of course, a lot more from Mama

Imka, about how a big love was waiting for her when she shed her old skin; something transformative with the power to change, not just her own circumstances, but others' too. Maybe she'd just been caught up in the moment but, through the cryptic mysticism that she'd been certain was all rubbish, Arno's snake tattoo refused to stop staring her in the face. It had taken on new meaning since then. Was it some kind of harbinger of transformation?

She kept telling herself she didn't believe in all that. That she was just projecting some hokum onto the first thing that seemed to reflect the woman's words. But still. It was difficult to look Arno in the eye without wanting to either run from him, or ask him what Mama Imka had said to *him*, *and* his father. He had kind of stared through her this morning when she'd asked, as if he was conjuring up something best left buried, which had set the alarm bells off in her head. Had something Mama Imka said to him, something *bad*, actually come true?

'Pass the iodine,' he was saying now, and when her fingers brushed his on the bottle between their chairs, she caught his eye and held it. Her heart revved as her hand seemed to linger next to his for longer than was probably necessary, all of its own accord, and she caught the hint of a smile on his mouth before they both turned back to their patients. Her pulse was a lump in her throat.

Maybe he didn't think she was an ice queen…

Across the mobile unit, Kimberley winked at her and Kaya rolled her eyes. She couldn't help the small smile that hovered on her lips a second though, before she bit it back.

She was assisting Arno, Kimberley and two other volunteers in seeing to the line of people that had formed as soon as the mobile clinic had pulled up. Arno had followed behind in his trusted Jeep. An hour in and they'd already diagnosed three respiratory conditions, bandaged several minor wounds, mainly to children's legs, knees and feet, and referred two cases of tuberculosis, which they'd done the same antigen tests for at the start of the week.

The Lindiwe Health Foundation's services were pivotal in maintaining the health of these small communities. What Arno had started was a miracle for these people, but what exactly, she wondered, had made him venture this far away from his family's wine business?

While she focused on her own patients at the next set-up station in the mobile unit, she couldn't help the way her eyes wandered to Arno. Every now and then she'd catch him looking at her too, as if he was trying to decode her or something, which sent her heart into a wild flurry of panic, excitement and adrenaline.

When he pulled her aside afterwards, and asked if she still wanted to go check on their garden plot, he looked as if he actively expected her to say no, which suddenly made her want to do the opposite.

'Why not?' she told him, and he raised his eyebrows, as if to ask if she was sure.

'Let's go,' she said, wondering exactly what was coming over her as she started towards the Jeep.

CHAPTER SIX

ARNO WATCHED AS Kaya used all her might to push the six-foot post into the hole in the ground. 'It's a little tight in this patch,' she said, heaving another breath. 'The ground is a bit too rocky.'

'Want some help?' He paused, wiping the sweat from his brow from the other end of the garden, where he'd just driven in another pole of his own in what would mark the end of the garden and the trellises for whatever vegetables Kaya wanted to plant.

'I'm fine,' she responded.

'Of course, you're fine,' he muttered under his breath, wondering when she'd admit she needed help. That pole of hers wouldn't last the night if they left it like that.

The afternoon sun was still beating down, even at five p.m. There were hints in the clouds that the sunset would be stunning, but he had to watch the time if he was still going to drop Kaya back, and then make it out to the estate to help Mama and her buyer with the sideboard.

'We could plant potatoes here,' Kaya was saying to a group of four young kids who'd gathered around her in curiosity. She'd abandoned her pole on the floor for now, and they seemed to be excited to dig in with their little shovels to help make the hole for it deeper.

Arno watched her crouch with her own little shovel, and

explain about spinach, and Swiss chard, easy root plants like carrots, radishes and beetroot. She seemed to know as much about broccoli, cabbage, cauliflower, and kale as she did about anything they'd discussed in the mobile medical unit this morning. He couldn't help smiling when he overheard the kids ask if she'd brought them any candy, and got a firm no in response.

Mapping out the entire plot for the vegetable garden hadn't exactly been his plan but when the villagers got excited about something, it was all hands on deck. He had, however, told the gang of three local men waiting on the sidelines that Kaya wanted to do as much herself as possible.

It wouldn't do to feed whatever fear Kaya seemed to have of people she didn't know getting too close. She hadn't said as much, but it was obvious something had happened to her back home that she didn't want to talk about. Luckily she seemed fine with their patients. It was just men that put her on edge, he reminded himself; him included, sometimes. Maybe not as much now as when she'd first arrived.

Arno felt his brow crease and he looked away as he caught her eye. It was none of his business...just as whatever Mama Imka had said to her the other week was none of his business, even though having to keep his distance was somehow making him want to get even closer to his new recruit. He cared about what might have happened to her, he realised, even though he barely knew her. She seemed to carry as many mysteries with her as his friends liked to say *he* did.

Intriguing.

'Kaya!'

Pausing with his spade, he turned to where Mama Imka was waving at her from behind the pigpen across the dirt patch, simultaneously swiping away the flies. They'd given her a check-up before moving on to the garden project, so he wondered what she could want with Kaya as the woman proceeded to walk towards her, lifting her skirts as she strode purposefully her way.

'Shouldn't you be resting?' he called to the old lady, but she waved him away, mumbling something about resting when she was dead.

He swiped his hands on his trousers, and set to work with the measuring tape, trying not to look as if he were earwigging on what the women might now be discussing.

Five feet by five feet would be adequate space for a couple of stacked beehives, which Kaya had insisted they should also source from somewhere, he mused, turning his ear to them but failing to hear a thing over the snorting of a nearby pig. As yet he didn't know who he'd source beehives from, but it was a good idea for a bonus community project…

'Snake!'

What? The word had him turning to Mama Imka again, only to find Kaya was covering her face with her hands, despite the dirt.

'Snake,' Mama Imka stated, this time gesturing to his arm from across the way.

'This?' he mouthed, rubbing a hand over his tattoo and leaving a muddy streak across the scales. 'What about it?'

'Nothing,' Kaya said quickly, ushering the woman away. He heard her say she really had to be getting things done here before sunset and when he wandered over, he was finally allowed to help her…and her face was still bright, flushed with embarrassment.

Together they heaved the post up and kicked the soil back around it, holding it between them like a third person while the kids helped shovel the rest of the dirt around the base, excited to be able to lend a hand.

Inches from her face, Arno could've sworn she was avoiding his eyes. Behind Kaya, Mama Imka was standing with the guys on the sidelines, eyeing him over her can of iced tea, prodding her biceps where his tattoo was on his.

'What was all that about?' he asked, amused.

'I think she just likes your tattoo,' Kaya said, and he studied the streaks of dirt across her cheeks, resisting the urge to wipe some away.

'I hope she's not planning on getting one at her age,' he followed, and she huffed a laugh he could tell didn't come from her heart.

'Who knows?'

Just then, a loud noise from beyond the fence, followed by a shrill scream, made them both start and the kids abandon their positions at the base of their pole. Luckily it was now firmly in the ground, because what Arno saw next, raging around the corner and almost flattening the last hut in the row of humble homes, had both him and Kaya staggering backwards and into each other in shock.

'Is that Alma?' Kaya couldn't believe her eyes. The rescue elephant she'd seen briefly during her last visit here was rearing into their garden plot with the ferocity of a speeding train. Thick chains around her tree-trunk-like back legs had come loose from whatever she'd been tied to, and a poor guy in jeans and a flimsy shirt was being dragged behind her, screaming for mercy.

'We have to help him!' Kaya was about to lunge forwards, anything to help this poor man, who was covered in blood already. 'He's hooked onto her somehow…we have to get him loose!'

Arno stood like an impenetrable wall in front of her, blocking her path, holding a hand up to stop anyone else from moving. His hand went to his belt, where he usually kept a gun and a tranquilliser dart, but he cursed to himself. He'd left it in the Jeep. No one had expected...this.

'Everyone stay where you are,' he instructed, his voice low and laced with caution that sent her pulse to her throat.

Snapping out of it, Kaya went to run the other way towards the Jeep. They needed medical supplies, fast, but Arno gripped her elbow, fast as lightning, just as the elephant trumpeted so loudly a flock of birds took off into the sky. Then, to her horror, it turned towards her, ready to charge. Arno leapt in front of her again, and she clutched his arm from behind, peeking out, half expecting a full herd to appear in a stampede.

Mama Imka let out a cry and a plea to the elephant to stop. She was clutching the hands of two young children who'd run up to her for comfort. The rest of the village had gathered now, shouting at full volume, waving their arms, making themselves bigger than the elephant.

Releasing her fingers from their steel grip around Arno's snake-tattooed biceps, Kaya joined in, flapping her arms in the air, yelling *shoo*, *shoo*, like they were, as if it were a mouse! The elephant staggered to the left, straight into the pole Arno had just pushed into the ground, and completely flattened it.

The elephant's poor victim was losing a lot of blood, mostly from his leg. A groan escaped his lips as he narrowly avoided being crushed by the pole. Kaya could see now he was hooked to the elephant by a chain around his own wrist. There was no way his arm wasn't broken too.

'I need you to help me,' Arno said to her.

Kaya was focused on the blood. The shock of what she was witnessing was only now registering—a wild animal gone truly rogue, stomping her disagreements out wherever she pleased, regardless of which humans here had shown her kindness or mercy up till now. No animals were really tame, none of them, she thought, not even Tande.

'Kaya.' Arno took her shoulders, and she didn't reel backwards. Rather, she felt grounded, hoisted back down to earth in one split second by his eyes. The groans of the man on the ground tore at her heart, especially since they couldn't reach him yet, but he was alive, and conscious.

'She's slowing down, she knows she's cornered,' Arno told her as the villagers closed in, still holding their arms high, fearlessly. 'We'll go in, together, do what I do,' he said, eyes darting past her to the Jeep. 'We need to get him to the vehicle. It's the safest place. We need to put an object between us...'

'OK,' she heard herself say, looking around for something and spotting the pole at the same time. She followed his lead, picked up the other end of the fallen pole, and together they walked as one giant barrier slowly towards Alma.

'That's it, slowly, you got this,' he encouraged her as they heaved the pole up together. It was the strangest, not to mention heaviest object she'd ever approached an emergency scene with, but an otherworldly strength seemed to possess her as they took slow but purposeful strides as one, towards the creature and her unfortunate victim.

As if sensing she was well and truly cornered now, Alma lowered to her fat, wrinkly knees in front of them. With one final trumpet she swept the floor with her trunk, and blew a shower of sand up around them, followed by a cascade of mud from a puddle on the ground, where a bucket had been spilled. Both Kaya and Arno were covered instantly.

A man appeared then with a tranquilliser dart...too little, too late, Kaya thought, struggling to hold the pole, as hot, wet mud trickled down her forehead into her eyes.

'Don't shoot!' Arno was adamant, blinking mud from his

own eyes. 'She's fine, this man is not her keeper, he was standing in, she must have just got spooked,' he explained, inching closer, and motioning for her to lower the pole. It hit the dirt with a thud and she finally ran for the Jeep, swiping at her face.

Crouching with the medical-aid kit, she helped Arno roll the man onto his back. He was conscious, but badly wounded. 'How far was he dragged?' she asked incredulously as the elephant seemed to sigh close by and put her head to the ground.

'Not so far, but she may have stood on his leg,' Arno observed, frowning at the flesh wound, the fragments of bone emerging from below his left knee. 'This is beyond us, Kaya,' he said grimly. 'He'll need to be airlifted out of here.'

He readied a tourniquet and she bandaged it as best she could while he radioed for help. A crowd of villagers had gathered around the elephant now. One bearded old man was bravely trying to get her up, to lead her away, while Kaya and Arno helped their survivor to the Jeep. The air ambulance would fly in from Cape Town, and as the seconds ticked past their patient groaned and clutched her hand, and insisted it wasn't the elephant's fault.

'He'll be OK,' Arno assured her, placing a hand on her arm gently. 'Will *you*?'

'I already am,' she said, searching his warm eyes. A moment passed…something realigned inside her like a shift between tectonic plates. Then Arno removed his hand, way too quickly, as if she were lava that might burn him.

Her fault, of course.

Kaya swallowed the annoyance at the way she'd inadvertently shunned him and, worse, made him think she was some little weak thing with issues, when clearly she'd just found the strength, somehow, to face off an elephant. All she'd felt at that touch was warmth, and a strange kind of certainty she wasn't used to: that not every man had the potential to hurt her. Some only had her best interests at heart.

Several women and children were crying, and, through the whirlwind of activity, Kaya noticed how Arno was nothing short of a hero, comforting their patient with her, consoling the poor man's wife when she arrived on the scene, ensuring that no harm would come to the spooked elephant.

Maybe she should've just told him what had happened to her back in Amsterdam, when she'd had the chance this morning. He wasn't the kind of man to dismiss her as an unsuitable employee because of it. He was a good person. The fact that something deep in her gut was thawing and learning to thrive again—albeit slowly—was giving her a spring to her step she'd thought she'd never have again, and he was partly the cause.

It hit her then, as the helicopter flew into view, that she hadn't told him anything because it wasn't just her professionalism she was afraid he might question. What Arno thought about *her* was starting to matter.

Her unfortunate crush was growing bigger by the minute, and that would have to be nipped in the bud. He was quite a few years older than her, she reminded herself, watching him lift his muddy shirt up over his head, revealing a body so muscled and toned she had to do a double take, then force her eyes away from his rippling abs. Sadly, he replaced his shirt with another from the Jeep, and went to address the paramedics.

They came from different worlds, she thought, packing up the equipment, rinsing her hands off with bottled water, glancing his way, catching him catching *her* watching him—again.

This is ridiculous.

He was not some saviour sent to sweep her up and fix her.

And even if he *was* attracted to her too, she was no good at relationships, or even hook-ups. Her instinctive reactions to being touched were so embarrassing she hadn't even *dared* to go on one date since Pieter had put a worse taste in her mouth than her perpetrator ever had, going behind her back with someone else—someone she knew, no less. What if he realised her ability to be intimate—in that way—was broken, and left her...?

Climbing back into the Jeep, her thoughts a mile a minute, Kaya realised with dismay that the garden plot would need to be entirely redone, and that *she* had no clean clothes to change into at all. She was absolutely caked head to toe in mud, and it was at least an hour's drive back to Thabisa.

CHAPTER SEVEN

ARNO SWIPED THE mud from his face as he drove back to the main road. The events of the last hour had put him on an adrenaline high, but now he was coming back down to earth and he saw only one option. He had no time to take Kaya to Thabisa before heading back to the estate to help his mama. She would have to come with him.

When he asked if she minded, she looked horrified. 'Like *this*?' She gestured to her filthy clothes and pulled the visor down, swiping another streak from her neck in the mirror. He couldn't help smiling. She looked kind of adorable, even now that she was covered in mud.

He should offer to hurry up in the house while she stayed in the Jeep, but no…that would definitely not be the right thing to do, he mused. She was his responsibility. She'd just risked her life in the face of an angry elephant, and he was doubting whether to let her use his mother's bathroom?

What is wrong with you, Arno?

'You can take a quick shower while I help Mama with the sideboard,' he told her, before he could even think. What would be the harm in that anyway? She wouldn't even see the blackened walls, or spend longer than three minutes with his mother, there would be no time for her to find out what an irresponsible son he really was… They'd be in and out, back on the road before it got dark.

Kaya's eyes grew wide as he swept the dirty Jeep through the gates of the Nkosi Valley Wine Estate. Nestled in the picturesque Blaauwklippen Valley, it was a highlight of Stellenbosch, even now, even though several areas hadn't ever been rebuilt after the fire.

'It's so beautiful,' Kaya enthused, taking in the sweeping rows of vines as far as the eye could see, framed by the mountains in the late afternoon sun. The yellow stone villa up ahead put a lump in his throat, but he forced indifference about bringing her here. She wasn't to know he hadn't let anyone here in a long time, for the one selfish reason that they might learn something awful about him as Bea had.

'Our ancestors had the vineyards planted on the slopes of the Helderberg Mountain, where the breeze comes in over the ocean,' he found himself saying, slowing down so she could take in the views. This would be the one time she'd see it, he supposed. 'The breeze helps add the freshness to the wines,' he continued, surprised at the tour-guide tone he was taking; it was just that she looked so enchanted.

'We used to have a cellar door, so people on tours would stop in and try the wines, have a meal at the restaurant...'

'There's a restaurant here? Ooh, what kind of food?'

Arno bit his cheek. 'Well, it hasn't been open for twenty years now.'

'Why not?'

Arno paused, pulling the Jeep to a stop. Here they came: the questions. Thankfully Mama was already sweeping down the front steps, dressed in her orange kaftan, covered in paint splotches as usual. She lunged for a hug the second he stepped onto the gravel.

'So wonderful to see you, my baby,' she swooned, pressing a palm to his cheek, making Kaya raise her eyebrows at him on the other side of the Jeep. 'I saw you from the studio.

It's good of you to come help. You know your father doesn't trust me not to give that old sideboard away for less than it's worth. He's probably right, it's just in the way...'

As she chattered on about the chore he was here to do, he found himself noticing a few more lines around Mama's eyes, a couple of new wrinkles around her mouth. A paintbrush protruded through her mass of thick, greying hair, where she'd stuck it behind her ear.

'You have more paint on you than we do mud,' he announced, clearing his throat, looking around for his father, even though he knew he wasn't there. He hated how being here made the guilt flare up ten thousand-fold, and that he couldn't seem to talk to Mama at all about it in case it *was* justified.

Mama only then seemed to realise they were filthy dirty. 'Goodness, you're right, what happened to you two?'

'We had a little brush with an elephant,' Kaya told her, holding out her hand. 'I'm Kaya.'

Arno winced. 'Sorry, sorry, Kaya, the inimitable Mama Annika Nkosi.' How embarrassing that he hadn't introduced her first; it wasn't as if he ever brought people home though, he was out of practice. He watched the women shake hands, the way Mama looked at her with her own special warmth, feeling the knot in his stomach tighten.

'I said she could take a quick shower, if that's OK?'

'Of course, go right ahead,' Mama said, ushering them both up the stairs to the veranda, and into the hallway. Kaya's eyes went to the family photos on the walls that stretched all the way up the staircase. Generations of Nkosis, who'd made the winery what it was.

'I'm making some tea, you'll have some first,' she announced, motioning them through to the kitchen.

'Oh, we don't have much time, we're just going to wait for

your man, he's due any minute, right?' Arno went to usher Kaya towards the bathroom instead. But she was already staring at the blackened walls around the barricaded kitchen door, which had once led into their beautiful restaurant.

They'd had the bedroom where his mother had been that night completely renovated. Even the restaurant walls had been reconstructed. On the outside it was good as new, but inside... His mother had insisted they leave the fire-licked bricks on show around the barricades to remind them to stay humble, to be aware that life could change in a heartbeat, and to always be grateful. She said she saw it like a piece of art.

'What's that?' Kaya said, wrinkling her nose quizzically at the bricks before he could even get her back to the door. 'Did there used to be a fireplace there?'

'That's where the restaurant was,' his mother said, pondering the wall with her now, twiddling a strand of her long, grey hair around the paintbrush behind her ear.

'Oh, right, Arno said it hasn't been open for a while?'

Arno felt his heart change gears in his chest. 'We'll take our tea to go, Mama. The bathroom is through there.' He pointed to the arched alcove across the terracotta floor, resisting the urge to put a hand to Kaya's mud-splattered back and guide her there even faster. 'Towels are in the cupboard; use anything you like.'

She shot him a look of mild annoyance mixed with confusion, but he plastered a smile to his face, just as his mother offered to get her some clean clothes.

'I can change when we get back,' Kaya started, embarrassed.

'Nonsense, you can't get back into dirty clothes, it's no trouble.'

Kaya nodded, seemingly unsure what to think, just as he was.

'She seems nice. One of your volunteers?' Mama said, turning to him with a choice of teas when Kaya was safely in the terracotta-tiled bathroom.

'She is,' he replied, picking out a rosehip tea he thought Kaya would like, and a mint one for himself, then letting himself sink into a wooden chair at the dining table. He fiddled with the wax on a melted candle, letting his eyes wander back to the kitchen wall. Sometimes he thought about painting over it, or having new bricks installed over the hotch-potch of wooden planks across the old doorway, so he wouldn't have to look at it. But that would be selfish. Mama had the right to remember things how she wanted.

He twitched again, remembering the plaque he'd designed but still hadn't had made. *Remembering Baby Kung.* That was what it said. He wanted it to go on this very wall...one day. He'd never got round to it, in case it brought back all the hurt. For all of them.

'Should we move the sideboard outside so your man can collect it easier when he gets here?' he said now, standing up before any more uncomfortable memories could wriggle back into his brain.

'Sure, but first let me grab some clothes. Your Kaya girl has a wicked figure, I have the perfect thing I want her to try on.'

'Mama, you really don't have to...'

His protest fell on deaf ears. His mother was already half-way out of the door.

When Kaya emerged fresh and clean from the bathroom, Arno and his mother were outside. Through the wide arched windows overlooking the sweeping vineyards and majestic mountains, she spotted Arno talking with a tall man, who seemed to be hosing down the Jeep. Mama Annika was on the phone.

Kaya couldn't resist a sneaky look around the lower level of the house. She'd never been to a winery before. This was in fact the hugest house she'd ever stepped foot in, though the charred-looking walls were a little strange. She wandered over, stroked a finger over the bricks, only to find soot on her fingertips. There must have been a fire at some point. Was *that* why they closed the restaurant? Arno seemed kind of… what was the word he'd used with her…*tetchy* about something, now that they were here.

She was still frowning at her fingertips when Arno strode back in, looking more than a little disgruntled. 'He can't come and get the sideboard till the morning now,' he grumbled as she wiped her hands quickly behind her back. 'Something about getting side-tracked by…'

He tailed off when he saw what she was wearing. Mama Annika had left her something pretty unexpected outside the bathroom door. Kaya literally saw his eyes wander from the scooped neckline of the chic olive-green dress, to the nipped in waist, right down to the hem just above her knees, and back up again to her still-damp hair.

Self-consciousness sent her questions about the closed-off restaurant rushing from her brain in a poof. She flushed in his stare. Usually, under this much scrutiny from a man, she'd want to run a mile, yet his eagle-like attention sent a shower of sparks right through her.

'You look…different,' he said, as if trying to fathom how there was someone mildly attractive under the mud, and the uniform tees she usually wore in his presence. She bit back a smile.

'Different, good?' she dared, surprising herself. Was she *flirting*?

He cleared his throat, picked up a flowery teacup quickly from the table and handed it over. 'Before it gets cold,' he said, just as Mama Annika walked back in and gave a rather more enthusiastic reaction.

'Oh, my sweet child, how good does that look on you?' she cried, practically dancing over and forcing her to take a spin on the spot. Her tea almost went flying. 'I had a feeling it would, I'm far too big for it these days. You keep it, it suits you, doesn't it, Arno? Doesn't she look amazing?'

Arno bobbed his head and mumbled his agreement, looking as if he wanted to run away. His mother seemed oblivious to her son's embarrassment. 'Now, I suppose Arno told you the sideboard can't be collected till seven a.m. tomorrow? You might as well stay for dinner, seeing as you're here now.' She beamed at her, clapped her hands together. 'Stay the night?'

Arno sprang from the chair. 'No, no, Mama, we really have to be going...'

'And drive all the way back here for me, first thing in the morning?' she tutted. 'Don't be ridiculous. I'll have the guest rooms made up, you can drive back right after he collects the sideboard in the morning, what's the harm? You can show Kaya the vines...and the tasting room, and the memorial.'

Memorial?

Mama Annika pottered over to the fridge, spouting delicious local food items she would prepare for them, and Kaya was amused at the way Arno looked completely mortified for a moment. It was almost as if he thought this was the biggest inconvenience on earth. It really wasn't that much of a big deal, and she told him so, taking a seat at the rustic farmhouse table with her tea. It seemed as if his mother liked having him around, and she'd never spent the night on a vineyard before.

He didn't seem keen on her being here with him though.

He probably thought this whole thing was turning into something completely unprofessional and weird. He simply couldn't say no to his mother; that was the only reason they were both still here.

But she hadn't been made to feel quite this sexy in a long time, nor confused about her feelings for someone. It was all new and suddenly quite exciting. Maybe she wasn't entirely broken, she thought as he sloped past her to take a shower, catching her eyes again and sending a flock of butterflies straight to her stomach. Maybe she'd just needed a real crush this whole time to bring her back to life. She'd taken Pieter's words to heart: 'frigid', 'cold'. She'd let them burn her, let them force an iron cage around her heart when she'd labelled herself undesirable and undeserving of love long before he ever did.

The shell was coming away, slowly, every second she found herself attracted to Arno. She was melting, she realised. This man was enforcing a kind of slow defrost and her crush was bringing her in from the cold.

But a crush was all it could be—Arno Nkosi was entirely off limits. He might as well wear a giant sign reading 'Do Not Touch'.

Kaya sighed, picturing the way the water must be sliding down his body in the shower. Then she recalled how quickly he'd pulled away from her, when he'd asked if she was OK earlier. Right when she could have sworn they'd been having a moment.

She still hadn't explained to him why she'd shut down on him a few times already; why it was hard for her to let anyone physically close to her, particularly men. It wasn't as if she'd spoken about the effects of the assault to anyone, not after Pieter cheated. It was all too humiliating.

But at least if she told Arno *something* about the attack,

he'd know it wasn't really *him* she was wary of. At least he'd know she didn't mean to insult his kindness.

The thought of having such a conversation sent chills through her bones, even in the warm kitchen.

CHAPTER EIGHT

ARNO'S PHONE RANG halfway through dinner—a contact at the hospital who found them after he'd told Thabisa they wouldn't be back. Their elephant survivor was doing fine post-surgery. He'd broken his leg and sprained a wrist but, other than shock, he'd been pretty lucky. Taking his seat again, Arno noticed his mother had moved away from the conversation he'd been trying to keep on the Lindiwe Health Foundation and Kaya's vegetable garden plans, and started asking Kaya about life in Holland.

'It's as you'd expect, pretty busy. I spent most of the time in the hospital with my work.'

'Don't people cycle everywhere? Is the cheese as good as they say?'

The questions kept coming, and while Arno was indeed intrigued to know more about her and her life, which she always seemed to keep close to her chest, he couldn't ignore that Kaya was clearly feeling less than comfortable in the spotlight.

Before long, he had her out on the veranda around the firepit, while his mother thankfully took a phone call from an old friend inside. The tension rose between them the second they were alone. He'd wondered if it would. Something seemed to have changed today and he didn't know if it was because of what happened in the village with the elephant, or

because she was here…at his family home…in that dress…
but he didn't quite know what to do with it.

'So, your mother mentioned a memorial somewhere?' she
said now, pulling the woollen blanket he'd given her tighter
around her shoulders. The moonlight played in her hair and
danced across her cheekbones and he wondered what her
lips would be like to kiss, even as his stomach clenched at
her words. He tossed another chunk of wood onto the firepit.
He'd been hoping she'd forgotten that.

'Is that, like, for a dog you had once? A cat? I know you
love your animals.'

He huffed a laugh. 'It's not for any animals,' he said.
'Mama had it built for…some people who died.'

'Here?' Kaya pulled a face and glanced out at the vines, as
if a ghost might suddenly pop up between the bunches of Sauvignon Blanc. He nodded, his heartbeat ratcheting up a notch.

'They didn't die in a fire, did they?' she said, frowning
at him over the flames now. 'Arno, what happened here?'

Arno sank to his haunches prodding the flames again, as
if he could get some tiny revenge on the element that had ruined the place; and would probably ruin what Kaya thought
about him, too, if he told her everything. She'd seen the walls,
heard about the restaurant, she'd put the pieces together.

Standing up, he beckoned her with him around the house,
down the now-dark pathway between the vines. She looked
a little nervous when he turned to check on her, and again
he had to force himself not to reach for her hand. 'It's OK.
Trust me,' he said.

'I do,' she replied, and the moonlight in her eyes as she
searched his threw him off track for a moment. Was it the
adrenaline, making him want to kiss her? The fact that
he'd never brought anyone out here? The last thing he'd ex-

pected when they left Thabisa this morning was this. But
here they were.

'What are you going to show me?' she asked, continuing
on with him towards the barn where the barrels were stacked
and the old bottles were gathering dust, and the new ones
still lured the tourists *and* the locals in for tastings. He slid
the giant door across, blinked with her into the blacked-out
abyss, breathed the familiar smell of tannins and oak, and
flipped the light switch.

Even without the restaurant, which used to be the un-
equivocal best restaurant around for miles, people still came
to Nkosi Valley. Mostly these days, they just wanted to see
the memorial.

'This is incredible!'

Kaya looped around the towering structure again, trying
to soak in the entirety of the spectacle she was looking at.
This was nothing short of a work of art. Framed photographs
of three people stood out in the tree-like tower, surrounded
by colourful trinkets that were all made from items related
to wine. Bottles, screw tops, a halo made from corks...

'Did your mama make this?' she asked, studying the photos. Each one had a name under it, fashioned from yet more
trinkets, coins and jewels. Marios, Anaya and Zen.

Arno, who'd said nothing up to now, walked up behind
her and folded his arms slightly awkwardly and told her yes,
it had all taken Mama Annika a year.

The memorial was at least eight feet high, stretching almost to the wooden beamed ceiling of the barn. Behind them,
rows and rows of barrels, shelves stacked with wine right up
to the rafters and a small circular bar with high stools around
it told her this was the heart of the estate. Or used to be.

'There was a fire,' Arno said now, pressing his hands into

his pockets. 'Twenty years ago. I was eighteen years old when it happened. These people worked for us.' He bobbed his head at the photos. 'They lost their lives that night.'

'I'm so sorry.' Kaya's heart had dropped to the pit of her stomach at the look on his face. 'That's how come the restaurant is closed…' she said.

'That's where the fire broke out. They mention reopening it every few years or so, but I think they're secretly afraid it would never be as good as it was. Restaurateurs are proud people, prouder of fixing people up than doctors are—that's what Mama said once.'

'Were you here when it happened?' she asked, resisting the urge to put a hand on his shoulder suddenly at his wry smile, realising she hadn't wanted to offer a man any form of comfort for anything in years; not till now, in this very moment.

'I wasn't home when it started,' he said tightly, avoiding her eyes. 'I should have been, but I wasn't.'

'Well, maybe you got lucky,' she offered, and he scowled darkly at the structure, scuffed up a fallen cork from the floor and strode past her to the bar.

'I should have been here. I was meant to get Mama up from her nap to eat. If I'd done that, then maybe we both would've smelled the fire next door sooner, before it spread.'

Kaya watched as he lifted a latch and stepped into the circular bar, closing it behind him.

'I got home to find it out of control. Mama somehow slept through it. I just managed to get her out. Marios, Anaya and Zen—the chef—were in the restaurant, trying to stop it spreading to the house; they were so dedicated to saving this place, they neglected to save themselves.'

'Arno… This is…' Kaya swallowed, trying to digest his words. What a tragedy! To think of what he, and all these people, must have gone through.

He reached for two wine glasses from the rack above him and she studied his movements, almost afraid to ask. But she had to.

'Where were you? That night.'

He sniffed. 'Out with friends. Drinking.'

She bit her cheeks and crossed to the bar, took a stool and watched him pour from a bottle. It wasn't wine. He hadn't drunk since he was eighteen, she remembered now. It must have been that night that put him off.

He pushed a glass towards her. 'Non-alcoholic,' he confirmed, resting an arm across the bar, putting the snake tattoo right in front of her face as he twirled his own glass and studied the pale yellow liquid inside. 'Nkosi Grape Elixir is one of our bestsellers.'

Kaya took a sip but she barely tasted it. His proximity and the severity of his words had left her in shock.

'I'm sure your family will want to reopen the restaurant one day. It has been twenty years,' she pressed.

Arno shrugged, chugging the grape juice back, then running his eyes over her mouth as she finally tasted it for herself. It was delicious, smooth, slightly tart…but she was more aware of how his eyes on her mouth had sent a little drummer boy right back into her chest.

'I can't help feeling responsible, you know,' he said, scanning her eyes now, as if he was looking for her to confirm that he might have been to blame.

'Why? You didn't start the fire,' she said.

'No, but, like I said, I might have been able to stop it. We lost the harvest that year, flames took out a whole pasture and the ash ruined the rest. The media were everywhere. I couldn't get away from their questions, especially after Mama lost…' He pulled back suddenly, swiped their glasses and turned his back to run them under the tap.

'Mama lost what?'

'Nothing,' he said quickly. 'I mean, everything, she lost everything. It felt like it anyway. Losing three staff members, seeing others injured... I guess that's what got me into medicine. I knew I had to help, do whatever I could, you know.'

'So that's how you started out with the foundation.'

'And I'll never go back.' He smirked then. 'You can't run a winery if you don't drink. You're not exactly a credible cheerleader for your stock when all you can rave about is the grape juice.'

Kaya didn't know what to say. What could she say?

'I'm so sorry you and your family went through all that, Arno,' she managed.

She didn't even know where she'd found the strength suddenly. Maybe it was hearing him share something so deeply personal, letting her see this remorseful, vulnerable side to him that she'd never seen before, but the words were coming out of her mouth before she could really think.

'While we're sharing the things that might or might not still affect us, something pretty bad *did* happen to me, too,' she said. 'I brushed you off when you asked before, because it's kind of...well, I didn't want you to think me unprofessional, or unsuitable for this job.'

Arno pressed a hand over hers, on top of the bar, sending a current up her entire arm. His warmth and the protective gesture flooded her senses, and as he went to pull his hand away again, she caught it in her own, held onto him. His eyes searched hers and she tried to pinpoint his expression. Sadness, empathy, anger on her behalf. It was all there, so clear it made her mind go blank for a second.

'I knew it,' he said, looking down at their hands. Kaya was suddenly glad the bar top was between them, or else she might have gone one step further and thrown her arms around him. He wasn't to know but, to her, initiating a continued touch like this was like leaping over a giant wall. 'What happened?' he asked her gently.

She took a deep breath. She hadn't spoken about it to anyone who wasn't in her immediate circle, let alone a man she barely knew. But Arno was different; someone she could trust implicitly. He'd been through pain as great as hers, and pain was a stronger bonding glue than anything.

'I was in a park in Amsterdam, late at night. A man came at me out of nowhere,' she said, and Arno's other hand came down over hers, clamping them together while she caught her breath.

'He threw me off my bike onto the ground, dragged me into the bushes. I thought he was going to kill me.' She swallowed, realising her hands had started to sweat and her voice was shaking. 'He tried to…he would have…he got into my underwear.'

'Kaya!' The rage on his face sent her pulse through the roof; he looked furious now, and she was struggling to maintain her composure.

'I managed to kick him off me,' she said. 'Some guys heard me shouting. They pulled up on their bikes and he got spooked and ran off. I never even saw his face. The police did nothing. They said there was nothing they could do.'

'It wasn't on camera?'

'There weren't any cameras in the park.'

His brow creased and he sucked in a breath through his nose and did not let go of her hands. They were silent for a moment. Then he finally lifted the latch and stepped out from the bar.

'That explains why you don't like to be touched,' he observed, stopping an inch from her shoes. Her hands were still hot from having his palms over them and strangely, she wanted him close again. She *wanted* his touch.

'Not usually,' she admitted, meeting his eyes again. She considered continuing, telling him what Pieter had said, how his words and actions had forced her further into her shell and left her with a fear of rejection so profound she'd never even considered dating again, till now.

Then again, Arno didn't need to know any of that. Pieter was the past, she was as much to blame for letting him get to her for so long, and this was…something different.

Arno stepped closer suddenly, as if testing her. He reached for both her hands, slowly and deliberately. 'Is this OK?' he said softly, turning her hands over in his as if they were precious, fragile items. Kaya felt another chunk of the glacier around her heart melt away.

'It's OK.' She gulped, thanking the heavens that he couldn't see into her brain. Suddenly, she'd never wanted a moment to last longer than this one, right now. It felt as if they were sharing something more than just the struggles they'd both encountered up till now. Her senses had never been so attuned to the movements of one person.

When he reached out to sweep a strand of hair from her forehead, the look in his eyes was so intense, so utterly surreal, it sent a jolt of fear through her like lightning. This was something big already. To her. It was something that could go very, very wrong, and potentially destroy her.

'We can't…' she muttered, pulling away quickly, leaving his hand in mid-air and turning to the barn door. 'I'm really tired…'

Within five minutes she'd shut herself in a guest room, where she lay awake for hours, wondering what on earth was happening to her.

* * *

As the weeks went past after that, Kaya did her best to maintain her professionalism around Arno, to tell her heart not to race in his presence. Just because they'd shared a few moments together, and he'd managed to crack a hole in the frosty cage she called her heart, it did not mean she could start obsessing over some potential fling.

This was a *temporary* position, a chance to feel alive, and useful and, OK, fine, maybe a little desirable every now and then after years of telling herself she could never feel that way again…but she was not here to put her heart in harm's way.

Arno was everything she didn't need to be all caught up in, and he was clearly still working through his own troubled past. It was so awful, what happened to those three people. He must think about it all the time.

Definitely better not to get any more personal, she told herself, about a thousand times.

However, the more she stayed away from Arno, the more he seemed to stay away from her, and before long, she barely had a thought left for the past. Confusion and frustration over her mounting attraction were occupying every neuron in her brain.

CHAPTER NINE

THE DAYS WERE flying by lately, things were so busy. From his set-up outside Betsy, the mobile clinic, Arno sneaked another glance at Kaya. She was looking particularly lovely today with her hair piled high on the top of her head, doing her kind, smiling thing for every single patient approaching her. But then, he thought she looked lovely every day, even in her blue shirts, as opposed to the olive-green dress Mama Annika had put her in that night.

She was a knockout.

He forced his eyes back to his patient's newly bandaged knee, right as Kaya caught him looking at her. Picturing her in and out of that dress had kept him up at night lately, as much as all the stuff they'd shared that night in the barn. He wished he didn't have to keep imagining her naked—she was not deserving of that, and she certainly wouldn't welcome it, maybe not from anyone, not after...what she'd been through.

She was walking over now, the afternoon sun in her hair. He pretended not to notice till she was literally standing behind his patient, in front of him.

'Sorry to interrupt, Arno, we're missing a box of leaflets for the presentation,' she said.

They were presenting together after this round at a rural primary school, part of his wider plan to have the foundation empower communities to act together with health, education and other social services like theirs. It wasn't like him to forget the handouts. Then again, he'd been pretty distracted lately, having Kaya around, knowing she knew what happened with the fire.

Did she know the rest?

It wouldn't be hard to find out about his dead baby brother. The media had lapped it up. All she'd have to do was search the Internet. She'd wonder why he didn't tell her that part.

'Arno?'

She was tapping her wrist now, and he realised his head was full of her, whether she was standing in front of him or not.

He dismissed his thankful patient, who hobbled away, grateful for the freshest bandage he'd had in a week. 'I'll go look in the back,' he said, annoyed with himself.

'I already looked,' she told him, stepping up into the vehicle behind him.

Alone in the mobile clinic, the walls closed in immediately. They didn't speak as they rifled through boxes, but the air was thick and the silence was loaded. Usually there would be other volunteers around, but Kimberley was sick with a stomach bug, and because of the presentation later, which Kaya had prepared for the school closest to this community, it had been the best thing for he and Kaya to kill two birds with one stone.

How could he deny his attraction to her? It was real, and affecting him daily, even if there was nothing he could do about it. She was no doubt several years his junior *and* she lived in the Netherlands, and she'd pulled away from him more times than he could count—not that he could blame her!

He was still kicking himself for the way he'd gone too far, reaching for her face like that, acting on the urge to be closer. Especially after what she'd told him about being assaulted—

that was a stupid move. Besides, he didn't mess with volunteers. He just…didn't. Whatever their age, or background, or how unnervingly beautiful and captivating they were, it was just a bad idea, mixing business with pleasure…wasn't it?

Now he wasn't so sure.

Maybe he'd let Bea mess him up more than he'd thought. Bea hadn't been a volunteer, but she was an exceptional woman he'd poured his heart out to, who'd deemed him unworthy and disappeared. Not a great feeling.

Ever since that night around the memorial, they'd both kept their distance. Only the occasional eye contact and blush on her cheeks told him she was feeling the same as him…as if they'd hovered on some dangerous precipice together and didn't know what to do next.

'I don't see the leaflets. We must have left them at base,' he told her now, accidentally brushing her arm as he moved another box. 'Sorry,' he said, flustered at her proximity after all these weeks.

'Sorry for what?' she said, a frown darkening her face. He shrugged, held up his hands, and she cast her eyes to the ceiling. 'I'm not some precious little broken flower, you know, Arno. Just because I told you what I told you doesn't mean…' She huffed back her next words, mumbling to herself as she opened another box too roughly.

'Woah,' he said, catching her arm this time. 'What's going on?'

She blinked at him. 'I shouldn't have told you what I told you, that night in the barn.'

'Why not?'

She scowled into the box, scrubbed a hand across her head. 'You've hardly said one word to me since. It's like, you're looking at me differently, and that's the last thing I wanted…'

'Kaya.' He stared at her, stunned. 'You haven't spoken to

me either,' he said. 'I thought I'd messed up. I thought I'd crossed some line with you I shouldn't have crossed. I was trying to be respectful.'

Arno's head was spinning now.

'Well…' She chewed on her lip, hands on hips, then blew out a sigh. 'I thought maybe *I'd* crossed a line by telling you what happened to me. It's not your burden to carry, you have enough going on, all by yourself. I wasn't trying to over-shadow what happened to your family and your friends in the fire.'

'I didn't think you were,' he said. 'It's not a competition, who's been dealt the worst hand. We were both just…being honest.'

Arno turned away before her eyes could probe him any further. *He* hadn't been entirely honest, purposefully omit-ting the part about Mama Annika being pregnant when the fire broke out.

Sure, he'd chickened out on telling Kaya the whole truth, completely negated to mention what a monumental error he'd *really* made, not being home that night with Mama, but he couldn't bear it if she started looking at *him* differently as Bea had. Being able to trust people was everything to Kaya.

'And for the record,' he added, feeling his fist clench at his side, 'I don't look at you any differently because of what you told me. Why the hell would I? If I'd known you when that happened to you, Kaya, I would've gone out with my rifle and knocked on every door in Amsterdam till I found who did that to you. And then…' He trailed off at the wide-eyed look of shock on her face, bit back the anger that was bub-bling up on her behalf. 'You don't even want to know what I'd have done then.'

Kaya was still staring at him in disbelief, the pile of boxes and missing leaflets forgotten. 'My boyfriend never said *any-thing* like that,' she told him quietly.

Boyfriend?

Arno gritted his teeth. How had he failed to imagine she might be in a relationship? Why did that suddenly matter?

'Dr Nkosi? We need you out here!' The voice that broke into the mobile unit was laced with urgency. Before he could ask her anything about her boyfriend, he was racing with Kaya back out into the heat.

Kaya squeezed the young woman's hand, then she and Arno lifted the stretcher into the mobile clinic, shutting the doors behind them. The last thing this poor girl—Lerato—needed was a thousand eyes on her.

'There's so much blood,' Lerato winced, lifting her soaked skirt and letting out a wail that pierced Kaya's heart and made Arno look even more determined than he had just now, telling her what he would've done to her attacker if he'd caught him. With a rifle.

She was still reeling from the severity of his words, even though she knew he'd have done nothing of the sort—he wasn't that crazy. But he did just admit to her that he cared, and that he'd been thinking about it, stewing on it, imagining what he'd have done if he'd been there.

'When did you start bleeding?' she asked Lerato, pushing the conversation that had just been interrupted from her head. This girl had to be no older than fifteen.

'Last night,' the girl managed, pressing a hand to her belly, then screaming out. Arno had to restrain her from wriggling off the stretcher in pain. 'I had really bad pain the last few days. Cramps, back ache. I thought it was normal. Then I saw the blood.'

Kaya spotted her bloated belly and caught Arno's eye. She

could tell he was thinking what she was: it was either appendicitis, or…she was pregnant.

So young, and pregnant?

Whatever it was, it was a miracle she was here. The poor girl had made her way to them unaccompanied. Apparently, a worried friend had told her that they were here. Five minutes later, and they might have already missed her. It didn't bear thinking about. Lerato looked disoriented now and complained that her shoulder was hurting worse than before. They studied her together under the lights. Arno's mouth was a grave, thin line.

'We'll have to check you,' Kaya explained, and the whole time they were helping her patiently through a blood and urine test she was hoping against hope that the girl *wasn't* pregnant. If she was, they couldn't give her much for the pain.

If she was, it might not have happened with her consent.

To Kaya's disappointment, the test was positive.

'She's so young,' she muttered to Arno over by the sink, and he shook his head, changing his gloves quickly without looking at her. He'd turned stone cold and silent, his concern for this girl mounting as much as hers, she assumed. The shoulder pain was a sign of internal bleeding…blood pooling in her abdomen. It was becoming evidently clear that Lerato was suffering a ruptured ectopic pregnancy. The baby inside her was already gone.

'Did you know you were pregnant?' she asked the tear-stained girl, helping Arno prepare the ultrasound.

'What?' The poor girl looked visibly shaken. 'No, no, no…'

Lerato was sniffling in both pain and what looked like confusion. The thought of how exactly she'd got pregnant so young was a whole other issue, but Arno was firing questions at her now, gently, kindly, in an effort to garner as much information as they could, while the girl crumbled in Kaya's arms and clung to her so tightly that Arno had to prise her off. The ultrasound confirmed she'd need surgery. Fifteen minutes later Arno was administering the anaesthesia.

The *beep-beep-beep* of the machines aligned with Kaya's own heartbeat. She was dutifully cool and collected on the surface, but the look on Arno's face told her this was serious, *and* that he wasn't impressed by whatever method this girl had come to be carrying a baby either.

'You'll feel better when you wake up,' Arno told the groggy girl gently, and while Kaya knew he was an expert, and had completed countless similar surgeries, she prayed he was right.

It was touch and go. With a ruptured fallopian tube, Lerato was losing a lot of blood. Kaya felt as if her own insides were being pulled taut as Arno announced what she was quickly realising herself: 'Blood transfusion.'

'I was hoping you wouldn't say that.'

'So was I.'

Kaya sprang into action, thanking the heavens that Arno had ensured the mobile facility carried blood-draw, laboratory, and blood-storage equipment and they wouldn't have to call an air ambulance again. The space was smaller than any OR she'd ever stepped foot in; she could see the village kids outside, pressing their faces to the windows.

At times like this the hospital she'd been so used to back home felt far too far away, but this mobile operating room was even equipped to perform laparoscopic surgery; it had tools and cameras, and now she was more grateful than ever that Arno's diligence towards bringing the newest, best equipment to their remote patients, along with their skills, was his top priority.

How many people were injured after that fire at Nkosi

Valley? she found herself wondering as they worked on the unfortunate unconscious girl. Arno, in blue scrubs, wore a look of iron indomitability, and looked visibly moved and even emotional as she cleaned the blood, and what was likely the unborn child.

It must take a lot to live through something like he had, she thought, and dedicate his life to saving lives as a result. Had he seen those three people who died in the restaurant, before it happened? Were they trying to get out? Had they died while he was trying to save them?

He must have seen so much, living out here. More than she ever had. Did it ever all get too much? At one point, she could have sworn she saw a damp tear slide from Arno's eye but she couldn't be sure. He was quick to swipe at his face and square his shoulders, and when he pulled off his gloves, leaving the girl to sleep off her anaesthesia, she asked him, 'Arno, are you OK?'

Kaya felt an unhindered urge to comfort him suddenly, and she didn't even quite know what for. He had an air about him now; something different. She could almost see his mind churning.

'I'm good,' he said bluntly, turning to wash his hands. She didn't believe him.

'I think we saved her,' she said, joining him at the sink, daring a sideways glance at his jawline as he pulled off his mask.

'I think so too.'

She frowned at the tap, scrubbing her hands. 'Have you... lost...many girls going through miscarriages here?' There had been articles and journals and statistics, of course, but now she wanted the truth from Arno's mouth; someone who'd been here for years, on the ground, witnessing it first-hand.

'Probably more than you've seen in the Netherlands, but

less since we got Betsy on the road.' He turned to her, yanking a paper towel from the dispenser, then seemingly without thinking wiped at something on her cheek with it. 'And since we started hiring people like you,' he added, while her mind spun.

Her hand flattened over his, across her cheek. She was more embarrassed by what must have splattered on her face than concerned by the fact that he was touching her. For a second she clean forgot where they were.

This time, he didn't apologise, and Kaya didn't flinch or move away. This felt so new, so strange. Some kind of change to her DNA took her breath away as she scanned the depths of his eyes. Another chunk of the glacier crumbled away.

'Looks like we may have to postpone the presentation,' he said then, busying himself with the radio, which was buzzing for their attention, no doubt confirming a place for Lerato's recovery in the nearest medical facility. 'We'll have to drive her to the hospital.'

'I don't want to leave her, anyway,' Kaya said, aware of how his touch had left her slightly breathless and flustered. Her hands shook as she pulled her hair from the bun and re-bundled it on top of her head. 'She came here alone, Arno. I need to find out her story. Young teenage girls don't just... Do you think she was...?'

The word left such a bad taste in her mouth that she couldn't get it out. As she turned to their patient, hooked to the IV, the memories of her own attacker were crashing back in now: the bulk of his body over hers on the cold mud, pinning her down, her whole life flashing before her eyes. The way she'd dragged herself home to Pieter, who'd forced her back out to the police station, where she'd been treated like just another statistic who'd been in the wrong place at the wrong time.

'I can't leave her till I know,' she whispered now, determination ebbing like an ever-expanding river through her bones. If she could help another victim find justice, or peace, or both, she'd do whatever it took.

'Breathe.' Arno put his hands to her shoulders, forcing her back to the moment. In spite of the tension between them, which was always there, no matter *what* the situation apparently, she found comfort instantly in his gaze, and she took a deep breath while he steadied her.

'I understand,' he said, tilting her chin. 'Kaya, we'll find out what happened, I promise.'

In that moment, she was overcome with relief that she'd told him what happened to her. He *did* understand why being here for this girl was important to her, and he was on her side.

CHAPTER TEN

FROM THE COLD plastic seats in the bleach-white waiting room, Arno watched Kaya taking in the modest clinic, which admittedly was only marginally better equipped than their vehicle, Betsy. Their young patient Lerato was stable, hooked to a new IV, in a bed of her own, but, of course, Kaya wouldn't leave until they'd spoken to a relative.

They'd been here two hours already. He was famished and exhausted, but no way was he leaving without her, and without knowing the girl would be OK. He kept sneaking glances at Kaya, aware of every time she adjusted her hair or twiddled her hands, trying not to look whenever she tapped at her phone. This was the first time they'd had a signal in a few days. Maybe she was texting her boyfriend.

He'd been trying—and failing—not to let that bother him. It'd been a long time since he'd experienced anything like jealousy and it didn't sit well. What would he have done with her anyway? Had a fling, before she disappeared from his life for ever? He snorted to himself. That was ridiculous. Kaya was so far off fling material it wasn't even funny. She was…special.

Maybe it was a good thing she wasn't single; it was getting harder to be around her without wanting to break every single rule he'd ever set for himself about making moves on volunteers.

Just then, the door blew open and a torpedo in the shape of a man, no older than seventeen or eighteen, came charging through. 'Where is she? Where's Lerato?' He looked as if he'd run a thousand miles; perspiration soaked his baseball hat and flapping shirt.

Kaya was on her feet in a heartbeat. Arno followed after her. 'How do you know Lerato?' she demanded, stopping in front of him so fast her shoes squeaked on the tiles.

'Where is she? Is she OK?' the guy urged her, putting his arms out to grab her in his desperation.

Kaya staggered backwards, just as Arno caught his forearms, holding him tightly away from her. 'It's OK,' he assured him, calmly, as Kaya composed herself at his side. 'No need to panic, Lerato is fine. Who are you?'

'I'm Navi, I'm her boyfriend!'

The commotion, now being witnessed by two doctors, a nurse and three other patients, seemed to have stirred the sleeping Lerato awake. She started calling his name. 'Navi! Navi, is that you?'

Navi pushed past them all and one of the doctors let him into the room. Kaya followed, peeking suspiciously through the glass door, and Arno's heartbeat regulated itself as it became pretty clear the two did indeed know each other.

'They're a couple,' Kaya whispered, nodding at the way Navi was cradling the now-crying Lerato, sitting at her bedside, swiping back tears. Lerato was gripping his shirt the way you only did if you never wanted someone to let go. Kaya wasn't even pretending to hide her relief that the pregnancy had been an accident involving two loved-up teens, and not some kind of violation, and he bit back a smile.

'Looks like they're pretty close,' he confirmed as another jolt of something like jealousy shook his senses—this time for the kind of love he'd never even got halfway close to having himself. He'd been too busy since Bea—telling himself he was too busy—but the truth was, he just didn't trust himself or his past not to mess it up.

Kaya was looking at him strangely now. He realised he'd been staring at her again, tracing the outline of her mouth with his eyes, lost in thought. Gosh, he was so tired, and all his bones ached, but they still had a pretty long drive.

'They are most definitely a committed boyfriend and girl-friend,' Kaya said. 'Even if they're far too young and prob-ably need a lesson on the dangers of unprotected sex.'

The dusty road stretched ahead of them as he steered towards Thabisa. Streaks from the hot, setting sun were starting to turn the sky into a coal pit of burning red embers above them. Eventually his growling stomach forced him to stop at a resting post that served them both grilled chicken, while Kaya talked about her plans for adding sexual-health aware-ness and sex education to her school presentations in future.

He nodded and murmured in the appropriate places, won-dering how much more she'd take on. The garden was al-ready a talking point—every community for miles that didn't have one already wanted to speed up planting one with the foundation's help.

He also couldn't help thinking she was filling every bit of silence on purpose, in case the awkward tension crept back in. In a way he was grateful she was taking the job off his hands. There hadn't ever been a volunteer he'd experienced this level of attraction to. Not only was it wholly inappropri-ate, but knowing she was taken added a whole other element to his predicament.

Back on the road, the silence enveloped them and, as pre-dicted, felt awkward. If she felt this attraction too, which he assumed she did, judging by her body language and the way she flushed red every time they locked eyes, or hands, she was probably feeling a little conflicted because of her boyfriend back home. Whoever he was. Lucky guy.

'Mud bath?' Kaya exclaimed suddenly, wrinkling her nose as they whizzed past the creaky old sign that marked the start of the old dirt track.

He smirked, stifling a yawn. 'Don't knock it till you've tried it.'

'Are you serious?'

Arno slowed the vehicle. The thought of a cool, relaxing mud bath right now was actually not a terrible one. 'It's good for your skin,' he said. 'Like a mineral mask. There are lots of them around. But only a few that aren't occupied by hippos.'

Kaya laughed; the first time he'd heard her laugh all day. In a moment of spontaneity he could only attribute to his exhaustion, he pulled a U-turn and rumbled the vehicle back towards the sign.

Since the time she'd been caught out and had to meet Arno's mother looking like a mud-splattered hurricane victim, Kaya had been careful to pack a change of clothes with her on every remote round.

She pulled out her spare bra and knickers now, glancing back at Arno from behind the scraggy bush, suddenly more self-aware than ever. He had to be the hottest creature to ever exist, and now he was pulling his shirt over his head, showing off those tight abs and slick stomach to absolutely no one intentionally, kicking out of his trousers, stepping into a pair of boxer shorts.

Oh, my God.

Kaya gasped as she caught a momentary glimpse of his round bare bum, whiter than white, like the moon against a sepia twilight. Committing it to memory for ever took less than a millisecond—it was without doubt the nicest bum to ever accidentally fall into her eyeline.

'Are you OK behind there?' he called now, yanking his bathing shorts up and turning around. Quickly she slid back behind the bush, hurrying on with her navy-blue underwear, glad it matched and wasn't too transparent, a giddy grin breaking out on her face. OK, so it wasn't a bikini, but was matching underwear better or worse? She must be totally exhausted and maybe a bit crazy after the heat and drama of the day, to agree to this.

Or maybe she was just besotted with a man she couldn't have? Clearly both. Why else would she have agreed to do something as potentially dangerous as taking a mud bath in the middle of nowhere?

'Are you sure there are no hippos?' she asked, stepping out into the clearing, still in her boots. She forced her arms not to hug her body out of Arno's view, and felt the wickedness seep further through her bloodstream till she was practically fizzing in his gaze. It felt good, actually, to be admired by him. Anyone else looking at her like...*this*...would probably have made her run a mile.

'Blue suits you,' he said now, without answering her question, and she watched his eyes rove like flashlights from her feet to her face. For just a moment, it looked as if he couldn't tear his eyes away. Thank goodness she'd kept up with her Pilates and kickboxing back in Amsterdam. It had all been an effort to keep her strong, and boost her confidence, but the results were evident in everything she wore...and didn't wear.

Was that a mild groan she heard from Arno's throat as he marched on ahead of her, telling her to stay close? She bit back another smile. Whatever was happening to her, it was definitely interesting. When was the last time she'd felt this alive?

'We're fenced in,' Arno explained, when he'd found his voice. 'The mud bath is part of the last village we passed. We're safe, trust me.'

Kaya studied his sculpted bare back and shoulders as he swiped at grass and branches ahead of her, and considered how the width equalled strength, and wondered if he'd carried anyone out of that fire he seemed to hate talking about so much. He'd only been eighteen. He carried them still, she thought—those people who lost their lives. He was troubled. Maybe that was why she was drawn to him, really.

Trouble invites trouble.

She'd been so determined not to feed her silly crush on him lately that she had perhaps come off a little cold herself since that night when they'd talked in the barn. No wonder he assumed he'd crossed a line and upset her.

Now that was behind them, thankfully, but the air was far from clear. You could slit it with an army knife the second things went quiet, which was why she'd done her best to make small talk about anything and everything till now—so much so that her throat was sore. It took a lot of effort to seem cool, when your heart was doing a tap dance.

'OK…time for your mud bath, milady,' he said from ahead of her, sweeping aside a final curtain of green foliage and beckoning her on past him.

His hand brushed the skin across her lower back as she crossed the threshold; the lightest, slightest touch intended only to guide her across the rough ground in her boots, but the skin-on-skin contact sent another bolt to her lady parts that she definitely had not been expecting. When was the last time a man touched her at all, while she'd been wearing so little? Arno would be shocked if he knew, no doubt about that. And she would be humiliated. Which was why she'd never, ever tell him.

'This is it?' she asked him, stopping just ahead of him. He walked up alongside her, studying the grey-brown pool of mud at their feet, surrounded by dust and dirt and fallen leaves and branches.

'This is it. It gets bigger after the rains,' he said, crouching down to the pool. It must be no more than six-foot squared, she thought, watching him scoop a handful of the gloopy substance into one palm and smear a little on one arm. How did he get all these muscles? she wondered as the late sun danced along the contours of his shoulder blades. There was a small gym at the resort, she supposed, and he did seem to wake up earlier than most people, most mornings. She knew because she'd seen him from time to time, going out to meet Tande, no doubt. Did he work out before or after that? What did he look like in gym gear? Maybe he did it shirtless. Maybe she should work out one morning and find out.

'Want some?' he asked her, interrupting her reverie.

Kaya blinked. 'That is why we're here,' she replied quickly as he stood, holding the mud in his hand between them. 'What do we do with it exactly?' she asked him, touching a finger to the squidgy goo.

'You cover yourself in it.' He smirked, as if she amused him. 'Like a hippo.'

'Are you calling me a hippo?' The flirtatious question slipped straight from her mouth as she bent and scooped some mud for herself, then flicked it at him.

'Hey!' Arno let out a laugh of surprise, which only set her off, too. A glob of sticky mud had landed straight on his neck, and no sooner had he smudged it in than he was flinging some back at her. Another giant glob landed right on her chest above her left breast and when she looked up, she realised he'd been watching her rub it in, smudging more mud across his own torso. Another spike of adrenaline tore through her.

The mini mud fight lasted less than a minute; it was hard to move when the stuff was sticking to her in every place she could imagine, but when a fresh glob trickled down her forehead and into her eyes, Arno stepped forward and reached a hand to her face; then, quick as a flash, pulled it back again, as if he was physically restraining himself from touching her.

Disappointment coursed through her veins. She turned her back, feeling his eyes on her as she covered her legs, one by one. *Look, but don't touch*—that was the vibe here. For both of them.

It wasn't as if she'd given Arno any reason to believe that the whole time she'd been actively keeping her distance from him, she'd been thinking about his hands in hers, and his arms around her, and just generally imagining what it would be like to sleep in a man's arms again—specifically his.

He'd been making her think all kinds of things lately, like how it would feel to actually trust someone implicitly after so long, knowing they only had her best interests at heart. Wouldn't it be nice to feel protected and safe with a man, instead of repulsed and/or terrified? It wasn't so hard to imagine all that whenever she looked at Arno... It felt as though another old demon got incinerated every time she laughed with him, or opened up, but he knew she was damaged. She'd told him about the attack and while it was nice knowing he'd been thinking about it, so much so that he'd imagined exacting some kind of bitter vengeance on her behalf, even if they weren't colleagues, with a certifiably big difference in age, he knew she wasn't someone he could ever really get close to. She didn't belong here, for a start.

Still…it might be high time to change the way people looked at her, she thought, and, come to think of it, the way she'd been looking at herself for far too long.

CHAPTER ELEVEN

THE MUD WAS cool relief across her skin, the more Kaya coated her arms, neck and stomach with it. Within minutes they were sitting side by side on the edge of the small pool, caked in the stuff like two happy hippos.

'Kaolinite, bentonite, magnesium, potassium, and all kinds of other stuff,' Arno explained, after she'd asked exactly what it was that was now crackling across her skin in the day's heat, still radiating off the ground. 'It gets rid of all impurities.'

She caught his eyes then, and he took a huge lungful of air and blew it out through his teeth at the sinking sun. 'Well, maybe not *all* impurities,' he added wryly.

Kaya's throat went tight. The air was thicker than the mud now. If she shuffled one centimetre closer to him, she could kiss him. She could actually feel his lips on hers, mud or no mud, if she wanted, if she dared…

She held her breath as he rested on his elbows next to her. Did he just imply that he was thinking impure thoughts about her? Or did she read that completely wrong? Hmmm. This wasn't something she was used to, exactly. Usually that kind of sexual objectification would send a storm of terror and horror and indignation raging round her skull and out of her mouth, but now she was kind of curious, and quietly turned on.

'I heard mud can also stimulate blood flow,' she said now, daring to study the trail of coarse, mud-coated hair down from his navel, straight into the waistline of his boxers as he kept his face turned to the sky.

'Affirmative,' he replied after a moment, glancing her way for a split second. She bit down on her lip, swallowed back her pounding heart from her throat.

'So, Kaya.' He folded his arms behind his head on the ground.

She braced herself.

'What does your boyfriend think about you being all the way out here? With me?'

'What?' Her heart skipped a beat, then started racing; where on earth did he get the impression she was in a relationship? The thought was almost laughable. She hugged her knees, the shock making her smile. 'I don't have a boyfriend!'

His eyebrows shot skywards. Then he turned to her, resting on one elbow, giving her his full attention. Behind him, three young kids hovered around a fence, as if they were contemplating interrupting them. For a second she prayed they would. The way Arno was looking at her now was so intense, almost as if he were probing her mind with his eyes.

'Why would you think that?' she followed carefully.

He drew a line in the mud between them with one finger, then looked up at her through his eyelashes. 'Back there, in the village, you said your boyfriend never went out and tried to find who did that to you, in the park.'

A deep frown cracked the mud around his forehead and she wondered how long he'd been stewing over this. A small thrill pierced through her reluctance to talk about it.

'I did have a boyfriend when it happened,' she admitted. 'What I meant was…well, it doesn't matter now, does it? It ended. Pieter ended things, about a year ago.'

Arno sat up next to her, mirrored her knee-hugging stance. 'Sorry,' he said. 'It's none of my business.'

'It's OK.' Kaya brushed at the hardened mud on her arms, watching the kids turn the other way and scramble back along a pathway, followed by a dog. What must they look like, sitting here like this? Suddenly she was all self-conscious again, solo in Arno's scrutiny. But she found herself talking anyway.

'Things weren't the same after the attack.' She sighed, fighting the urge to hide or run, as she always did. 'Pieter wanted me to act like I had before and I just…couldn't.'

'I get it,' Arno said, nodding darkly at the pond.

'It was like something froze in me. I didn't want him, or anyone to…'

'I get it,' he said again, and the gravity of his tone silenced her.

Did he? Did he really get it? She wasn't going to spell it out—that she hadn't been able to get intimate with her ex. Or that she'd moved in with her parents, or that Pieter went on to cheat on her with one of her friends from work.

Ugh, it had all made her feel so bad, as if she were less of a woman somehow. She'd carried that thought for three whole years, till now. Till someone had looked at her as Arno was looking at her now.

The sun was sinking like a melting ball of fire. Orange hues stained the sky and brought flecks of gold to his eyes. Now her crush had multiplied by a hundred thousand, and she was sure he could see it.

'I know what it's like to feel a bit broken,' he said after a moment. 'After the fire, things weren't the same with my parents. I felt like everyone was judging me.' He paused and Kaya's curiosity spiked as high as her heart rate. He hardly ever talked about the fire, or how it must have affected him.

'I felt like everyone was looking at me differently,' he continued.

'But why? The fire wasn't your fault,' she said, releasing her knees. 'How could you have stopped it, even if you had been there? Those other people tried, and they couldn't stop it.'

'I could have got Mama Annika out sooner,' he said. 'She was my responsibility. She was p—'

He shut his mouth, as if he'd suddenly said too much, then sighed through his teeth again, getting to his feet. 'We should wash this mud off and get back,' he said, holding a hand down to her.

Without thinking she took it, letting him pull her up, and suddenly they were face to face like two muddy monsters emerging from a swamp. Maybe it was the mud blocking every other feature on his face, but his eyes held more intensity, more bottled-up emotion than she'd ever seen, as they stood there, his hand still firmly in hers.

'Mama Annika was what?'

'The past is the past,' he interjected, as if he could possibly erase all the questions about *his* past that were spinning like a merry-go-round in her brain. 'What I meant to say was, I wish to hell that didn't have to happen to you, Kaya.'

One side of his mouth curved into a self-deprecating smile as he traced her mouth with his eyes. 'I shouldn't say this, but I'm also kind of glad you're single, too.'

Kaya was so shocked she let out a sound that was half gasp, half laugh, and turned her face to the ground. Thank goodness she was covered in mud, so he couldn't see her blushing.

'No, you shouldn't say things like that,' she agreed quietly, but she let him hold her hand the whole way back along the path to their vehicle, under the mutual guise of him leading the way. She even let him hose the mud off her back with the mobile unit's water supply and he did so slowly, carefully, as if it was his one main mission to have her emerge fresh, clean, his own personal achievement. She'd felt so wanted and desired, and so impossibly changed from the woman she'd been just a few weeks ago.

There was one moment, when she was washing the mud off his broad shoulders from behind, when time seemed to slow right down. It was only them, two normal, unbroken individuals enjoying the sensuous act of washing each other... right before he seemed to trip clumsily on the hosepipe and right himself, as if he was so distracted by her being there that he'd lost his balance.

It all made her feel seen, and attractive, and hopeful in a way she hadn't in ages. Damn this crush. OK, so he felt it too, clearly, but it wasn't as if either of them were in a position to do anything about it. He knew he shouldn't. He'd said it. *She* knew they shouldn't... They were here to work, not flirt.

Neither of them went any deeper than small talk on the drive back to Thabisa but her heart was like a wild zebra bucking in her chest, every single time Arno looked her way. She couldn't help the smiles breaking out on her face, and she didn't miss his either, no matter how much he might be trying to bite them back.

When they were finally back at the resort, the sun had set fully on the day and the volunteers eyed them in interest from their camping chairs around the fire pit. She was still fighting the urge to ask him more about the night of the fire; something told her there was more to it than him showing up drunk and too late. Something about Mama Annika that he'd been about to tell her and held back on. Maybe she should search online—he was bound to come up. But no, that didn't feel right. If he didn't want her to know something, he must have his reasons.

Besides, the Internet out here was terrible.

'Where have you two been all day?' the Australian lady, Kimberley, called out, urging her over. Kaya watched Arno slink away like a cat and fought not to let the disappointment overshadow her good mood as she took a seat. Someone was playing guitar. The others were chatting quietly.

'We had an emergency, in one of the villages. Arno had to operate,' she whispered, searching for him in the shadows.

Kimberley frowned at her suspiciously in the firelight. 'What's that on your cheek?' she asked suddenly. 'And in your hair!'

'Oh.' Kaya brought a hand to her face, touching a patch of crusty mud she'd clearly just missed in her haphazard flirt-fest back at the mud bath. Obviously it was still caked in her hair too—it wasn't as if they'd had shampoo.

'Did you fall in a river?'

'Not exactly. We went to a mud bath.'

'We?' Kimberley lowered her voice conspiratorially. 'You mean, Dr Nkosi took you for a spa treatment?'

'It was an outdoor mud bath,' she explained, compressing her lips and folding her arms over herself to cover any more unfortunate splatters that might have made it onto her clothing when she'd put it back on. 'As in, *natural*. It's not like we went to a *spa*.'

God, how did this look to the others? Not good, probably.

'Look at you, getting all the special treatment.' Kimberley bit her lip. 'Maybe I should ask if we can all go get a spa treatment tomorrow, huh?'

Kaya shuffled in her seat, wishing she'd just gone straight to her room and washed her hair, as Arno probably did. 'It wasn't like that, it was just there, on the way back.'

'It doesn't exactly sound part of the package.' Kimberley was only teasing her the way anyone would if they discovered their colleagues might be hooking up, but Kaya didn't miss the beer cans around the fire, the way Kimberley was loose in her seat now, as if she might swivel off it at any moment and fall. How long had they been drinking?

'What's going on?'

Kaya's stomach dropped as one of the guys got up from his chair and crossed to them, waving a beer can. Mark from Canterbury, a tall, lanky med student who wanted to be a dentist, was renowned for being the more vocal amongst the volunteers at the best of times. 'Did I hear something about you and Arno? Are the rumours true?'

Rumours? Kaya swallowed, getting up from her seat.

'I think they might be. First she gets to stay the night at his winery. Now she's going for mud baths with him…'

Kaya cringed as they talked between themselves as though she weren't there.

It was harmless fun, but clearly they'd been talking about her and Arno all this time, and probably thought they were doing more than they actually were. Plus, they were way too drunk for her to be comfortable.

Kaya turned to go, but Mark had other ideas.

'Ah, come on, Kaya! Stay with us. You're always such a stick-in-the-*mud*—get it?'

'I have to go, it's been a long day,' she insisted as her defences rose like a drawbridge at his proximity.

'Have some fun with us! Or are you saving all that for your alone time with the doctor?'

He caught her elbow. She pulled away but he did it again, trying to make her stay, and suddenly his leering face in the firelight was all she could see. Kaya froze, feeling the tears flood her eyes as the flashbacks assaulted her one by one. The teeth up close, the odour of alcohol on his breath, the clammy hands…she was back there.

Kimberley was cackling from her chair. Mark was trying to dance with her now, telling her he was only teasing her, wrapping an arm around her waist. Her feet wouldn't move; he was that man in the park, all over again, leering and jeering and smelling of booze...

'Get your hands off her!'

The booming voice sounded out like a bomb behind them, shaking her to her senses. Arno stormed towards them and past her like an angry bear, and suddenly she was free and Mark was staggering backwards, hands in the air, beer spilling everywhere.

'I heard you all, acting like animals,' Arno seethed. 'What the hell are you doing? Are you drunk?' His eyes scanned the circle and she watched him take in the beer cans, the scattered biscuits and discarded plates. Everyone was on their feet now, stunned into a sheepish silence. She'd never seen him so angry.

'Are you guys serious? Is this what happens when I leave the property? This isn't some kind of party!'

'We were just...' Kimberley trailed off, awkwardly.

'You were just *drinking*.' Arno glowered, swiping up a can, then tossing it hard into the blazing fire, which spat in instant disapproval. 'Did I not specifically state when you all arrived that we don't drink here, not in the week, not when we have patients to see first thing in the morning, people who might *need* us?'

The group muttered their apologies as Arno simmered. Kaya could tell he was doing his best to swallow the rage that had just consumed him.

'They were just having a bit of fun,' she tried, although she could still feel Mark's hands on her; and everything that 'bit of fun' had thrown to the forefront of her memories. He'd held her so tightly just now, the white marks from his hand on her flesh had turned to red.

Arno wasn't looking at her. He was glowering at Mark, who was backing off towards the rooms slowly, as you'd try to escape a rhino itching to pierce your lungs with a lethal horn. She put a hand to Arno's arm gently. 'Arno, it's all right.'

'Are *you* all right?' he said now, turning to her in front of everyone.

She nodded mutely, rubbing her arms, then remembered to stand tall. She'd done nothing wrong; let people talk, let people think what they wanted about her—*them*. She was done being some precious flower, stuck in the shadows. And Mark should not have put his hands on her under any circumstances—he knew that. She could tell he was already regretting it.

Arno's face was still dark as a storm cloud.

'Everyone out of here, now,' Arno barked, and the group scattered on command, till it was just the two of them, standing by the fire in the dark.

'I saw his hands on you,' Arno hissed into the crackling fire. 'I saw red.' He sank to a chair, kicked another can and pressed his hands to his head. She didn't know what to do, except touch a hand to his shoulder from behind him. Somehow it felt as if it was Arno who needed comforting right now.

She helped him clean up the cans, while he muttered things about how much he loathed drinking, how it ruined everything, how he shouldn't have overreacted. She bit her tongue. From what he'd said earlier, he blamed himself—a little—for being out drinking when that fire broke out at the winery. It made sense, why he'd overreacted, but he'd also been worried about her. It was everything combined.

This thing, whatever it was, was growing between them, stronger by the minute. Maybe he was as frustrated as she was.

As he walked her back to her room, Kaya toyed with the notion that once the panic over Mark's behaviour had subsided, and Arno had appeared to defend her honour, she'd probably never felt so turned on in her life. This was all so confusing.

'Get some sleep, you must be exhausted,' he said, swiping at his eyes on her doorstep.

'Thank you, for tonight,' she replied, hoping he knew what that meant. She got lost in his eyes in the light from the porch, wishing the night wouldn't have to end. A distant cry of a night bird pierced the air and he squeezed his eyes closed, pretending to bang his head against the door.

'I shouldn't have been such an ogre with them.' He winced against the wood. 'They'll hate me now.'

'No, they won't. They'll respect you even more.'

'Drinking against my rules is one thing, I can forgive that, I know they were just letting loose, but when I saw Mark's hands on you, after what you said, what you had to go through…'

She stepped towards him, courage pushing her to the tips of his toes. 'That's the funny thing about having someone's hands on me. If it's *you*, I really don't mind.'

Kaya touched a palm to his cheek, caressing the softness of his face, allowing one finger to sweep his cheekbone before he covered her hand with his. The warmth of him washed deliciously over her fingers and she swore she could feel his pulse quicken. She'd read a study once that said that when a person was attracted to another, their heartbeat synchronised with that of their lover. It wasn't just science, it was chemistry. This was something she had *never* felt this strongly. Not even with Pieter at the start.

Kaya drew a jagged breath as his eyes narrowed speculatively. 'What about if I kissed you? Would you mind that?'

'I don't know.' Nervous excitement pulsed through her, like a million fingers tickling her heart and belly. She rested her hand against his heart, stepped closer till her hips were pressed to his. 'You can always try?'

Arno traced a feather-light thumb over her lower lip, and she swallowed against the sensation of her heart skyrocketing up to her trachea and getting stuck there.

'Do you trust me?' he asked her, his mouth so close she could almost taste it already.

Her fingers found the fabric of his shirt. Arno ran his hand caressingly over the curve of her waist and she clean forgot where they were as he bent to kiss her. Time stopped when his lips landed on hers...softly, gently, as if he was testing the waters. And while it was a much lighter kiss than she actually desired, hunger throbbed and shot through her loins, making her gasp for a breath.

'Maybe we shouldn't.' Arno groaned, releasing her, obviously mistaking her rush of desire and pleasure for another disturbing flashback.

A rapid pulse beat a new song in her throat. A dull ache nagged at her insides as she reached for him, and dared to press her lips to his again, opening her mouth this time, welcoming his tongue. Just the smallest flick of it against hers was enough to breathe new life into her. Just one sensual touch between tongues made her feel as if she were shooting back to the surface after months underwater. A ripple of laughter escaped her throat and she clutched fistfuls of his shirt, pressed her forehead to his heart, relieved she could still do it, that she could still kiss and be kissed, and enjoy it.

'Was that too much?' he asked her now, and she shook her head.

'It wasn't enough.' She smiled into him, releasing a sigh into his chest as his big arms looped around her. They stayed that way a moment, in a spill of moonlight that felt almost magical to Kaya, until Arno prised her hands away, moved to the steps of the porch.

'Get some sleep,' he said again from the step below her, curling a lick of muddy hair behind her ear. This time she was the one to emit a groan. He was leaving. Correctly so—this was already a disaster waiting to happen. But by the look of his trousers now, he wanted more, too.

'If I stay one second more, I will do something I might regret,' he said, confirming her thoughts. He scooped her by the nape of her neck, and pressed his lips to her forehead this time, leaving a hot trail of tingles in his wake. Looking deep into his eyes, she saw how much he wanted her, but in seconds he had disappeared into the night, leaving her breathless on the porch, haunted by the taste of him.

CHAPTER TWELVE

'KAYA, I NEED YOU!' Arno shoved the radio back in its holder and held a hand up at her over the ruckus of teens all clamouring around her, outside the school.

'What's up?' she said, heading his way in her uniform blue T-shirt, swatting a fly from her face while a teenager talked at her a million miles an hour. He watched the sun play on her cheekbones as Kaya took her shoulder gently. 'Honey, I'll be back very soon, you can ask me any more questions then.'

She was good with kids, whatever their age. It was hard not to notice.

'Looks like there's been a road accident up ahead. We're the closest medics, we need to go now,' he said gravely, opening the Jeep door and resisting the impulse to put a hand to her back or steady her as she climbed up quickly, issuing a hurried goodbye to the girl, who was *still* trying to talk to her about her boyfriend.

They'd just given the presentation at the school that had been postponed a week ago, and the bit about safe sex, by Kaya herself, had sparked a barrage of questions that he'd done his best to answer, but let Kaya handle for the most part. Now it looked as if they were needed for something more pressing. Hopefully it wasn't too serious.

In seconds he was swerving out of the schoolyard and Kaya was gripping the handle.

'I'll never get used to your driving.' She grimaced as he hurtled through a puddle, and he battled a laugh at the look on her face, told her she would *have* to get used to it eventually, then realised she probably wouldn't, seeing as she was leaving at the end of her six-month placement.

Which was exactly the reason he hadn't made another move on her since that kiss last week. Why go down that path with a volunteer?

It wasn't easy, staying professional, when all he wanted to do was taste more of her. The other night, when the November rains had slashed his windows and kept him awake, he'd wanted to go to her so badly, but then, she hadn't made another move either. So here they were, at some kind of torturous stalemate that thickened the air every time they were in the same room...or Jeep. Like now.

A female in her mid-twenties, who'd been established as Sarah from the UK, was sitting on the roadside when they pulled up. A smashed-up hire car lay smoking on its side in the vines. Officer Marlo—whom Arno had known for years—ran at them from the overturned car, shouting something about the back seat. Sarah was crying uncontrollably, clutching her stomach and chest.

'There's someone in the back seat,' Marlo panted, sending Arno's heart straight up to his mouth. 'Her partner, Daniel. I couldn't get the door open. Looks like there's blood.'

Arno grabbed his backpack, told Kaya to stay with Sarah. The girl was sobbing wretched sobs, struggling for air. Whiplash from the seat belt was evident on her skin, but there could well be internal bleeding. Kaya would check.

'He wasn't wearing a seat belt,' he heard Sarah sob, and dread seized Arno's chest as he peered through the broken window. The guy, Daniel, lay whimpering in shock on the back seat. Marlo was right; blood had soaked his white shirt and pooled onto the seat. He pulled at the twisted door, but it was no good. Running to the other side, he tried the other one and yelped as broken glass slashed his hand.

Dammit.

'It's not moving,' he yelled at Marlo as Kaya ran over to assist. Quickly he hid his bleeding hand from her. He would address that later. Getting this guy out was imperative. Kaya went for the door handle, but he darted in front of her. 'Kaya, no, there's too much glass…'

'I want to help,' she told him. 'Sarah is stable. What do we do? Where are the first responders?'

'We are the first responders,' he said, checking the mangled back window now. 'The roads are too narrow. Look, this might be our only way in.'

Stepping over broken glass and twisted vines, Arno picked up part of a broken fence post, assessing the best way to use it to get into the car. Kaya followed him to the back, one hand over her mouth. Behind them, Sarah was hugging her knees ten feet away, rocking like a baby, but at least she was fine and conscious.

The car was smoking profusely now. Marlo was still tugging at the other back door. Inside, Daniel groaned, his face pale, shrouded in smoke.

'They were drinking. These damn wine tourists, it's always the same,' Marlo growled, before cursing loudly at the jammed door again. 'No idea what they're messing with, coming out here…'

'Help me with this,' Arno barked, tossing him another piece of fencepost. He ordered Kaya to stand back as they took the wooden posts to the remaining back windscreen. He bit his tongue as his thumb throbbed with the impact, but Kaya was ready with blankets, fearlessly shoving them against the jagged edges, creating a smooth exit.

'We need to be fast,' he told them both, but the pain in his hand was unreal now. Scarlet blood oozed from his thumb down his wrist.

Ignore it. You're fine.

'Arno, I'll crawl in, I'm the smallest,' Kaya said now, making for the hole they'd just forged in the back of the car. He barred her with his good arm.

'No.'

'Let me!'

'No.'

There was no way he was letting her in this vehicle, not on his watch. He was already fighting the memories of the arms flailing from the restaurant windows that night—the giant restaurant that was already too choked for three people to escape from. He might be wounded now but he was still the strongest. She battled his decision with narrowed eyes and he turned from her before he broke, and scrambled through the window to the back seat.

Smoke made his eyes water as he assessed the damage up close in the tiny space. No time to linger. Daniel was conscious but the blood was pooling from his upper-left chest area—he had to keep him talking.

'Stay with me, you're fine. Tell me the date, tell me your girlfriend's name... Kaya, get me something to tie round him,' he called out.

Kaya pushed another sheet towards him. Good enough. 'Left upper anterior open chest wound,' he told her as her face appeared in the shattered window to his side.

'Arno, hurry up!'

She didn't have to tell him that. Making a quick job with the makeshift occlusive dressing, he clocked the open bottle of wine in the back seat, and the rest of the bottles that had been thrown and smashed in the accident. There was enough booze in here to spark an inferno.

An angry hissing sound from somewhere near the front of the car sent his mind reeling back to that night—the black-as-night smoke clamouring for oxygen from the restaurant windows, shattered glass, employees on their knees, calling for the ones they'd lost, Mama Annika gasping for breath as he pulled her out, the sirens wailing in the distance. Adrenaline claimed his throat with the acrid smoke as he hoisted Daniel onto his lap.

Kaya and Marlo took his arms. Daniel slumped, a heavyweight against his chest, and Arno willed the pain away from his own throbbing hand as he handed Daniel out to them as steadily and quickly as he could.

'Get him away from here,' he yelled at them, clutching his hand as the car made an ominous creaking sound. The memories rushed at him; seeing his mother, running in drunk and stumbling, dragging her out on the strength of pure willpower, just before the roaring fire shot through her bedroom.

Focus, focus, focus, Arno.

Kaya and Marlo were running, dragging Daniel between them towards Sarah. Heaving himself through the window again, clutching his bloodied arm, Arno had barely made it three steps from the wreckage when the car burst into flames.

Kaya used her body as a shield. Crouching over Sarah and Daniel, she and Marlo dropped to the ground as the heat from the explosion threatened to scald them all. A distant siren wailed. A woman in a red dress she didn't recognise was rushing towards them now through the vineyard, arms in the air, but she kept losing her in the smoke.

'Arno.' She coughed, searching the wreckage for him with her eyes. 'Arno?' She stood on wobbly legs. Where was Arno?

Fear took her entire body hostage. The siren wailed closer, louder, louder than the crackling fire that was now burning wildly where the car had been. He was still inside?

'No, no, no...' Tears flooded her eyes, and burned like the smoke. She scanned the scene for him. Did he make it out? Oh, God...no...surely not...

Then, there he was, staggering towards her, like a super-hero at the end of an action movie! All the breath left her body as she met him in the middle of the road and threw her arms around him, just as a fire truck and an ambulance screeched up beside them. Arno let her hold him in a blur of firemen and hoses and paramedics and spraying water; let her inspect him, let her lead him over to the others and sit him by the roadside. He was breathless, weaker than she'd ever seen from breathing all that smoke.

'I'll help you to the ambulance,' she said. His face was black as soot, his shirt was ashen and bloodied. Daniel's blood?

No, *his* blood.

'I don't need them, I have you,' he managed, and she stared at him helplessly. Blood was streaming from his hand.

Kaya grappled for the med kit on the ground, hands shaking. Behind them the fire was almost out. Daniel was being strapped to a stretcher, while Officer Marlo seemed to be explaining something to the woman in red, who'd run to the scene through the vineyard. She looked distressed to say the least. The car was now a mangled black wreck, steaming into the bright blue sky. They were all lucky to be alive.

When she got him to the Jeep, Arno slid to the ground at the wheel, catching his breath, pressing the oxygen mask to his own mouth till the colour flushed back to his cheeks again. Her heart made a lump in her throat as she cleaned out his wound, checking for shards of glass, all the while giving the paramedic who approached them as much info as she could about what just happened.

'You might need stitches,' she told Arno, when he'd gone.

'I'm fine,' he mouthed, through the inhaler.

'You're not fine. We should go with them to the hospital.'

He tore the mask from his face. 'It's not that bad, Kaya, I'm telling you. I don't need that.'

She scowled at him, pulling the bandage tighter, making him suck in a grimace through his teeth. 'Stubborn idiot,' she snapped, standing up as the tears sprang back into her eyes. 'You scared the crap out of me.'

'I'd rather scare you than let you crawl in a car that's about to blow!'

Arno clenched his good fist, and she bit back her next words about it being OK for him, but not for her. Swiping at her face, she cursed under her breath, turned to the sky.

Breathe, Kaya. He was trying to protect you.

Her emotions were getting the better of her. She cared so much about him and hadn't been able to do a single thing about it since that kiss. They hadn't even mentioned it since. It was killing her. They shouldn't have let things get so messed up. Of course she'd be the one to suffer—*of course* he didn't want to start something with a volunteer, and neither should she, but it didn't mean she could switch off her feelings.

'Kaya.' He reached for her now, urged her down to his level. Embarrassed by her tears, she couldn't look at him. Arno scooped the back of her neck gently and drew her closer, pressed his forehead to hers. 'Kaya,' he said again, sincerely. 'I'm sorry.'

She swallowed as his jagged breathing slowed and soon she felt her heart rate matching his. Damn him, she couldn't even be mad at him for scaring her. Their chemistry got the better of them both, it seemed. She liked him so much.

'You were brave,' he told her, swiping a tear from her cheek with his good thumb.

'*You* could have been killed.'

'Not *"You were brave, too, Arno"*?' he teased.

Then he laughed softly and coughed again, and she sighed out her relief through her nose. He'd inhaled too much smoke, and his hand would bother him for a while, but he'd be fine. He'd also gone out of his way to protect her, again, she thought helplessly as he searched her eyes, and scanned her lips in a way that made her heart ache and her throat even drier. He was everything she'd ever wanted; someone who'd always have her back, and her best interests at heart. The opposite of Pieter.

Standing up, she tore her eyes away, emotion trembling through her. They might not be indulging in any more overtly intimate moonlit moments, but he was the one she trusted, the only one she'd trusted fully in a long time—how could she not want him, when he acted like this?

What kind of mess had she landed herself in now?

The ambulance had rumbled off with their patients. Three firemen were hoisting bits of the mangled car onto a second truck already, and the hot sun beat down on her head, making her dizzy. She would likely have to drive them back herself, no thanks to his hand, or to the hospital, but she was thirsty and running out of energy fast.

The woman who'd been talking to Officer Marlo hurried over, taming back her wild dyed hair. Her vivid red dress was a beacon against the sky. 'I hear you saved that man's life,' she said to them, her hands running nervous trails along the chain of blue beads around her neck. 'We saw the explosion from the window. This is our property.'

Arno got slowly to his feet, accepting her help to steady him. Kaya gripped his arm; noting how his forearm took both of her hands to hold, and how the snake tattoo still seemed to taunt her, even covered in dirt. 'Yeah. Sorry about that, Mrs Wistuba,' he said, with another cough. 'I hope it didn't take out too much of the harvest.'

The woman frowned closer at Arno through her glasses, then her eyes widened in recognition. 'Arno Nkosi?' she cried in shock, pressing a hand to her mouth. 'Is that you? My goodness, does your mother know you're today's hero yet?'

CHAPTER THIRTEEN

KAYA WATCHED THE firemen remove the rest of the burnt-out car from her place on the front porch of Wistuba Winery's cellar door. She could barely make it out from this distance, but poor Mrs Nina Wistuba had been pouring her prize-winning Cabernet Sauvignon for the tourists behind closed doors when she smelled the smoke, then saw the explosion.

Arno drank a coffee in silence next to her, using his one good hand to grip the cup. Nina chattered into the phone by the steps, doing an interview with the local newspaper below several hanging baskets that were overflowing with the most magnificent shades of magenta and yellow Kaya had ever seen.

Nina, Arno's mother's closest friend, was refusing to let them leave until they'd rested a while longer, though it was obvious from his stance that Arno couldn't wait to get out of here.

'How's the hand now?' Kaya asked him softly, eager to break the silence.

'Fine.'

'You're not burdening me with anything by letting me help, you know, if that's what you're thinking,' she told him, realising he probably thought he'd just put her through enough—not that it was his fault! 'I'm going to have to check it later, in case you need stitches,' she added.

'You're welcome to, Doctor, but I won't.'

'How do you know that?'

'I know my own hands.'

'Why do you have to be so…?'

His phone chirruped like a cricket, and he fished around for it in three pockets before he found it, cursing at his hand while he did it. Kaya bit her tongue and studied the flowers, listened to him discuss the guy they'd pulled from the car, Daniel. His injuries were being treated in Cape Town. Thankfully it sounded as if he'd be OK, and he had his girlfriend with him. Maybe they'd think twice about driving tipsy or without their seat belts in future, she thought, disapprovingly. No wonder Arno was so against alcohol, if that was the kind of thing they saw regularly around here.

This tension between them was palpable. He was probably wishing he'd never kissed her and made things awkward. Already they were bickering.

No sooner had he hung up than his phone was ringing again.

'Popular,' she quipped.

Kaya saw *Mama Annika* flash up on the screen, but to her surprise he flipped his phone over and ignored it.

'You're not answering to your mother?' She couldn't keep the concern from her voice. 'She must have heard what happened, she's probably worried about you.'

'I'm alive, aren't I?' he said, crossing to the edge of the porch, away from her.

'Don't you think she'd like to hear that from you?' she said, but he merely shrugged, with his back to her. Damn him, shutting her out, and his mother, what was his problem? Kaya could almost see the weight on his shoulders as he rested his arms on the wooden railings and stared out across the vines.

Annoyed, she focused back on the hanging baskets, wishing she had her own phone with her. It would've been nice to send a message to her parents right about now. Something worse could have happened if she'd been just a couple of feet closer to that car when it exploded. And they worried about her, after everything she'd laid on them after the attack.

She'd been so distant after it, and living at home for three months afterwards hadn't helped her relationship with them... or with Pieter. Glancing at Arno, still staring at the vines, she wished she could see into his thick head. Why did she have to be falling for someone harder than she'd *ever* fallen for Pieter, especially someone she couldn't be with, especially out *here*, where she certainly did not belong?

Then again, where exactly did she belong? The more she thought about it, the less she knew. Going back home to her old job, working the night shift, where *she* was, the girl who'd seduced Pieter, wasn't a particularly encouraging thought.

Life was playing one big fat prank on her lately, throwing Arno into it like this.

'Now then, Kaya, how are you doing now? Have you had enough water? More tea?'

'I'm OK, thank you, Mrs Wistuba.' She smiled, gratefully. The kind Nina was done with her interview, hovering around the table, glancing between her and Arno. She lowered her voice. 'I hope that one's not giving you any trouble?'

'Who, Arno? Giving me trouble?' Kaya's stomach clenched. Maybe she'd heard their mild bickering—it certainly couldn't have looked professional.

Mrs Wistuba slid into the seat next to her, swiping at her brow. 'He can't much enjoy anything to do with cars going up in flames, not after what happened. But don't let his bad mood bring you down, it's nothing personal.'

'Oh, I know that,' Kaya said, flicking her gaze onto him, all hunched shoulders and sombre silence. Her heart went out

to him suddenly. She'd been thinking about their personal…
situation…but of course, he'd put himself in the line of fire
again. 'I know about the fire at Nkosi Valley. All the people
who died. It's awful, I saw the memorial.'

Nina Wistuba sat back in her chair, drumming her nails
on the table. 'He showed you that?'

'Yes, when I stayed at his home.'

Nina was silent for a moment, seemingly trying to deci-
pher her. 'Then you know it was all over the news,' she said.
Her tone conveyed a fresh sadness that crept across the space
between them into Kaya's bones. 'His poor mother. Losing
her staff like that was bad enough, but when Annika lost the
baby, nothing was quite the same for that family. I'm happy
to see he's at least talking about it with someone now.'

Baby? Kaya blinked at her. 'Mama Annika lost a baby?'

Nina pulled a face, as if she'd accidentally revealed a secret. She lowered her voice even further, as perspiration tickled Kaya's neck. 'Are you two…together?'

'No, I'm a volunteer with the Lindiwe Foundation.'

'But he took you home? Annika says he never takes anyone home.'

Kaya kept her voice cool, even though her heart was a
drum. 'Well, we had a run-in with an elephant and he had to
run an errand there, after. So, there was a baby?'

Nina pursed her lips. Weirdly she didn't seem fazed about
the elephant. 'Well, it's not really for me to say…but yes. Annika was pregnant when it happened. She was sleeping and
she didn't wake up. Arno pulled her out. Annika was fine,
but the baby… It was the smoke, they said.'

Kaya's hands found their way to her mouth. Her head was
spinning.

So that was what Arno felt so bad about; what he'd failed
to tell her. It was none of her business, and not his preroga-

tive to tell her at all, but the pieces were falling together. He blamed himself for not being there. He thought it was unforgivable, going out, getting drunk, not being home when a pregnant Mama Annika needed him. His *older* pregnant mother, she realised now. He was only eighteen when it happened, twenty years ago.

Was he so caught up thinking it was all his fault that he never took anyone home in case they found out about it? He'd definitely seemed less than comfortable about her being there, that night. Couldn't get her away from his Mama fast enough. And he did say that before…that he felt as if people were judging him after the fire.

'What are you two gossiping about?' Arno broke into her thoughts, crossing the porch back to the table, eyes narrowed suspiciously. Kaya got to her feet before Nina could tell him what she assumed was something he wasn't too keen on sharing.

'We were just talking about…the flowers,' she said quickly, gesturing to the hanging baskets above the steps. 'I was just saying how I could do with some like this, for the garden.'

Thankfully, Mrs Wistuba seemed to read the room. Her beads swished as she stood, ushering them both from the porch into the barn, past the bar and barrels of wine and abandoned glasses, while Kaya wrestled with what to do about the barrel-load of new information she'd just received. If she told him she knew about Mama Annika and the baby, he might turn on her or stop talking to her altogether. He had to want to trust her and tell her himself.

'If you like those flowers, dear, wait till you see out the back,' Nina said, swinging open a huge, creaking wooden door at the back of the barn. 'I think you'll really like my sunflowers.'

* * *

Arno followed Nina Wistuba and Kaya through the garden he'd played in as a kid, with Nina's daughter, and vaguely heard them discussing different plants and flowers. His head was foggy, and his cough wasn't going away yet.

The eight-foot-high sunflowers towering over the pathways were impressive, and Kaya seemed excited to have seeds for her garden project, but he couldn't really concentrate on flowers right now. He felt bad for ignoring Mama Annika's call.

So bad.

But the last thing he needed was to have an emotional conversation with Mama in front of Kaya. She'd be upset, and rightly so, he might have been blown to pieces in a burning car. No doubt Nina had told her he was here, and what had happened on her property.

He was kind of torn up, if he was honest. The fire…the explosion. He'd put Kaya in a dangerous situation and now she was worrying *more* about his hand. Letting on that he was upset to Mama on top of all that—no. What right did he have to cause Mama any *more* concern?

Also, if he was totally honest with himself, he didn't want to be flung back to that day, when Mama's wailing could have taken down the hospital walls. He and Dad had had to bring her home to the charred house, all frail and broken; then Dad had gone off at him, telling him it had been his responsibility to look after her, to be there, to *protect* her. He'd never seen either of his parents cry before the miscarriage. *His* fault.

They never really spoke about it all. He tried not to, in case he ever saw the same blame in her eyes that he'd seen in his dad's, but maybe he *did* need to talk to her about it, for her sake.

Kaya had looked horrified just now, seeing him reject

her call, and she was right to think him a selfish arsehole. She was right. Apart from Bea, Kaya was the only woman he'd ever let meet his mother; she'd seen the memorial too. She knew how the fire had affected them all...but she didn't know his brother died before getting the chance to live, because of him.

Watching the sunflowers arching over her ahead on the path, he felt suddenly compelled to tell this beautiful, honest woman the full extent of why he still found it so hard to be at home. Maybe he would if she wasn't going to be gone before her own sunflowers even blossomed in Mama Imka's village garden...

Arno stopped dead in his tracks.

Mama Imka.

Sunflowers.

'What's wrong? Is it your hand?' Kaya was at his side now, looking at him imploringly. Nina was halfway up the path, en route back to the house. Kaya took his hand and he let her study it, taking in every bit of her face, her mouth. Those predictions, whatever they were that Mama Imka had people so captivated by, weren't real.

'Arno? You've gone pale.'

This was a coincidence. Just a coincidence that they were standing here now in a garden full of sunflowers and she had him thinking things he'd never let himself think till now.

He realised he was staring at her, and he pulled his hand back quickly. 'I was just thinking I should go call Mama back,' he said. 'You're right, she's probably worried.'

Kaya's frown deepened. Her expression held the kind of perplexity that rattled his insides as the swaying sunflowers and their shadows seemed to mock him. 'Arno, I know we're not...talking about what happened,' she started. Impulsively he took her fingers in his, with his good hand.

'It was wrong of me to kiss you, and then act like it didn't happen,' he said.

'I did the same thing.'

'You don't let many people close to you, and neither do I. But that's no excuse, not after you told me what happened to you.'

Kaya smiled, shook her head at the grass. 'I don't think I knew what to do with it all either.'

'This is just all new to me,' he admitted. 'I don't usually do this with... I'm not sure what's right and what's wrong here.'

'Well—' she laced his fingers through her own '—I was just going to say that, even if nothing like that ever happens again, if you need someone to talk to about *anything*, I'm here. I'm your volunteer. I'm volunteering to hear you out.'

Arno rubbed at his chin, looking at their hands entwined, her slender fingers in his, the sweet tenderness in her eyes. The way she'd emphasised *anything* was almost as though she knew he held more demons inside him than he was willing to let escape. It didn't feel great, keeping such a big part of his story from her...but it would feel worse, seeing her react to the damage his selfishness had already done. He'd been through all that with Bea.

'Talk to me,' she said now. Her tone was nothing short of demanding. 'Did that car accident and the fire bring stuff back up for you? Is that why you didn't want to talk to your mother just now? It's OK to show a little emotion, you know, Arno, you'd be no less of a man for it. And you know by now, I'm a mess sometimes myself!'

'You make a mess out of me.' He groaned. She'd be gone before long; before her sunflowers got anywhere near this tall. Why tell her anything to help her change her mind about him now?

Kaya gasped softly as he swept her face closer with one

hand. Her eyes fluttered shut and her lips looked so inviting he could hardly help sweeping a thumb from her cheek
to her chin.

Maybe it was everything that had just happened, or the
strange coincidence that had them standing here, having this
conversation in the sunflowers, that got to him. It was quite
possible that he didn't want to face *any* emotions right now
in front of anyone, but kissing her again felt more right than
wrong.

This time she didn't seem to want to stop at soft, light
and tender. Her hands smoothed his cheeks and head, then
brought his face forcefully forward, begging wordlessly for
more from his lips as her hips crashed to his.

He loved the way her soft curls were bouncing around
his face as they found themselves hidden from the house
behind a tree. The warmth of her mouth rushed through to
his heart, chasing away all the doubts, and he almost forgot
how cold he'd felt this past week, telling himself he shouldn't
do this again.

He was so caught up in the moment, and their mouths and
lips and tongues, that he went to lay her down on the soft
warm grass, where he could taste more of her, as much as
she wanted him to taste. No one could see.

Kaya pulled away. His stomach plummeted as she sighed
into her hands, then shot him a sheepish look that sent his
hard-on right back to ground zero.

'I went too far with you.' He winced, scrambling back to
standing.

'No, no, it's just…the grass, I don't know.' Kaya looked
nervous now, leaning against the tree, touching her hair,
looking up at the sunflowers, embarrassed. Arno could have
kicked himself. This wasn't just any hungry, sex-obsessed

woman who wanted him, this was someone who'd been taken advantage of and violated; he had to watch himself.

'It's not you,' she started, grimacing, hugging her arms around herself. 'I wanted you to kiss me, it's just…sorry.'

'I'm the one who should be sorry.' Arno was mortified for his behaviour, for the thoughts that had momentarily shoved his common sense aside.

'Not at all, Arno. This is so embarrassing.'

'Don't be embarrassed,' he told her, angry on her behalf now. What the hell did that guy do to her? He dared to reach for her, coaxing her slowly into an embrace, where hopefully she'd feel safe. She was so slender, so strong, but yet so frag-ile. Her bones felt like delicate branches he suddenly wanted to shield from every single storm. The need to protect her against all evils rose in him and coursed like fire through his veins. He was in out of his depth.

He wanted Kaya and wanted to be the one she turned to, at least while she was here, which meant he should probably tell her what had been eating at him since the day of that fire. She knew he was keeping something back; and she'd told him more than she probably ever meant to already, about herself.

This was it, he realised. Trust equalled trust. He had to trust she wouldn't turn away from him if she found out the truth about the pain he'd caused—the full reason he'd turned to medicine. Whatever happened from this point forward, and it would have to happen very, very slowly, if at all…all he wanted now was for her to trust him. If only it weren't so ingrained in him to keep all his emotions locked in a water-tight box in the pit of his stomach.

CHAPTER FOURTEEN

KAYA RAN HER hands along Tande's coarse fur and closed her eyes. She was doing her best to project a sense of calm, although every time she met with the lioness it felt as if she were in the opening scene of a wildlife documentary before the brave and reckless tourist wound up as dinner.

'She likes you,' Arno whispered into her ear as Tande yawned, and stretched out on the ground next to them, her huge paws kicking up the dust.

'I hope so.' She sighed, resting her head back against his broad chest in the soft grass, feeling the first few rays of sunlight start to warm her skin. She'd forced herself to be OK with grass. After what had happened the other day in Mrs Wistuba's sunflower garden, when she'd made a fool of herself and ruined one of the best kisses of her life, she'd worked on it, sat outside amongst the birds and bees, sometimes alone. Sometimes with Arno and Tande, like this.

Grass didn't have to remind her of her faceless perpetrator, shoving her hard onto the damp ground and...ugh. No. Grass was good. Grass was hope, and peace and comfort, and a piece of the natural world she could love and trust again because of Arno. It was Tande's favourite thing, next to raw meat.

'Thank you for meeting me here, every morning this week,' Arno said now, dropping a lingering kiss to the side of her head that made her stomach perform a backflip and her coffee flask almost slip from her hands. Five-thirty a.m. had never been so good. It had become a routine, this past week or so. He'd kiss her goodnight at her door, in secret under the stars. She'd meet him again out here first thing in the morning to watch the sun rise with Tande. Then, they would go to the gym.

He liked to work out with his shirt off. Even with his bad hand he managed to lift weights with the other one, and every time she watched him grow a little bit stronger, a little bit more like the shield she never knew she'd been looking for, she got the kind of starry eyes that made her wonder if tonight would be the night he asked if he could stay in her room. Or ask if he could talk to her about what was really going on with him and his mother.

He never took her up on that listening ear. And he never asked if he could stay over.

If she wasn't trying her best to live in the moment for once, she'd be infuriated at all the things she still didn't know, and might never know, but she had to keep her head on straight.

'Are you coming with us on the outdoor expedition?' he asked her now, stroking a finger along her bare arm, and leaving a stray butterfly flapping around her heart.

The butterfly died suddenly at his question. She'd been wanting to go along on this weekend's trip, designed to introduce a group of school kids to survival tips and first aid in the wilderness, even though it was her weekend off, but Mark had signed up to go. So had Kimberley.

No one had said anything more about her and Arno since that night when Mark had grabbed her by the fire and got an earful from Arno in return. At least, not to their faces. But the last thing she needed was to be stuck in a tent with one of them, pretending things weren't totally awkward.

'Mark cancelled, he has to fly home for a birthday,' Arno told her, a sly smile on his lips. Was he reading her mind?

'Will I get my own tent?' she asked him as her heart sped up.

Silence.

She stroked her hand across Tande's back and waited for Arno to say she wouldn't need one, that they could share, but instead he nodded quietly, eyes narrowed. 'Everyone gets their own tent. We leave tonight after dinner.'

The whole day, on their rounds at two different villages, Kaya saw to her TB patients, administered treatment for a lung infection, and answered another barrage of questions about sex from teenagers at the school where they'd given their talk, all the while trying not to think of how torturous it would be this weekend, being so close to Arno without being able to touch him.

He'd watched like a hawk this afternoon, from the other side of the garden as she'd pressed the new sunflower seeds into the earth with the kids, as if he were worried she would fly away too soon. But he wasn't making any real moves beyond kissing, and she didn't quite know how to feel about that. If someone had told her just a couple of months ago that she'd be imagining herself in bed with a South African doctor, her mentor no less, she'd have laughed.

No, she wouldn't have laughed actually, she'd have been terrified. The thought of all that had been terrifying for so long; it felt strange to *want* to be touched. But he wasn't initiating anything. And it was probably best. The last thing she needed was for all those hormones to rush back in and render her attached to a man she had no business getting any more attached to.

* * *

Back at Thabisa, Kimberley poked her head around the door as she was packing for the camping expedition, in a red baseball cap to match her rosy cheeks.

'Got everything?'

'Yes, ma'am,' Kaya answered, grabbing a book she knew she'd bury herself in at nights, alone in her tent; anything to stop herself wanting to go to Arno.

'I'm glad you're coming,' Kimberley said, hovering in the doorway. 'Have you forgiven me yet, for what happened that night, when Mark…you know?'

Kaya sighed. She couldn't avoid this for ever. 'I hold no grudges against either of you. You were just asking me what's going on with Dr Nkosi. I suppose you have to work with us, and you're not blind.'

'So, there's an "us"?' Kimberley cocked one eyebrow, stepping further into her room. 'It will go no further, I promise. I kind of hoped there was. You two make a cute couple.'

Cute. Ugh. What a word.

Kaya huffed a laugh she didn't really feel. 'There's no "us",' she told her, carefully. 'But there's *something*, I guess.'

Kimberley dropped to her bed and eyed her, throwing a sweater and camo trousers into her bag with her toothbrush. 'What will you do when you have to go home?'

Kaya's heart lurched. Tears sprang to her eyes without warning and she bit down on her cheeks, pausing with her packing. Hearing it spoken out loud by someone else made the truth sink in. She wasn't staying here, she didn't belong. Arno's life existed on a whole different continent, and he couldn't exactly up sticks and move to the Netherlands with his lioness.

'Nothing,' she said, forcing her voice to stay neutral, turning away from Kimberley's intrusive gaze. 'I'll just keep living my life, like he will.'

Kimberley snorted indignantly. 'Listen to you,' she said, slapping a hand to her heart dramatically. 'God, girl, if I scored someone like *him*, I'd never let him go.'

'But…we live in totally opposite hemispheres!'

'So? Didn't you say something about your mama being from here, in one of our intro sessions? She moved to be with your dad, didn't she?'

Kaya's heart had started to go a little haywire. She sank to the bed next to Kimberley, suddenly grateful the brash Australian had reached out with a new perspective on her whirring inner monologues. Yes, her mother crossed the world to be with her dad after their whirlwind romance, but that was then, and they were different.

Kimberley chatted at her while she finished packing, and she did her best to focus, and not to let herself think along those lines about herself and Arno—he didn't want to start some relationship with her, surely. He couldn't even open up to her about his past after she'd given him the chance. He didn't *want* to get that close.

It was a tender, loving, intimate, temporary thing that was helping her self-confidence, and making his days less lonesome, that was all.

'You don't have much time left to snare him.' Kimberley grinned.

'I'm not trying to snare him!'

'Well, maybe you should.'

Kaya crinkled up her nose—there was nothing worse than being put on the spot like this. But maybe she *was* looking for excuses not to get that close herself. This was everything she'd felt for Pieter at the start multiplied by a million. Being cheated on had left some kind of nasty scar around her heart, and if anyone else ever did that…if Arno ever did that, or even just called it off, the pain of it all might just kill her.

The questions from the kids were flooding in as usual. Arno usually loved this part of the first night of camp, when everything was fresh and exciting. They were sitting around the fire under the moonlight on the disused logging trail behind the Berg River Dam, listening to the croaking frogs.

He'd started a discussion about plastic bags and their choking effects on small streams, how they smothered the larvae of unborn frogs and cut off their sun and air. Kaya was listening to everything intently, scribbling in her notebook as much as the kids, and he was glad she was here, even if she wasn't pleased with him.

Not pleased at all.

She'd seen him ignore another call from Mama Annika, right before boarding the bus from Thabisa. She asked him why he'd done that, again. He told her he would text Mama Annika, that he needed to talk to her face to face in private, and clearly, Kaya felt excluded. She reminded him that they were going off grid into the wilderness with no reception, but still he'd shrugged it off, like a selfish idiot, and refused to explain why the need for privacy—they were too close for secrets now, and his was eating him up but it was something he needed to face alone.

'Can we go for a night swim?' one of the girls was asking now.

He was about to answer the girl with a resounding 'No, not tonight' when she turned to Kaya and asked her the same question.

'I don't think that's the plan for tonight, right, Arno?' she said tactfully, casting her eyes at him for confirmation.

The girl pouted, her friends jeered *boo*, while Arno replied, 'Right.' But he held Kaya's eyes like glue. It was the first thing she'd really said to him since arriving.

A moment passed.

Then she tore her eyes away, leaving him cold.

'Let's discuss the critters, shall we?' he said, squaring his shoulders, inviting more questions. They all wanted to know about the spiders and usually he loved to enlighten them on identification, habitat, and first-aid treatment of their various bites and stings.

Now, though, Kaya's eyes held the sting of a thousand scorpions. He still owed her an explanation as to why things were so tense with Mama Annika; she was probably more insulted that he was clearly keeping something from her when she'd opened up to him about her own issues...which were worse, and way more recent.

He'd almost told her several times. All those mornings she'd sat with him watching the sun rise over the mountains with Tande this past week, he could have just told her then, put his trust in her, as she'd put her trust in him.

But what if she pulled away from him, as Bea had?

Coward!

OK, yes, he was a coward. He liked her too much, already. It should probably stop—this thing, whatever it was turning into—but, just as selfishly, he didn't want it to.

'What's the most venomous spider out here?' Kaya was asking now. He shoved his hands into his pockets, wondering why such an innocent question seemed so loaded.

'That would be the six-eyed crab spider,' he said. 'They might be the most venomous spiders in the world, but they're pretty solitary and secretive creatures.'

'Oh, yes. I know those kinds of creatures,' she said thoughtfully. 'Solitary. Secretive...'

Arno cleared his throat, ignored a smirk from Kimberley

and moved the subject matter on to the first aid. 'You'll be learning some really essential life-saving techniques this weekend, starting tomorrow. How to care for a sprained ankle, how to stop a bleeding nose, what to do and what not to do with a fractured limb...'

Kaya was unnerving him. Talking to a group wasn't as easy as it usually was and he recognised his guilt again, plaguing him as it had for years every second he lost focus.

He'd called Mama Annika several times since they'd pulled the tourist from the car wreck; more than usual, in fact, which was kind of nice after all this time. She definitely appreciated hearing from her son more often, and talking about her art. Likewise, he liked to hear it.

Only now she was asking for him to go visit again, and to bring Kaya—Nina Wistuba must have mentioned something about them coming back to the porch a *long* time after she'd left them in her garden—and he was stalling.

He'd already decided to face her about the fire, thanks to Kaya, really. She'd got him thinking, without really knowing the full extent of what he'd done. It *was* time they talked it out, time he admitted Dad was right that night, he should've protected her and his soon-to-be brother, time he heard it from her too and apologised and maybe even tried to put it behind them.

But whenever he decided to do it, he backed out. Things were good right now. Shouldn't he just enjoy the time he had left with Kaya? He wasn't ready to break down the past just yet.

Excuses.

Kaya stuck her hand up again. 'What do I do if my tent won't stay up?'

'What?'

She gestured with a finger to where he'd helped her put

the tent up, just thirty minutes ago. Sure enough, Kaya's tent had doubled in on itself and was inexplicably crumbled in a heap of useless canvas on the groundsheet.

Arno stormed across to it, inspecting the material while the kids broke into laughter and chatter behind them. Kaya was at his side now.

'I don't get it,' he said, dashing a hand across his head in confusion. This had never happened before. These were military grade tents and he'd been using them for years with no issues. Maybe it had been on its last legs on the last trip, when they'd suffered through that mountaintop gale, and he hadn't noticed.

'I can't sleep in this. It's broken,' she mused. 'Maybe some-*thing* has broken it.'

Her eyes grew round in fear.

'What if it was a lion, or a cheetah?'

'Cats around here don't attack tents, they're not even in this national park,' he said. He'd never bring this group somewhere that unsafe, or Kaya, for that matter. The look she gave him, all big, beguiling eyes, struck his core like a thunderbolt. He wouldn't be *that* guy.

'You can sleep in Kimberley's tent,' he told her, before he could invite her into his. 'Not mine.'

'I wasn't suggesting I sleep in *yours*,' she shot back haughtily, dropping his arm and grappling for her sleeping bag amongst the canvas, but he didn't miss the hurt in her eyes.

He pulled out her backpack and crossed to Kimberley's tent with it. Kaya followed and tossed her sleeping bag through the doorway, heavily.

Zipping the tent up roughly, he felt her eyes lasering his back, and when he stood, she was right there, arms crossed, an inch from his lips, almost daring him to change his mind.

He resisted the impulse to reach for her waist in the shadows, and strode back to the group, picked up his spider talk.

All night around the fire, he kept on catching her eye, searching for a sign that she wasn't mad at him. Oh, man, she was mad at him. Maybe even more annoyed than before, but he would not be swayed, not on this matter.

Of course, he wanted her in his damn tent, but they were out here *working* and, besides, he wasn't about to put either of them in that situation. She wasn't ready for what he'd want to do with her so close, even if she thought she was, and he wasn't going to be the one to initiate anything, not after what had happened the last time he'd got careless and let his impulses override his chivalry.

It wasn't all about his refusal to get physical anyway. Something else was keeping him away. Their work here was dangerous. There were fires, and storms and guns and animals and other bad people out there... She was one brave woman, considering what she'd endured, but he couldn't always be there to protect her, even if he wanted to be. Bea might've thought he'd let her down eventually, one way or another, and left before he got the chance. Kaya could do that too.

OK, so he couldn't predict the future, but he could start by not putting her in danger of *him*.

CHAPTER FIFTEEN

KAYA YAWNED, HER SLEEPINESS causing her to stumble on the hiking trail. Sweeping the branches out of her face, she tried to stay focused on the young boy from Johannesburg she was walking beside, who was telling her about practising first aid on his dog, but all she wanted to do was slump in a heap on the ground.

Kimberley had snored the entire night in her ears. She'd lain awake in the deplorable volume of it, wishing she could just be braver and go to Arno's tent instead. But he didn't want her there; he didn't even want to *talk* to her about anything real, like the reason he found it tough to be around Mama Annika.

That ignored phone call had played on her mind all night, too. The fact that for whatever reason he didn't want her to know the full story about the night of the fire was almost worse than it would've been, not knowing anything herself. He was holding back on talking, on trying to take things further, because she was difficult to be around—obviously—and because this thing was getting out of hand. She was leaving, *soon*. His reticence was totally understandable. He didn't want to invest emotionally *or* physically. Neither should she.

Last night, in the maddening vibration of Kimberley's snoring, she'd decided to call it off with him. No more sunset meet-ups, no more kisses. It was all just getting too weird and complicated. Her heart wasn't designed to handle this!

If only he didn't look so damn hot out here, out of his uniform T-shirts, leading this group on the trail along the dam and into the bush, like an expert commander in his hiking boots, all muscles in his sleeveless shirt.

Groan.

Damn him, sending her heart into a fluttering mess every time she tried to be mad at him. She should tell him. *I want this thing between us to be over.* But she couldn't seem to find the words to tell him something she didn't quite mean.

Soon, it was lunch time, and he caught her while the kids were chattering noisily over pre-packed boxes of chicken and rice by the river. The sky was dotted with fluffy white clouds, just a hint of grey she hoped wouldn't turn to rain later.

'How was last night?' he asked her, handing her a coffee. She must have looked as if she needed it.

'Great, if you like sleeping next to a chainsaw,' she told him, and his mouth twitched.

'I thought you looked tired. I can give you some earplugs for tonight if you like.'

Kaya scowled over the coffee cup, wishing she weren't so drawn into his twinkling eyes, and enchanted by the shape of his way too kissable mouth. This would be the perfect time to tell him what she'd decided last night—that when they got back to Thabisa there would be no more making out, no more cosy gym sessions or sunrises, but she couldn't do it.

'No earplugs?' he said now, running his eyes over her lips in a way that turned her bare knees to jelly. He reached a hand to her hair and swept it behind her ear, and for a second his eyes seemed to glaze over, before he remembered where they were. He pulled his hand back, leaving her heart racing.

'I'll get them from you later,' she told him, putting her cup down, flustered. 'Don't worry, I won't come into your tent.'

He muttered something under his breath, stepping closer, then he ushered her quickly away from the group, down to the reeds along the riverbank.

'You know why you can't stay in my tent, don't you?' he said, cupping her face in his hands.

Her heart leapt to her throat as the reeds tickled the skin around her shorts. The frogs were so loud, messing with her head. His gaze was all intensity, threatening to unravel her resolve.

'Not just because we're working, and the kids are here, and—'

'Listen,' she said, cutting him off before she chickened out again. 'You don't want to take things any further with me. I understand, Arno. I probably freaked you out last time we tried...'

Arno's eyebrows shot to the sky. 'You think I don't *want* to take things further?'

'I'm a difficult person to get close to.' She lowered her voice, shook her head, trying not to be swayed by his closeness or her attraction to him, which was flying through the roof just being in his hands.

'But so are you, Arno. You don't trust me.'

He frowned. 'What do you mean?'

'It doesn't matter now. You don't want me to get close to you, and I get it, I do. I'm leaving. This should all probably stop, Arno, it won't end well. It's too much for me.'

Arno searched her eyes and she saw helplessness, desperation, before it was shuttered out by the usual stubbornness. His lips drew into a thin line.

'If it's too much for you, then yes, we stop. Now.'

She felt sick, suddenly. Was that the only part he'd heard?

Kaya forced herself not to reach for him as he stood with her. She felt like saying that wasn't *exactly* what she'd meant...the physical stuff didn't feel like too much, but the thought of having it, and loving it, then losing it was definitely too much. Pieter flashed into her mind—as he always did at the worst of times, but now she was starting to see the situation differently. He'd backed into Claudette's arms, but only because she had pushed him there by hating herself too much to let him touch her. She'd felt dirty, as though a part of her were always unclean, and only now was she starting to feel whole again, and worthy—because of Arno!

But she couldn't quite articulate all that, and he was already pulling away. She could literally feel him letting her go.

It was better this way, she told herself. This was a whole different situation; she could hurt even worse, way, way worse if she fell for this one and couldn't make it work. Her parents made it work, the voice in her head yelled, but that was their story, not hers. Aside from everything else her whole life was in Europe, and this man's most definitely was not. The Band-Aid way was the only way. Get it over with fast so it wouldn't hurt.

By late afternoon, the kids had practised how to do basic life-saving mouth-to-mouth breathing and cardiac massage. Arno had patiently demonstrated how to feel for a pulse, to listen and to look for signs of breathing, and also how to alleviate the excruciating stings and bite wounds left by various creatures in the wild.

It was excruciating being out here, knowing she'd never touch Arno or kiss him again. Every time she met his eyes, adrenaline pumped like petrol through her veins, making her dizzy. Was she too hasty earlier, pushing him away? Was she just annoyed over his secrecy, scared that he was pushing her away first? This was all so confusing.

Nothing had ever been so confusing in her life. Kimberley kept asking what was wrong. 'I'm just tired,' she told her.

'Was I snoring?'

'A little,' she replied tactfully, but poor Kimberley looked embarrassed, which made her feel even worse about the day.

Somehow Kaya took over the part of the session at camp where she explained the mantra of good first aid: *First do no harm...you'll be more help if you just stay calm.*

She was just about to explain the many ways in which a helper in a hysterical mindset could lead to an even bigger injury when the little boy—Stefan—she'd been talking to on the hike about his dog, called out to her.

'Kaya!'

She frowned, noticing his suddenly pale face.

'My hand hurts.'

She exchanged a glance with Arno, just before the boy started screaming and clutching his arm. 'Now my whole arm hurts!' he yelped, before hunching over on the ground.

For a second, everyone froze and stared. Except herself and Arno.

'What's the matter?' she demanded, rushing over, taking his head onto her lap on the grass, while Arno raced for medical supplies. Stefan could barely keep his eyes open now and was clutching his arm to his chest as if he were worried it might fall off.

'It's some kind of allergic reaction,' Arno said, back at her side, checking the boy's eyes with a torch. In the background Kimberley was ushering the remaining panicking kids away to the riverbank, where they couldn't watch and be frightened. Then, Kaya saw the size of Stefan's hand. It was swollen so much now it was almost twice the size as normal.

'Arno, look!'

Arno's eyes narrowed next to her as she cradled Stefan's head. Together they inspected the bizarre but telling black dot, circled with a white ring on the back of the boy's right hand. 'Spider bite,' he said gravely. Stefan was frothing at the mouth now, slurring his speech as he tried to complain. 'Shh,' she soothed. 'We're going to help you...you'll be OK.'

She lowered her voice. 'It's not the six-eyed crab spider, is it?' she said, watching Arno fish around in the bag for a syringe. The boy was struggling to breathe already and seemed to be slipping into some sort of fever dream in her arms.

'I don't know. I don't think so, it looks like a black widow bite.'

'Black widow?' Kaya's mind reeled as she held Stefan closer, protectively. 'That's almost as bad, isn't it?'

'Not quite, we caught it just in time.'

The boy was sweating but felt cold and clammy to the touch. Arno pulled the cap off a bottle of liquid and told her to hold him still. In less than twenty seconds he'd administered the full vial of antivenom, and Kaya realised she was trembling with adrenaline, sitting on the muddy floor. Were there other spiders here, ready to issue venomous bites to everyone else? How on earth had they missed this?

'Stefan didn't say anything about his hand till just now. It must have all happened so fast!' she said out loud. She bit her tongue as Arno met her eyes, remembering the talk she had literally just given the kids on staying calm.

She was the opposite of calm, suddenly. Was she to blame here? She'd been too distracted by Arno, all afternoon, torn over her decision to call things off, to notice *anything*.

'I should have seen this sooner.'

Arno must have seen the look on her face. He put a hand to her arm gently. 'There was nothing to see, it came on so fast. It's no one's fault. He's already getting colour back in his cheeks, look.'

'Arno,' she whispered, cradling the boy even closer. 'People can die from black widow bites.'

He nodded, packing up the syringe in its wrapper. 'Small children, people who are already sick, and very old people, maybe, but he's fine, this antivenom works at short notice, don't worry.'

'You've seen this before?' Kaya couldn't keep the shock from her voice.

'Of course, I have. This isn't Amsterdam.' With that, he snapped the bag shut, motioned to her to follow him with it, and took the boy gently from her arms. Stefan was coughing and clasping his arm, which thankfully was already decidedly less swollen. 'He'll need half an hour or so for the drugs to take full effect. We'll dress the wound on his hand with antibiotic cream. He'll be OK.'

She followed as he carried the boy to his tent.

This isn't Amsterdam. Did he really just have to highlight how they were from two different planets? The most dangerous things in Amsterdam were the trams and the cyclists... and weird, stoned, drunk men in parks at night, she thought with a chill. She was out of her league here, way out of her league and of course he knew it. Sure, there were moments when she dared to think she had this life all worked out, mostly gazing at some romantic sunrise, but she'd barely scratched the surface of Arno's world and she was way too green, at the end of the day, to ever live somewhere like this for ever. The thought left a dull ache in the pit of her stomach.

She helped him apply the cream and wrapped Stefan's hand with a gauze while Arno checked his blood pressure. 'He's fine, he'll sleep it off. If he wants to go home later, I'll take him.'

'I don't want to go home!' the boy mumbled groggily, and Arno huffed a laugh.

'Tough guy, huh?'

'Need me to watch him a while?' she asked.

Arno got to his haunches. 'I'll stay with him for now. Go tell the others he's OK, we handled it.'

She sighed and slunk back outside, feeling helpless and searching the ground at her feet for spiders. Always some different new drama out here; it really wasn't Amsterdam. Home would be considerably less interesting after all this.

Arno's pride had probably taken a kicking, hearing her call things off as she had done; she hardly expected things between them to be fine straight away, but till now she hadn't really considered what a culture shock it would be, going *home* after this.

She could learn something new every day if she stayed longer, carried on working with Arno…maybe there was some kind of future, like Mum and Dad had made happen for themselves. They could always visit, if she stayed on. They'd love visiting here more often, spending time with all the animals, and the kids. Mum would love Tande, she thought dreamily, before kicking herself.

Ugh. What was she even *thinking?* She must be delirious—definitely needy—after years of thinking she could never need anyone like this, also scared he'd go cold on her from now on when she was here to grow a backbone—alone.

The rest of the night, while poor Stefan rested and she, Arno and Kimberley took turns to monitor him, her head continued to hurricane around the notion of actually ending this volunteer position, or extending it, maybe with another foundation or facility.

It wasn't just about Arno! She might be too old for her parents' concern by most people's standards, but they knew what she'd been through. Mum had said more than once in her emails how dangerous it could be here, if she stepped foot in the wrong direction at the wrong time. Come home soon... stay safe out there...don't do anything silly... All the things a worried mother could say were right there in her emails. A million different ways to say they missed her.

God knew she'd put them both through enough after the attack. It wasn't fair that they'd still be worrying about her every day out here. There was also work. The hospital had offered her a new position, no more night shifts with Claudette. She was over that anyway. Claudette was welcome to Pieter; even if she did see her at the hospital, she was *much* stronger now, with or without Arno!

She jutted her jaw out, clenched her teeth.

OK, so it wasn't ideal. But it was *something*, till she figured out what was next. She could do a lot now she'd finally got her backbone back! This place had been good for her but home was calling. She'd done the right thing distancing herself from potential heartbreak, she told herself resolutely, glancing at the greying sky just as the thunder rumbled ominously from the mountains.

'Looks like we might get some rain tonight, guys,' Arno told the group, prodding at the embers of a dying fire. 'Make sure you zip your tents up properly.'

He threw her a lingering gaze that crept deep into her bones and probed at her soul. His eyes spoke volumes about wanting her, despite all the weirdness between them. For a split second she forgot she'd called things off. A flashback struck, him kissing her in that sunflower garden; the softness of his lips on hers, then hard and hungry, the start of something new. She'd fallen for him irrevocably then, and she could have sworn he felt the same.

If her ex's kisses had been ice cream and honeycomb and

all the candies she could've wanted, Arno's were strengthening pulses and nourishing juices and all the things she *needed*. He filled her up and left her satisfied. The most incredible kisses of her entire life so far had been with him. Oh, to have one more kiss with him like that, and *feel* like that, and not ruin it next time.

She groaned to herself, breaking his gaze. There couldn't be a next time! What was the matter with her? Had she not just decided?

Better for her to go to bed.

She was so exhausted, so tired of trying to figure out what was right, and what was wrong. But all she wanted, she realised, was to lie down and sleep for a week in the arms of the man she'd pushed away.

CHAPTER SIXTEEN

ARNO SMACKED A fist to his pillow, trying to get it just right. Damn camping pillows were always too small, they never fitted his head right. Not that he would've been able to sleep; the rain was almost deafening and Kaya was refusing to get out of his head.

'It won't end well. It's too much for me.'

Just those words had felt like a bullet to his chest. He'd pushed her too far; with the early morning meet-ups and kisses and caresses. They were verging on becoming a couple, sex or no sex, which was never going to end well for either of them. Volunteers never stayed long.

But that wasn't the real issue here.

He pummelled the pillow again as the thunder rumbled outside, brought it down over his head and growled into it, deep, guttural. She thought he didn't trust her. That was the killer. Was it that obvious he was holding back? He should've told Kaya when he had the chance, trusted her, let her in.

'Arno, are you awake?'

He threw the pillow aside. 'Kaya?' She was standing outside his tent in the rain—was she crazy? Quickly he won the fight with the zip at the door and she stepped inside in a pair of night shorts and a vest top, brushing the rain from her bare arms.

'Sorry… I couldn't sleep again. I came to get the earplugs.'

He stared at her from the warmth of his sleeping bag as she dropped to her knees. His brain wasn't quite registering she was actually here.

'Right, of course, I have some…' Rummaging through his backpack, he became aware of her breathing, short, sharp, as if she was nervous. The small tent shrank around them and the frogs outside intensified their rain song. Where were the damn earplugs?

'Sorry if I woke you,' she said now, sniffing against the cold.

'You didn't, I couldn't sleep,' he admitted. His fingers closed around the tiny plastic box and he clasped it in his palm as the rain on the canvas quickened in fury, a thousand hands pummelling the canvas. She said nothing but her teeth were chattering. He zipped up the open door behind them quickly, grabbed the extra sleeping bag, wrapped it around her shoulders tightly, then handed her the earplugs.

'Wait a minute at least. You'll be soaked if you go out now,' he said, resisting the urge to wipe a raindrop from her eyelashes. She sucked in a breath, an inch from his lips. He'd never seen her in sleep shorts, all tiny and fragile and sleepy, and suddenly he wanted to draw her close, nuzzle up to the warmth of her and have her protect *him* from his own incessant thoughts, and tell her…everything.

'What did you mean when you said I don't trust you?' he started.

Kaya frowned into the sleeping bag as she brought it up to her chin. She sighed through her nose. 'I know Mama Annika had a miscarriage after the fire, Arno. I know about the baby who died.'

What?

Arno sat cross-legged his sleeping bag, facing her with

his heart in his throat. So much for finally telling her himself. 'How did you…?'

'Nina told me. She thought I knew about it. I know you feel bad about that. You think Mama Annika blames you, and that's probably why you're not as close to her as you could be, right? Why you ignore her calls?'

'She said that?'

'Not all of it, no, I figured it out, from the way you are.'

Arno was speechless. He ran a hand over his jaw, thrown. She'd known all this time? Not just what happened, but she'd figured out the guilt that followed him around, strapped to his ankles like leaden chains. He didn't know whether to be angry, or relieved, or impressed…what was this feeling?

'I gave you the chance to talk to me about it,' she said now. 'Stupidly I thought maybe I'd be the one to make you realise you shouldn't feel guilty about anything. You were eighteen, you were just living your life, how were you to know a fire would break out? But I don't think you wanted to tell me anything at all, did you?'

He balled his fists around the sleeping bag, let the rain fill in the silence. This was not how he'd expected this to go. 'I didn't want you to look at me differently,' he tried to explain. 'It's my fault I wasn't there to get her out, Kaya. I know that. My brother died because of me. It's not exactly something I'm going to shout from the rooftops when I *like* someone.'

Kaya's eyes shone fiercely in the slip of moonlight creeping through the tiny mesh window.

'No one died because of you, Arno. They died because there was a *fire*.'

'That's not what my father thinks,' he said.

She blinked. 'What do you mean?'

'He blames me. When we got back from the hospital with

Mama, he told me I should have been there to protect her, and he was right.'

'Those are two different things, Arno! When did he actually say he blames you for Mama losing the baby?'

Arno paused, reliving the conversation from all those years ago in his head. They'd both been emotional, his dad especially. He'd almost lost the love of his life. Looking at Kaya, Arno could see it all now, from his father's perspective.

'I'd bet my life he doesn't blame you,' Kaya said. 'You just decided that the miscarriage was your fault and took on all the shame. The same way I told myself Pieter ditched me because I wouldn't sleep with him. You made me see this, Arno, the way you've been so good and patient with me, even knowing *everything* about what happened! Pieter dumped me because I let the shame of it all ruin the way I looked at myself. I turned into someone else, someone even *I* couldn't stand, and for what purpose?'

Her voice was wobbling now, almost setting him off as he shuffled closer impulsively, wrapped his arms around her. 'I mean, how did that serve me, Arno? He cheated on me, with one of my friends!'

The emotion in her voice now was unbearable. He held her closer, tighter, and she sank against him. 'I don't want to be someone who can't be touched,' she continued, pressing her face to his heart. 'I don't want *you* to look at *me* differently, like Pieter did. I want you to trust me and talk to me and make love to me...' She trailed off, blew air through her nostrils. 'Because you're amazing. You shouldn't feel guilty about anything, you did what you could at the time and look at everything you're doing now. You're...amazing.'

'Kaya...'

'But at the same time, I don't want you to trust me and

talk to me, and make love to me, because I don't belong here. Soon I'll never see you...'

'Is that why you called things off?' He choked into the top of her soft head. He realised he was willing his own voice not to tremble now; he wasn't used to all this emotion. It was exactly what he'd swallowed back all these years in case a tidal wave of it consumed him. But he'd severely misinterpreted what Kaya was going through. Even letting him get this close to her was a bigger deal to her than he'd ever imagined, and he'd paid her back by insulting her intelligence.

Kaya pushed him off her and scrambled out of the sleeping bag, swiping at her eyes. Arno's vision was blurry; what the hell just happened? 'Baby, what are you doing?'

She was tugging at the zip on the door now, desperate to get out. He scrambled after her. 'Kaya, stop!'

'Thank you for the earplugs,' she said, finally managing to dislodge the zip. She almost tripped on her way out, leaving her boots behind in the doorway, and Arno followed her barefoot into the rain, cursing that he couldn't call for her in case he woke everyone up.

He caught her halfway to Kimberley's tent, took her hips, swung her around. Her hair dripped rain into her eyes that slid from her eyelashes as she gasped in surprise.

'Is that why you called things off?' he said again, scooping her face closer. 'Because you think once you're done with this position, I'll never want to see you again?'

She shook her head, flattening her palms to his bare chest as the thunder cracked above them. 'It's impossible.'

Arno's stomach clenched. Maybe she was right, but he couldn't bring himself to imagine never wanting to see her again, not even if she *was* on the opposite side of the planet. She knew everything about him now, and she still wanted to see him, still worried deeply about losing him. It had been for ever since anyone had known the real him, maybe no one ever had, and Kaya wanted him anyway.

He lifted her chin, pressed his lips to hers and kissed her, to hell with the rain, and impossibilities. She responded with heat and hands and passion that made the knots inside him unravel. 'Whatever happens, I'm here for you,' he said. 'Would I kiss you like this if I wasn't? Would I even be here?'

He gestured to the rain and she shook out her arms, then looped them back around his shoulders, half laughing with the cold and emotion. 'I didn't mean to give you any reason to think I'd keep things from you… It's just, twenty years of carrying that around, it's not so easy to talk about it with anyone.'

'I see you,' she said, and she kissed him again, and again, crashing her tongue to his in the rain, till they were staggering back to his tent, falling through the door, arms and legs a wet, tangled mess on top of the sleeping bags.

The tent didn't feel too small any more as they kissed, and kissed, and wrapped their bodies around each other. It felt right to Kaya, like their own protective bubble. She was drenched, just like Arno, but the cold couldn't reach her here.

Straddling him on the sleeping bag, she leaned over him, pressed her mouth to his again, soaking in the hot deliciousness of his kisses. To hell with her fears getting in the way. No one had ever made her feel like this.

He groaned softly beneath her and she felt his hardness through her shorts. Thrilled, she wondered how this had happened so fast; she'd broken things off, but he wasn't going anywhere. Arno wanted her, even though she'd dredged his deepest darkest secret out into the open. He still felt guilty, she knew that much, but he wouldn't for ever, not if she could help it.

She slid her languid palms along his torso, along his arms, around his navel, memorising the feel of his flesh against hers, committing his contours to memory in the half-light. His hands came up in her hair and she arched her back, then slid her vest top up over her head.

Arno stilled beneath her. She felt the rise and fall of his chest between her thighs, the heady thrum of his heartbeat, same as hers. Taking his hands, she covered them with hers and traced them up over her stomach, stopping just below her breasts.

Drawing a slow, deep breath, she closed her eyes and continued inching his hands, in hers, up slowly over her naked breasts, where she paused, waiting...waiting for what?

The fear and nausea never came; the panic refused to find her. Desire flooded her belly as she pressed his hands to her breasts, wondering at the feel of them, big, warm, protective, cupping all of her, as if his hands were built to hold her.

He slid them back down her stomach, over her hips, up and down her spine slowly in wonder, exploring the feel of her skin tentatively as she rocked atop him, marvelling at the feel of his hardness against her shorts, all for her. Something to love, not to be afraid of, something that would never hurt her.

'Will you please make love to me?' The words left her mouth without a thought. Lowering her mouth to his, letting her hand slide down to the band of his shorts, she trembled in anticipation as she went to reach for him. She was ready to touch him; ready to be touched. Finally, here was everything she'd ever wanted.

With a frustrated sound, Arno clasped her hand, then removed it.

'No, Kaya,' he said, bringing her fingers to his mouth instead.

'I *want* you to. I'm saying it's OK.'

'I said no, not here.' Arno sat upright, lifted her easily from astride him and laid her down gently onto her back, arching over her.

She froze beneath him. His face was obscured by the shadows, a faceless force, and she gasped for breath, scrambling up and away from him, covering her face in her hands as fresh mortification consumed her.

Breathe, breathe, breathe... It's Arno. It's not him!

'I'm sorry,' she cried, devastated. 'It's not you...'

'I know, it's OK, calm down.'

'I was fine, when I was in control, when I was on top...'

'This is why I'm not doing it,' he said gruffly, reaching for something in the dark. To her horror he pulled on a shirt, rummaged around for something else, and in a second he was shining a torch up at the roof. He held out his hand, eyes narrowed in compassion, and just the tiniest bit of annoyance—at himself, no doubt—and there was the nausea, swirling through her stomach, chasing all the butterflies out. She'd done it again. Proven she was broken.

'You're not ready,' he said to her softly, kindly, still holding his hand out to her. 'It's OK, Kaya, you can't rush it and I won't let you.'

But we don't have time not to rush, she felt like saying, but she couldn't even muster any words.

She took his outstretched hand in the torchlight, and he helped her into a sleeping bag, snuggled up close to her in his own, draped an arm around her. Moving into his big protective spoon, she tried not to blame herself. How could she? Besides, he understood, he knew everything, and he was there for her...

This was *exactly* why she was falling for him, she thought in dismay as his breath ruffled her hair. This was why this would only hurt her more when it was over. It hadn't gone to plan today at all, ending things for good with Arno.

What exactly was she supposed to do, now?

CHAPTER SEVENTEEN

THE DAY DAWNED bright on the last morning of the expedition, and Kaya left his tent before sunrise, quietly, so no one at camp would be any the wiser. He heard the zip of Kimberley's tent, then he heard her start the fire, the clang of the pot for their coffee. He lay there alone for a few minutes, studying the canvas ceiling, gathering himself together.

Her sweet scent was all over his pillow.

Whatever had happened last night had thrown him all out of whack, but he had a bush survival skills class to teach before it was time to pack up and head to Thabisa, and he had to pull himself together.

Pulling on his clothes, he could still taste Kaya, still recall every inch of herself she'd revealed to him...the curves of her breasts in his hands, the look on her face when he'd told her no. The hardest damned thing he'd ever done!

He tore the zip up roughly, stepping into the sunshine. She handed him a tin cup of steaming coffee.

Lucky that he did say no last night, he thought, eyeing her profile in the morning light against the backdrop of glistening wet leaves and craggy mountains. *Beautiful,* he thought. Mama Annika would love to paint her, just like this, if she had the chance.

'How are you feeling?' he asked her.

'I don't know,' she admitted, but she hid a small smile in

her hair, and his lips curled in response as he clocked her still flushed cheeks, her swollen lips.

'You were a gentleman,' she said next, quietly. He wasn't sure if that reassured her or provoked the same deep agonising urges in her as it did him, even now, but they sank to the camping chairs and drank in silence in the ring of tents, tapping their boots against each other's.

He'd been right, she wasn't ready for more; not in the way she wanted to be. It only lit a fire in him, to be a better man for her. That Pieter guy cheated on her? After what she'd been through? The thought of it made his blood boil. No wonder she found it hard to let people close.

However long he had her for, he could still strive harder to be the kind of amazing she thought he was...which, of course, he wasn't. Not to Mama anyway. Not yet, but he would change that. No more cowardly avoidance.

She turned to him suddenly. 'Arno, we should probably talk about—'

'Kaya?' Their spider-bite survivor, Stefan, was stepping out of his tent now, yawning sleepily. She shot Arno an apologetic look as she put her cup down and rushed to Stefan, got to her knees and checked his hand.

It was back to normal, as Arno knew it would be, and the kid still insisted he wanted to stick it out for their final day. Kids round here were brave; they had to be. Sometimes he wondered if his volunteers had seen half the strength from kids where they came from, as they saw out here.

Kaya was brave last night, too, he thought. He watched her while they set up the cereal station for breakfast, wishing he could go back to last night and stop himself sooner, before she'd even got the chance to try and give herself to him like that... What was he even doing, letting it go that far?

He'd got carried away, he supposed.

She probably just wanted to tell him it had to go slower, but she didn't need to. They wouldn't be doing anything more, even though the thought of abstaining was torturous enough. She was worth waiting for.

How ironic that the theme of today was survival, he mused, feeling the caffeine slowly render him ready for the day's lessons as the kids emerged slowly from their tents. As much as she'd made it clear that they could be there for each *other*, he felt as though all he was living for now was to make things good for Kaya and keep her safe from the world.

He rolled his eyes at himself. God, he was in trouble.

Survival and its various techniques were clearly a favourite subject for Arno, Kaya thought as the kids took furious notes and clamoured to be part of his hands-on demonstrations. She was listening in, buttering bread for lunch-time sandwiches.

'Breaking survival down to its basics, it's all about three life-saving elements: shelter, warmth, and water,' he was saying now. 'Without any of these, you'll fade fast in the wild before you can have any hope of rescue.'

It wasn't anything she didn't know but, even with her knowledge of first aid and emergency care, she wouldn't stand much chance here, without Arno around. It wasn't Amsterdam. The more she thought about that, the more she didn't want to go home so soon. Would he ask her to stay?

She smiled to herself, smothering peanut butter onto a slice, letting her mind wander. She couldn't stay, she'd already decided that, but she felt a little better, a little more in control of her life. Maybe it *was* possible to get out of her head, and just enjoy him.

It was the sexiest thing on earth watching Arno construct a shelter from sticks and stones with his bare hands, encouraging the kids to help. She couldn't get the image of their kiss in the rain from her head, or what had happened after, unfortunately, when she'd asked him to make love to her and he'd refused.

She cringed, catching his eye over the makeshift shelter.

'A shelter will protect you if the wind and cold or even the sun get too much,' he said, holding her gaze a second too long as he snapped a branch in his hands, sending her mind back to the seductive thrill of his fingers trailing the circumference of her navel, the sparks that had set her insides on fire the second his hands had cupped her breasts. She could still feel the length of him hardening between her legs.

She swallowed, realising Kimberley was grinning at her from her place, folding towels by the tents.

'The shelter will provide a vital element of protection in an otherwise desperate situation,' Arno told the group. 'If you're lost, the shelter will be your protective environment while you wait, whether it's hours or days or maybe weeks...'

Hours, days, weeks...

Kaya bit hard on her lip, stabbing a knife back into the peanut-butter jar. How long would she have to wait to feel him so close again? She didn't have much time, but he was right, she couldn't be rushed. Couldn't even rush herself, not when the slightest, stupidest shadow was enough to set her back.

'We'll need a fire next,' he was saying. 'Heat and flames can send a signal to potential rescuers.'

She was hot, without the fire, she realised, swiping at her clammy forehead. Just the memories from that tent, and the way he'd kissed her in the rain as though their lives depended on it, were enough to get her burning up.

In minutes, their little fire was crackling. Kimberley winked at her over a towel, bobbed her head suggestively towards Arno, and Kaya felt her face flush. Kimberley had heard her come back from Arno's tent this morning, but all she'd said was, 'Did you get lucky with the doctor?'

'Depends what you mean by lucky,' she'd replied. Lucky he didn't kick her out then and there for being a tease. Lucky he'd come back even after she'd tried to push him away.

'Does anyone know what we can add to that fire, to make smoke?' he said, shoving his shirt sleeves higher up his arms, showcasing the snake with its fangs on his arm.

A flurry of hands shot up at his question and it sucker-punched her, the cold, hard fact that she was totally, irrevocably smitten. That stupid snake tattoo...maybe Mama Imka was onto something there. She didn't have to rush; like a snake, she could go slowly. He *had* been a gentleman. But if they went any slower now she'd scream.

'That's right,' he was saying, passing a bunch of green leaves to one of the girls. 'See what these do to the fire.'

The leaves sent a cloud of smoke high into the sky. The kids all clapped. The young girl beamed from under her sun-hat as if she'd solved a riddle and scored a prize, and Kaya ran her eyes over his lips from afar, conjuring back the taste of him.

They hadn't even gone all the way, but the embarrassment of her little turn had faded now; she was more determined than ever to have him make love to her, at least once, before she had to go home. She'd always wonder if she didn't! So what if it made her miss him more, or she got attached? That was all called being alive, and being a woman. Finally, she was starting to feel like a woman again, thanks to him.

A chorus of *'Ew...'* and *'Gross...'* almost cancelled out the frogs in the river and she startled from her thoughts, only to discover he'd explained that their own pee could also be used on a fire to make smoke.

He sure knew everything there was to know about fire.

Kaya frowned at the slice of bread before her now. Did she get through to him at all, last night?

Mama Annika didn't blame him for that miscarriage, surely, the way she was always reaching out to him. He'd just taken his dad's words to heart, even though the man was probably an emotional mess at the time. She hadn't met him but, judging by the love she'd felt in that home, every scrap of Arno's guilt was unwarranted. If he'd only talk to them both about it, instead of making all these excuses not to be around them, they'd have him shed that truckload of guilt in no time…

Kimberley was calling her over from the tent. Dropping her peanut-butter duties, she wandered over.

'Help me with this one, will you?' she said, gesturing to the end of a cotton tablecloth. 'I can't believe how fast this weekend has gone already!'

'Me neither,' Kaya said as the kids cheered at something Arno said behind them.

'Is he as good to you as he is to them?' Kimberley pried, gesturing to him over the giant tablecloth. Kaya sighed. These days, she had no energy to even deny it.

'He's everything to me,' she admitted.

'Then snare him!'

CHAPTER EIGHTEEN

TODAY WAS THE DAY. Arno had already decided. It was less than a month now till Kaya and the rest of the volunteers were due to board their planes back to their respective countries. Usually he'd be excited to welcome a new group, but this was different. Time was ticking by too fast; he had to ask if she wanted to stay longer.

Just come out and ask her already!

He should have asked by now, he thought, finding her across the mud and grass that constituted Mama Imka's village's football pitch—where they'd set up their temporary medical centre for this afternoon's treatments. But he'd been trying to enjoy the moment. Every moment with her.

The weeks they'd spent together since that camping expedition were a blur that could bring a goofy smile to his face any time, anywhere. He'd shown her how to fire a gun, hit a moving target with a tranquilliser dart. She knew the names of the birds who sang in the new dawn, and at the top of Table Mountain he wished he had half his mama's skills, so he could paint her against the sunset, so he'd never have to stop looking at her face.

It was all new to him—a year with Bea hadn't even compared to the depth of his emotions now after just a few months, but if he asked her to stay and she refused him...

They hadn't even had that conversation—it was as if they'd

both silently agreed to enjoy this for what it was, without worrying about the future, and the last thing he wanted was to pressure her.

Could he even commit to something serious, with someone so much younger, from an entirely different country? Could he keep her safe and protected long-term, as she deserved and needed?

That was the real issue that was keeping him up at night. He couldn't stand the thought of letting her down in any way.

'Mama Imka is ready for her medicine,' she said now, walking over to meet him in her uniform blue T-shirt. His eyes lingered on her hair, then the smooth caramel flesh on show inside the V of her collar. 'Do you want to do it, or shall I?'

She fiddled with her necklace suddenly and he sighed to himself, getting up from his seat, wishing just the sight of her didn't turn him on so much in public—a result of abstaining from sex all this time, he supposed. She'd got him so wound up, so utterly frustrated that no wonder his head was a carousel of questions around her.

'You don't want to?'

'I don't mind,' she lied, looking at the floor.

She was nervous being around Mama Imka, because of whatever she'd told her, or *predicted*, when she'd first arrived. Sometimes he wondered if she'd predicted something to do with *him*.

'You still haven't told me what she said to you,' he reminded her, crossing the grass with her, past the kids playing football, towards the hut.

'That's for me to know, and you to find out,' she said cryptically, but he didn't miss her gaze flickering to his forearm, where his tattoo was peeking from his shirt sleeve. He stopped, shoved his sleeve up and studied it, looking for a fly or a tick, or something.

'What?' he asked, confused.

She shook her head. 'Nothing. Why don't we both go in to her?'

'Deal,' he said.

'You know...' She paused. 'You haven't told me what she said to you, either. Before I even got here.'

'What makes you think it was about you?' he teased, and he touched a hand to her back, to guide the way.

His touch seemed to stop her short in her tracks. Kaya crumpled his shirt sleeve up tightly in her hand and sighed so heavily through clenched lips she could have uprooted a tree. He could read her sighs by now. Kaya thought she was ready for more. She was chomping at the bit; probably more frustrated than him, but he'd refused her, over and over, and over.

Maybe he was crazy...but it was better than having her react badly and feeling as if he'd pressured her. Maybe he'd give into her, if she wanted to stay longer.

'How are we feeling today?' she chirruped as they entered the hut together. Kaya was clearly trying to appear indifferent in front of Mama Imka, he mused now. Her nerves made his pulse quicken; she was right, he hadn't ever told her about the real significance of their encounter in the sunflower garden. In truth he was still struggling with that one himself.

'Ah, the two of you together, what a delight.' Mama Imka looked worryingly pale today, and frailer than she had done even last week, when he'd come with one of the other volunteers.

'She has a cough, and chest pains,' her daughter croaked from the doorway. Then she lit three candles and Arno knew Kaya was thinking the same thing. The meds were just keeping her stable now. HIV and TB together had weakened her immune system; even the smallest illness or bug could wreak havoc on her fragile body.

'I'm fine,' Mama Imka insisted, before hacking into her hand.

'We may have to move you to the hospital,' he said gently, and the old woman tried her best to sit up, waving Kaya's hands away as she offered her another blanket.

'I'm not going anywhere,' she said, adamantly. 'I told you that, Dr Nkosi. This is where I belong.'

'But if you get worse, you won't have the help you need here,' Kaya tried as Arno prepared her medicine. The six-month course was almost up, and while she had good days and bad days, the bad days were catching up with her.

He felt Kaya's frustration as the woman insisted she wouldn't go, not even if she was at death's door. Then she insisted she was fine with death welcoming her, as it had done her husband several years ago.

'I don't know what to do, she's so stubborn,' Kaya told him outside, when they were packing up the Jeep. 'Are you sure the two of you aren't related?'

'Very funny,' he said. Then he saw the genuine concern on her face. 'Some people round here, especially from the small villages, don't put much faith in traditional medicine. They believe in…other things.'

She pouted, thoughtfully. 'We must be able to force her. She needs full-time care by professionals.'

'We can't force her to do anything,' he told her. 'I wish we could.'

'But she'll die here.'

'That's her choice.'

Kaya was silent. She climbed up into the Jeep with a jaded sigh, and he wished he could reassure her, but she didn't know how these things worked out here. It wasn't as if it were where she was from. There was a lot she still didn't know about life here. Not all of it was saving lives, most of it was just making it a little bit more comfortable.

He searched for something positive to tell her.

On the road, he almost let on about the plaque he'd finally had made in honour of his brother. The copper memorial had arrived just last week—*Remembering Baby Kung*. He was planning to present it to Mama Annika, and maybe even suggest they open the restaurant again. He would help, of course. It was time. But he was still procrastinating…it needed to be the right time. Kaya would tell him to drive there right now if he brought all this up. That was the problem. These were conversations he had to have with Mama *and* Dad, in private, especially after all this time.

Speak of the devil. His phone was ringing. They must have driven into range; the signal was so sporadic out here.

Swiping it from the dash, he answered on speakerphone. He knew better than to ignore her these days, and actually it felt pretty good to know that their mother-son relationship was slowly getting back on track; even if it was mostly small talk.

'Dinner, with you and Dad tonight?' he answered her now. 'Me and Kaya?'

Mama Annika wanted them to stay over, too, and he paused before answering. It was best not to refuse. His recent efforts to be a better son weren't going unnoticed, why refuse a nice dinner invitation?

How was she to know he'd been planning to take Kaya to dinner himself tonight, and ask her if she'd stay on, somewhere quiet where they wouldn't be interrupted?

'I'd love to,' Kaya said into the phone, much to his surprise. She had never met his dad before, and even though she'd insisted he probably didn't blame Arno for what happened to Mama, Arno had yet to talk to him about it. Their relationship had been based on small talk for so long he wasn't sure what they'd all find to say. Either way, Arno saw his plan fly straight out of the window.

Kaya hadn't quite been expecting the spitting image of Arno—an older, greyer version of him at least—to welcome them into the house and talk her ear off about the wine industry around the kitchen table, and now that she was here, something didn't feel right.

She realised, halfway through her plate of white bean casserole, that she'd accepted in anticipation of a very different introduction by Arno, especially as she was meeting his father, but he'd still called her his *volunteer*.

He reached for her fingers under the table the second her parents got up to fetch themselves more wine from the cellar. 'Sorry about him,' he said.

'I like hearing your father talk,' she said, releasing his fingers quickly, the second they walked back into the room.

He threw her a look she knew meant *What's wrong with you?* But she concentrated on her napkin. Maybe he was wondering why she was suddenly awkward, but the longer she was here, the more uncomfortable she was, not knowing what this *thing* was. If it was just a fling, should she really be here, getting to know his parents?

Where did she stand?

She shouldn't have come.

'I was kind of hoping we could talk tonight, somewhere else, alone,' he whispered now, while his parents discussed the vintage bottle excitedly, opposite them.

'Oh?' Kaya's heart sped up as the butterflies struck her belly. She was about to ask what about, when Mama Annika started talking about the restaurant, how she'd been thinking about opening it again, how a new hot chef had expressed interest, and what did Arno think? Could he help locate a structural engineer? Could they move the memorial there, where it really belonged?

Arno looked as though someone had just put a live cable into his bathtub. 'I was going to suggest the same thing, but, Mama, Dad, I think we all need to talk—'

'Maybe Kaya can plant us a little restaurant garden,' Mama said next, cutting him off in her excitement. 'How long do we have you for, lovely Kaya?'

Kaya's heart leapt up to her throat.

'I do hope you'll be back again to visit? Or maybe Arno can visit you in Holland?'

Arno sat back in his chair. Kaya waited again. Now might be a nice time for him to confirm that either suggestion would be nice, but he mumbled a non-committal *maybe*, staring at the blackened kitchen wall, drumming his fingers on the table.

Her stomach plummeted right through the bottom of her chair. Of course he wasn't going to visit her, he had far too much going on here…and now this. Not that she could blame him; she should be happy he seemed to be getting more involved with his family. It was what she wanted for him, but…

He threw her an apologetic look and she forced a smile, even as fear struck her like a thunderbolt. She'd been here before, she'd felt it, right before Pieter announced he was seeing Claudette and didn't love her any more.

'I have a few weeks left here yet,' she explained quickly, forcing an air of indifference she prayed they bought. 'My parents have planned a big welcome-home party already. The hospital where I work have asked for confirmation of a return date, so I guess it's all set.'

'You're going back to the hospital?' Arno's brow furrowed instantly next to her. She had his full attention, and a thrill darted through her as she straightened up. She'd told him Pieter's new girlfriend, Claudette—the one he cheated on her with—worked there. 'Is that a good idea?'

'It's a good opportunity.' She bristled. 'A promotion. No more night shifts.'

'I was hoping you might...' He trailed off, frowning at his plate while his parents looked between them in interest.

'Might what?' she pressed. Any second now, he would say it. He'd say he wanted her to stay, with the foundation, with this new restaurant launch, whatever that might involve. With him.

'I think he wants you to stay,' Mama Annika cut in with a grin at his dad, and Arno blew air through his lips, dragged a hand across his head.

'Mama!'

Kaya's cheeks flamed. Talk about putting them on the spot. She wanted to hear that from him, not them. And he hadn't said a word about it, much as he wasn't now. Gosh, she was an idiot.

'Well, I'm afraid I can't stay,' she forced herself to say firmly as her heart convulsed in her chest. 'Even though I do love...' she glanced at Arno '...love...it here, I have a lot going on back home.'

Excusing herself, she hurried to the bathroom, splashed cold water on her face and scolded herself in the mirror for her tears. She was here to grow a backbone, not crumble over a man.

The rest of the evening was torture.

Arno—even quieter than usual—tried to put his arms around her in the bedroom, and this time, for the first time ever, she removed herself from his embrace, told him she was too hot and needed a proper rest. He didn't argue. Didn't ask why she wasn't trying to throw herself on him as usual. Maybe, all things considered, he was glad she was backing off.

Eventually, in the darkness, he said, 'Are you really going back to that hospital?'

'Is that all you want to say?' she snapped, annoyance getting the better of her.

He was silent for a long time. 'I don't know what to say, Kaya. I know your life is somewhere else. And mine is here; it will always be here.'

He sounded sad, and her heart broke into a million pieces. 'I know,' she said again, forcing her voice not to shake. 'It is what it is, Arno, we both knew that, going in.'

Lying with her back to him in the tension, Kaya cursed her stupidity. She should have known this would happen. That she'd fall hook, line and sinker, only to be left in a pile of wreckage. No wonder he wouldn't sleep with her. For a second, back there at the table, she'd thought by 'talk' he'd meant something else, because she'd been dying for him for weeks. He'd been fending her off, as if he was afraid he might break her if they tried again, and it was getting to be intolerable. Now, she was starting to understand.

He'd been here for her, as he'd said he would, but as for wanting to see her after this… That was all just wishful thinking in a moment of passion and wrought emotion. He was already anticipating her departure. He'd accepted they were far too different for this to be anything real and lasting. It was time she did the same.

Arno Nkosi was enough of a gentleman that he wouldn't just sleep with her and abandon ship, not after what she'd been through, but as for wanting anything more than a temporary fling, well… This was not her own parents' love story. This was her own, and it was not going to have a happy ending.

CHAPTER NINETEEN

TANDE WASN'T AT the gates, waiting for him at sunrise as she usually was. Arno couldn't help but see it as an omen. It was never going to be a great day—the day Kaya was leaving.

The morning round was perfunctory at best, just himself and Mark: a spate of jabs, some meds to be administered, one fractured wrist. He stopped by the village to check on a withering but steadfast and stubborn Mama Imka, took a few Polaroid shots of the blossoming sunflowers and plump beans that were almost ready for picking in the veggie garden. Kaya might like to take them home.

It wasn't exactly the parting gift he'd had in mind for her, but with things the way they were she hadn't really given him much time or attention since they'd left the winery that night. Switched off might be the better term, and his own self-preservation had drawn a deeper line between them.

She was leaving today.

He drove back to Thabisa slowly, watching the clouds make faces at him over the mountains.

That night had been driving him crazy ever since. So much for getting her alone, to talk to her. First his father had talked her ear off, which had surprised him—he hadn't brought anyone home in so long he'd clean forgotten how they both still thrived amongst company. Then Mama had thrown a bombshell about wanting to reopen the restaurant. His words had got all tangled.

He had been about to just come out and say it, right there in front of Kaya and Dad too—that he was sorry he hadn't been strong enough for her up till now, sorry about not being there when she needed him that night, and all the years after, sorry for waiting so long to give her the damn plaque. It had been right there in the Jeep, waiting for him to hand it over.

Then Kaya had announced she was going. Everything he'd been building up in his head had just flown out of the window.

She was so sure about it. Even about going back to the hospital. She had a life back home that didn't involve him, and he had one here. The whole time he'd been thinking of asking her to stay, she was already accepting a new job in Amsterdam!

He wasn't about to try and pressure her into anything. That wasn't the way to handle her. So that was it. It had been fun. More than fun. The best thing that had ever happened to him, even without the sex, and that was something he'd never thought he'd say.

Now he just had to suck it up and put it in the past. Somehow, he had to say goodbye.

By the time he returned to Thabisa, the farewell cocktails were well under way. He slunk past the group, catching Kaya's eye briefly. The long, lingering look she gave him twisted a knot in his stomach, which stuck the whole time he was showering and changing. He sat in a towel on the bed, pulled out the best Polaroid to give her. Picking up a pen, he hovered it over the back.

Should he?

Well, at this point he had nothing to lose.

He wrote on the back, kept it brief, kept it neat.

Then he changed his mind. He couldn't give her this! It would mess with her head; she'd made a decision. Who was he to stand in her way? She deserved more anyway...someone who at least knew how to look after a woman.

Standing, he felt the fury at himself grown tenfold. The plaque taunted him from the dresser. He hadn't even faced his own parents yet. It had been nothing but excuses. Enough was enough. Grabbing it up, he swiped the Jeep keys and drove like a bat out of hell to the estate. He'd be back before the group left, but he was damned if he'd put this conversation off one moment longer. Yes, he'd let Kaya slip through his fingers, but he was still his mother's only son.

'Where's Arno?'

Kimberley went to hand her another drink but Kaya refused it, eyes scanning the forecourt. The bus would be arriving to take them to Cape Town in less than an hour, and she was starting to worry he wouldn't even say goodbye.

'I don't know,' she admitted as her pulse spiked. Around her, the volunteers were laughing, toasting a job well done, talking excitedly about plans for home, but she was worried. OK, so they'd cooled things off, but it wasn't like him to just disappear.

'What happened with you two?' Kimberley asked her again. She'd been asking for days but Kaya wasn't sharing. She didn't really know herself. Nothing, she supposed. They'd slipped right back to being colleagues since that night at the winery and she assumed that was fine by him. It was for the best, all things considered, but to not even say goodbye?

Now she was just...angry.

Excusing herself, she walked to his room, stood at the bottom of the porch steps. The lights were off inside, but what if he was in there? Anxiety gnawed at her insides. What if he was sick?

'Arno?' The door opened in front of her right as she knocked, and she braced herself. But he didn't answer. He'd just left his door unlocked.

She stepped inside, looked around for the Jeep keys. If those were gone, she'd know he'd driven somewhere himself. The room smelled of him, his unmistakeable scent. Weakened by what she'd lost, she stopped and caught her breath. She'd got so used to his scent in her nostrils, and the time she'd spent without it lately had felt empty, bland, boring, but what was she supposed to do?

'Where are you?' she growled as emotion rose in her and threatened to consume her. Then…what was that?

Sinking to the bed, she picked up what looked like a postcard. No, a Polaroid. Her hand flew over her mouth. It was a photo of the vegetable garden, and three sunflowers. They must have just come up this week, from the seeds she'd planted.

When did he take this? Why did he leave it here?

There was writing on the back. Kaya's hands trembled as she read it. Suddenly, she was struggling for breath.

Kaya,

Mama Imka told me a great love would bloom with the sunflowers. She was right. I think I'll love you for ever.

Arno x

Kaya swiped at her eyes. This was not happening!

How on earth was this real? Not just the prediction about the sunflowers, but him writing *I think I'll love you for ever.*

He had never told her that. Why hadn't he told her?

'Kaya, are you here?' She sprang from the bed at the

voice outside. Kimberley was racing up the porch steps. 'Where's Arno?'

'I don't know,' she said again. 'He's not here, his keys aren't here!'

Kimberley looked frightened suddenly. 'When did you last see him?'

'An hour ago, I'm not sure, I was outside with you, I just saw him pass by, and now he's gone again. What's happened?'

Dread pulsed through her. Kimberley's face wasn't helping. 'There's been some kind of attack,' Kimberley said, panting in the doorway. 'They found a man. He's unrecognisable, they said. It just came through on the radio. They think it was a lion. You don't think it's... Tande?'

A tear-stained Mama Annika, in her paint-splattered kaftan, loved the plaque. She hugged Arno closer than he'd let her get in years and put it straight on the wall by the kitchen door. When Dad walked in, his words got caught in his throat, but he forced them out.

'I always thought you blamed me for what happened to Kung. So I blamed myself, all this time.'

His father pulled him into him, along with Mama. They stood there for what felt like for ever while Dad told him what Kaya had: that he'd spoken from the pain and loss and anger at *himself* for not being there either, and had in no way intended for Arno to carry the blame.

'I should have been there for you that night, Mama. Dad was right about that.'

'We're so proud of you, son. You took what happened that night and you turned it around. Look at all the lives you save now.'

Mama would have none of his apologies for the years he felt as if he'd shut her out. All she had ever wanted was for him to be happy. It was as if he'd shed a blanket made of concrete on the kitchen floor.

Relief flooded through him in the arms of his family, right before he remembered he'd just lost as much as he'd gained.

Mama asked him, 'Isn't Kaya leaving today?'

'She's all packed up.'

Mama Annika gasped and started ushering him out of the door. 'Go, go! I thought you would ask her to stay longer!'

He tried to explain. 'You heard her. She has a life to get back to.'

Mama Annika just crossed her arms and closed her eyes, and shook her head at her feet, and he knew then, he'd really messed it up.

'Son, you need to learn a few things about us women. She was waiting for you to show her you want her! Go get her. That is an order.'

Arno didn't need telling twice. Already he could feel the concrete blanket was back around his shoulders, thinking it was too late. She might already be on that bus, to Cape Town.

Kissing Mama goodbye and shaking his father's hand with a promise to be back soon to take a look at the restaurant plans, he sped back to the Jeep, only to find his radio buzzing off the hook.

An emergency, something to do with a lion, a man…an attack. Bashing the co-ordinates into the satnav and praying to God this wasn't the reason why he hadn't seen Tande today, he roared out of the driveway, checking the time. He'd go straight to the airport after this—he'd go get Kaya. Or at least tell her how much she'd changed his life.

Because of her, he might actually have a great relationship with Mama *and* Dad going forward. Because of her, he'd at least shed the guilt of being someone who couldn't protect what was his. He'd done all he could at the time. Mama had even said, *'If you hadn't dragged me out, I'd be dead too!'*

The body, when he got to it, no longer even looked like a human. A village of people were crowded round, panicking, screaming. 'It went that way, the lion went that way!'

Arno's heart bucked. What if it *was* Tande? Something could have happened…anyone might provoke her.

The pathway through the mountains was overgrown jungle, but there was a village at the end of it. One that would have no idea a lion might be heading for them.

Arno gathered his gun and tranquilliser darts from the Jeep and sprinted into the bush.

The emergency rescue vehicle, with just herself and two male staff members from Thabisa, was speeding down the gravel road. Kaya's butt should be bruised and sore from the lack of suspension in the back, but she barely felt it. No one could reach Arno.

His radio seemed to be out of range. Someone had seen him at the scene of the attack; they said he'd gone off alone into the mountains. Probably looking for Tande.

Somewhere ahead, a plane soared over the mountains. Maybe it was hers, she didn't care. The others had left once they knew the person who'd been mauled wasn't Arno, but she'd hugged Kimberley goodbye and joined the rescue crew. It had been four hours now, and there was still no sign of him. Gut-wrenching loss made a mess of her make-up; her heart felt as if it might explode.

The conversation around the dining table played out again in her head as she scanned the roadside for him, the siren blaring. She'd thought about that night a million times since, but now she could see it so differently.

He'd been dealing with his parents coming at him about reopening that restaurant; that would have been a tough subject for him, all things considered. And she'd only thought about *herself* in that moment, read him all wrong. All she'd done was panic and project her stupid fears of rejection onto him, made him think she didn't even want to be there, or with him.

And now he was gone…possibly in the wilderness with a lion that might or might not be Tande. Mikal had confirmed they hadn't seen Tande all day—maybe she had escaped and got hungry. Kaya couldn't even entertain the thought that Tande would do something like that, let alone to Arno…

'I see something.' Their driver pulled the vehicle to a stop. Sure enough, she could see something flickering, a torch, maybe. They'd come a different way from the route the guys at the scene said he'd taken on foot, and now they were stopped at the entry point to what must be the most remote village she'd ever seen. The pathway was so narrow, they couldn't drive it. She leapt from the vehicle and didn't even flinch when Mikal tried to grab her wrist to hold her back.

'Be careful!'

He was right. Kaya drew a deep breath, quoting herself on the outdoor expedition: *First do no harm…you'll be more help if you just stay calm*. She took the tranquilliser gun from the door and shoved it into her belt with a purpose, swallowing down her galloping heart.

Then, she ran for the light, swiping the bushes as they lunged for her, and only stopped dead when a deafening roar ahead splintered her senses.

CHAPTER TWENTY

THE LION'S ROAR could have started an avalanche and Arno's heart was a freight train as he motioned for the mother and her two small children across the small clearing to stay quiet.

'Where are you, buddy?' he whispered to the beast, scanning the shadows. It was close, judging by that sound.

The woman held her kids close, huddled in a doorway to one of three tiny huts, pitched around a campfire. The men, they said, had gone to another village for supplies, and left them with no gun, but the hunk of animal meat on the spit above the fire must have lured the predator close.

Just then, a crack of a branch ten feet away sent his pulse roaring louder than the lion. 'Get inside,' he told the cowering woman, poised with one hand on his holster.

It wasn't a lion that emerged slowly from the bush, clutching a gun with two hands. It was Kaya. Mikal was close behind her. 'What are you doing here?' he snapped. 'It's dangerous!'

'Looking for you,' she said, and in less than a second flat she'd sprinted across the circle, past the fire, to his side. She was panting heavily, her dress was crumpled, her forehead clammy. She was supposed to be on a plane! For a moment he was totally thrown.

'Are you crazy?' he said, coming to his senses, just as Mikal's voice echoed out in the night.

'Arno, watch out!'

He darted in front of Kaya as the two kids screamed and shrieked from the doorway. A giant lion, almost the size of his Jeep, pounced from the roof of one of the huts and landed with a thwack on the dirt between them, its huge paws less than six feet away from Arno's toes.

'Don't move,' he said.

Across the circle, Mikal pointed the gun as the lion stalked the slab of meat in the firelight, shaking his mane. Kaya's breathing was a ragged scratch behind him and he wanted to yell at her for putting herself in danger, for making him responsible for her. Because his heart quite literally would not handle it if anything happened... But she'd come for him. Instead of getting on that plane.

One of the kids sniffed, and the lion looked up, seemingly turning his attention to a new target. 'Not the kid,' Kaya cried now, going to step out from behind him. The movement made the lion spin and take a new aim. Right at them.

Arno drew a breath, then loaded a dart. Neither of them made a sound. Its black eyes glimmered in the firelight. Time slowed to nothing, then a surge of fury took a hold of him. There was no way in hell he was letting any harm come to Kaya, or anyone here!

'Want me to shoot?' Mikal was poised.

'I'll do it,' he said.

One finger on the trigger, he made his body a shield for Kaya. He hated to shoot, even with a tranquilliser, more than anything, but if he didn't have a choice...

Just then, another rustle in the bushes drew the lion's gaze away, and before Arno could quite tell what was happening, another big cat was on top of their stalker, wrestling the lion to the ground.

'Tande!' Kaya grabbed his arm. He made quick work while

the cats were distracted and backed with her around the fire, away from the wrestling match. Screaming kids pierced his ears as the family of three ran to Mikal. Arno told him not to shoot.

Tande must have heard them and come to his rescue. His usually gentle lioness was biting and clawing and scratching her way to victory, until, as quickly as she'd arrived, she'd shooed the giant lion off, sent it packing the way it had come. They watched from the ground as it leapt, defeated, back onto the roof with a growl and darted off into the night.

They were left there, breathless, while Tande helped herself to the meat around the fire, lounging on the ground with it between her paws, like a contented cat.

'Unreal,' Kaya whispered, dropping her gun to the ground and turning to him. 'What just happened?'

He cupped her beautiful face in his damp hands, and kissed her before he could even think, half in relief, half in desire, mostly in desire—she'd never looked better. She kissed him back, deeply, hungrily, told him sorry, over and over and over.

'I saw the photo you took, on your bed,' she said after a moment, searching his eyes. 'I went looking for you when you didn't come say goodbye. Why didn't you tell me?'

'Tell you what?' he asked her, smoothing her cheeks. He could hardly believe she was still here, or indeed what had just happened. It could have turned out a completely different story. His brain wasn't working.

'That you think you'll love me for ever,' she said, taking his hand, pressing it to her heart. 'You've changed everything, Arno. I shouldn't have ever made you think I didn't want more than… I just got caught up in my own head. I didn't want you to end things first. You wouldn't sleep with me…'

'I had my own stuff going on in my own stupid head,' he

replied with a wry laugh, and she kissed him again. God, he'd missed these lips, the feel of her hair tickling his face, her eyes. 'And you have no idea how it killed me, not sleeping with you.'

She bit her lip, looked up through her eyelashes. 'What do we do now? I missed my flight.'

'You can keep on missing flights,' he told her, taking her hands, then claiming her mouth again with his. In truth, he had no idea what was next, except the bedroom, but as long as she was looking at him like this, and kissing him like this, he knew they would work it out.

EPILOGUE

One year later

'MY PARENTS ARE obsessed with you,' Kaya exclaimed as they left the house on Kerkstraat and made their way across Leidseplein towards the canal.

'Well, who wouldn't be?' Arno joked, bringing her hand to his mouth and placing a light kiss on her fingers.

'I'm serious. I think my mum's reliving her childhood there, through you. They're going to want to come and stay longer next time.'

'They're welcome to,' he said, and Kaya's heart swelled to the size of a watermelon as they strolled hand in hand in the twilight, stopping while she acted like a proud tour guide for Arno. He was seeing Amsterdam at its absolute best today, right before sunset, when the sky was streaked red and golden, as it often was in South Africa.

Her parents had stayed there for a whole month last time, half at Thabisa for safaris, half at Nkosi Valley. They had even helped pick tomatoes and leeks, and plant more seeds in the Mama Imka Memorial Garden, which had strangely blossomed beyond belief since they had lost her, seven months ago.

Their mothers had acted like long-lost friends, so much so that she and Arno had often left them to chatter for hours, while they had gone and done...other things.

They were pretty good at the other things, she thought now as a tram rumbled past and someone on it eyed up Arno as if he were a hunk of meat. She didn't mind; it was nice to be the one who'd snared him, as Kimberley said.

He'd been patient. More patient than her.

'Your mama's a great cook,' he said now, patting his full stomach and guiding her across the street, towards the park. 'She should talk to Mama Annika again, put a Dutch dish on the restaurant menu when it opens next month.'

'Mmm…' she said, though now she was distracted. She could see the treetops from here over the chocolate-box houses and a fluttering in her belly tried to warn her, this was not where she wanted to be. Arno didn't know that.

She held his hand tighter, trying not to think about it. Usually she wouldn't walk this way. But this was Arno's first time, meeting her family on home turf, seeing the city she'd left behind to move to South Africa and be with him. He deserved to see the park—it was beautiful. A city highlight. At least, he could see the outside of it.

He stopped with her at the tall, wrought-iron gates, letting the cyclists hurry past them into the park, as if sensing her apprehension. 'I know you don't like this place,' he said softly. 'Your mother told me it was here but…'

Kaya took a deep breath, then released it through her mouth, right before he kissed her. 'Trust me,' he said, and his warm eyes steadied her heart. Of course she trusted him.

But… Oh…

What was he doing…dropping to the floor…getting his jeans all dirty…going down on his knees? On *one* knee.

Oh, my God.

Her hands flew to her mouth, right as the tears sprang to her eyes and almost blurred the moment from her vision. The box, the ring. 'Are you serious, Arno?'

'Marry me,' he said now.

'Yes!' she cried as he slid the silver studded band from the velvet clasp onto her finger, where she knew she would never, ever take it off.

He picked her up as if she were a weightless feather and spun her around, making several people stop on their bikes and cheer.

'I love you,' she breathed into his neck, wrapping her arms around him, and the crowd of clapping strangers grew around them as they kissed for what should have been an embarrassingly long time. They were almost deafening in their support. Suddenly this was not the same park—only *good* things happened here.

'Let's go inside,' she said a moment later, surprising herself. Never in a million years did she think she'd be suggesting this.

'Are you sure?' Arno smoothed her hair, and took her hand, admiring the ring on it.

'I'm sure, now you're with me,' she assured him. 'What can happen?'

The park was as beautiful as she remembered. They stopped at the pond, where the ducks left their trails in the water. Took photos by the sculpture shaped like a fish and watched the joggers and the dogs run around. He led her to a bench by the rose garden where they sat with her head on his shoulder, watching the world go by. The scent of the petals and the jasmine bushes tickled her nostrils and as Arno kissed the top of her head she felt complete, and free of fear for the first time in years, maybe ever.

Arno was the best person to be here with; no one could hurt her while he was at her side, not here or anywhere.

* * * * *

COMING SOON!

We really hope you enjoyed reading this book. If you're looking for more romance be sure to head to the shops when new books are available on

Thursday 8ᵗʰ June

To see which titles are coming soon, please visit

millsandboon.co.uk/nextmonth

MILLS & BOON®

Coming next month

TWIN BABIES TO REUNITE THEM
Ann McIntosh

A tidal wave of arousal crashed over Saana as her gaze dropped to that full, wide mouth—unsmiling now, but no less sinfully sexy for that fact.

Against her will, her head suddenly filled with scenes, scents, sensations of being held in Kenzie's arms. There, her every sensual need had been met, ecstasy lifting her higher and higher, until it became irresistible and she was flung into the stratosphere.

Taken to the stars.

Suddenly weak-kneed once more, Saana knew it was time to bring this surreal encounter to an end. The sustaining anger had waned, leaving her floundering and sad.

But she wouldn't allow that to show.

The one person she'd ever completely trusted had betrayed her and deserved nothing but cool dismissal.

Getting a grip on both her emotions and her traitorous body, and although her legs still felt weak, she walked around the car to the semicircular staircase leading to her front door.

"Well," she said, aware of Kenzie's gaze following her

and refusing to meet it again. "This has been delightful, but I'm afraid it's time for you to leave."

She was two steps up when Kenzie replied.

"Saana, I need your help."

Pausing, Saana felt the words echo, shockingly, between them. In fact, it was almost impossible to believe she'd heard them correctly.

Unable to resist, she looked over her shoulder, saying "As surprising as it is to hear you, Miss Independence, say that, I'm sorry. I'm not interested in offering assistance."

Then, as she turned to climb to the next step—wanting to hurry now, to get away—she heard Kenzie say, "I'm pregnant with twins. And I really need your help."

She froze where she stood, trying to process the words, her first impulse to spin around and look at Kenzie to judge whether she was telling the truth or not. To let loose all the questions firing around her brain.

Pregnant? By whom? Had she started a new relationship without telling Saana? Decided she wanted a family with someone other than the wife she'd promised to love and cherish always but had then left behind?

Continue reading
TWIN BABIES TO REUNITE THEM
Ann McIntosh

Available next month
www.millsandboon.co.uk

LET'S TALK
Romance

For exclusive extracts, competitions
and special offers, find us online:

f MillsandBoon

𝕏 @MillsandBoon

◉ @MillsandBoonUK

♪ @MillsandBoonUK

Get in touch on 01413 063 232

MILLS & BOON

THE HEART OF ROMANCE

A ROMANCE FOR EVERY READER

MODERN
Prepare to be swept off your feet by sophisticated, sexy and seductive heroes, in some of the world's most glamourous and romantic locations, where power and passion collide.

HISTORICAL
Escape with historical heroes from time gone by. Whether your passion is for wicked Regency Rakes, muscled Vikings or rugged Highlanders, awaken the romance of the past.

MEDICAL
Set your pulse racing with dedicated, delectable doctors in the high-pressure world of medicine, where emotions run high and passion, comfort and love are the best medicine.

True Love
Celebrate true love with tender stories of heartfelt romance, from the rush of falling in love to the joy a new baby can bring, and a focus on the emotional heart of a relationship.

Desire
Indulge in secrets and scandal, intense drama and sizzling hot action with heroes who have it all: wealth, status, good looks…everything but the right woman.

HEROES
The excitement of a gripping thriller, with intense romance at its heart. Resourceful, true-to-life women and strong, fearless men face danger and desire - a killer combination!

To see which titles are coming soon, please visit

millsandboon.co.uk/nextmonth

JOIN US ON SOCIAL MEDIA!

Stay up to date with our latest releases, author news and gossip, special offers and discounts, and all the behind-the-scenes action from Mills & Boon...

 @millsandboon

 @millsandboonuk

 facebook.com/millsandboon

 @millsandboonuk

It might just be true love...

MILLS & BOON

MODERN

Power and Passion

Prepare to be swept off your feet by sophisticated, sexy and seductive heroes, in some of the world's most glamourous and romantic locations, where power and passion collide.

MILLS & BOON
Desire

Indulge in secrets and scandal, intense drama and plenty of sizzling hot action with powerful and passionate heroes who have it all: wealth, status, good looks…everything but the right woman.